THE
BEAST
WARRIOR

NAHOKO UEHASHI

Translated by CATHY HIRANO

HENRY HOLT AND COMPANY

NEW YORK

JEH

SHEEMIYA — HUSBAND

MEEMIYA

WIFE — YOUNGER BROTHER

DAMIYA

THE DIVINE KINGDOM OF LYOZA

HUSBAND

HALUMIYA — HUSBAND

DAUGHTER — HUSBAND

SEIMIYA — SHUNAN

YUIMIYA   YONAN   CHILD

THE YOJEH FAMILY TREE

To all my readers

Henry Holt and Company, *Publishers since 1866*
Henry Holt® is a registered trademark of Macmillan Publishing Group, LLC
120 Broadway, New York, NY 10271 • fiercereads.com

Text copyright © 2009 by Nahoko Uehashi
Translation copyright © 2020 by Cathy Hirano
Illustrations copyright © 2020 by Yuta Onoda

Library of Congress Cataloging-in-Publication Data is available.
ISBN 978-1-250-30748-4

Our books may be purchased in bulk for promotional, educational,
or business use. Please contact your local bookseller or the Macmillan
Corporate and Premium Sales Department at (800) 221-7945 ext. 5442
or by email at MacmillanSpecialMarkets@macmillan.com.

First edition, 2020 / Designed by Trisha Previte
Printed in the United States of America

1   3   5   7   9   10   8   6   4   2

PART ONE

THE QUEST

FROM IALU'S DIARY

I still ponder the meaning of what happened on Tahai Azeh. And its effect on your future, Elin.

Where will the path you have chosen lead you?

And where will the path I have chosen lead me?

When the rebel army clashed with the Aluhan's forces on Tahai Azeh, I was driven by a longing for change, but now I wonder if I made the right choice.

Generations of Yojeh had protected this kingdom's purity by renouncing the corruption of war. Their unwavering integrity and sanctity were the soul of this land, the very heart of its people, making Lyoza rare among nations. But it was wrong to maintain that purity through the sacrifice of others' blood.

Even though each successive Aluhan chose defilement willingly to protect this realm on the Yojeh's behalf, only those who lived in Aluhan territory were forced to kill and be killed. The Yojeh and her people should have considered more carefully what that meant.

Like the Toda, those ferocious beasts whose blood-drenched fangs decimate enemy troops and rout their cavalry, the Aluhan and his people were feared, despised, and carelessly discarded, even though they had protected this country for centuries. It was only natural that they should long for change.

So many choices were made that day on the plain of Tahai Azeh. Uncertain of the answer, yet guided by their own convictions, each person made what seemed the only possible choice. And now those choices have generated a relentless surge of change.

I doubt you can escape that wave unscathed, Elin.

On the plain of Tahai Azeh, the Aluhan witnessed how easily a Royal Beast could slaughter his 'invincible' Toda troops. We all knew that those majestic creatures, the symbol of the Yojeh, could kill Toda. But we believed they could not be tamed or controlled, and so the Aluhan had never thought to fear their existence. On that day, however, he saw you command Leelan to vanquish the Toda.

If Royal Beasts can be controlled by man, that changes everything.

The Yojeh vowed never to use them as weapons again. As her promise is sacred, I am sure she will try to keep it. But that does not change the fact that you and the Royal Beasts are in a precarious position. If people in other countries learn what you have done, someone is bound to try to capture and use the Beasts. Although the skills required to handle them cannot be acquired overnight, the day will come when a rival country develops its own Royal Beast corps. And when it does, this kingdom will be threatened with extinction.

The young Aluhan will never overlook such a risk. He will arise to protect his army of Toda, the symbol of his power and the key to this country's safety. And whatever steps he may take, they will most certainly impact you, Elin. The only person in the world who can control the Royal Beasts.

ONE

VOICE FROM THE PAST

I

THE KIBA CHAMBER

For a split second, the sky lit up like it was midday, followed moments later by a deafening crack of thunder. Before the last stomach-wrenching rumble had faded, the rain began to fall—a torrential downpour, as though the bottom had dropped from the heavens.

The officer sitting in the carriage reached out and closed the window with a crooked smile. "Well, that's inconvenient," he said. "We'll have to pull up at the entrance to the Stone Chambers unless we want to get soaking wet."

The woman sitting across from him, however, stared vacantly out the closed window without responding. Running a hand through his salt-and-pepper hair, the officer regarded her silently for a moment before trying again. "Lady Elin. You told the driver to stop before we reached the entrance, but it's pouring. Shall I tell him to drive us to the entrance after all?"

Elin started as though waking from some reverie and turned her eyes toward him. "Pardon me? What did you say, Yohalu?"

A faint smile rose to the man's lips, but he repeated what he had just said. Elin cast him an apologetic look. "You're right," she said. "We will get sopping wet. But it's forbidden to bring horses too close because it could excite the Toda."

Yohalu blinked. "Yes, I know, but surely the horses' scent wouldn't reach inside in such a downpour."

"You are probably right," Elin said. "But Toda Stewards hate to break the rules."

At this, Yohalu nodded. "True. I suppose we must get wet, then." He reached down, picked up two conical hats of braided sedge that lay on top of a bag between his feet, and handed one to Elin. "Although I suppose these won't do us much good in this rain," he said.

Elin took the hat but did not put it on even when the carriage stopped. Instead, she placed it gently on the seat. Seeing the frown on Yohalu's face, she said, "I appreciate your concern, but the Stewards don't like people to enter the caves with their faces concealed. You are wearing a uniform, so in your case, I'm sure it won't matter. But I had better enter with my face bare."

She bowed and then reached out to open the door. Yohalu gently moved her hand aside and raised the handle himself, pushing the door open. "After you," he said.

Elin bowed once more and then stepped into the onslaught. Although she was drenched in seconds, she silently thanked the chill rain that soaked her body, dripped from her hair, and ran down her forehead. This way, no one would know if the drops that poured down her cheeks were water or tears.

The smell of wet trees and grass enveloped her. The huge rock face was split by a black fissure, the entrance to the caves where the Toda were kept. It loomed ominously through the haze of rain, and the figures hurrying in and out of that crack reminded her of ants scurrying to and from their nest.

Yohalu stepped down from the carriage to stand beside her. Catching sight of him, the guards outside the entrance snapped to attention. The sweet scent of Toda slime, which not even the rain could erase, wafted toward Elin, and she gripped the collar of her robe tightly. As she made a dash for the entrance, taking care not to slip in the mud and conscious of the curious stares directed toward her, she fought to shield her mind and keep herself from being swept into the maelstrom of memories that surged inside her. Even so, she heard once again the mourning wail of the Toda, a shrill keening sound like wind whistling through a broken pipe. With it came the memory of a dawn more than twenty years ago that had changed her life forever. She shuddered.

Although this was not the Toda village where she had been raised, the caves were built just like the ones she remembered from her childhood: A large cavern inside the entrance, known as the Hall, branched off into multiple caves called the Stone Chambers. Torches in wall brackets burned vigorously, sending shadows dancing across the damp stone.

The Toda Stewards, who were gathered in the Hall, stared at Elin, wariness evident in their faces. Enormous Toda carcasses lay on straw mats spread across the floor. Five days had already passed since their deaths, and the mucous membrane that cloaked their bodies had dried, making them appear like wooden carvings coated in glue rather than the bodies of once-living creatures.

All Toda were fearsome beasts that could bear warriors swiftly across the battlefield, scattering cavalry before them, but the largest and strongest were the Kiba or "fangs." These formed the vanguard, and they could massacre enemy troops.

Five days ago, every single Kiba in the village of Tokala had been found dead, a disaster for the Toda Stewards that managed the Stone Chambers. It was the chief inspector's job to investigate the cause of death and punish those responsible. Soon after the news had reached him, he arrived in the village and seized the man responsible for their care. But for some reason, the man's punishment had been deferred by order of the Aluhan, and a new inspector had been summoned. It now dawned on the Stewards that the new inspector was a woman, and their consternation deepened.

Shifting her eyes from the Kiba carcasses, Elin walked over to where the Stewards stood along the wall. "Who is your chief?" she asked.

A white-haired man jerked, then inclined his head timidly. When she drew near enough for him to see the color of her eyes, surprise suffused his face.

"I am not an Ahlyo," Elin said quietly before he could speak. "My mother was, but she was expelled by her people when she chose to wed my father. My father was a Toda Steward."

The man's eyes flickered, and he frowned as though trying to dredge up some distant memory. Suddenly, his eyebrows shot up. "So you . . . You're the one? From Akeh Village?"

Elin nodded. A murmur rose behind him. The younger Stewards looked puzzled, but the elders could not conceal their shock. Tokala was close to Akeh, and many of them had kin there. Despite the strict ban on even mentioning that incident, they had all heard about the Ahlyo woman from Akeh who had been blamed for the death of the Kiba and executed by being thrown into the Toda swamp.

Hearing a commotion at the entrance, Elin turned to see the guards move aside. A man robed in red with a wide ornate sash stepped into the cavern. The chief inspector. She drew in a sharp breath and felt her scalp tighten. A wave of fierce loathing rolled through her.

He must have heard that she had arrived. There was a suspicious look on his arrogant face as he marched boldly toward them. Even though he could not possibly be the same man who had executed her mother to protect himself, just the sight of his robe set her pulse racing.

Returning her gaze to the Chief Steward, she said quickly and quietly, "I didn't come to punish any of you. I came to prove that you weren't responsible for the deaths of the Kiba. Please lend me your aid." The man's eyes widened slightly.

"I heard that the Aluhan's envoy has arrived," the inspector called out in a booming voice. "Where is he? In the Stone Chambers?"

Elin turned to face him. "Chief Inspector, I am his envoy."

The man halted and gaped at her. "You?"

8

"Yes."

A frown twisted his features, and he took a step forward, as if to intimidate her. Elin stood her ground, returning his gaze calmly. At that moment, Yohalu ambled over to stand beside her. He nodded at the inspector and said, "So you're the son of Yalaku? You look just like your father. It must be two years now since he passed away."

The inspector looked puzzled, but when his gaze fell upon Yohalu's sash, his eyes widened. "Sir! You . . . You're a member of the Black Armor?"

"No, no," Yohalu said, waving his hand. "I no longer wear the black armor. Too old for that now. I just serve as a companion for the Aluhan when he needs someone to talk to." He placed a hand on Elin's shoulder. "And sometimes I serve as an escort. I suppose it must be hard to believe that a woman could be an inspector, but I can assure you that she was indeed sent by the Aluhan."

The inspector blinked rapidly. "I beg your pardon, sir, but the fact that a new inspector was sent . . . Was there some aspect of my work with which the Aluhan was displeased?"

Before Elin could respond, Yohalu shook his head. "No, not at all. There's no need for you to worry. Your task is to manage and inspect the Toda Stewards. In other words, your job is to investigate the mistakes made by men. But she has been sent here to investigate the Toda, not men at all."

As she listened to Yohalu smoothly allay the man's fears, Elin reflected once again that he was no ordinary bodyguard. The Black Armor was an elite band of warriors that protected the Aluhan, and she had heard that they were chosen from his own kin for their exceptional intelligence and military prowess. If Yohalu had been a member of the Black Armor, then he must be Shunan's blood kin.

She gazed at his calm, friendly features. Maybe he was sent to keep an eye on me, she thought. Shunan would have chosen someone of such high rank because he trusted Yohalu. Although she had already guessed that the Aluhan felt she needed not just protection but also supervision, her heart sank every time she confirmed this suspicion.

She took a breath and pushed these thoughts away. There's no point in dwelling on it. You chose this path yourself. Thanks to that, there are still things you can do.

She turned toward the row of carcasses.

Elin had reached the Aluhan's castle, Aluhan Ula, in the morning three days earlier. With little time to prepare for the journey, she had been thrust on a horse almost as soon as she had received the Aluhan's summons. Although she did not know why she had been summoned, the sight of his castle, surrounded by formidable walls of enormous stone and watchtowers that pierced the sky, had filled her with a strange, crushing dread that made her feel very small.

A fortress for men who wage war, she had thought. It was a far cry from the Yojeh's palace, which was surrounded not by walls, but by a forest in which birds warbled.

She passed under the magnificent gate built by master craftsmen, walked along a colonnade that stretched far into the distance with a ceiling so high it caught her breath, turned down a passageway, and climbed a flight of stairs. By the time she reached the Aluhan's sitting room, she felt almost dizzy. The room into which her escort ushered her, however, was surprisingly small.

Through the wide-open windows she glimpsed the tops of slender tohk trees. Their small white blossoms were bathed in the soft light of early spring, and when they swayed in the breeze, the light danced across the floor. The room was empty, and once her guide had left, the only sound to be heard was the rustling of leaves. As she stood gazing absently out the window, she heard the door open. Shunan strode into the room followed by a tall, middle-aged man.

"Hello, Elin. Sorry to have kept you waiting when it was I who summoned you here." At the sound of his voice, Elin hastily knelt on the floor and placed both palms to her forehead in a proper salute.

Shunan acknowledged her greeting with a smile and gestured for her to sit in a chair by the fireplace. Examining her face closely, he said, "You haven't changed a bit."

Elin's cheeks dimpled. "I wish that were true, but I'm already past thirty and feel sure that I must have changed a great deal."

"Well, you haven't. Although I hear that you're a mother now. How's your son?"

"Too well, I'm afraid. Sometimes I don't know what to do with him."

A father of two himself, Shunan grinned appreciatively. "I can imagine. If he's anything like you, we can expect great things in the future."

Elin looked away at this, but Shunan's keen eyes must have caught the shadow that crossed her face, because he changed the subject smoothly. "And how about you? Do you have any stiffness in your back from that old arrow wound?"

Elin shook her head. "Thank you for your concern, but fortunately, no, I have not had any problems with it."

The arrow that had struck her when she had shielded Shunan had penetrated deeply into the muscle, but a bone had stopped the point before it could damage any organs. Even so, it took a long time for her to move her arm without pain. Both the Yojeh Seimiya and the Aluhan Shunan had granted her request to return to the Kazalumu Beast Sanctuary to heal. Eleven years had passed since then, and during that time, Elin had fallen in love, wed, and borne a child. Back then, she could never have imagined that such changes would happen in her life.

During the last ten years, the kingdom had also changed. Yet there were times, such as on a quiet summer's afternoon, when she could almost imagine her life would go on like this forever. The grim-faced guards stationed at the Beast Sanctuary, however, always reminded her that this was merely a transient peace. When the Aluhan's messenger had arrived unannounced, her first thought was that the time had finally come.

The morning light etched shadows on Shunan's face. His expression was gentle, but the muscles around his eyes were tense. He probably wasn't getting enough sleep, she thought. His sallow skin exposed an underlying fatigue.

On Tahai Azeh, Shunan's younger brother had murdered his father. When he realized that he had been used, he had hung himself by his belt in his cell without waiting for judgment. Shunan's mother had lost her mind, unable to bear the tragic deaths of her husband and younger son. Alone, without any parent to bless him, Shunan had succeeded to the position of Aluhan and married Seimiya. Having wed the woman he loved and launched a new era with his own hands, he should have been a happy young man, but he had lost so much to achieve that union. Although he had willingly accepted all this suffering to gain a brighter future for the kingdom, the fruits of his efforts had been far from satisfactory.

The Aluhan's union with the Yojeh had taken a great weight from the hearts of those who lived in Aluhan territory. Many were deeply moved that the Yojeh had chosen to wed him. They rejoiced at the new opportunity to qualify for posts in the central government, a path formerly denied to them, and longed for this marriage to erase the resentment and sense of misfortune that had smoldered in their breasts for generations.

But the revulsion with which the people of the Yojeh's territory had greeted the marriage was far greater than Shunan had anticipated. Viewing the increase in the Aluhan's authority as a threat, the nobles took issue with his policies at every turn and sought to restore the Yojeh's control over him. People whispered that the Aluhan had angered the god by defiling the Yojeh. They claimed that this was the cause of successive crop failures and the epidemic that had spread from Aluhan territory throughout the kingdom, taking many lives. It was the threat of foreign invasion, however, that shook the kingdom most. The horse riders of Lahza had stepped up their attacks on the caravan cities that were governed by Lyoza, and Elin had heard that the lives of many warriors had been lost in these skirmishes. Shunan and Seimiya shouldered the burden of all these things.

The silence in the room was so profound that Elin could hear the wings of the birds that flitted in the treetops. Shunan's voice barely disturbed the quiet. "If I had asked you to come when I was still at the palace, it would have been a little closer for you, but I needed to talk about this here. You stayed at the Silver Branch last night. Did you sleep well?"

Elin had barely slept at all, but it wouldn't do to say so. "Yes," she replied. "Thank you for arranging such luxurious accommodation."

Shunan smiled reassuringly, as if he sensed the uneasiness beneath her words. "You must be thinking that I summoned you about the Royal Beasts, but I didn't. To tell you the truth, I still don't know what we should do about them, although I do know we'll have to address that issue soon."

Elin blinked. He didn't call me here about the Royal Beasts? The rod of tension inside her loosened, and her shoulders relaxed. Although she knew the decision was merely being deferred to a later date, she was glad that at least for a little longer, things would stay the same for Leelan and the others.

But if this isn't about the Royal Beasts, why would he wish to speak with me when he's so busy?

As if he could read her thoughts, Shunan said quietly, "I summoned you because I received a report that all the Kiba in the village of Tokala were wiped out."

As the meaning of his words penetrated her mind, Elin froze. She felt as if a hand had reached out from the past to seize her heart. Her face paled, and Shunan looked at her with pity in his eyes. "Your mother was blamed for the loss of the Kiba and sentenced to death, wasn't she?"

Elin opened her mouth, but couldn't find her voice. Swallowing to moisten her throat, she answered hoarsely, "Yes, that is correct."

Shunan gave a short nod. "The records show that the Kiba were wiped out in a single night, which is exactly what happened this time. They were quite healthy the day before, swimming around as usual, but by dawn, every single one was dead."

Elin's eyebrows drew together. She remembered that after her grandfather had cursed Sohyon for letting all the Kiba die, her mother had told her not to worry—because it had happened before.

Elin looked up. "Does this kind of thing occur very often?" she asked.

Shunan's mouth crooked. "If it did, our army would be rendered impotent in no time."

Elin blushed. "I see. Pardon me for asking such a foolish question."

Shunan shook his head. "No, it's not foolish. That's actually an important point." He turned to the tall man who had accompanied him into the room. "Yohalu, please give me those."

The man handed him a sheaf of papers.

"Here, Elin," said Shunan. "Read these."

There were holes along the right edge of the pages as if they had been taken from a book. They were all written in the same format, and most were yellowed and brittle with age. Elin stiffened when she saw the title on the first sheet.

"Those are from the records preserved by Toda villages in every district," Shunan continued. "We took only those pages that recorded mass Kiba fatalities."

Although Elin heard him, her eyes remained glued to the page. The title read "Concerning Sohyon's Improper Management of the Kiba in Akeh Village and Her Punishment." She read the words beneath, then her eyes blurred, and she could no longer see the page. The content was so blunt and simple.

Despite having been entrusted with the care of the Kiba, the female Toda Steward, Sohyon, failed to maintain water quality in the Pond. As a result, the Kiba died of poisoning. She was strictly punished to prevent this from happening again.

That was all. Nothing in those words conveyed the brutality of her punishment, the way she had been thrown into a swamp to be devoured by wild Toda, or her grief at orphaning her young daughter.

Closing her eyes, Elin bowed her head and took a slow breath.

"The inspector who sentenced your mother died long ago." Elin raised her head at the sound of Shunan's voice. "But what he did was inhumane. The maximum sentence for someone who lets the Kiba die is the loss of their right arm. To feed her to the Toda was a gross injustice. We've never monitored the judgments of inspectors in each district, so in some ways perhaps I am responsible for your mother's death. I intend to review whether inspectors should be allowed to pass a death sentence."

Shunan's red-rimmed eyes and tightly pressed lips revealed his anger at the ignorant cruelty of the officer and his remorse for having let men like him do as they pleased. His expression made him appear so unbearably young that Elin averted her eyes.

"But I didn't summon you here to apologize," he said. He pointed at the documents. "Take a look through the rest. There's not much time so just skim them. You can read them more thoroughly later."

Elin flipped through the papers. There were nineteen pages, all reporting mass Kiba deaths. As she focused on the dates, locations, and numbers, she felt a growing excitement. She sensed that there was some kind of regularity to their deaths. Although the intervals between the incidents varied, making it hard to pin down the correlation, the deaths had occurred in several villages at once. The year Elin's mother had been killed, all the Kiba in the neighboring village of Yoson had also died.

She raised her head and looked at Shunan. He nodded. "That's right," he said. "These mass fatalities were not the fault of the Toda Stewards. It would be unthinkable for Stewards in multiple villages to make the same mistake at the same time. There must be another cause."

Something hot gushed from a point deep in Elin's chest, and she bit her lip.

"I want you to find out what it is," Shunan concluded.

There was a dull ringing in Elin's ears.

Did Mother know?

The disturbing doubt she had carried in her heart ever since she was a child reared its head again. In her mind's eye, she saw her mother in the dimly lit Stone Chamber, standing up to her chest in icy water as she gently stroked the dead Kiba. In her face, there was no trace of surprise or bewilderment, while in her eyes, there was only a profound sorrow.

Another scene floated into view as though pulled by a string, and Elin's heart began to race—the last time she had seen her mother, when she had played her finger flute to command the Toda and save Elin's life.

Her mother's words came back to her as clearly as if she had just spoken them. "Elin," she had said. "You must never do what I am going to do now. To do so is to commit a mortal sin."

Elin gripped her knees. Mother could control the Toda. She knew things that not even the Stewards knew.

Of course she did. Because she was an Ahlyo, one of the People of the Mist. As a descendent of the Toga mi Lyo, the Green-Eyed Ones, she had inherited the knowledge they had brought with them from the other side of the Afon Noah, the Mountains of the Gods, where they had once raised Toda as weapons.

If so, then why? If she knew that the Kiba deaths were not her fault, why didn't she tell the inspector?

Elin closed her eyes. She could think of only one reason: because it was taboo. Whatever had killed the Toda must be related to the knowledge the Ahlyo had been forbidden to share, even if it meant death. Although Sohyon had been banished by her people, the rigid laws of the Ahlyo, designed to prevent another tragedy, had remained firmly rooted in her heart. If the cause of the mass deaths had touched upon those laws, that would have silenced her. Just as the Royal Beast Canon had been designed to conceal the true nature of the Royal Beasts, there must have been some reason for concealing the nature of the Toda.

Elin stared at her hands, which lay clasped in her lap. This was a turning point. If she continued in this direction, she would open yet another door that should remain shut. Even though she knew this, however, she could not suppress the burning urge that flared inside her. She longed to unravel the mystery of the Kiba deaths, to find out what her mother had given her life for.

Raising her face, Elin looked at Shunan. "Please send me to Tokala. I will try to determine the cause of the Kiba deaths."

2

THE SECRET OF THE WASHU

Once the inspector realized Elin had not come to find fault with him, he left without protest, but the Stewards remained. Elin could tell that they were eager to see what she would do. Although they occasionally shuffled their feet or cleared their throats, they made no move to leave. Their stares disconcerted her at first, but she soon became so engrossed in her work that she forgot they were there.

She inspected the nearest carcass carefully, touching the hard scales that covered it. The slimy membrane had dried, and some of the scales had hardened like resin, but the surface of many seemed blistered. Perhaps some change had occurred in the mucous film that protected them. She moved around to the Toda's head. Shoving her arm inside its mouth, she pressed against the tongue with her elbow to open the jaws wider. The skin inside was also blistered, as if it had been irritated by a strong medicine.

She frowned. Could they have had a toxic reaction to the tokujisui because the membrane in their mouths had thinned? Although the Stewards in this village probably wouldn't have noticed, she found it hard to believe that her mother would have been so careless.

She paused and stared at the beast. But why would the membrane have thinned? Pursing her lips, she brought her face closer to peer at the scales, only to pause in surprise. Instead of the sweet musk-like odor of Toda slime, the smell reminded her of new grass. A memory from her childhood leaped into her mind. Elin knew this scent; she had smelled it the day she stood beside her mother and stared at the dead Kiba in the water.

Pressing her palm against forehead, Elin searched her memory. She recalled asking her mother if the way Toda smelled changed when they died. Elin's mother had jerked around, her eyes boring into Elin as she asked what had made her think that.

What did I tell her?

Torches flickering in the dark. Her mother's shadow wavering each time the light moved. The faint glimmer of washu, glow bugs, swarming around the Kiba corpses that floated like logs in the Pond. When she reached this point in her memory, she snatched her hand away from her forehead.

Insects! That was it! The swarm of bugs had caught her attention because she had never seen them in the Chambers before. She had thought they might have been attracted by the scent of the dead Kiba.

And Mother told me . . . not to tell anyone what I thought!

She rose and bent over the carcass to peer at the scales, running her eyes over every inch of the Toda's body until her gaze was drawn to a single point.

There . . .

The body of a small insect lay stuck in the mucous membrane. Although there weren't many, she found more insects stuck to every carcass. She looked over her shoulder at the Stewards. "Who discovered that the Kiba were dead?" she asked.

The men shifted, their eyes darting to one another's faces. A young man stepped forward. He was quite a bit shorter than the others. If he was a Toda Steward, he would have to be at least eighteen, but he only looked fourteen or fifteen, perhaps because of his boyish face.

"I did. My older brother is responsible for the Kiba's care, so I always come a little earlier than him in the morning to prepare the food. I was the first to enter their Chamber that morning and . . ." His face twisted.

Elin stood up. "Did you notice little insects swarming around the corpses?" she asked.

The young man's brow furrowed. "Insects? I think there were some washu, but . . ." He fell silent for a while, as though searching his memory. Finally, he said, "Yes. There were little bugs flying around. I'm sure of it."

"They were probably just attracted to the light of the torches," a middle-aged Steward interjected.

The young man shook his head. "No. Although they flew around the torches, too, they were swarming around the bodies of the Kiba. I thought it was because the Kiba had died. Did those bugs have something to do with their deaths?" he asked eagerly.

Elin shook her head. "I can't tell yet. But you don't usually see them around, do you? Not here in the Stone Chambers?"

All the men agreed except one, who cocked his head. Elin looked at him. "Have you seen these bugs before?"

Looking a bit flustered, he said, "Yes, but not in the Stone Chambers. I've seen them a few times in Ukala Swamp."

When he said this, the other men murmured in agreement. "He's right," one of them said. "I've seen lots of them swarming around Toda in the swamp."

"In the swamp? You're talking about wild Toda, then?" Elin asked.

He nodded. The Chief Steward, who had said nothing up to this point, frowned. "You're talking about when they lay eggs, right?" he said. "It's true that they swarm around wild Toda during egg-laying season. But they never come around Toda raised inside the Chambers. It's too far from the swamp. And besides, it's too cold in here."

Elin stared at him. She felt a thrill of excitement creeping up inside her, raising goosebumps on her skin. "Egg-laying season . . . And when is that?"

"Around this time of year. But I'm talking about wild Toda. The Toda in the Chambers never mate."

"Yes, that's true," Elin murmured. She rubbed her arms as she gazed down at the carcasses. "I wonder what sex the Kiba are."

The Chief Steward's eyebrows rose. "Male, of course. Although I've never actually checked."

Elin's eyes widened. "You don't check their sex?"

The man gave her a sour look. "No, we don't. Not unless we want to break the Toda Laws. 'Never choose which to raise. Whether male or female, Toda are Toda.' But you're from Akeh Village. You ought to know that."

Elin shook her head. "Well, I don't. I left when I was ten."

The Chief Steward's face clouded. "Ah, I see. Well, anyway, that's how it is."

Elin glanced at the corpses, then looked at him again. "Would it be all right if I check their sex?" she asked.

He frowned, but before he could answer, Yohalu, who was standing behind Elin, spoke. "Please feel free to investigate anything you feel is necessary. There is no need to worry about the Laws."

She turned to Yohalu in surprise. "The Aluhan instructed me to let you do as you wish," he told her. "So please, investigate whatever you like." He turned to the Chief Steward. "You should keep that in mind, too."

The Chief Steward pursed his lips, then nodded stiffly. The Toda belonged to the Aluhan, and his word was absolute. But the rules governing Toda care had been imprinted on the Chief Steward's bones; Elin guessed that it must be repellent to him to see those broken.

"Chief Steward," she said. "To determine the cause of death, I am afraid that I will have to break many of the Toda Laws. I will not only need to identify their sex, but also to dissect them and examine the condition of their organs." The man's eyes bulged. "As that could be very painful for you and the other Stewards to watch," she continued, "please feel free to leave. When I'm finished, I promise to report everything I learn."

With knitted brows, the man turned to the others. The same disgust was reflected in their faces. An elderly Steward growled, "I can't bear to watch her do something so accursed as to slit open the Kiba."

The Chief Steward turned back to Elin with a determined look. "We will leave," he said hoarsely. "You can do as you please once we have gone."

Elin bowed. With a curt nod, the man turned on his heel and strode away. The others fell in behind, but the young man who had discovered the dead Kiba stopped after a few steps. "Sir!" he called out. "I . . . I want to stay behind. May I?"

The Chief Steward turned to him.

"I don't want my brother to be branded a criminal!" the young man said, his voice shrill. "Please let me stay and help."

Gazing down at him, the Chief Steward rubbed his chin. "If that's the case, give her a hand."

The young man's face brightened. He bowed and ran back to where Elin stood.

With the Stewards gone, the Stone Chamber seemed cold and deserted. "So where shall we start?" the young man asked, his eyes shining. "Should we turn them over?"

Elin hesitated. As a beast doctor, she was used to dissecting animals, but this was certainly the boy's first time. When she slit their bellies with her knife and the entrails spilled out, the stench would be overpowering. Even if he steeled himself for it, she wondered if he could stand it. But to ask him would question his resolve.

Making up her mind, she said, "Yes. I want to check their sex first. Let's start by rolling this one over to expose its belly. Please give me a hand."

The cold, rigid corpse of the Kiba was so heavy that it didn't budge even when Elin and the young man set their shoulders against it and pushed with all their strength.

"Here, let me help." Rolling up his sleeves, Yohalu strolled over and placed his hands on the Kiba's flank.

"Careful!" Elin said. "Toda scales have edges as sharp as knives."

Yohalu smiled. "Yes, I know that very well. I was a Toda Rider myself, remember? Now, I'll put my shoulder here so that we're spread out at equal distances. Are you ready? Let's push on the count of three."

They pressed their bodies against the corpse. Slowly, it began to move, then flipped over to expose its underside. One part gleamed pale white where there were no scales.

Staring at its belly, the young man exclaimed, "Woah! Wait a minute. It's a female?"

He was right. There was no sign of any male reproductive organs, just an opening for laying eggs. Elin probed the area around this hole to make sure no male organs were concealed inside.

"Let's turn the others over," she said, and the two men nodded. They swung themselves over the Kiba's tail and proceeded toward the next corpse. By the time they finished, they were drenched in sweat, but they had discovered that every Kiba was female.

"Well, who would have thought?" the young man said, his chest heaving. "I was sure that the Kiba were male." He looked at Elin. "What's next? Are you going to dissect them?"

Elin stared for some time at the row of corpses that now lay belly up, then shook her head. "Let's leave that for tomorrow. There's something else I want to check today. Did you bring a Silent Whistle with you?"

Understanding dawned in the young man's eyes. He pulled on a string that hung around his neck and drew out a whistle from his robe. "You want to find out the sex of the other Toda, do you?"

She nodded, impressed by his quickness. "Exactly. I want to check the Toda that are still alive. The fastest way to find out what killed the Kiba is to determine how they differed from healthy Toda."

Yohalu's eyebrows flew up. "Do you plan to examine all the living Toda?"

"Yes."

"Well, well," Yohalu said with a wry smile. "The Aluhan picked the wrong man as your escort. If I'd known we'd be doing so much hard labor, I would have suggested he assign someone much younger."

The young man grinned, rolling up his sleeves. "If it's youth you want, you've got me. This time, though, we'll be looking at Toda floating in the water, which will be a lot easier."

Yohalu rolled his eyes. "We have to get in the water? Now that's asking too much."

They spoke lightly, but all three knew how dangerous live Toda were. If the paralysis caused by the Silent Whistle wore off while they were still examining them, they would be devoured in no time.

After planning out the procedure in careful detail, they began checking the Toda in each Chamber. There were more than a hundred, and working in the frigid water for hours on end was draining. When they had finished the fifth Pond, Yohalu said, "Lady Elin, how about leaving the rest for tomorrow?"

The sound of his voice jerked Elin back to her surroundings. Looking up, she saw that the lips of both men had turned blue, and exhaustion was etched on their faces. "Of course," she said hastily. "Let's finish tomorrow."

Now that her concentration was broken, the cold overtook her, and she began to shake violently. They could barely haul themselves out of the water and had to help one another onto the ledge. Through chattering teeth, Elin gasped, "It's cold, isn't it?"

The two men glanced at each other and burst out laughing. Clearing his throat, Yohalu said, "I wish you had noticed that a little earlier." He rubbed the left side of his chest. "I have been worried for quite some time that my heart was turning to ice."

The young man laughed and slapped his thigh. "I was worried I'd freeze my bal—" He stopped, blushing furiously.

Yohalu raised his eyebrows. "Yes, well, I must say I know exactly how you feel. However, that's really not something to mention in front of a lady."

The droll way he said this sent Elin into a fit of laughter. She knelt with her hands on the stone floor, her shoulders shaking. Still quivering with cold, the two men burst out laughing again as they helped each other to their feet.

The effects of the Silent Whistle wore off, and the Toda began swimming around the enclosure. Elin and her companions sobered as they stood staring at them.

"The Toda in these five Chambers were all male," the young man remarked.

Yohalu rubbed a hand across his frigid lips. "Does that mean the Kiba died because they were female?" he asked.

"Perhaps," Elin said. "I won't know until we've checked all the others, though."

Yohalu cocked an eyebrow at the young man. "How about getting some of the other young Stewards to check their sex tomorrow?"

"Good idea," the young man said. "If I try to keep up with Lady Elin, here, I may never be able to take a wife." Elin snorted.

The young man stamped his feet to get the blood circulating. "I'll run ahead to the baths and tell them you're coming," he said. "I'll drop by my house, too, and get Mother to fix you some dinner. Please stay with us tonight."

He turned to go when Yohalu stopped him. "Wait! You haven't told us your name. Without that, how are we supposed to find your house?"

The young man blushed. "Forgive my rudeness. I'm Chimulu. The baths are on the west side of the village. You'll know by the high chimney. Please go on ahead. I'll meet you there later."

"Wonderful!" Yohalu said. "And if you don't mind, could you also tell our coachman where we'll be? He stabled the horses at the Chief Steward's place. That's where he'll be staying tonight."

The young man bowed, then dashed off. Watching him sprint away, Yohalu sighed. "Youth is a wonderful thing, isn't it?"

As they exited the cave, they were wrapped in the soft glow of the setting sun. The heavy rain had lifted, and the bright sky was dotted with a few sunset-colored clouds. The only sound on this mild spring evening was the chirping of the birds returning to their nests.

The guards bowed, and Yohalu stopped to greet them before setting off with Elin. The two walked silently along the forest path toward the village, avoiding the puddles made by the earlier downpour. Just as Chimulu had said, they saw the bathhouse chimney immediately. Watching a thin thread of smoke rise from it and disperse into the sunset sky, Elin bit her lip.

How often she had walked with her mother to the bathhouse at this same time of day. Holding hands, they would chat about nothing as they strolled along. Her mother would have spent at least half the day in the icy Ponds, and her hand was always frigid. Although many years had passed since then, Elin could still remember the coldness of her skin.

"Now I can appreciate why all the Toda villages have such magnificent bathhouses," Yohalu said, a smile crinkling the corners of his eyes. "The water in those pools chills one to the marrow. Your mother must have been quite something to have worked for so many years in that freezing water."

Elin nodded shortly. In retrospect, it was surprising that her mother never got sick. As a child, Elin hadn't given it a thought, but standing chest-deep in water so cold it numbed the body must have been hard on her mother.

The man in charge of the baths was waiting for them at the entrance.

Outsiders were normally not allowed in the bathhouse. Although he looked a little uncertain, the man greeted them kindly and showed them inside. "This is the men's bath," he said, "and that's the women's. The villagers're all done, so you can have the place to yourselves. Please take your time. Chimulu told me you were coming, so I cleaned the water. The temperature should be just about perfect."

He handed them each a towel. As the man left, Yohalu gazed at the one in his hand. "Where did he get these from? He couldn't have had time to get towels from someone's house."

Elin smiled. "They always keep extra on hand because children who come on their own are likely to forget theirs." As the words left her mouth, her son's face popped into her mind. No matter how much she scolded him, the little rascal often scampered off without his towel on purpose. She wondered what he was doing right now. Probably helping Ialu prepare the evening meal. She could picture him climbing onto his father's back as he crouched in front of the oven and fed wood into the fire.

Yohalu draped the towel around his shoulders and cocked an eyebrow at Elin. "They think of everything, don't they? Let's get warmed up." He disappeared into the men's changing area, while she entered the women's side.

The warmth of people just out of the hot tub still permeated the room. Elin removed her wet clothing and placed it to one side, then descended the steps to the bath area beside the large tub. She poured a dipper of water over herself. It felt scorching hot against her frozen skin. Recalling how her mother had taught her never to dirty the bath water, even if they were the last ones in, she washed herself thoroughly before sliding into the tub. She shivered with pleasure and let out a long sigh as the warmth spread through her body. Gazing absently at her pale legs floating in the hot water, she let all that she had seen and heard that day flow through and out of her mind.

I wonder why only the Kiba were female . . .

This point bothered her. The Stewards couldn't have deliberately selected females for the Kiba because they never checked their sex. If so, then why were they all female while the rest were male, almost as if they'd been handpicked? And what made a Toda into a Kiba in the first place? Did any of the wild Toda grow so large?

Maybe they tell them apart when they're in the egg. Perhaps when they stole them from the nests, they picked ones of a certain size for Kiba and those were all female.

She got that far in her reasoning and then muttered to herself, "No. That's impossible." From what the Chief Steward had said, it sounded like he had seen wild Toda mating. This made sense because collecting Toda eggs from the wild would have been an important task for the Stewards. They couldn't steal any eggs unless they kept their eye on where the Toda lived and knew where they laid them.

If they had seen Toda mate, then they should know if there were any features that identified sex, such as one sex being larger than the other. In that case, however, they should have responded immediately that the Kiba were female when she'd asked. Yet not only the Chief Steward, who strictly adhered to the laws governing their care, but Chimulu as well had assumed that the Kiba were males. This could only mean that there was no obvious trait that distinguished males from females in the wild.

The last rays of sunlight shone through the ventilation window, casting a rosy glow on the white wall of the bath.

Besides, if the Kiba were always females and sex had anything to do with their deaths, mass Kiba die-offs should have occurred more frequently.

The deaths had been sudden. Those that had died must have shared some unique characteristic not found in the other Kiba.

Elin sighed and rubbed her face with her palm. No matter what line of reasoning she followed, she simply did not have enough knowledge. She would have to learn as much she could from the Stewards. That would be her starting point.

Her arms glowed white in the shimmering water. She missed holding her son, Jesse, on her lap. He was always on her mind. The littlest thing would remind her of his face and the softness of his skin. Had she always been on her mother's thoughts like this?

She could almost see her mother's arms wrapped around her, the way they had when she'd sat on her mother's lap. Her mother had left this world with so much still locked away inside her. Yet, even so, each thing that Elin discovered about the Toda might teach her what her mother had left unsaid.

She wiped a hand over her face once more, then rose and stepped from the bath.

3

CHIMULU'S HOUSE

"Oh, I do apologize. Our house is really not suitable for people like you. It's such a mess. So cramped and noisy." Chimulu's mother ducked her head repeatedly as she pushed her children aside and beckoned Elin and Yohalu into the house.

The homes of Toda Stewards were all of similar structure: a large dirt-floored space with a sink and a clay oven that led straight into a raised wooden-floored room with a hearth. A corridor alongside this led to other rooms in the back. Elin had lived in a similar house with her mother. But she remembered it as being more spacious than this, perhaps because it had only housed the two of them.

Chimulu's family was large, and six children were staring wide-eyed at Elin and Yohalu, fingers in their mouths. "I've got seven brothers and sisters," Chimulu said. "But these ones will stay at my grandparents' tonight."

He turned and shooed them out. "Off you go now. Stop making such a racket!" But even when he gave them a swat on the bottom, they didn't budge, remaining rooted in the entranceway, chattering excitedly as they stared at the visitors.

Chimulu's mother finally spread her arms and swept the children out of the house. The door snapped shut, and everything grew quiet. "Phew!" She sighed as she faced her guests. "Sorry for all that noise. I meant to send them off before you arrived, but I wanted to feed them first, and then it got too late."

Like Chimulu, she was short with a bright, energetic disposition. Although talkative, she never stopped working. Having heard from Chimulu that they had come to save her eldest son, she showered them with hospitality.

"My husband passed away," she said. "During that malaria epidemic a few years back, if you remember. So my eldest son took his place as a Steward. He was always a smart boy, and earnest, too. That's why he was chosen to help care for the Kiba."

While she talked, she filled their bowls with steaming-hot rice. Her eldest son supported the household now, she told them, and he worked hard, despite his youth. At this she choked up, and her eyes filled with tears.

Yohalu glanced at Elin and then turned to Chimulu's mother. "Unless he was clearly negligent in his duties, your son won't be accused of any crime. There's no need for you to worry so much. You must be patient and wait a little longer."

The woman nodded. Chimulu chimed in, "He's going to be all right, Mum. I'm sure of it. I know how carefully he took care of the Kiba. If these people investigate thoroughly, I'm sure they'll be able to prove that it wasn't his fault." He looked at Elin and Yohalu with a defiant light in his eyes. "I'm so relieved you've come. My biggest fear was that the inspector might accuse him to avoid being blamed himself."

To voice any doubts about the inspector was to question the Aluhan's ability to rule, but the challenge in Chimulu's eyes made it clear that he knew this and had said it anyway.

Yohalu expressed neither sympathy nor rebuke, but simply picked up his chopsticks and ran his eyes over the food on the table. His face brightened. "What a feast! Shall we dig in?"

The table was laden with dishes typical of mountain villages. Slices of grilled pheasant basted with miso and minced tsushi, tenderly stewed bamboo shoots, and sweet-and-sour pickled oolika fruit. When grilled, the slightly bitter tsushi-miso had an aromatic fragrance that made normally gamey meat rich and savory and the fatty layer under the skin succulent and delicious.

Elin took a mouthful of rice. Tears welled suddenly in her eyes, and her nose stung. The food brought back her childhood. Since the day she had washed ashore in Yojeh territory, she had eaten only fahko, an unleavened bread made of mixed grains—never rice and rarely any miso.

"Don't you like it?" Chimulu's mother asked.

Startled, Elin looked up and said, "Oh, of course I do! It's delicious." She tried to smile, but couldn't keep the quiver from her voice. She drew a deep breath and tried again. "I'm sorry. It's just that this food tastes so familiar. It really is delicious."

"Ah. I forgot," Chimulu's mother said. "You're from Akeh."

"Is this what they eat in Akeh, too?" Chimulu interjected.

Elin nodded. "Yes. We ate tsushi-miso often at this time of year. I used to go down to the stream in the spring with my friends to dig up the shoots. My mother was always delighted when I came back with an armful."

Chimulu laughed. "Really? When I was a kid, I hated them. I never went tsushi picking, even when my friends asked me to go along. They're so bitter, you see. I only found out how good tsushi-miso tastes recently. After I was old enough to drink. That's when I realized it's really quite delicious. Weird."

As he talked, he leaned over and poured them wine. They chatted about different seasonal dishes for some time. Toward the end of the meal, Elin said, "Memories from my childhood have been coming back ever since I arrived here, but they're mostly insignificant little details. Even though my mother was a Steward, I don't know anything about the Toda." She looked Chimulu in the eye as she spoke. "There's so much I need to learn. Would you be willing to teach me? About the work of the Stewards?"

Chimulu's face shone. "Of course! I'd be glad to tell you everything I know." He paused and laughed, looking a little embarrassed. "But I'm just a novice. If it were my older brother, now, he could tell you everything."

His mother piped up. "You're right, there. You don't have any experience, and you tend to be a bit careless. Unlike your brother who—"

"Hold on now!" Chimulu said hastily, raising his hand for her to stop. "No need to go on so much about my brother." He turned to Elin. "Pardon me. What is it you wish to know? Ask me anything. I will be only too glad to answer. I was being modest, but to tell you the truth, I know at least as much as my brother."

Elin couldn't help laughing. "All right. I won't hold back, then. First, tell me about the Kiba. How are they chosen? Can you tell the difference between them and the other Toda when they're still in the egg?"

Chimulu slapped his thigh. "That's exactly what I've been thinking about this whole time! You know what surprised me most? That all the Kiba were female. The strange thing is, the eggs they hatch from are no different from those of the other Toda. It's impossible to tell which are female and which are male. The ones that will be raised as Kiba aren't chosen for any characteristic of their eggs. We simply raise all the Toda hatched every five years as Kiba."

Elin raised her eyebrows. "Every five years?"

"Yes. We collect eggs every year, but once every five years, we put all the eggs gathered into the Kiba Pond and raise the hatchlings with tokujisui. They grow quicker and larger than the other Toda and have big, strong fangs. In other words, the only difference is that Kiba are given tokujisui while the rest aren't. When we found out that all the Kiba were female today, I was shocked. Do you think that giving them tokujisui turns them into females?"

As Elin mulled his question over, her thoughts were drawn to the Royal Beasts. Those raised on tokujisui never fully matured, but Leelan, who had been raised without it, had matured and mated with Eku to produce their cub Alu. She frowned. Alu and her siblings should have reached maturity by now but had not. Esalu had said that there was no need to worry just yet: with large animals like Royal Beasts, there was quite a bit of physical variation. But Elin couldn't help feeling that something important was lacking in Alu and her siblings' environment.

Elin had raised them without tokujisui in conditions very similar to those in nature, so why hadn't they started mating yet? Perhaps with Royal Beasts there were multiple factors, complexly interrelated, that affected sexual maturation. Even so, it was clear that tokujisui affected reproduction. That must be why the Kiba, as well as the other Toda, which were given a diluted version known as hakujisui, didn't mate and reproduce.

But was tokujisui really powerful enough to determine sex? If it was and all the Kiba given heavy doses became female because of it, then it was unlikely that tokujisui caused the mass deaths.

Elin raised her face and looked at Chimulu. "Do any Kiba die of old age?"

Chimulu nodded. "Yes, of course." He glanced at Yohalu. "But they're surprisingly susceptible to disease, and many are killed in battle, too. I've only seen two or three Kiba that died of old age."

Yohalu gave a wry smile. "Because Kiba form the vanguard. The Kiba troops lose the greatest number of Toda Riders, too."

Elin stroked her chin. "But some Kiba do die of old age. In that case, the fact that all the Kiba were female may not be the direct cause."

Chimulu and Yohalu looked taken aback. "Ah, I see," Yohalu murmured. "If being female is what caused their deaths, mass die-offs should occur much more often."

"You're right!" Chimulu exclaimed. "And while they may not live to be that old, many live ten years or more."

"How old were the Kiba that died this year?" Elin asked.

"They were all three."

Elin frowned. "They were all the same age? Do you mean that you kept only one generation of Kiba in the Stone Chambers of this village? Weren't there any older ones?"

Chimulu grimaced. "No, there weren't. Like I said, they're more susceptible to disease and more often killed in combat. The last of the older ones were all killed in the most recent battle. There were six of them, eight years old and thirteen years old—"

"Hang on a second." Elin stopped him as she tried to catch the tail end of a thought. She pressed a finger to the spot between her eyebrows, and gradually, the idea came back. Eyes bright, she gazed at Chimulu. "The Kiba that died this time were all three years old," she said slowly. "But the older ones that you had left, which would've been the eight-year-olds and thirteen-year-olds, were still healthy before the last battle. Excluding those that had already died of illness or been killed." Chimulu nodded, looking a bit perplexed. "The Kiba that died this time were all three-year-olds," Elin repeated as if to herself, her eyes still on Chimulu.

"Yes. What about it?" he asked.

But Elin didn't hear him. The dead Kiba were all born in the same year. If so, something may have happened that year that led to their deaths. Maybe some difference in the weather or the water temperature when they had hatched had caused some kind of physical change. Hope dawned in her heart. There were still too many unknown factors to judge, but she felt sure this line of reasoning could help her find the cause of the mass deaths.

A hot rush of excitement warmed her skin, but she quenched it; when a breakthrough seemed within reach was when she needed to use the most caution. If she became obsessed with exploring a single path, it could blind her to other possibilities.

They knew so little about the Toda. She had to collect facts, one by one, and think them over. Still, she was happy to have found a clue that would serve as a starting point. She would take her first steps from there. The path she had glimpsed through the mist might be a mirage, but she would never know until she followed it.

4

ESALU'S CONCERNS

A chill spring wind rustled through the grass, which was wet with morning dew. In the meadow, two Royal Beasts rubbed their heads against each other, sniffing each other's chests, then looked up and trilled in fluty voices. *Lululululu.*

Esalu, headmistress of the Kazalumu Royal Beast Sanctuary, gazed at this scene with a twinge of anxiety. Based on past experience, she knew that Leelan and Eku would take their mating flight today or at the very latest tomorrow. And if they did, Leelan would most certainly conceive. Over ten years had passed since Leelan had borne her first cub, Alu. She hadn't mated again for another two years, but when three Royal Beasts at the sanctuary had died the following year, she and Eku had mated and conceived a second cub as though trying to fill the empty spaces. That cub, Kalu, was now fully grown, and his younger sister Mina, born a few years later, was growing well and romping about the plateau.

Overjoyed by the births, the Yojeh and the Aluhan had not only granted the sanctuary a generous sum of money each time, but had also sent healthy wild Royal Beast cubs. Celebrating each birth with a lavish banquet, they had proclaimed far and wide that it proved the god was pleased with the new Yojeh's rule. Esalu guessed that they sought to allay people's uneasiness about the Yojeh's marriage to the Aluhan, a union unheard of in the nation's history.

It was the gift of the wild cubs that particularly worried Esalu. Royal Beasts raised at the sanctuary on tokujisui never mated. At Elin's insistence, however, Leelan had never been given tokujisui, and she became the only Royal Beast in captivity to reach sexual maturity. When Eku, a mature wild male, was brought to the sanctuary to be treated for an injury, she had come into heat, mated, and conceived. This fact had captured the interest of both the Yojeh and the Aluhan.

Seimiya had never commanded Elin to breed more Royal Beasts. When she had begged Elin to fly Leelan in order to save Shunan from death at the hand of his younger brother, she had vowed never to use the Royal Beasts as weapons again. But it would be foolish to assume the rulers of this land would be indifferent to creatures powerful enough to vanquish the Toda. Esalu knew this and was sure that Elin knew it, too, though she never mentioned it. Everyone had believed that Royal Beasts could never be tamed. But the sight of Elin flying Leelan into battle and single-handedly subduing the Toda troops was seared into their minds, along with the possibility that Royal Beasts could become invincible weapons.

So when the Yojeh and her husband sent wild cubs to Kazalumu to commemorate the births of Alu, her younger brother Kalu, and little sister Mina, Esalu couldn't help but suspect an ulterior motive. Had they sent them so that the newborn cubs would each have a mate when they matured? Were they hoping that the Royal Beasts would multiply?

She looked at Nola, a female sent as a gift at Kalu's birth, and Ukalu and Tohba, both males. They stood slightly apart, watching with keen interest as Leelan and Eku nuzzled each other. Tohba, who was not yet fully grown, showed no change, but the chests of both Nola and Ukalu had flushed to a delicate pink in response to the scent of the courting pair.

There was a rattling noise, and Esalu turned to see Tomura, one of the teachers, wrestling with the gate. When they neared mating, Royal Beasts could become aggressive. To prevent anyone from disturbing them, Esalu had asked the custodians to erect a temporary fence around this part of the field. Perhaps it had been put up too hastily, because the gate always got caught on the frame.

After a brief struggle, Tomura succeeded in opening it and came to stand beside Esalu. "They're so lovey-dovey, it's almost embarrassing to watch, isn't it?" he murmured, gazing up at the pair. With a slight frown, he added, "It looks like they'll take their mating flight soon, don't you think?"

"Yes, could be anytime now," said Esalu.

Tomura shifted his gaze to Ukalu and the others. "Their courtship seems to be affecting those youngsters over there. Do you think Ukalu will fly when Leelan and Eku mate?"

Esalu folded her arms. "He might. Male animals often fight over a female in heat, although we don't know if that's true for Royal Beasts." Her eyebrows drew together. "Even small animals like tomcats will fight ferociously for a mate, but between Royal Beasts, such a contest could be ghastly."

Tomura looked at Esalu. "But they wouldn't go so far as to kill each other, would they?"

"Probably not. As long as one backs down, the fight will end. In the animal world, that is. Only humans go so far as to kill each other over a female," Esalu said caustically. Her face grew thoughtful. "Still, when it comes to Royal Beasts, we just don't know. While they might not kill each other outright, the wounds could be fatal. We'd better be prepared."

The Royal Beasts in the sanctuary were the property of the Yojeh, and Esalu, as the headmistress, was responsible for their protection. It was unlikely she would be blamed too harshly if anything happened. Because there had never been more than one pair ready to mate before, no one could expect her to anticipate the consequences. If they weren't prepared, however, that would be a different story. This thought caused a constant tightness in Tomura's chest for he had been entrusted with the care of Leelan and the others in Elin's absence, but Esalu, who had decades of experience at the sanctuary, betrayed no trace of concern.

Tomura glanced at Alu, Kalu, and Mina, who were some distance away from their parents, and his face clouded. "Alu hasn't come into heat yet, has she?" he said. The three siblings frolicked in the sunshine, apparently oblivious to the scent of their parents or of the wild Beasts. As Esalu watched Alu patiently endure her younger sister Mina's playful tugging, she felt a heaviness fill her chest.

She'd been concerned about them the last few days as Leelan, stimulated by Eku, came into heat, and Ukalu and Nola showed signs of response. Alu and her siblings had never been given tokujisui or been frozen with the Silent Whistle. In that sense, they'd been raised in conditions closer to those in the wild than Leelan had. Yet they showed no interest at all in the scent of the wild Royal Beasts and no sign of sexually maturing.

Esalu shook her head slowly. "Let's worry about them later," she said. "It may be that Royal Beasts mature at different times. Humans do. Not all women begin their periods in the same year."

"That's true," Tomura said. He sighed. "What a time for Elin to be absent. It's been quite a while since the Aluhan summoned her. Has there been any word about when she'll return?"

Arms still folded across her chest, Esalu heaved a sigh. She'd heard nothing since she had received a brief letter from the Aluhan explaining that he had sent Elin to investigate the cause of some Toda deaths. Considering that any information related to the Toda was top secret, she hadn't expected to hear more. But she couldn't help worrying. She opened her mouth to speak, but then paused, eyebrows raised. Her eyes had caught a movement among the trees at the edge of the broad expanse of forest that stretched behind the Beasts. Squinting, she realized what it was. One of the Aluhan's soldiers, who guarded the sanctuary, was waving to her. She could tell from the motion that it wasn't an emergency, but when she turned in the direction to which he pointed, she clicked her tongue.

Tomura cast her a quick look of surprise, then followed her gaze. "Not again," he muttered with a frown. A little figure was creeping through the meadow toward Alu, crawling on all fours like a pup. He probably thought he was concealed by the long grasses, but from here, he was clearly visible.

"He must have snuck around from the valley," Tomura said with an exasperated look. "Though I suppose I should at least give him credit for having guts."

No one was allowed in the sanctuary without permission. The front and back gates were well guarded, and people who climbed the road up the hill from the village couldn't get through without being detected. Even if they did, because Leelan was nearing her mating flight, they would need a key to open the gate through the fence.

The dorm students were keenly aware of how dangerous the Royal Beasts were, and none, no matter how rebellious, would dare to approach them. Still, the fence had been built to discourage climbers. The only way for someone coming from the village to get near the Royal Beasts was to approach from the rear through the forest. This meant traveling a long way around to ford the mountain stream and climb the steep cliff on the other side, before hiking through the trees, where the Aluhan's soldiers kept watch.

The soldier who had waved signaled that he was leaving the intruder in their hands. Tomura took a step toward the boy, but Esalu stopped him and strode off, making a wide arc so as not to get too close to Alu and the others. Alu and Mina paused in their play and stared at Esalu as she walked purposefully past them. She gripped the Silent Whistle that hung from her neck, prepared to blow it at any moment.

When he realized that he had been discovered, the boy rose from his hiding place behind Alu. For a moment, he looked as if he was about to run, but to do so could startle the Royal Beasts, and he appeared to reconsider. Rather than dashing off, he began to back away slowly. He looked so comical that laughter rose in Esalu's throat, but she forced it down. Keeping her face stern, she strode up to him and grabbed him by the collar. Silently, she hauled him some distance away from the Royal Beasts, then glanced at Alu.

Although Alu and her siblings were watching her curiously, they made no sign of approaching. The Royal Beasts were wary of Esalu, and never came up to her or cooed the way they did with Elin. Once she confirmed they wouldn't follow, she turned back to the boy. "Surely you realize what you're doing, Jesse?"

He pursed his lips and looked up at her. His short-cropped black hair and dark eyes were just like his father's, but the way his eyes gleamed and the stubborn set of his jaw reminded her of Elin when she was younger. His hair was tangled and his soft cheeks were scratched, as if he had crawled through a thicket.

"Answer me, Jesse."

The boy cringed at the sharpness in her voice, but his eyes showed no sign of being cowed. "I just came to see my brothers and sisters!" he said. "That's all!"

Esalu's eyebrows rose. "Your brothers and sisters?" For a moment, she struggled to grasp what he was talking about, then sighed. He'd been coming to this meadow ever since he was a baby on Elin's back and had been playing with Alu and the others for as long as he could remember. She supposed that to him they must seem like family. Elin had raised him very strictly, and whenever he was with her, he wore a solemn expression as if to say he understood very well how dangerous the Royal Beasts were. But how could a boy of just eight possibly understand their true danger?

Esalu opened her mouth to give him a good scolding, only to close it again in futility. No matter what she might say, he was simply too young to understand why he shouldn't go near Alu and the others. Plus, his stubbornness was formidable. If he believed he was right, he wouldn't budge.

Changing tacks, she decided to strike his weak side. "I see," she said, feigning disgust. "Well, I'm really sorry to hear that. I had no idea that you cared so little about your family. It doesn't even bother you that your actions are going to make them suffer."

Jesse looked puzzled for a moment. "What do you mean?" he snapped. "I'm not going to make them suffer."

"Yes, you are. Because of you, I'll have to lock Alu and the others in the stable. If there's a possibility that an intruder—and by that, I mean you, Jesse—could approach them, I can't let them out into the pasture. What choice have you left me but to keep them inside? From now on, I'll have to shut them up in the dark. They won't like it, but it can't be helped, can it? As long as there's someone like you around who just can't obey the rules."

Jesse's expression changed to one of shocked disbelief. Then his face crumpled. Though young, he was old enough to understand Esalu's logic. He looked at Alu and the others, then raised his eyes to Esalu's face. The coldness of her expression told him that she was quite serious, and tears sprang into his eyes. He sniffled hastily and struggled to suppress his sobs, but his lips trembled.

"I'm sorry!" he shouted. Startled, Alu and the other young Beasts swiveled their heads toward him. Esalu raised the Silent Whistle to her lips, but Jesse stretched up, grabbing her hand in his small one. "Don't blow it," he whispered fiercely. "Please! Don't! I promise I won't come here anymore. So please, please don't shut them up in the stable. That would be too cruel."

Esalu kept her gaze stern, resisting the urge to smile. "You expect me to believe that?" she said. "You already promised once before that you wouldn't come again, yet here you are. Do you expect me to believe someone who breaks their promise for their own selfish reasons?"

At this, the tears rolled unchecked down Jesse's cheeks. Hiccupping, he wailed, "I'm sorry! I'll never break my promise again, so please, please don't lock them up! I'll keep my promise! Really, I will!"

Esalu glared at him. Although still hiccupping, he never let his eyes waver from hers. At last, she said quietly, "You're sure I can trust you?"

Jesse nodded emphatically. His face deadly serious, he raised his index finger and pointed to his chest, a gesture that meant if he broke his promise, she could kill him.

Esalu bit back a laugh, but couldn't keep a lopsided smile from her lips. Placing a hand on his small shoulder, she gave him a little shake. "Then I won't lock them up. Now come. I'll ask Professor Tomura to take you home to your father."

Nudged by her hand on his shoulder, Jesse had fallen into step beside her, but now he scowled. "I can go home by myself, you know."

"I'm sure you can," Esalu said coldly, "but there's no guarantee you'd go straight home. Especially as you probably disobeyed your father's orders by coming here."

Jesse's shoulders drooped, and he heaved an exaggerated sigh. Craning his neck, he stared at Alu, as though reluctant to leave her.

"Do you love Alu so much?" Esalu asked gently.

Jesse gave a cocky shrug. "Of course I do. She's my big sister." He looked up at Esalu. "Will Mother be home soon?"

Esalu blinked. "It looks like she'll be away a little longer. I'll let you know as soon as we receive any word. I'm sure you must miss her, but try to be patient."

Jesse pressed his lips together and stared at the ground, but his mouth was trembling. Esalu's chest tightened.

5

AUTOPSY

Dissecting the Kiba took a long time. Toda hide was so hard it could repel arrows, and no ordinary knife could penetrate where it was covered in scales. With a small, sharp dagger used by the Toda Stewards, Elin made her incisions in the underbelly. It was scaleless, but no easy task to cut through. Chimulu offered to do it for her, but Elin declined, partly because she knew it would be painful for him to insert a knife into the Kiba he'd helped raise from hatchlings, but even more so because she wanted to learn everything she could, including the feel of the hide, the layer of subcutaneous fat, and the flesh beneath.

Even if she dissected the Kiba, there was no guarantee that she'd be able to determine their cause of death. In fact, it would be almost impossible to determine if there was no obvious internal damage. The care of both the Toda and the Royal Beasts was bound by countless taboos. Everything had to be done strictly according to the Toda Laws or the Royal Beast Canon, and no deviation was permitted. Toda had never been dissected before, and no records of their anatomy existed, so she wouldn't be able to compare her findings with previous cases. Yet she had decided to dissect them anyway to pursue a hunch.

If tokujisui was involved in their deaths, then the most likely cause would be a reproductive abnormality. As all the Kiba were female and it was egg-laying season for wild Toda, some change, such as ovulation, could have precipitated their deaths. She had to find out if her suspicion was right.

Slowly and methodically, Elin dissected the first carcass and checked the various layers of tissue between the hide and the reproductive organs, examining them thoroughly and recording everything she saw. The work was much harder than she had expected. The protective slime that covered their hides was toxic and could have disastrous effects if she cut herself and got any in the wound. Just in case, she kept a cloth drenched in an antidote close at hand. Each time she stopped to pick up her pen, she had to wipe her hands first, which made the work much slower.

All the while, she was conscious of Yohalu's presence beside her. Like Elin, he had covered his mouth and nose with a cloth, and he stood silently watching her, showing no trace of emotion, even at the sight of the decomposing innards or at the ripe stench. He only left her side to relieve himself.

As she examined the innards, Elin measured the intervals between Yohalu's bathroom breaks. When she approached the reproductive organs, she took her time with other tasks, waiting for him to get up and leave. But this time it seemed like he never would. Not knowing what else to do, she began carefully feeling each vein with an expression of intense concentration, as though they intrigued her.

"Is there something strange about those veins?" Yohalu asked from behind her.

Without looking at him, she said, "Sometimes poison can cause lesions on the veins."

"Hmm," Yohalu said, as if interested. Then he murmured, "I must be getting a bit chilled in here. If you'll excuse me for a moment."

As he left, she began cutting swiftly near the reproductive organs. Although she was in a hurry, she bit her lip and forced herself to slow down, moving the knife with care. Suddenly, her eyes widened.

What's that . . .

The Kiba's fallopian tube looked swollen and deformed. She slit it open and found that it was plugged with multiple hard lumps. Her knife touched something different. Slowly, she explored the spot, and a round, fist-sized ball slipped out onto her palm. She stared at it.

An egg. This Kiba, raised in an unnatural way, had reached maturity and produced unfertilized eggs without mating.

Footsteps sounded at the entrance to the Chamber, and Yohalu returned to her side. He peered over her shoulder at what lay on her palm. "What's that?" he asked.

She glanced up, and their eyes met. For an instant her gaze wavered, and she regretted looking at him, but it was too late. Yohalu's sharp eyes hadn't missed her inner turmoil.

"That's an egg, isn't it?" he asked.

She nodded. She wished that she could have a little more time to think before she told him, but there was no way to avoid it now. Besides, if blocked fallopian tubes had killed the Kiba, she couldn't lie to him anyway.

"Was it pregnant?" he asked.

Hearing the excitement in his voice, Elin shook her head. "No. I believe this is an unfertilized egg." She pressed the point of the knife against the lumps in the tube. "Look here, and here. Here, too. Do you see these?"

"Yes."

"These growths blocked the fallopian tube, preventing the egg from passing through. The death of organ tissue spreads out from here. I can't say for certain yet, but I believe this is what caused their deaths."

Yohalu fixed his eyes on hers. "But what could have caused such a change? Poison?"

Returning his gaze, Elin shook her head slightly. "I don't know. And until I determine whether any other pathological change occurred, I can't tell if this is what actually killed them."

She kept her eyes downcast as she spoke, grateful for the white cloth that masked her lips, because she couldn't keep them from trembling.

Tokujisui!

Although she had no conclusive proof, there was no doubt in her mind. It was tokujisui that had caused this deformation—because that was the only difference between the Kiba and wild Toda. Shivers rose in waves from the pit of her stomach. Unable to suppress them, she stood up. "If you'll excuse me, I'd like to step out for some fresh air." Bobbing her head once in apology, she hurried from the caves.

The guards bowed to her as she passed, but she did not see them. Only when she was inside the forest did she stop. Birds warbled, and sunlight filtering through the leaves dappled her face. Pressing her back against a tree, she closed her eyes.

Tokujisui. What a dreadful potion. It turned living creatures into aberrations, yet, for centuries, they'd been giving it to the Toda to make them into powerful giants.

The sunlight played on her closed lids. An image of her mother's face rose in her mind, and she could hear the echo of her voice. "Tokujisui makes their fangs harder and their bones larger than Toda in the wild. But at the expense of other parts."

She realized now that her mother should never have shared such thoughts with her young daughter, but she'd probably been unable to stop herself.

Think about it, her mother had said. What can Toda in the wild do naturally that Toda raised in the Ponds can't? I'm sure you'll find the answer for yourself one day.

Mother knew.

She had known that it would kill female Toda to give them the tokujisui that made them into Kiba. The chill that gripped Elin intensified. The Toda Stewards had no idea what effect the tokujisui would have, but her mother did. The change in the slimy membrane occurred during the egg-laying season. And with that change their odor probably changed, too, attracting winged insects.

That's why she told me not to tell anyone they smelled different.

Which meant that her mother had noticed the change in the membrane. She'd noticed, yet had still given them that potion, even though such a high dose would encourage ovulation and turn the tokujisui to poison.

Elin didn't need to ask why she would do such a thing. If she had told the Stewards they should stop using it, she would have had to explain why. And that was something she could never do. If she did, people would learn that Toda could be bred and multiplied by humans. Tokujisui and its diluted version were designed to prevent that. If the Toda were raised without tokujisui under conditions similar to those in the wild, they would mate and reproduce, just like Leelan had.

Even though Mother was expelled by her people, she still . . .

Adherence to the Law had been that important. Long ago, her mother's ancestors had used Toda as weapons, destroying a nation that had flourished on the other side of the Afon Noah, the Mountains of the Gods. Filled with remorse, the Ahlyo, the People of the Mist, had lived ever since in strict obedience to the Law to prevent such a tragedy from recurring. Born and raised an Ahlyo, Elin's mother would have tried to prevent others from breeding Toda, even if it meant her execution.

But . . .

Although Elin could follow her mother's reasoning, emotionally she couldn't accept it. How could she have done that to the Toda? It was so hard to understand. She pressed her palm against her forehead.

Could I do that? Could I bring myself to give Leelan and Alu tokujisui to prevent them from being used as weapons?

Just the thought of it filled her with revulsion. She doubted that she could ever do it. Even so, maybe it was something that had to be done.

Another scene rose in her mind. Her mother's face when she had thrown the Silent Whistle into the fire, her eyes and cheeks lit by the glow of the flames in the oven.

"What I've done will make life so much harder for you," she had said. "Yet, to be honest, I'm glad that I'll never have to use that thing again . . . I hate watching the Toda freeze whenever I blow it . . . To see wild beasts controlled by humans is a miserable thing. In the wild, they would be masters of their own destiny. I can't bear to watch them grow steadily weaker when they live among men."

Beneath her closed lids, Elin's eyes burned. It must have been so hard for her to bear.

Elin squeezed her eyes tight. Yet, despite that pain, despite her abhorrence for what she was doing, in the end, her mother had still chosen to continue perverting the growth of the Toda.

Elin covered her face with her hands.

If I had never been conceived . . . If she could have continued living as one of the Ao-Loh, the People of the Law, the true name of the Ahlyo, instead of becoming a Toda Steward . . .

Surely her life would have been much easier, and so different. Would she have been freed of such dilemmas? Her mother, a Steward with the heart of an Ao-Loh, had been forced to witness firsthand just how cruelly the Law perverted the Toda. What had she been thinking as she stood chest deep in the chill waters of the Pond day after day? Had she ever doubted the wisdom of the Law?

Once again, she saw her mother inside the Stone Chamber; saw her kneel on the frigid stone floor and bow her head to the Kiba as water from her sodden garments spread in a dark pool around her. That cold, dark water seemed to seep inside Elin and pool at the bottom of her chest. Knowing her mother, she had been begging the Kiba to forgive her. For killing them with tokujisui.

What am I going to do?

Now that she knew what her mother had known, what should she do? Should she conceal the secret of the tokujisui to prevent people from breeding Toda and make up some plausible explanation for why their eggs had been blocked? Or should she continue to investigate and, once she discovered the whole truth, confront it head-on?

For the sake of the Toda, she would rather find a road that would keep them from being used as weapons. But there was no way that the Toda army, the kingpin of the country's defense, could ever be dismantled.

So what should she do? What *could* she do?

Behind her lids, she saw the lifeless, infertile Kiba. She opened her eyes and gazed up at the dappled light. The leaves fluttered in the breeze, but the trunk stood steady. Narrowing her eyes against the light, her face grew calm.

I can never give living creatures something that deforms them and prevents from ever bearing young.

That much she knew. She took a deep breath and pulled away from the tree, feeling the cool breeze caress her sweat-drenched back.

A twig cracked beneath someone's foot, and she turned. In the shadow of a tree stood a woman.

6

A MESSAGE FROM THE PAST

The woman was slender and looked to be about fifty years old. She stood with a basket in her arms and stared at Elin as though she wanted to talk. Although she was a stranger, something about her seemed familiar. She opened her mouth, then hesitated. At last, she seemed to gather her resolve and stepped out of the tree's shadow.

"You probably don't remember me," she said, walking slowly toward Elin. "I've been coming here as often as I could, hoping that I might have a chance to speak with you. I can't enter the Stone Chambers, and it would be hard to talk where others might be listening."

"Excuse me, but who are you?" Elin asked.

The woman flushed. "Oh, I beg your pardon. I should have introduced myself first. We're actually related. I'm your father's cousin, although I don't know what relation that makes us exactly."

Elin stared at her openmouthed, feeling as though she had been hit in the chest.

"It's true," the woman said, her words tumbling out. "We've met before. I used to play with you quite often, you know. But I married a man from this village when you were only five, so you've probably forgotten." She smiled suddenly, as if remembering that time. "You couldn't pronounce my name properly so you called me Auntie Chacha. My name's Tsulana."

The name Auntie Chacha echoed in Elin's ears, jogging a distant memory—the blurred brightness of day, a laughing voice, a flowered apron.

"I remember," Elin murmured hesitantly. "Not clearly. But I do remember. Did you wear an apron? One embroidered with yellow flowers or something?"

Tsulana's face brightened. "Yes! Yes, I did! I'd completely forgotten about it, but I used to wear an apron like that then. Amazing! So you do remember me!"

The tension between them dissolved, and they smiled at each other. "I'm so glad!" Tsulana said. "I wasn't sure how I was going to explain things to you. I mean, I never dreamed you'd remember me, and it would be so odd to have a stranger tell you they're your father's cousin."

"Yes, you really took me by surprise," Elin said, finding her voice. "But I'm so glad you came."

Tsulana nodded. "Me too. I thought you'd died with Sohyon, so when my husband told me you were here, the shock knocked the breath out of me. Of course, I was thrilled to know you'd survived." She stopped and gazed at Elin, then added, "You look so like your mother. Not just your eyes, but your mouth and your build, too. Your eyebrows and nose, though, remind me of my cousin."

Elin could hardly remember her mother anymore, yet Tsulana could see Sohyon in her face. And her father, whom Elin didn't remember at all. Goosebumps rose on her flesh, and her lips trembled.

Tsulana's face twisted. "It was just so cruel. And Sohyon was so young, not even thirty."

Elin realized with a shock that she had not even known her mother's age. She had been only ten at the time, and to her, Mother was just her mother. It had never occurred to her to wonder about her age. "How old was she?" she asked with a quiver in her voice.

"Twenty-seven, I think," Tsulana answered quietly. "Because she was only seventeen when she gave birth to you."

That young?

Elin pressed her hand against the tree to steady herself. Many girls married at sixteen, so it wasn't unusual to bear a child at seventeen. Yet the thought that her mother had been only sixteen when she'd chosen to abandon her people and marry a Toda Steward pierced Elin's heart.

Tsulana seemed to be thinking the same thing. "My cousin died at eighteen and Sohyon gave birth to you at seventeen," she said. "They were both awfully young, weren't they? I was just sixteen then, too, but Sohyon seemed so grown up, I never thought of her as being just one year older than me. I knew their situation was awkward, but I'd always liked my cousin. Of course, I was a bit frightened of Sohyon at first. I mean, she was an Ahlyo, and that in itself was somehow scary . . . But she was a good person. The more I got to know her, the more I understood why my cousin had fallen in love with her. I really loved those two."

Elin listened, barely breathing. She wanted to hear anything she could about her mother and father, like how they'd come to be married or whether they'd had a wedding.

"What was my father like?" she asked.

Tsulana's eyes shone softly. "He was such a warm person. He didn't talk much, but when he smiled, he brightened up the world around him."

Muffled sounds came from the distance, and they both stopped, startled, turning their heads toward the noise. Yohalu had come out of the caves and was looking at them. Elin took a step toward him, but he raised his hand and waved her away, as if to say not to worry about him. He turned and began talking to the guards in front of the entrance.

"Do you think it's all right?" Tsulana murmured, peering anxiously toward Yohalu.

"Yes. It should be fine. I can tell him later."

Despite this reassurance, however, Tsulana continued to frown, staring in Yohalu's direction.

"Auntie," Elin said.

Tsulana shifted her eyes toward her. "I'm sorry," she said. "It's better if we don't talk too long, although I know there must be so much you'd like to ask. And so much I'd like to ask you, too."

"But—"

Tsulana shook her head. "I'm sure you know that in a small village like this, rumors tend to spread. Because people are afraid." She thrust the basket she carried toward Elin. "Here. Take this. I made some rice cakes with shizu petals for you."

Wedged between the rice cakes and the edge of the basket was a parcel wrapped in brown paper. Tsulana flicked her eyes toward it and whispered, "If I couldn't meet you, I was going to ask someone to give you this. There's a letter in that parcel and something else that I think will make you very happy. Read the letter when you're alone, though."

"Thank you," Elin said. With her back still turned toward Yohalu, she took the package and slipped it inside the front of her robe.

Handing her the basket, Tsulana gripped Elin's hand. "I'm so glad I was able to meet you. Please take care of yourself. Live long and well for the sake of your parents who died so young."

Elin squeezed her hand in return. She didn't want to let her go, but she understood all too well her reluctance to stay and chat. This was a Toda village where people were sworn to secrecy. Anything even slightly out of the ordinary would seem suspicious and cause them to overreact.

Still holding Tsulana's hand, Elin said, "Thank you so much. I will treasure what you shared with me today forever. May you also have a long and prosperous life. I will pray for your happiness from the bottom of my heart."

Tsulana bowed her head and gently released Elin's hand. She waved goodbye and walked away as though reluctant to leave. Elin watched her until she finally vanished among the trees before returning to where Yohalu waited.

Yohalu finished talking with the guard and cocked an eyebrow at her. "I knew you'd be safe with these fine men here to guard you. I was just a little concerned that you might not be feeling well."

"My apologies. A woman who said she was my father's cousin brought me a basket of petal rice cakes." She showed him the contents, and he smiled.

"Mmm. They smell lovely. Why don't we take a break, then?"

One of the guards took a kettle of boiling water from over the fire and made them some tea. After the long, grueling hours in the cold cave, the hot tea tasted delicious. But even as she sipped the tea and munched on the petal-scented sweets, Elin couldn't take her thoughts from the letter inside her robe. Tsulana had told her to read it when she was alone, but the only time that happened was when she went to the outhouse or soaked in the bath. Otherwise, there was always someone around. She even slept in the same room as Chimulu's mother, so finding an opportunity to slip the letter out and read it was not going to be easy.

It was not until dawn of the following day that she finally got a chance to open the parcel. Chimulu's mother was still asleep when the first light of morning cast a thin glow through the window. Listening to her rhythmic breathing, Elin turned away onto her side and slipped the parcel from under her pillow. She unfolded the outer wrapping cautiously so that it wouldn't crackle. Inside was a three-page letter and another parcel wrapped in oiled paper.

She turned the letter to catch the feeble morning light that fell through the window. Words had been scrawled across the pages by a hand clearly unused to writing. Elin could almost see Tsulana, who had never gone to school, struggling to recall the letters her parents had taught her when she was young. The content was the same as what she had told her today—that she was Elin's father's cousin and had played with her when she was little. But as Elin peered at the words, trying to decipher them, she suddenly caught her breath.

The parcel wrapped in oiled paper, Tsulana had written, *is a memento from your mother, Sohyon. Your neighbor, Mistress Oki, sent it to me. Do you remember Saju, the little girl you used to play with? Mistress Oki was her mother. Sohyon left behind many notes, but no one could read them. Your grandfather was afraid they were evil Ahlyo magic, so he burned them all. Saju's mother felt bad that everything Sohyon had left was burned, so she saved some pages that she found in the ashes. But there were only a few. She was afraid that if she kept them, her husband would be angry, so she sent them to me, Sohyon's friend.*

With trembling fingers, Elin unwrapped the oiled paper. Inside was a sheaf of yellowed pages the size of her hand. Although more than two decades had passed, they still smelled faintly of smoke. The edges were charred black in places. Flipping through them, she saw that they were covered densely with neat handwriting in an odd script. Breathing shallowly, Elin stared at the pages.

She saw her mother sitting in front of the clay oven late at night, writing. Tears filled Elin's eyes, blurring her sight so that she could no longer make out the letters. She wiped her tears away with her fingertips and stared intently at the page in the white glow of the morning.

The script did look odd. That alone would have unnerved her rigid grandfather who had despised the Ahlyo. But the language was actually one that he and everyone else knew well. She reached out to grasp the small hand mirror that lay by her bed and placed it so that it reflected the page. Although the cursive handwriting was a little hard to read, the script in the mirror was the same one she used all the time. Mirror writing. Elin had thought it was magic the first time her mother had shown her. Choking back tears, Elin followed the writing across the page.

The first line recorded the condition of the Toda's scales and the second line was the date.

It's her diary.

The book must have been so thick that the flames never reached the middle, leaving these pages intact. Skimming through them to the end, she saw that this remnant covered a period of ten days, two years before her mother was executed. Most of the entries were short and simple, describing the condition of the Toda that day. But there was one spot, a few lines, in which her mother expressed her feelings like a sigh.

. . . The rot that has set in on these scales could be cured by applying a solution made of ground tsuma grass roots. I'd like to try it, but I'll have to be careful because this cure has not been taught to the Toda Stewards. It couldn't cause any harm to heal scale rot, so why on earth weren't they taught this? There is so much missing from the knowledge given to the Stewards. Oh! How I wish I could go to the Valley of the Kalenta Loh, the People Who Remain. Oh, Paleh, the valley fragrant with flowers. If I could go there, I might learn why the knowledge was passed on in this way this . . .

The Valley of the Kalenta Loh, Elin thought. What had her mother meant by that? What was in this valley that smelled of flowers?

Chimulu's mother groaned behind her and stretched. Hastily, Elin pulled the covers over the pages. Closing her eyes, she listened to the woman rise while letting her thoughts run over what her mother had written. This record had survived fire and twenty-some years to reach her hands. She was struck by the strangeness of this coincidence. Although barely ten pages had survived, the fragments of this diary contained her mother's thoughts when she was alive. Her voice came through so vibrantly because she hadn't intended these words to be read by others.

When I leave this world, how will Jesse remember me when I was alive? What kind of traces will I leave behind?

For a long time, Elin lay listening to the birds chirping busily outside the window as she let her thoughts roam.

In the late afternoon, two days later, she finally finished dissecting the Kiba and binding their bodies with fabric to cover up the incisions. After wiping her hands on a cloth, she exited the Stone Chambers with Yohalu. The shadows of the trees stretched long in the honey-colored light. Removing the mask that covered her nose and mouth, she savored the sweet, refreshing breeze.

Walking slowly beside her, Yohalu murmured, "You've finished your investigation. It looks like all of them suffered damage to the same organ."

Elin nodded. "Yes. I didn't see any other notable pathological changes."

"Which means," Yohalu concluded, "that's what must have killed them. What we need to find out next is what caused this change in their bodies."

Elin opened her mouth to respond, when someone shouted, "Lady Elin!" Chimulu dashed out of the caves and came racing up. "I'm sorry," he said, his face clouded. "But I have bad news. The Toda in Ponds eleven and thirteen are all female. The Kiba weren't the only females after all."

Elin's lips crooked in a smile. "But that's good."

Chimulu's eyebrows rose. "It is? Why? Doesn't that mean the cause of death is no longer certain?"

Elin shook her head. "If there'd been no other females at all, then it would've meant one more factor we needed to investigate, so actually, I'm relieved to know there were others."

Seeing his perplexed expression, she added, "The fact that the Kiba weren't the only females proves that tokujisui doesn't determine the Toda's sex."

"Oh!"

She was about to explain to him what had caused their deaths, but then glanced up at Yohalu. "May I tell Chimulu the results of the autopsy?"

Yohalu gazed down at Chimulu for a few moments before responding. Finally, he said, "You've worked hard and helped us well, Chimulu, so I'll let Lady Elin share with you her findings at this stage. But you must not tell anyone else until the inspector officially announces it. Do you understand?"

Chimulu nodded silently, and Yohalu gestured for Elin to go on.

"The cause of death was necrosis of the organs resulting from blocked fallopian tubes," she said. "That explains why all five died at the same time. They were all the same age, right? They all reached the breeding age at the same period, and they all died from egg-binding."

Chimulu's face brightened. "Egg-binding? You mean that eggs blocked their tubes? That proves it wasn't my brother's fault! That's fantastic news!"

Elin could not keep from smiling. A warmth flared in her chest at the thought that by discovering the cause, they had proven his brother's innocence. She wanted to jump up and down for joy just like Chimulu, but knowledge of the cause did not erase the fact that the Kiba, the gems of the Aluhan, had been lost. To let him rejoice now before the Aluhan had passed judgment would be cruel. Placing a hand gently on his shoulder, she said, "I promise to explain to the Aluhan that your brother wasn't at fault. And I'm sure that he will make a wise decision. But as he has not yet confirmed your brother's innocence, please don't tell your mother for now."

Chimulu's expression sobered for a moment, but then he patted his chest as if to encourage himself. "It'll be all right. Not one of the Stewards ever suspected that Toda raised in the Ponds might bear eggs. There's nothing in the Laws about their care that takes that into consideration. I'm sure the Aluhan will understand."

Elin nodded. "I think so, too."

Chimulu's face brightened, and they set off together. "Even so, it's strange," he continued. "Why were all the Toda born in the same year female? Don't you think that's odd? The females we found today, too, were all hatched from eggs collected the same year. If all the eggs laid in one year are either male or female, then do they reach reproductive maturity in different years?"

"I know," Elin said. "That question has been bothering me, too." His quickness of mind impressed her. The children of Toda Stewards had no opportunity to go to school. It seemed such a shame not to give someone as smart and curious as Chimulu the chance to study. There could have been many other Stewards in the past who were just as bright as him. If they had been allowed to study the lives and natures of living creatures from childhood, one of them might have questioned the Kiba deaths and discovered the cause much sooner.

Elin's face tightened at this thought. Of the entire artisan class, only the Toda Stewards and the Royal Beast Hunters were not allowed to attend school. This had never struck her as odd before because both of these groups lived in isolated villages, which made it impossible for them to attend school. Now, however, she couldn't help but think there was some cunning design behind it.

Reaching the edge of the forest, they stepped out of the gloom beneath the trees into the light of open space and set off along the village path. Thin threads of smoke rose from the village houses. The women must have been in the midst of preparing the evening meal.

"I'll run on ahead and tell my mother to prepare a hot meal for you," Chimulu said. "You can take your time."

Elin gazed after him as he dashed away. "I wish he could study at Kazalumu School."

Yohalu smiled. "I know what you mean. He's a clever young man." The amber light bathed his face. "But he's a Toda Steward. He can learn everything he needs to know here and nowhere else." He narrowed his eyes, squinting against the sun. "As you're a teacher," he added quietly, "I'm sure there's no need to say this, but it wouldn't do to give knowledge to everyone equally. It's by controlling what those who belong to each profession learn that this country maintains its current order, don't you think?"

Elin stared at him. He was a strange man. She was sure what he was thinking far exceeded what he put into words. "With all due respect," she began, but he laughed and raised a hand to stop her.

"There's no need to tell me," he said. "I can guess what you're thinking without you saying it. Our positions are different. We would just be arguing on different planes." He laid a hand lightly against the small of her back and urged her forward, then changed his tone. "Well then, have you thought about which Toda village to investigate next?"

His question came like a blow to the chest. She already knew what had caused the egg-binding. The time had come to tell him. Her pulse quickened, but she took a deep breath to steel herself. "No," she said. "As I was about to tell you before, the answer is already clear. There's no need to visit any other villages."

At this, Yohalu gave her a light pat on the back. "True. We know what caused their deaths. But"—he smiled and looked her straight in the eye—"you have not yet solved the riddle Chimulu raised, have you? The mystery of why Toda hatched at the same time are all the same sex."

Elin frowned slightly, taken aback. "Yes, but—"

"I know what you're going to say," Yohalu interrupted. "You've completed the task that was asked of you. From now on, if we check the Toda's sex and choose only males as Kiba, we can prevent this problem from recurring. But since we've come this far, it seems a shame not to continue. I would love to thoroughly examine other things about the Toda that are as yet unknown."

Elin stopped and stared at him. Anxiety surged in her chest, grating coarsely. If she went to other villages, her return to Kazalumu would be delayed for quite some time. "I'd like to find out those things, too," she said finally. "But the Royal Beasts in my care at the sanctuary will be mating soon. I don't want to delay my return any longer if possible."

"In that case," Yohalu said reasonably, "how about just one more village? There's one in particular where I would like to take you. Oohan. I am sure that you will find it fascinating. Let's stop there first before I escort you back to Kazalumu."

His expression was mild, but there was something in his voice that brooked no argument. Elin continued to stare at him, her brow furrowed. This man had belonged to the Black Armor, the highest-ranking unit within the Aluhan's army. She was sure that he really did want to learn as much as he could about the Toda. And yet, although she didn't know why, she was just as sure that that was not all.

A smile rose to Yohalu's lips. Once again, he tapped her on the back and urged her forward.

TWO

SEIMIYA'S DAYS

I

THE VOICE INSIDE

The gossamer curtains billowed in the warm spring breeze. Outside, the light was slowly fading. Music ebbed and flowed in the distance like the murmur of the sea, but in her seat by the window, Seimiya sat lost in thought with no ears to hear. The voices of her children who were playing with their nurse and maidservants rose sharply, but even then, she did not twitch an eyebrow.

"Mother! Mother!" Her daughter, Yuimiya, ran from the other side of the room and grabbed her by the knees. "Mother! Yonan says he saw a frog! A frog, Mother! But there are no frogs, are there? Not in the garden!"

Tall for her five years, she still tripped over her words sometimes, and her cheeks were flushed as she accused her brother of teasing her.

Yonan rushed over, looking flustered. "Yuimiya!" he scolded her. "Mother's not well. You shouldn't shake her like that." He would turn nine this year and still looked young, but already he had the quiet air of his father.

"Does your tummy hurt, Mother?" Yuimiya asked.

Seeing the frown on her daughter's face, Seimiya smiled gently. "No, it doesn't hurt, dear. I'm just being quiet because your little brother or sister is sleeping inside me."

Yuimiya reached out a hand to stroke her mother's belly with her fingers. "Be a good baby, now," she said solemnly. "Don't be mean to Mother."

Seimiya stroked her daughter's hair. It was smoother than silk.

The trill of a flute sounded through the thick door, announcing the arrival of her husband. The door opened, and Shunan entered dressed in formal attire, although without his sword.

Yuimiya leaped up at the sight of him. "Father! Father!" she cried. Running over, she wrapped her arms around his waist and jumped up.

"Hey there, little Princess," said Shunan. "Careful, please. I'm all dressed up today."

Yonan came over, trying to act grown up, but his cheeks glowed as he gazed up at Shunan. "Father, have those foreigners arrived yet?"

Shunan raised his eyebrows. "You mean the prince of Tolah? He arrived just a little while ago." His face grew stern. "But, Yonan, it isn't right to refer to an official delegation from another country as 'those foreigners.' They've followed every protocol and come seeking our friendship. We must greet them with the same courtesy."

Yonan blushed. "Yes, Father."

Handing Yuimiya to her nurse, Shunan walked over to Seimiya and knelt beside her chair. "How are you feeling?" he asked.

Seimiya looked up at him, her face wan. "I'm fine. Thank you," she said weakly. Then she added, "It's not because I'm ill that I am not joining you in the hall tonight. You do understand that, don't you?"

The skin at the corner of Shunan's eyes grew taut. "Yes, but—"

Seimiya cut him off, her voice low and sharp. "Say no more. I have permitted foreigners to set foot in the Yojeh's sacred palace for the first time since this country's birth. We should attempt no more right now."

Shunan remained silent for a long while, then stood up slowly and said, "Yes, it is just as you say. It would be going too far to do more than that at this time." He took a breath. His eyes softened, and he bent low to kiss her cheek. "It'll be all right. We can do this," he said in a voice only she could hear.

Seimiya's face stiffened, and she turned her head toward the window. Silence rolled like a wave, heavy and ponderous, through the large room. Even Yuimiya kept quiet, watching her mother from her nurse's arms.

At that moment, the strumming of a lakkalu undulated softly, floating toward them on the breeze. It sounded completely different from the music played before.

"So Rolan's here, is he?" Seimiya murmured.

Shunan nodded. "Yes. His lakkalu works magic." He sighed and touched his wife's hand gently. "I will ask him to play for you, too. Although I doubt that he can do so tonight." Seimiya shifted her gaze to his and nodded.

Turning his head, Shunan fastened his eyes on his son and regarded him thoughtfully. "Yonan," he said, "you should attend the luncheon with me tomorrow."

Yonan blinked. Mixed emotions crossed his boyish face. Joy at being permitted to join such an important gathering and nervousness at his first encounter with people from a foreign land. "Yes, Father," he said, his voice faint, then glanced at his mother. Shunan also cast her a questioning look.

Seimiya gazed at her son, his arms and legs still childishly slender. "It will be a good opportunity for you, Yonan," she whispered.

Their first son would be the Aluhan, their first daughter, the Yojeh. That is what she and Shunan had decided when their children were born. There was no need to even discuss the possibility of Yonan becoming the Yojeh. That position was passed down from mother to daughter. Likewise the position of Aluhan was passed down from father to son. Yonan could never become the Yojeh. As he would one day be the Aluhan, Seimiya believed he should learn about the outside world, but it pained her now to see the uncertainty in his face. He looked so very young. She wished that she could give him a little more time to be a child.

Yuimiya, who sat perched on her nurse's lap, and Yonan, who was trying so hard to be grown up, would bear an arduous load once they reached adulthood. Pity welled within her as she thought of the merciless path ahead of them.

These children . . .

She must strive to lessen their burden even a little. Struggling to lift her spirits, which threatened to sink at any moment, she raised her chin and looked at her husband. "Shunan." He turned toward her, his face still bearing traces of the young man he had once been. "I will bless your negotiations with the kingdom of Tolah so that they may go smoothly."

Shunan's eyes shone. Smiling, he pressed his palm against his breast in gratitude. He gave his son's shoulder a quick squeeze, then turned and strode to the door. Just as the servant reached to open it, however, they heard the sound of a bell outside.

Yuimiya leaped down from her nurse's arms. "It's Auntie's bell!"

Stepping into the hall, Shunan cocked an eyebrow at his younger sister, her slender form garbed in an attractive gown of twilled fabric. "What are you doing here, Oli?" he asked. "The banquet's starting soon."

She shrugged. "I'll only be a moment. I heard that Seimiya wasn't feeling well, so I brought her some chimi fruit stewed in honey."

Seimiya's face brightened at the sound of her voice. "Oli?" she called out.

Oli saluted her brother with her eyes and slipped past him into the room. Dropping to one knee, she bowed to Seimiya and the two children, then rose and walked over to Seimiya's side. "How are you feeling, Your Majesty?"

The Yojeh smiled. She loved this young woman whose skin glowed with health and who, still single at almost twenty, spent every moment she could out riding. "Thank you for your concern," she said. "It's just morning sickness. I always get it. I'm not actually ill, so there's no need to worry."

Oli's lips twitched at this. "Morning sickness is a perfectly respectable illness, Your Majesty, so please feel free to rest." She turned to her maidservant who was carrying a basket and took a small jar from it. Placing it on the side table by Seimiya's chair, she opened the lid. Yuimiya and Yonan trotted over and peered inside.

"Oh, how pretty!" Yuimiya exclaimed.

Oli smiled at her. "A large chimi tree grows in the garden of the Aluhan's castle, Aluhan Ula. It's so laden with fruit that when they drop in autumn, they cover the fallen leaves. We take those and stew them with honey. They're delicious and good for your health, too."

Oli's maidservant removed three plates from the basket and scooped out some golden fruit from the jar with a spoon, deftly arranging them on the plates. A refreshing citrusy aroma wafted through the air.

"What a lovely smell," Seimiya said softly. Nami, her lady-in-waiting, glided forward and looked at her. She nodded, and Nami scooped one of the fruits off a plate with a spoon and daintily slipped it into her own mouth. She had been serving as Seimiya's food taster for so long that each movement was made with natural grace and no trace of hesitation. When she finished, she removed some utensils from a pouch she always carried with her and placed them on the side table. These were reserved solely for Seimiya's and her family's use.

Seimiya took the small plate of fruit Nami offered her and popped one of the glistening golden orbs into her mouth. A fresh aroma coupled with a delicate sweetness spread across her tongue. She had been unable to eat properly for so long that the sweetness seemed to seep into every corner of her body. "They're delicious," she said.

"I'm so glad you like them," said Oli with a broad smile. She turned to look at the servants. "I brought a jar for all of you as well. Please have some when you take a break."

Seimiya's servants looked uncomfortable. Although more than a decade had passed since Seimiya's wedding, they were still unable to accept the freedom with which the Aluhan's kin, who in their eyes were unclean, entered the Yojeh's chamber. Oli was fully aware of their feelings, but she never seemed to let that upset her and always treated them kindly.

The children's nurse strode forward. Bowing, she thanked Oli and took the jar. Noticing the woman's expression, Seimiya was caught by surprise. Although the nurse had schooled her features to conceal her emotions, her eyes betrayed a glimmer of remorse, as though she was ashamed of the coldness with which they treated Oli. The change was minuscule, yet it made Seimiya think that Oli's generous nature might be affecting the hearts of her servants after all.

This brought back memories of her grandmother, Halumiya. Regardless of her age, she had always stood straight and tall, smiling at everyone and addressing them as if they were her kin. She had been open to all without ever losing her quiet, illustrious dignity.

Grandmother . . .

She had probably been the last true Yojeh, Seimiya reflected. With that thought, the sounds in the room receded, and she was left alone in the silence, confronting the fear that plagued her mind.

If I am not the Yojeh . . . then who am I?

Seimiya woke in the dim light of dawn and laid her slender arms on top of the bed. She stayed that way for some time, feeling her skin, accustomed to the warmth of the covers, grow cold. Slipping her arms back under, she closed her eyes. But sleep did not come. She stretched under the soft quilt that covered the wide bed and sighed.

Her gratitude at being alone was greater than the loneliness of missing her husband beside her. These last few years, she always tensed when he gazed at her. Not knowing what face to show him, confusion made her stiffen. Despite her awkwardness, Shunan's attitude never changed, but his kindness just added to her burden.

His face and that of his sister rose in her mind.

Shunan and Oli. They're both so strong.

They bore such a heavy burden that pain sometimes etched their faces, yet they still had the strength to take another step. It was probably their unwavering conviction that had reminded her of Halumiya.

Grandmother never doubted, even for a moment, that she was the Yojeh. That's what made her so strong and generous and radiant. She was convinced that she was descended from the god who had crossed the Afon Noah and that her very existence brought this kingdom blessings. It was this that had made it possible for her to stand firm and unshakable, like a great tree, arms spread wide to embrace her people.

Seimiya sighed and ran a hand over her belly. Shunan thought it was their marriage that was making Seimiya suffer, the knowledge that she had thrown her people into confusion by wedding the Aluhan, whom they considered unclean. Even after all these years, the people still believed every calamity that assailed the kingdom was caused by his defilement of the Yojeh, and the palace was still in turmoil.

But he was wrong. If, like her grandmother, she had still believed without a trace of doubt that she was the Yojeh, she would have held her head high, regardless of the criticism unleashed against her. She would have taken his hand and together faced the difficulties that beset them.

With unseeing eyes, she stared at the blue dawn light wavering at the bottom of the thickly woven curtains. It was the Yojeh's task to decide foreign policy, and she was fully aware of the importance of diplomatic relations with Tolah, a rich land, bordered on the south by a long coast. Establishing strong bonds between them would deter Lahza, a country that mushroomed like a black cloud on the eastern plain, and contribute greatly to the kingdom's security.

But the nobles of Yojeh territory did not welcome relations with Tolah. If trade between the two kingdoms increased, it would be the lords and merchants of Aluhan territory, which already had ties with Tolah, that prospered. The nobles of Yojeh territory profited through taxes on goods that traveled the ancient highways joining this country with the caravan cities scattered along the grassy plains in the east. They feared that if bonds with Tolah were strengthened, traders would start using that route instead, reducing their profits.

The nobles were bound to create friction at the banquet just to cause Shunan trouble. To make sure that the banquet concluded peacefully and uneventfully, she, as the Yojeh, should be present. Yet even though she knew just how important this was, she could not bring herself to greet the prince of a foreign country. Not because she found the criticism of the bigoted nobles distasteful, but simply because she was afraid. Afraid to appear before the people and sit on the throne as the Yojeh, the ruler of this nation.

The source of her fear, the origin of her anguish, was emptiness, a lack of any solid foundation beneath her feet. No matter what she tried to say or do, she couldn't make up her mind. She couldn't see what was the right thing to do.

That night . . .

She closed her eyes, frowning. The tale Elin had told her the night she had appeared on the back of a Royal Beast had gouged a gaping hole in Seimiya's heart. She longed to believe that Elin had made up that story to save the Royal Beasts. But once the seed of doubt had sprouted in her mind, it had refused to wither.

If the Yojeh aren't descended from a god, then the belief that my very existence brings my people happiness is no more than a myth.

Since childhood she'd been certain the pure blood of the gods ran in her veins, but once that conviction vanished, all that was left was a vulnerable woman, no different from any other. Around the time that Yuimiya was born, Seimiya had begun to hear a voice murmuring in her ear whenever she sat on the throne and spoke to the people. A voice that called her an imposter.

It was not her union with Shunan or the resentment of her people that caused her anguish, but this voice that whispered deep in her mind.

2

SPRING BANQUET

Bathed in soft spring sunlight, a large round table stood in the garden. Glass dishes piled high with colorful fruits and freshly baked sweets sat upon the pristine white tablecloth. Guests sat around the table, chatting quietly, while behind them, servants bustled back and forth, bearing sizzling platters of roasted meats and bowls of steaming vegetables, which they deftly slid onto the table.

Seated on the left of the Aluhan, Yonan had barely touched his food. His face was tense with nerves, and he kept glancing at the foreign guests.

Beside him, Shunan was engaged in an amicable conversation with Tauloka, the prince of Tolah, who sat on his right. Sitting across from them, the nobles of Yojeh territory remained silent, occasionally whispering among themselves. Kin to the Yojeh, they loathed Shunan and deeply resented the drastic changes he had caused. To invite foreigners into the sacred palace was equivalent to trampling through a holy place in muddy boots. Given the choice, they would not have attended either the banquet the previous evening or this luncheon. But they couldn't protest when the Yojeh herself had given these events her blessing, and so they applied themselves to their food with glowering faces.

Oli sat next to Yonan. "Your Highness, you should eat," she murmured.

Yonan, red-faced, hastily cast down his eyes and picked up his spoon. Oli focused on helping her nephew to navigate his first official luncheon, forcing herself not to look at the nobles. Just the sight of them made her so angry, it killed her appetite. Inwardly, she cursed them.

Fools! The people of Tolah were probably already aware of the situation in this country. Still, why would the nobles demonstrate their discontent so openly? They were unhappy about strengthening ties with Tolah. She knew that, but their reasons were purely selfish—they feared that their own profits would decrease. Maybe they wanted to declare through their rudeness their opposition to the negotiations. Or to embarrass the Aluhan by showing that he'd failed to win their confidence. But couldn't they see how this put the country at a serious disadvantage?

"Is that so? This palace has wonderful pastures, too."

Picking up the words of Prince Tauloka's interpreter, Oli turned her attention to the conversation between him and her brother. Robust and deeply tanned, the prince was so short that the nobles had almost laughed in his face when they had met him last night, and he looked so boyish, he seemed far younger than his twenty-three years. He laughed often, and his big dark eyes darted here and there. But as she watched him, Oli began to suspect that, contrary to his appearance, he was sharp-witted, picking up every subtlety.

Once again, he spoke, his voice penetrating, and the interpreter quickly translated. "How unfortunate that I could not meet Her Majesty, the Yojeh, to present her with our finest steeds in person. However, if you have a pasture so close to the palace, why not ride with me after lunch? The five horses we brought for you were trained on the beaches of our coast and are strong-legged. I would be honored if you would test them yourself."

Silence spread around the table. Under the steady scrutiny of the nobles, Shunan paused, seemingly unsure how to respond. Toda Riders considered horses to be inferior mounts. Warriors were trained in horseback riding, but while Shunan might ride in a carriage, he was not a skilled horseman and did not ride horses for pleasure. Well aware of this, the nobles waited, eyes glittering spitefully, to see if he would accept this invitation, which would surely end in humiliation.

But before Shunan could speak, a bright voice rang out. "What a splendid idea! If you wouldn't mind, I would be delighted to accompany you," Oli said. Ignoring her brother, who had turned to her in surprise, and keeping her eyes fixed solely on Tauloka, she pressed her trembling fingers together beneath the table and smiled. "Ever since last night, when you showed us those wonderful horses, I have been longing to ride one."

Tauloka looked at her with an arrested expression. The warbling of the birds sounded loud in the hush that had fallen over the garden. Finally, the prince inclined his head gracefully. "What an unexpected pleasure it will be to ride with the sister of the Aluhan," he said. "Please do join me."

A murmur of indignation rose from the other side of the table as the nobles demanded to know why the younger sister of the Aluhan should ride horses that had been gifted to the Yojeh. Their voices, however, were interrupted by music, which suddenly poured forth from among the trees. All eyes turned toward the sound. In a spot that a moment before had seemed empty stood a lone musician, his finely chiseled features framed by shortly cropped brown hair. Leaning against the trunk of a sasha tree beneath a halo of pale pink blossoms, he strummed a lakkalu.

His russet-colored eyes narrowed, and he bowed his head slightly over the instrument, focusing on the music, as he raised his gentle voice in song. Wafting toward them like the spring breeze through the blossoms, the tune touched some forgotten place deep within their hearts. It was a joyful song, celebrating spring, and by the time the last ripples had faded away, peace had settled over the group assembled at the table. Even the nobles had lost the desire to grumble.

The meal ended, and, after seeing the guests off, Oli told her maidservants to go on ahead. Alone, she walked over the grass toward the musician where he sat perched on a tree root loosening the strings of his lakkalu. "Thanks, Rolan," she said.

The man raised his eyebrows and smiled, his eyes crinkling. "Always at your service, Princess."

Oli scowled. "Stop calling me that."

Rolan scratched his chin and cast her a teasing look. "But I can't go on calling you Omli forever, you know. It wouldn't do."

"Omli is just fine. We were playmates from before we were even out of diapers. It feels weird to hear you call me Princess." She frowned at him sternly, but his mouth quirked.

"Then Omli it shall be. But only when no one else is in earshot." He cradled his instrument as tenderly as a baby and slipped it into his knapsack. "You're going to ride with the prince, are you?" he murmured.

Oli didn't answer. Rolan rose slowly, looking down at her. Aware of his gaze, she sighed. "Yes. I'm going with the prince. For a long ride this afternoon." Raising her eyes, she stared up at him. Her face twisted. "Time goes by so fast. It seems like yesterday that we were playing tag together."

Rolan stood silently, watching her eyes fill with tears. She wiped them away hastily, then nodded as if to herself. "Yes. Time has passed. I'm a woman now, old enough to be a man's wife." Thrusting her chin forward, she looked at him with a fierce gleam in her eye. "We mustn't let that prince take our country lightly. If we can establish a strong bond with Tolah, I'm sure my brother will use that good fortune to protect this land. You've spent years painstakingly building this connection. I'll make sure we tie that knot well."

Renowned for his spellbinding voice, Rolan was invited to palaces in every land and had used his position to serve as a bridge. He looked for people who could be of use to this kingdom, took time to subtly move their hearts, and built slim but precious connections between Lyoza and other countries.

He gazed wordlessly at Oli. She knew this visit from the prince of Tolah was due to his hard work. And she was telling him that she wouldn't let his effort go to waste. He nodded slowly. As the younger sister of the Aluhan, and the sister-in-law of the Yojeh, she was a trump card in the game of diplomatic relations. His daring, cheerful childhood companion was telling him she would play that card well. Yet all he could do was nod.

Prince Tauloka stayed three short days and, in the end, offered only a promise of friendship between the two kingdoms. No doubt during his visit, his shrewd eyes had grasped the country's internal instability. In the agreement they made, there was no mention of an alliance that would involve military action.

Shunan was discouraged by the results, but the visit had yielded one opportunity to deepen their relationship. After his long ride with Oli, the prince had invited her to visit Tolah as a guest of the state. From her efforts was born this single bond, slim but highly promising.

THREE

DESCENDANTS

I

THE ROAD TO OOHAN

The sasha trees were in full bloom, their pale blossoms floating like a cloud above the road. Petals quivered in the barely perceptible breeze as the carriage passed beneath.

"Ah, spring is the best season." Yohalu sighed, inhaling the delicate fragrance that drifted through the window.

The mellow trill of a flute was followed by a burst of cheerful music. Several musicians were playing beneath the sasha trees. They had set out a large box to collect the coins of passersby, but no one stopped. Although the musicians had chosen a well-known tune and played with skill, something was lacking. One of the instruments was a little off-key.

What a waste, especially when the flute sounds so nice, Elin thought.

"That lakkalu player must be an amateur," Yohalu said with a grimace. "His strings are loose. They won't make much in this town. People here are used to far better."

Elin looked at him in surprise. "I had no idea you knew so much about music."

"I don't really," Yohalu said with an embarrassed smile. "I just listen to a lot of it." His face softened. "My son plays the lakkalu, you see." Saying no more, he looked out the window.

The road was lined with many kinds of stalls, and the people crowding the street were garbed in diverse styles of clothing. Carts piled high with sacks of wool lumbered by, swaying drunkenly each time the wheels struck a rut in the paving stones. Although firmly secured with ropes, the bags lurched precariously, as if they might tumble off. The drivers were mostly men with thick beards and long, intricately braided hair coiled on top of their heads.

"I wonder where they're from," she murmured, round-eyed.

Yohalu grinned. "They're Asheh, from the grasslands. We're near the border, so it's quite common to see them here."

Elin stared at him. "The border? But you said that Oohan wasn't far."

His eyes twinkled. "That's right. Oohan is near the border. Although, to be precise, the closest border is about three days from here by horse and boat. Does that seem odd?"

Elin shook her head. Toda villages were located far from other settlements and kept a closely guarded secret. The Stewards only dealt with the nearest villages and were never informed of where the others were—a precaution taken to prevent hostile nations from discovering their location.

A sasha petal fluttered through the window and landed on Elin's shoulder. Yohalu reached out and plucked it off. "Oohan is the oldest Toda village," he said. "Where the first Toda were raised."

"Really?"

Holding the petal between his fingers, Yohalu said, "I'm sure you've heard the tale of the first Toda Rider and Aluhan, the hero Yaman Hasalu."

Elin nodded. Yohalu released the petal out the window and pointed east. "This is a land of ancient history, where the Victory of Amasulu took place. Beyond those hills flows the great Amasulu River, the one that

Yaman Hasalu crossed on the back of a Toda to defeat the invading Hajan army.

"Even though he saved our country, Yaman Hasalu was defiled by the blood he had shed," Yohalu continued. "Because of that, he never returned to his homeland on the other side of those mountains, which then formed the border. To reward him for his loyalty, the Yojeh bestowed upon him the title of Aluhan, grand duke, and gave him the territory from here to the mountains." Yohalu swept his hand toward the west. "So you see, this is where Aluhan territory began."

His hand traced an arc toward the rear of the carriage. "At first, it was just a small piece of land, a fief between the river and the mountains that could have been blown away with a single breath. And it stayed that way until the time of Yaman Hasalu's grandson, Oshiku Hasalu. He began raising Toda to create the army that would conquer, one by one, the lands of the Hajan kingdom."

Yohalu looked at Elin. A light burned deep in his eyes, and he broke into a smile. "In one sense, this is where our kingdom started. In a different way from how it began on Tahai Azeh."

Elin regarded him silently for a long moment. "You're very proud of this land, aren't you?" she said finally.

Yohalu's smile deepened. "Of course. This is my homeland." She looked at him in surprise. He nodded, then shifted his gaze out the window again. "This road is very well maintained. Do you notice how it twists and turns so you can't see ahead? It was designed and built in anticipation of enemies invading. This is the kind of place in which I was raised. I'm a Toda Rider to my very bones."

With that, he fell silent, eyes focused on the passing scenery. As he had said, the road was well kept, and the slope had been built at the perfect incline to ease the uphill passage of horse-drawn carriages. This made the ride smooth and pleasant, and they reached the top of the hill by noon.

Yohalu ordered the driver to stop and invited Elin to step outside. Descending from the carriage, she gasped. Below her spread a wide plain rimmed with mountains and bisected by a great river. At the foot of the hill on which she stood lay a large town. White sails dotted the river, and she guessed that they must be merchant vessels. Rice paddies encircled the town and spread far into the distance. Fed by the abundant waters of the Amasulu River, the plain was a prosperous rice-producing district.

Pale, wispy clouds drifted across the bright blue sky, and birds flitted busily to and fro. Caressed by the refreshing spring breeze, Elin gazed down, squinting against the hard, silver light glinting on the river's surface.

"That's the Amasulu, which Yaman Hasalu crossed on his Toda to scatter the Hajan troops." Yohalu stretched out his arm and pointed toward a spot where a smaller river merged with the larger one. "Do you see that tributary?" he asked. When Elin nodded, he said, "Oohan, the village where we're going, is at its head, although you can't see it from here."

Elin looked up at him. "Pardon my ignorance," she said, "but is the Amasulu the border?"

Yohalu shook his head. "No, not anymore. The eastern border is some distance away. In the past, the broad Amasulu River plain belonged to the kingdom of Hajan. The territory the Yojeh gave to the first Aluhan, Yaman Hasalu, only went as far as the riverbank on this side. It was tiny. He stayed here for the rest of his life, continuing to protect it from Hajan invasions. It wasn't until his grandson's time that the other side of the river became part of our country."

Yohalu stared at the narrow strip of land. "The Hajans finally stopped attacking us when Oshiku Hasalu developed his Toda army and conquered not only the lord across that river, but also the lords of Hajan domains much farther east. He signed a pact with the king of Hajan, who ceded those lands to our country on the condition that we advance no farther."

Shifting his eyes to Elin, he said, "In Yojeh territory, people speak of Oshiku Hasalu as a man who laid waste to other lands from selfish ambition. But if he hadn't crossed the Amasulu, everyone in Lyoza would still be destitute and living in constant fear of invasion. Oshiku knew his name would be reviled through the ages, but rather than protecting his reputation, he chose to lay the foundation for this country's stability and prosperity."

Elin remained silent for a long time, staring down at the plain. Slowly, she raised her head and looked at Yohalu. "But in the end, Hajan was destroyed, wasn't it?" she said.

Yohalu's eyebrows rose. "You're well informed."

He looked as if he would say more, then paused, but Elin could guess what he was thinking. The Yojeh's subjects were rarely told anything about the enemy that now threatened the caravan cities to the east. Yohalu was probably thinking that someone had tried to persuade her to use the Royal Beasts against them by telling her the fate of Hajan. Having seen the momentary flash of consternation on his face, however, she was sure he had some other reason for expounding upon the feats of the Aluhan's ancestors.

Yohalu gave a small sigh. "Yes, the kingdom of Hajan was destroyed. It was swallowed up by the Lahza horsemen who control the plains far to the east." He pointed eastward. "The prosperous caravan cities of Hajan that we seized lie some distance in that direction. The Lahza attack them frequently. Until now, their attacks, though fierce, have not been large in scale. They've just been testing us. Without a doubt, however, they hope one day to seize our kingdom."

Elin frowned. Looking at this beautiful, spacious world, she found it strange that anyone would want to invade another country. "Why would they want to conquer us?" she murmured.

Yohalu smiled wryly. "Because—" he began, but then stopped and grew sober. He scrutinized Elin's face for a moment, then shook his head lightly. "We should go. We've tarried here too long. By the time we reach the foot of this hill, the sun will be starting to set. The road to Oohan leads into the mountains and is quite steep. Let's stay the night at the bottom of this hill."

Catching sight of Elin's expression, he added, "As for your question, let's wait until we have time to discuss it properly."

The next morning, they left the inn and headed toward the village, accompanied by four of Yohalu's men. Around noon, they veered off the main road and began climbing the path that led to Oohan. Elin was now keenly aware of why Yohalu had avoided traveling in the dark. Far too narrow to travel by carriage, the mountain trail was typical of those used by woods-men and hunters. It followed a deep, churning river that seemed to go on forever.

Elin reached down to rub her knee as her horse plodded along behind Yohalu. She was used to riding. When she had lived with Joeun as a child, she had often ridden his mare, Tochi, and in Kazalumu, she usually rode when she went to town. But this mountain trail was so steep in places that she had to raise her hips and lean forward with her chest against her horse's neck. Her legs had begun to ache, then her hips and even her back.

Perhaps he had heard her labored breathing because Yohalu slowed and glanced back. The two soldiers who were following Elin slackened their pace as well. "Are you all right?" Yohalu asked.

"Mmm, maybe not. My legs are starting to cramp," Elin said with a rueful smile. "How much farther is it?"

Yohalu grinned. "There's still quite a way to go, but this is the last steep part," he said. "Hang on a little longer."

Just as he had said, the trail soon leveled off, and Elin could catch her breath. Her mount seemed to have found it a hard climb as well. Its hide was sweaty, and steam rose from its flanks. She patted its neck. "Well done! That was quite a climb. Thanks for carrying me up." The horse's ears flicked in her direction, and it shook its head as if in agreement.

Yohalu swiveled around, a grin on his face. "Terrible trail, isn't it?"

Wiping away the sweat that trickled down her temples, Elin sighed. "I thought that the village of Tokala and the one where I was born were deep in the mountains, but the trails there are nowhere near as steep as this, and they're both closer to town. The villagers here have it pretty hard, don't they?"

Yohalu nodded, toying with the Silent Whistle that hung around his neck. It was the kind Toda Riders used, much shorter than those of the Stewards. As he fingered it, he looked down at the rushing river at the foot of the cliff. "This area's crawling with wild Toda. Even hunters avoid it. That's exactly why Oshiku Hasalu chose it as the place to raise his army. His first concern was to make sure no one discovered where it was."

Still talking, Yohalu dug his heels into his mount, urging it into a walk. "Even so, it's possible for enemies to sneak across the border into the mountains and steal the eggs. And then there are the smugglers who sell eggs to other countries despite the penalty of death. But no one from any other country has been able to train the Toda and ride them into battle. In other words, the real gems of the Aluhan are not the Toda but rather the skills of the Stewards and the Riders. We have to make sure that these two things never fall into foreign hands."

Shielding his eyes from the sunlight shining through the leaves, he smiled. "Living so deep in the mountains makes life that much harder. In other villages, the Stewards feed their Toda goats, but it's difficult to raise goats here or bring them in from outside. Instead, the Stewards of Oohan feed them mainly fish, which means they can only raise a limited number. There also isn't much room to practice riding them. Oshiku discovered many things that needed improving while raising the first Toda here. That's why the villages that were built later are in more convenient locations."

Elin was so intrigued that she forgot her aches and pains.

"Oohan has only a little over ten Toda," Yohalu went on. "That's not enough to form a troop. There are three other Toda villages in Amasulu territory, and most Toda that are ridden into battle are raised in those villages."

Holding the reins in one hand and deftly guiding his horse with his legs alone, Yohalu looked back at Elin again. "The other three villages are closer to Tokala, but I wanted you to see Oohan, the first Toda village."

Elin bowed her head. "Thank you very much," she said fervently. Although she still wondered why this old warrior had brought her here, her heart leaped at the prospect of seeing the village upon which all the others had been modeled.

Squinting, she looked down at the sunlight dancing on the river's surface. When the men of this village were summoned to battle, they probably rode their Toda down this river. And when the war was over, rode them back up again. This was where the Toda army had first begun.

As the light shining through the foliage began to pale and the sun started its descent toward the horizon, the trail they were following came to an abrupt end. A sheer cliff towered in front of them, and a cascade plunged over it with a deafening roar, falling into a wide pool beneath. The emerald-green water was so clear that Elin could see fish swimming under the surface. Waves fanned out from the waterfall and lapped against the reeds in the shallows at the pool's edge. As Elin drew near, the color of the water intensified. It must be quite deep, she thought, because the bottom was shrouded in darkness.

The water carved an arc as it fell from the height of the cliff, sending up a shower of white spray. On the wind raised by the thundering water, Elin caught a faint sweet scent. Softly, she grasped her Silent Whistle. At intervals around the pool, she noticed deep purple shrubs called ogulu. "This is the gate, then, is it?" she asked.

Yohalu nodded.

There was always a place like this on the trails leading to a Toda village; a swamp or a pool where Toda too old to bear a Rider were kept. These served as a barrier against intruders. Toda hated the smell of ogulu. Unless there was some dire emergency, they would never go near these shrubs, and the Stewards called them Toda stoppers.

To an unsuspecting traveler, this spot would look like an ordinary pool. But Elin had been raised in a Toda village; she understood that these shrubs had been planted at strategic points, such as where the Toda could slip from the pool into the river, to keep them from leaving the area. When the Toda swam out to battle, the Stewards probably got into the river and pushed the shrubs aside to make a passageway.

She heard a ripple of water and saw the reeds along the pool's edge sway. Having picked up the scent of horse and human, the Toda were on the move.

"Dismount and hold your horse's bit tightly," Yohalu told Elin. "Then follow my footsteps."

Elin slid off her horse, as did Yohalu's men, two in front and two bringing up the rear. They looked at Yohalu as if awaiting orders. When he slipped his whistle inside his mouth and gripped it between his teeth, his men followed suit. That motion brought back a day long ago when Elin's mother had taken her to send off the Toda Riders from her village. That's right, she thought. Toda Riders carry the Silent Whistle in their mouths because they need to use both hands.

An enormous shape slithered out of the reeds, and Yohalu raised one finger. Elin presumed it was a signal that he would blow the whistle. She heard a hiss of air from his mouth, and instantly the Toda stiffened. Yohalu led his horse past the giant form, which stayed as motionless as a rock. Elin followed, soothing her mount, which was rolling its eyes in fear.

Yohalu led his horse gently across the gravel of the shallows, making sure that its hooves didn't slip. Elin and the guards walked behind him, their senses alert for any movement. When stalking their prey, Toda swam slowly, but when they attacked, they moved as swiftly as a flash of light. At a distance, they were impervious to the Silent Whistles, so timing was crucial. Unless one could read the ripples that radiated from their bodies as they swam beneath the surface and gauge their speed to judge their distance, it would be impossible to stop them with a whistle. Even experienced Stewards were occasionally torn to shreds because they blew their whistle at the wrong moment.

The party walked carefully around the pool, conscious of the musk-like odor that mingled with the scent of water. When they neared the waterfall, a trail that had previously been concealed by the trees came into view. Just as she was thinking that it must be the path to Oohan, Elin heard something charging through the reeds toward them. Not from the pool but from the bushes along the shore. She waited for a breath, and when the muzzle of the beast appeared from the reeds, she blew.

The Toda jerked upward as though it had run full force into a rock wall. Rigid, it fell with a thud onto its belly, and its sharp-clawed feet twitched spasmodically. Elin frowned. Turning, she saw that Yohalu also looked perplexed as he watched its quivering limbs. "Did you blow your whistle, too?" she asked.

Yohalu shook his head, and his men hastily assured her that they hadn't either. "Then why?" Elin muttered. Puzzled, she stared at the Toda. Blowing a Silent Whistle too soon after a Toda recovered from paralysis could cause convulsions and even death. Both Stewards and Riders were careful not to blow too frequently. The fact that this Toda was suffering from whistle shock meant someone else had used a whistle not long ago.

"Maybe a villager passed through," one of the soldiers said, his voice muffled by the whistle still clenched between his teeth.

"Maybe," Yohalu said. "But there was no sign of anyone ahead of us. Let's ask the guards."

2

THE TOGA MI LOH

They traveled on until the sound of the waterfall receded and they came to a large saya tree. Here, the road forked. One branch headed downhill toward the sound of flowing water. Judging by the fresh ruts in the grass along it, Elin guessed that it led to the river from which the villagers caught fish for their Toda.

They proceeded along the road on the other side of the saya tree. Gradually, the trees grew thinner and the forest brighter. Suddenly, the way before them cleared, revealing a valley with a village at the bottom. Terraced fields covered the slopes down to the village, where threads of smoke rose from the chimneys of the houses that nestled together. The building with the tall chimney set apart from the rest was likely the baths.

The road into the village was blocked by a guardhouse. Two young soldiers sat in front of it, but they leaped to their feet at the sight of strangers riding toward them. Spears at the ready, they opened their mouths to challenge them, only to freeze at the sight of Yohalu.

"Sir!" one of them cried. They snapped to attention and saluted.

Yohalu gave them a nod. "Thank you for your work," he said. "Where is your commander?"

Still saluting respectfully, one of them said, "Sir! Captain Aoolu is out on patrol!"

"Hmm," Yohalu said. "Is the gate included in your regular patrol?"

The soldier looked puzzled. "No, sir. That area is not included in the regular patrol because it is dangerous, sir. But if there is anything unusual, the patrol will go there, too."

"I see. Tell the captain to report to me when he returns. We'll be staying a few days, and I want to tell him our plans and why we've come. We'll be at the chief's house."

"Yes, sir!"

Sturdy retaining walls of black stone bordered the terraced fields. Tiny blue flowers poked between the stones and waved in the gentle breeze. The glow of the westering sun filled the valley, and the pleasant scent of freshly tilled earth wafted on the air. Women were working in the rice fields, bent over at the waist, but when Elin and the others rode along the path between the terraces, they straightened and gazed down at them. Children helping their mothers gaped like round-eyed puppies, then set off at a dash down the road. Elin guessed that they were heading for the chief's house to let him know guests were on their way.

Suddenly, the women raised their voices in song. At the sound, a wave of nostalgia gripped Elin's chest, and her hands tightened on the reins. Long ago, she had heard the women of her village sing like this. The welcome song, a greeting sung when peddlers entered their village with permits hanging from their necks to show they were allowed in. The tune was slightly different, but very similar. Perhaps the song had originated in this very village and then been passed on to each new Toda village when it was built.

People emerged from houses scattered in the valley and looked up at the visitors. Chickens fled squawking, startled by the horses, while children climbed onto the railings of a sheep corral, pushing and shoving one another as they tried to get a better look at the visitors. Four people stood smiling outside the chief's home. Elin guessed that the elderly man in the center, who looked to be over sixty, must be the chief. His short hair was liberally peppered with gray, but he stood straight and dignified. As he peered at Yohalu's face, his eyes grew round with recognition. "Well, well!" he exclaimed.

Yohalu grinned. "It's been over ten years since I last visited. I've aged since then, but you haven't changed a bit."

The chief shook his head. "No, no, I'm getting old, too," he said. Then, as if recollecting himself, he announced formally, "Welcome to our village. We were just saying that today something auspicious would happen because last night was such a lovely starry evening."

His voice rang as he pronounced these ritual words of greeting, and Yohalu bowed deeply in response. The women beside the chief clapped their hands and broke into a merry rendition of the welcome song.

"Thank you," Yohalu said when they finished. "It's wonderful to see you all looking so well. I'm sorry I didn't let you know we were coming in advance, but I hope you'll let us stay a few nights."

"Of course! Of course!" the chief exclaimed. "What greater happiness could we ask for? As you know, we have only our humble home to offer, but please stay with us for as long as you like." He ushered them inside, betraying no trace of curiosity for why Yohalu had come or why he had brought Elin with him. Yohalu's men went off with some of the villagers to take care of the horses.

When Elin stepped inside the chief's house, she was momentarily disoriented by the darkness. Inside the entrance was a large earthen-floored space with a high ceiling. On the left was a kitchen with several big clay ovens. The women appeared to have been preparing the evening meal. There were freshly washed greens and chopped riko onions sitting in baskets. The walls and round beams in the ceiling were blackened with smoke and soot from cooking, showing the building's age. Elin's mother had sometimes taken her to visit her grandfather, and his home had been much like this. The lives of the Toda Stewards seemed to be the same everywhere.

They washed their feet and stepped up into the spacious living room.

The windows on the far wall were open, and sounds floated in from outside. The wooden floorboards were so well polished that they gleamed, and thick winter rugs had been laid around the hearth in the center of the room.

"Even at this time of year, it gets cold at night," the chief said, as he invited Yohalu and Elin to sit. He told the women to hurry and bring some tea.

Lowering himself onto a rug, Yohalu glanced toward the corridor that led to other rooms in the back. "How is Kamalu?" he asked.

"Ah. Grandfather is very well. Although he sleeps a lot these days. In fact, he's sleeping now. Shall I wake him?"

Yohalu shook his head. "No. There's no need to disturb him. I can talk to him when he wakes up and his mind is fresh."

Yohalu chatted with the chief about different people they knew while the women prepared the meal. By the time the last light had disappeared, the large pot that hung over the hearth had begun to bubble, and the delicious smell of miso-flavored stew permeated the room.

"Let's fill our stomachs with a hot meal. Nothing special, I'm afraid." The chief spoke less formally now. Half rising, he took some eggs and broke them into the pot, one by one. While they were still soft, he deftly ladled these along with vegetables and meat into generous bowls of steaming rice. While he did this, two women poured tea for everyone. Elin assumed they were his daughters or daughters-in-law.

"This looks delicious. Thank you." Yohalu picked up his chopsticks and, mixing the contents together, began to eat. Following his cue, Elin bowed her head in thanks and picked up her bowl. She broke the egg with her chopsticks, and the golden yolk spread into the stew. The rich flavor of the stewed vegetables and meat permeated the fluffy rice along with the creamy egg. It was so delicious she wanted to shout.

Once their hunger was satisfied, they sat sipping tea while Yohalu explained to the chief what had brought them here. The chief seemed fascinated, and the women, who had begun peeling fruit, paused in their work.

When Yohalu finished, the chief cocked his head to one side with a puzzled look. "All the Kiba died? That's very strange. And there've been mass Kiba deaths like that in other villages as well?"

"You mean it's never happened here?" Elin asked.

The chief shook his head. "No. Not even once."

"It's just as he says, Lady Elin," said Yohalu. He withdrew a sheet of paper from the bag that lay beside him and handed it to her. "Mass Kiba deaths have never occurred in this village. That's one reason I wanted to bring you here."

The chief and the others exchanged puzzled looks at the deference with which Yohalu treated Elin. Seeing their expressions, he laughed. "This lady is the one who saved the Aluhan's life."

Elin glanced at Yohalu in surprise. She had thought that he was speaking to her with deference to conceal his identity and pass as her bodyguard. But if he really treated her this way because he thought that . . . Rather than pleasing her, this made her feel so uncomfortable, she bowed her head.

Oblivious to how she might be feeling, a broad smile spread across the chief's face. "How wonderful! Of course she would be a Toga mi Loh. We are truly honored to welcome such an illustrious person into our home."

Elin blinked. Toga mi Loh? She rolled the words over in her mouth, wondering what they meant. A shock ran through her. "Excuse me, but did you just say 'Toga mi Lyo'?" she asked hoarsely.

The chief's brow furrowed. "Did I say something strange?" he said.

Elin shook her head. Her forehead felt numb, and her lips trembled. "You said 'Toga mi Lyo,' didn't you?"

The chief nodded, rubbing his chin. "Well, actually I said 'Toga mi Loh.' You have green eyes, you see, so I assumed you must be one."

Elin stared at him, dumbfounded. There was no mistake. The Toga mi Loh he was talking about were the Toga mi Lyo, the Green-Eyed Ones.

But why? How could he have known? Filled with remorse for the tragedy they had caused on the other side of the Afon Noah, the Toga mi Lyo had kept that history carefully sealed away, never sharing its secret with the people of this country. Here, they were known as the Ahlyo, the People of the Mist, from a land far away. The only ones who knew the truth were the Ahlyo themselves. And now Elin, along with the Yojeh, the Aluhan, and Ialu.

Her eyes met Yohalu's. He was watching her reaction with a bland expression. He knows, Elin thought. Her mouth grew dry, and she struggled to breathe. Yohalu had known that if the chief saw her, he would mention the Toga mi Lyo. That's why he'd brought her here. She was overcome with confusion. The world around her seemed to warp and bend. Desperately, she struggled to maintain her composure.

"Are you all right?" the chief asked with a look of concern. "You look pale."

Elin shook her head. "I'm fine. I was just a bit surprised, that's all." Her eyes darted toward Yohalu and back to the chief. "Where did you learn the name Toga mi Loh?" she asked in a trembling voice.

The chief blinked, as though wondering why she would ask such a question. "Where? Nowhere. We've always known. When a child with green eyes is born in this village, we say they're Toga mi Loh."

Elin's eyes widened. "There are children in this village who are born with green eyes?"

The chief nodded, looking a bit taken aback. "Yes indeed. Not that many, but yes. My granddaughter is a Toga mi Loh." He turned and said something to the women. One of them rose and, stepping into the corridor, called someone's name. A young girl of about ten appeared and timidly approached them. She had probably been in the next room all this time.

"Come," the chief said, and she stepped forward with a shy smile. Kneeling in front of Elin and the others, she bowed. When she raised her head, Elin stared at her eyes. As the chief had said, they were green.

After dinner, the women began preparing the bedding for the guests, and Elin slipped outside. The chill night air caressed her skin. She drew a deep breath. Darkness enveloped the valley, and the lantern light seeping from the houses twinkled like fireflies. Above her, the night sky was ablaze with stars. Gazing at the heavens, which seemed to suck her in, she let her thoughts flow like a rushing stream.

The first Toda village. A place where green-eyed children were born and called Toga mi Loh. Her thoughts sped in the direction to which these things pointed. She trembled.

Why did something so obvious never occur to me before?

The Yojeh had given the sacred treasure, the Toda whistle, to Yaman Hasalu and permitted him to ride the Toda. Yet that was impossible. The Yojeh's ancestor was a Royal Beast Rider, not a Toda Rider. It was the Toga mi Lyo, not the Yojeh, who knew how to control the Toda.

And besides . . .

The first Yojeh and the Toga mi Lyo were mortal enemies. They'd fought to the death on the other side of the Afon Noah. Why hadn't she seen this? Why hadn't she noticed how strange it was for Toda to have been used in a country built by the Yojeh?

Somewhere along the way, the tale passed down through the generations had been twisted. Something was missing. Where and when had Jeh, the first Yojeh, learned to control Toda? The knowledge bequeathed to the Stewards and Riders was far too detailed to have been learned from hunting wild Toda as food for the Royal Beasts. Or from fighting them. Clearly, the knowledge that could transform wild Toda into weapons had belonged to the Toga mi Lyo. If so, then who had given this knowledge to the Stewards and the Riders?

Not the Ahlyo. That was unthinkable. Vowing to protect the Law until the end of time, the Toga mi Lyo had become the Ao-Loh, the People of the Law, who were now known as the Ahlyo. They were the only ones she knew who could have passed on this knowledge, yet they would never have done so. Even her mother, who had been disowned by the Ahlyo, had despised using the Toda as weapons and had guarded the Law with her life. If they had known that the Toda would be used to fight for this country, the Ahlyo would never have shared the Handler's Art that allowed people to control them.

Were there Toga mi Lyo in this country other than those who had become the Ahlyo? At this thought, a memory fragment shifted deep inside her brain. The smell of smoke, the light of dawn . . .

Ah, that's it . . .

As if a flame had been kindled in her mind's eye, she saw the scorched pages of her mother's diary. The strange lines in the middle. The words she had read so many times they were now seared in her memory.

Oh! How I wish I could go to the Valley of the Kalenta Loh, the People Who Remain. Oh, Paleh, the valley fragrant with flowers. If I could go there, I might learn why the knowledge was passed on in this way . . .

Shivering, Elin hugged herself. Who were the Kalenta Loh, the people her mother, an Ahlyo, had longed to meet?

At that moment, she heard the rattle of a door behind her. Turning, she saw Yohalu silhouetted by the light spilling from the house. He strolled up and stood beside her. Stretching, he took a deep breath of night air, then smiled at her.

"You knew that there were people in this village with green eyes, didn't you?" she murmured.

"Yes, I did," he answered. "The girl's great-uncle had green eyes, too. I was surprised when I first met him. Unfortunately, he died in an accident eight years ago."

"Her great-uncle?"

"Yes, the chief's younger brother. In fact, I just learned that the daughter of the chief's brother was the girl's mother. She married her cousin, the chief's son."

"Both the chief's granddaughter and his younger brother have green eyes? They seem to be rather common in his family."

"There's a reason for that," Yohalu said with a wry smile. "It's not something they want to boast about, I'm sure. I'm guessing the chief didn't tell you because he hadn't explained it to his granddaughter yet. Would you like to hear it?"

Seeing her nod, Yohalu launched into the tale. "When Oshiku Hasalu decided to build the first Toda village here, he left everything up to a man

84

that he trusted completely. Oshiku told him to take any men who wished to become Toda Stewards into this mountain valley along with their families. They built the Toda Hall and Chambers and raised Toda hatched from eggs. This man trained the first Stewards, teaching them everything they needed to know.

"He must have had exceptional talent to be so trusted by the Aluhan, but he appears to have been rather loose with women. It took them several years to build the village, and during that time he got the wife of one of the Stewards pregnant. That must have gotten him into trouble. Once the work reached a certain point, he left and never came back."

"And the child that was born was—"

"That's right. The chief's ancestor."

Elin rubbed her cold hands absently. Was he a Toga mi Lyo? It seemed very likely that a Toga mi Lyo, and one who was not an Ahlyo, had come to this country to raise Toda as weapons. If so . . .

Suddenly, Yohalu grabbed her by the shoulders and shoved her behind his back. "Who's there?" he barked, his voice splitting the darkness. "Step out into the open!"

A figure appeared from behind the stable. A man. With a sword hanging from his belt. It was too dark to see his face clearly. He walked slowly toward them, then brought his heels together and bowed.

With his hand still on the hilt of his dagger, Yohalu snapped, "Who are you?"

In a muffled voice, the man replied, "Captain Aoolu."

Yohalu scowled. "Captain Aoolu? You were supposed to report to me as soon as you finished your patrol. Why're you so late?"

"I came but you were in the middle of your meal," the man said sullenly.

Yohalu waited for him to say more, but he remained silent. "So?" Yohalu demanded. "You're saying you didn't want to bother us?"

The man nodded.

"What were you doing over there?"

The man shrugged. "I was waiting for you to finish," he said.

Yohalu glared at him. "Without a light, behind the stables?"

The man shrugged again. "This village is like my own backyard," he said, his voice flat. "I can see well enough by the light of the stars."

Yohalu scowled, but then sighed as though to dispel his irritation. Removing his hand from his hilt, he said, "How long have you been posted here?"

"Ten years."

"I see," he said, his voice still tinged with annoyance. "Did anyone pass through the gate before us this afternoon?"

"No. No one."

Yohalu gave him a piercing look. "But someone must have, because one of the Toda clearly went into whistle shock."

Although his face was only a blur in the darkness, Elin could tell that the man's expression didn't change. "There's one Toda that often goes into convulsions," he answered in a low voice. "He's been at the gate a long time. It was probably him."

Yohalu finally nodded. "All right. That's all I wanted to know. Thank you. You may leave now."

The man bowed and shuffled off, vanishing into the darkness.

"There're many like him among the soldiers who serve in remote regions like this. He must have some skill as a Rider to have been given the post of captain. But if he's been here ten years already, he likely made a mistake, or did something wrong, and was posted here to redeem his honor."

Ten years. To redeem his honor . . . Elin sighed inwardly. To be separated from one's family and forced to live in this isolated village for so long. No wonder he behaved like that.

A bird called somewhere: a long, thin whistle that crossed the darkness, then melted away.

3

AN ARROW SPLITS THE DARK

The old man pointed his cane toward the entrance to the caves that spread out deep within the mountain. "Welcome to the oldest Toda complex in the country," he said with evident pride. "Please come in." Stooped with age, he tottered forward on unsteady feet.

The chief hastily grasped his elbow. "Father, please, allow me to walk beside you." But the old man brushed his hand away irritably.

Yohalu broke into a smile. "Master Kamalu, how old are you now?"

Kamalu turned and gave him an almost toothless grin. "I'll be eighty-eight this year!" he said. "Not bad, huh? But enough chatter. Follow me." He set off, and the chief hurried after, casting Yohalu and Elin an exasperated look as he held the lantern high.

The Stone Chambers were naturally formed caves. The only places that showed the trace of human hand were the channels that led out of the caves. It was damp inside, and water dripped from the ceiling. Distracted by the surroundings, Elin slipped and almost fell.

"Whoops!" Yohalu reached out and steadied her.

Elin blushed. "I'm so sorry. Thank you."

Yohalu chuckled. "I expect these Chambers are different from the ones you're used to."

"Yes. I was just realizing what a lot of work must have gone into the ones I know. The floors are smooth, wall torches keep down the damp, and smoke holes clear the air."

As they moved deeper inside, the moist smell of moss and the scent of Toda grew stronger. Elin sensed movement and heard the muffled sound of voices. The Stewards must be tending the Toda, she thought.

"Here we are," announced Kamalu from up ahead. "This is the Kiba Pond." As Elin stepped inside the Chamber, a raw stench assailed her nostrils. With a fish in each hand, a middle-aged Steward stood gaping at them, then ducked his head in a bashful greeting. At his feet was a basket full of fish.

"It's all right, Kolu. Carry on," Kamalu said. The man nodded and began throwing fish into the dark pool one by one. They arced through the air and fell out across the water. The first had barely touched the surface before a large head reared up and swallowed it whole with a great spray of water. Three other Toda rose, mouths opened to expose sharp fangs. They pushed against one another as they vied for the fish.

Elin frowned. They're so small. They were at least a whole size smaller than the Kiba she knew. And if these were the Kiba, then the other Toda would be even smaller. Yet their movements were swift and powerful.

"The Kiba of Oohan are known for their small size and agility," Yohalu said. "So much so that it's the custom to use them for scouting missions and night raids." The other men beamed with pride.

"Do you only feed them fish?" Elin asked.

Kamalu scowled. "Of course. I've heard that the villages built after us feed their Toda goats, but in the end, that'll make them sick. Toda were originally fish eaters, you see."

The chief cleared his throat and cocked an eyebrow at Elin. "Wild Toda do eat animals sometimes, but ordinarily, they eat fish. So that's what we've always fed the ones we raise here."

"What about tokujisui?"

"Of course we give them tokujisui. We give the Kiba plenty."

With the chief's permission, Elin put her face close to a tub of it in a corner of the cave and sniffed. It smelled just like the solution she was used to. She asked the men many questions, which they answered willingly, but the only difference between the Toda of Oohan and those in the other villages seemed to be their diet of fish.

When she expressed the wish to check the Kiba's sex, Kamalu's eyes almost popped out of his head. The men's respect for Yohalu, however, was deep, and when Elin slipped into the cold pool and began examining the paralyzed Toda, the chief and Kolu jumped in to help. The Kiba were all male.

"I guess that means the problem must be their diet," Yohalu said as they exited the caves, squinting in the light.

Elin, her purple lips quivering, shook her head. "Possibly, but I have a feeling that it's something else. The fact that they only eat fish could cause physical differences, but even so, it still leaves an unsolved riddle."

"Oh?" Yohalu said. The two other men also paused to stare at Elin.

"It was egg-binding that killed the Kiba in Tokala village. In other words, they died because they were female. But in this village, there has never been a mass die-off of all the Kiba. I can think of only two possible reasons. The first is that Kiba females that eat fish don't suffer from egg-binding. But I think we can rule that possibility out."

The chief raised his eyebrows. "Why?"

"Because even though you don't check their sex, if any Kiba had been female and remained healthy after maturation, there should've been reports of them laying unfertilized eggs. Yet neither you nor Kamalu mentioned anything about that."

"You're right," Kamalu said. "I've never heard of such a thing."

"And the second possibility?" Yohalu urged.

"That there have never been any female Kiba here. But the probability of that happening for over two centuries seems incredibly low. Especially when the method for choosing Kiba is exactly the same as that in the other villages."

Yohalu and the chief both frowned. "I see," Yohalu muttered, stroking his chin. "Then what's the difference between this village and the others?"

"From what these people told me, there seems to be absolutely no difference at all," Elin said. "However, it may be something so slight that it would normally go unnoticed. Or it could be related to the location. Where they're born and the natural features of the place in which they're raised can have a big impact on the bodies of living creatures." The three men listened intently. "There may be some natural mechanism in Oohan that prevents people from choosing eggs containing females, even though they aren't consciously aware of it."

Kamalu nodded. "Have you ever been egg gathering?" he asked.

"No. Never."

"Then you should get them to take you. It's always best to try things for yourself. When you see with your own eyes and hear with your own ears, things look different. It's egg-laying season, and although it's still a little early for gathering, you might learn something just by seeing where the nests are."

Elin's face shone. "Yes, please. That would be wonderful!"

At this, the chief spoke up. "In that case, I'll take you." He paused, then added, "But there's one thing you should know. Egg gathering can be dangerous. Toda get very excitable once they've laid their eggs, so we only go after the temperature drops and they're sluggish. That means going to the river when it's pretty dark, either at evenfall or dawn. If you miss your footing, you could slip into the river and drown." His face clouded.

Catching sight of his expression, Yohalu murmured, "That's how he died, wasn't it?"

The chief nodded. "He was always so careful, too. He went off with two others to collect eggs, but he was the only one who never returned. They heard him cry out once and then a splash. After that, nothing."

He glanced at Elin and sighed. "We're talking about my younger brother. He was a Toga mi Loh. You met my granddaughter yesterday, right? He was also her grandfather, on her mother's side. He was a cautious man, but kind, and a very good Steward."

Kamalu cleared his throat. "Let's not speak of it. Talking won't change anything."

The chief gave his head a quick shake as though to dispel his gloomy thoughts, then set off toward the village, his clothes still dripping with water. Elin was about to start after him when she felt as if she was being watched. Turning, she saw a group of soldiers talking near the trees beside the entrance to the caves. Among them, one figure stood looking her way, his face surly.

That's the man from yesterday.

She hadn't been able to see his face clearly in the dark, but from his build and behavior, she guessed it must be Captain Aoolu. Under his thick eyebrows, his narrow eyes were trained on Elin and her companions.

Kamalu predicted that there would be heavy mist the next morning, so they decided to look for eggs that very evening. The chief had insisted that he would take them, but Kolu, the Steward who had fed the Kiba, offered to go instead. The chief had already spent a long time in the icy waters of the Pond, Kolu said, and another cold soak in the river might aggravate his sore hip. Although the chief protested that his hip didn't bother him at all, he appeared grateful and agreed to let Kolu be their guide.

Yohalu and Elin followed Kolu through the last light of day toward the river. By the time they began descending the narrow trail that led off from the big saya tree, the sun was slipping behind the trees, and the breeze had turned chilly.

"This is the river where you catch fish, isn't it?" Elin said, eyeing the ruts left by cart wheels.

Kolu nodded. "Yes. The children catch them in the morning and bring them to the village."

The sound of rushing water grew louder, and the river came into view. It was a fast-flowing stream that sprang from the top of the mountain. Elin guessed that the rock in this area was quite solid because the river snaked along the contour of the land. In a large bend, the water slowed and pooled into a deep pot-shaped well, then overflowed and cascaded down in multiple steps. Mist drifted above the water, and the dry reeds surrounding the edge of the pool rattled each time the water pushed against them.

"This way," Kolu whispered, beckoning them with his hand. He stood on a spot slightly away from the rushing river where water lapped over the bank, making the ground muddy. Thick reeds, taller than a man, grew there. A sickly sweet scent filled the air, and the hairs on Elin's skin stood on end. If they were attacked by wild Toda, Silent Whistles would be useless.

Toda raised by men had their ear flaps cut off while they were still young, but not wild Toda. Even if she managed to stop the first one with her whistle, the rest would plug their ears and keep on coming. Still, she and Yohalu held their Silent Whistles at the ready as they made their way toward Kolu.

"This is the time when Toda are the most docile," Kolu said. "See?" Peering toward the shadowy reeds where he pointed, Elin saw the tip of a tail. "When they're like that," he explained, "they won't budge even if they hear noise or smell humans."

He pointed to another spot. In the dying light, Elin saw a mounded shape. A Toda nest. She glimpsed what looked like several eggs nestled in the pile of reeds and grasses. It was damp with water that overflowed from the pool.

"Are those the kind of eggs you gather?" Elin whispered, and Kolu nodded. "For Kiba, too?"

Kolu started to nod, then shrugged. "This isn't a year for choosing Kiba, but if it were, we wouldn't use eggs from that nest."

Elin blinked. "Why?"

Kolu gave a wry smile. "It may sound superstitious, but we have a saying that eggs from the upper basin don't grow as well."

"Basin?"

Kolu pointed toward the stream. Elin realized he must be referring to the pot-shaped pools at each step of the waterfall. The one at the top level was small and shaded by thick branches. Although water pooled where the river plunged into it, it quickly overflowed, cascading down to the pool below.

"We call pools like that at the base of each waterfall 'basins.' All the eggs taken from the same one are raised in the same Pond. But that nest is too close to the upper basin, so in years when we collect Kiba eggs, we take them from nests a little farther down." He stopped and pointed to a spot deep within a patch of reeds. This pool was much larger, and the water looked darker and more sluggish. Where the water flowed out of it onto the shore, Elin saw a hump of wilted reeds. "We would choose a nest like that one."

Elin stared at the nest for some time, then she crouched down, pushed aside the reeds, and stepped into the swampy water along the shore.

"Elin?" Yohalu said in a startled voice, but she didn't stop. She pushed her way slowly toward the first nest he had pointed to and slipped her arm inside it to feel the water and the eggs. Then she turned and carefully climbed down to where the second nest was, once again feeling inside.

It's warm!

The water inside this nest was warmer than that in the first one. There were no branches above this pool. During the day it would be exposed to the sun, which would heat the water. The nest was built with packed mud mixed with Toda saliva and slime and covered with withered grass and reeds. Soaked in water, the vegetation may have begun to ferment, which would also generate warmth. The nest on the upper level, however, would be constantly filled with cold water, which would suppress heat.

She brought her face closer to the nest to get a better look, when suddenly she heard the twang of a string. Startled, she turned and saw Yohalu stagger. An arrow protruded from his back.

"Yohalu!" she cried.

"Run!" he shouted hoarsely.

Far from fleeing, however, Elin ran toward him. From the corner of her eye, she saw Kolu pushing through the reeds as he escaped. When she reached the spot where Yohalu knelt concealed among the reeds, the sun had completely set, and his figure was only a vague blur. She probed the arrow gently, checking its position in relation to his shoulder and chest. Trembling, she breathed a sigh of relief.

"It missed your vital organs," she whispered, and Yohalu nodded. Like her, he was trembling. Although he must have been in great pain, he clenched his teeth to keep from crying out. Raising a finger to his lips, he peered into the darkness.

Elin heard a rustle of movement near the forest and then voices. The intonation seemed strange, and she couldn't understand the words they said.

A foreign language?

Someone clicked their tongue. It sounded surprisingly close. "Over here!" a man barked impatiently. "Hurry! He's been hit. Find him!" Elin's eyes widened. Captain Aoolu!

She heard the sounds of several men moving this way, speaking in some foreign tongue.

"Lazy brutes!" Aoolu muttered. "How many times do I have to tell them to speak our language?" Then he yelled out, "Don't kill the woman. She's worth far more than any Steward you might catch." He said something more but she couldn't hear it.

The dusk deepened. Although she could see no one, she could tell by the noise that the men were pushing through the reeds toward them. If she and Yohalu stayed here, they would be captured. But if they moved, they would give themselves away.

She heard the faint sound of metal and guessed that Yohalu had unsheathed his dagger. Terror caught in her throat, strangling her. Her mind raced.

What was going on? Why had they been attacked? What were foreigners doing here? She pushed the panicked confusion whirling around her brain to one side and focused on what she should do.

Yohalu was wounded. If they fought, he would surely be killed. And she would be captured . . .

"Don't kill the woman. She's worth far more than any Steward . . ."

These words kept echoing in her ears. If they caught her, she would be taken away and used. She would rather die than let that happen. The faces of Jesse and Ialu rose in her mind, and tears welled in her eyes. She clenched her teeth.

The men were coming closer. Mingled with the sounds they made, she heard something else. The hair rose on the nape of her neck.

Toda!

The Toda were on the move. Had they caught the scent of Yohalu's blood? Stealthily, she raised the Silent Whistle to her lips. The touch of the cold metal coupled with the stench of Toda wrenched her back in time, conjuring up a memory so vivid, it cut her heart like a knife.

Toda circling.

A dagger clenched between her teeth.

Her mother's pale hands.

And with that memory, an idea flashed through her mind. She grasped Yohalu's hand, and he looked up at her in surprise. "Can you run?" she whispered in his ear. Yohalu nodded. "Then trust me and do as I do."

She rose and dashed in the direction of the river. The ground was invisible in the darkness, and she ran without knowing what lay beneath her feet or what slashed her legs.

Behind her, she heard shouts and men crashing through the reeds, closing in. The roaring of the river grew louder, and the cloying odor of water and Toda engulfed her. Yohalu followed closely, his breath coming in painful, ragged gasps. The reeds blocking their path vanished, and the ground beneath their feet turned hard. Rocks. Elin slipped on a clump of moss and stumbled. Although she didn't fall, she banged her fist and couldn't help letting out a sharp cry.

The glow of the night sky gilded the river's surface. Long dark shadows slithered into the water with a quiet splash. She stepped into the river. The current was much stronger than she had expected, pushing against her legs.

"You'll never make it by river," Yohalu gasped. "It's too fast. And the Toda—."

There was a loud thud, and his voice was cut short. Elin turned and ran back. "Yohalu!" she cried. He groaned and struggled to rise. Elin slid beneath him and, hoisting him onto her back, staggered doggedly toward the water.

A large shape forged against the current, and the waves cresting around its head glowed faintly. Nearby, she felt more Toda stirring. The men who had followed her must have felt them, too, because they stopped among the reeds, and began arguing.

"It can't be helped," Aoolu yelled. "We can't let him live! Shoot! It doesn't matter if you hit the girl."

Bows twanged, and a flurry of arrows sailed through the air. Elin heard a loud whirring by her right ear, and a burning pain shot through her earlobe. A shock ran through her left elbow, as if it had been hit with a club, followed by a fiery agony.

She heard the sound of a heavy weight mowing down the reeds. Twisting her head, she saw several Toda slither from the reeds into the river. Her pulse pounded like a warning bell. She pressed her fingers to her lips. As she did so, she saw her mother's face; the sorrow in her eyes. She seemed to say, "You know what will happen if you use the finger whistle, don't you?"

Mother.

For a moment, she closed her eyes and gazed at her mother's face. Then, she opened them again. Just as the Toda reared and bared their fangs, she blew.

The notes of her finger flute rose shrill and clear. The high, complex melody rang across the river's surface and faded. The dark shapes stopped. Like hunting dogs awaiting their master's signal, they gazed straight at Elin.

She blew again, high and low, finishing with a flourish of strong, complex modulations. The shadows of the Toda surged forward, racing to her like a pack of dogs. Still bearing Yohalu on her back, she grabbed the horns of the nearest one and climbed on. "Yohalu!" she cried. "Hold on to me!" With a groan, he wrapped his arms around her waist.

The creature began to run. Water splashed Elin's face and within moments they were swimming down the river. Arrows rained down. Elin gripped the horns desperately, but she had no strength in her injured arm, and it slipped off. Instantly, the Toda began thrashing about.

We'll sink!

At that moment, a thick arm reached out and grasped the left horn. "The right one, too," Yohalu gasped. Elin relinquished the other horn. Yohalu slid his hands up to a certain point, turned his wrists at an angle, and gripped both horns strongly. The Toda jerked, then began swimming straight ahead as if it was fleeing for its life.

"No one," Yohalu murmured into her ear, "can beat a man of the Black Armor when he grips a Toda's horns."

Riding the torrent, their mount came to the lip of a plunge pool. Kicking with its feet, it crossed the ledge and slid nimbly down the river. The moon had risen, and the water gleamed palely. The Toda glided across the surface as if it were flying.

4

THE LORD OF AMASULU

With each break in the branches overhead, the silver moonlight flashed through, only to vanish again as the darkness closed in. Elin and Yohalu sped through that darkness, entrusting their lives to the Toda.

It had taken more than half a day to climb the trail to the village, but the Toda swept down the rushing stream with astonishing speed. Where the stream joined the tributary of the Amasulu River, the lights were still on in the houses that lined the road.

The Toda beneath them began to sink, and Elin blanched. The water was so deep she could not touch bottom. The weight of two adults had taken a toll on the poor creature. It writhed and twisted as it swam, raising its jaw above the surface.

Yohalu's rasping breath had sounded in Elin's ears throughout their journey, but now it came in quick, short gasps. Turning her head, she said, "Hang on. There are houses ahead. Let's stop somewhere along here and get help."

Yohalu muttered something, but the gurgling water drowned out his words. "I'm sorry. What did you say?" Elin asked.

"Let's go to Amasulu," Yohalu gasped. "There's a little channel just before this tributary joins the river. Let's pull in there."

Elin nodded. This was Yohalu's home. He knew it best. Relief at seeing houses must have released her taut nerves because the throbbing in her arm became intense. The arrow must have cut deeper than she had thought, and the loss of blood made her feel weak and cold. Yohalu's breathing grew even shallower. She feared he wouldn't make it to the channel.

The river flowed more slowly, and the Toda struggled to stay afloat, sinking and rising and sinking again. Silently, Elin urged it on. Just a little farther now. I'm so sorry. You must be so tired.

When the broad surface of the Amasulu River appeared ahead, Yohalu suddenly yanked the beast's horns to the right. It turned into a narrow canal thickly lined with reeds and overshadowed by branches that plunged them into darkness. The channel was barely wide enough for a single Toda to pass. Gradually, the trees thinned, and then a wide vista opened before them.

Elin blinked. A smooth lawn spread along both sides of the channel. Up ahead she saw a stately manor that looked like it must have belonged to the ruler of the domain. Lights shone in some of the windows, and the smell of hearth fires wafted on the air. A small hut stood by the channel.

"Go . . . ," Yohalu gasped. "Get help . . . Tell them . . . my name."

Elin ducked under Yohalu's arm and slid her rigid body off the Toda's back. She slipped into the water gingerly, unable to see the bottom in the dark, but it was shallower than expected; the tips of her toes touched ground when the water reached her chest. Placing her sound arm on the edge of the channel, she wiggled her way out of the water onto the grass. She tried to rise, but her knees gave out. Gritting her teeth, she crawled to the hut, then pounded on the door with her fist.

The door swung open, and she heard a gasp. Light flooded around her, and she squinted.

A man knelt beside her. "Who are you?" he demanded. "What's going on?"

"Help. Please. Yohalu . . . in the channel."

The man dashed off, and Elin rested against the doorframe. Through her fading consciousness, she heard the man say something to Yohalu. He ran back to the hut and picked up what looked like two pieces of fence that were leaning against the wall. Hurrying back to the channel, he placed one piece at each end of the Toda, then angled them so they pressed against the animal's head and tail.

A Toda weir. Elin had seen the Toda Riders tether their mounts in the channels like this when she was young. For some reason, Toda became quite docile when the fence touched their head. She stayed conscious long enough to see the man pull Yohalu from the Toda's back before she fainted.

For a long time, she lay at the bottom of darkness, listening to faint strains of music that came from far away. The strumming of the strings changed to Leelan's voice. She saw Leelan fly up into the air, her fur dazzling.

Ah, she's going to mate again. Joy and sorrow pierced Elin's breast.

She heard the cheerful voice of an official. "The Yojeh is overjoyed to know that the offspring of the Royal Beasts are increasing."

Yet for those in power, that was not just a blessing, but also a threat. Which path would they choose: to multiply the Beasts, or destroy them?

As Elin followed the thread of what would happen and what she should do, she came upon a different memory. The forms of Leelan and Eku disappeared, and she was in a dimly lit room. Someone's breath brushed against her ear, and a voice groaned, "We shouldn't do this. Our child will be doomed to bear a cruel fate."

Elin shook her head. Sorrow turned to anger, erupting from the bottom of her heart, and tears poured down her cheeks.

I will never wish that I hadn't been born. Even if I knew the life I would lead before I came into this world. We can't choose when or where we're born. Every living thing has to live the best it can wherever it happens to drop . . . Is that all you feel about your life? Regret?

To conceive a life with the one she loved—how could such an act be an abomination? She would never accept that, even if the child were bound by the fetters that constrained her own life.

But when she saw her son's face for the first time, when she heard his cry and cradled his warm little body in her arms, a fierce regret tore her heart. This child would have no choice but to be swept up in his parents' fate. The thought of how much he would suffer made Elin want to scream with fear. Confronted with her red-faced, bawling son, her feeble logic was no support at all.

Her arms and legs hurt.

Suddenly she was running through the darkness. Her body felt as heavy as mud, and dense reeds barred her way.

"Don't kill the woman. She's worth far more than any Steward . . ."

Squirming shadows rushed up from the depths of darkness. Elin ran for her life. She couldn't let them catch her. She couldn't let Jesse suffer the grief of losing his mother.

Sobbing, she twisted and turned until she shook off the leaden dream. Her breath came in gasps, and she wiped away the tears that streaked her cheeks. The dregs of the dream lingered, and she gazed stupidly into the air, unable to register what she was seeing. Gradually, it dawned on her that she was looking at a ceiling decorated with wooden squares. Each one framed three delicately carved flowers.

She turned her head, and groaned as pain shot through her. Fumbling, she tried to touch her ear but instead encountered a thick cloth that was bound around her head. With that sensation, memory came flooding back.

That's right . . .

She remembered being carried into a large room where a doctor, a plump man, had tended her wounds. He had smelled faintly of wine, and she supposed that he had been interrupted in the middle of a bedtime drink. But he'd sewn her up deftly. Her suluma, women's trousers, had been shredded by the Toda's scales, and deep scratches covered her legs. The doctor had washed them thoroughly with shilan solution.

"Imagine riding a Toda without tsuppa to protect your legs!" he had grumbled. "Of all the foolhardy things to do!" He had rattled on like this, but Elin had been too exhausted and weakened from blood loss to care.

The noises around her had faded to an indistinct murmur that seemed to come from very far away. After she had been given a sedative, she remembered nothing. She supposed they must have carried her to this room. Though small and bare, it was pleasant, and each time the breeze filled the curtains over the window, she caught the faint scent of flowers and grass.

It must be early afternoon, she thought. She had no idea how long she had slept, whether half a day or a day and a half.

Somewhere, the soft strains of music sounded again. A quiet tune, like surf washing against the shore. It eased her mind. She half closed her eyes and gave herself up to the melody. Waves rolling in and rolling out . . . Gradually, the tangled remnants of her dream unwound, and all that was left was a deep lethargy.

Footsteps approached, and the door opened quietly. It was the doctor. When he saw she was awake, his face brightened. "Ah! You've come around," he said. "I thought you might be awake by now." He lowered himself onto a chair beside the bed and took her pulse on the wrist of her good arm. "How are you feeling?" he asked.

Elin moistened her lips and said hoarsely, "Quite a bit better. Thank you."

The doctor placed a hand on her forehead. "Hmm. Your fever's gone down. Let me have a look at your legs."

He pulled back the covers and unwound the bandages. "Those scratches were covered in mud. I was worried they might fester, but the swelling's almost gone. Shilan's very effective." With pudgy fingers, he began redoing the bandages.

"How is Yohalu?" Elin asked.

The doctor raised his eyebrows. "He's fine. His fever has gone down, too." His lips twitched. "But if I were you, I wouldn't call him that in front of anyone else. They might not like it."

"What?"

"The man you so lightly call 'Yohalu' is none other than Lord Yohalu Amasulu, who governs this domain."

Elin gazed at the doctor silently. Having suspected something of the kind, she was not particularly surprised. But the uneasiness that had lurked in the bottom of her mind now turned to sharp suspicion. If he was lord of the land where Aluhan territory had begun, then his rank and authority must have been substantial. Why would such a person serve as her bodyguard?

A cold lump began expanding inside her, only to be interrupted by a bright flurry of music. It sounded very close. Elin and the doctor looked toward the window in surprise. A shadowy figure visible through the white curtains wavered each time they fluttered.

The soft thrumming of the strings reminded Elin of spring sunlight. The musician played a single verse of a love song, then let the tune fade. After a short pause, he said, "My father is worried about you, Elin." His voice was pleasant; clear yet deep. "It was his duty to protect you, but instead he placed your life in danger." The man chuckled. "I'm sure you know what my father is like. He has been complaining bitterly that he has disgraced the Black Armor."

"Please," Elin said hastily, "tell him not to think such things."

The shadow beyond the curtain nodded. "Thank you. Please rest and let nothing trouble you. I will have them prepare a hot meal that will restore your strength. Eat and sleep well."

When the shadow disappeared, the doctor stood up. Looking a little uncomfortable, he left the room, muttering to himself. In the silence, Elin stared blankly at the bright sunshine-filled curtains.

5

YOHALU'S CHILDREN

It was not until the evening of the second day that Elin finally saw the person who had spoken to her from outside the window. Hearing that Elin was recovered enough to be up and eat proper meals again, Yohalu's children invited her to have supper with them.

The lady-in-waiting, who came to escort Elin, helped her to dress. "The dining room is not far," she told Elin. "It's just on the other side of the great hall. But unfortunately, the hall is full of soldiers, so I'm afraid I'll have to take you through the garden and then around by the covered walkway."

The commotion inside the hall was so loud that Elin could hear it as they crossed the garden, and the men who passed them along the walkway on the other side wore fierce scowls. A faint musk-like scent hung in the air as the men went by. Elin frowned. The smell of Toda permeated their clothing. They must be Riders, she thought.

"Is the manor always like this?" Elin asked.

The woman shook her head with a wry smile. "No, not at all. Although the castle is located on the same grounds, this manor is Lord Amasulu's home. He usually governs affairs from the castle." Then she lowered her voice. "He really should rest a little more. He was seriously wounded, but he keeps on summoning soldiers and giving orders even while his bandages are being replaced. It makes us ill with worry to think about it."

"How is he?" Elin asked.

"He says that it's nothing. But he's paler than usual. And a wound that bad couldn't possibly have healed so quickly."

While they talked, they came to a large door. "Here we are." The woman pulled a string that hung beside it, and a little bell rang. She opened the door and gestured for Elin to go inside, then closed the door behind her.

The room was large with a high ceiling, yet it felt comfortable and pleasant, as if it was a place where the family often gathered. The floor, built a step higher than the passageway outside, was covered in a thick luxurious rug. In the center was a large low table with a recess beneath it for people to put their feet. In winter, the space underneath would have held a charcoal brazier to keep everyone's legs warm.

Seven legless chairs were arranged around the table, and two men and a woman were already seated. But when Elin walked through the door, one of the men rose and, coming around the table, extended his hand.

Elin murmured her thanks but froze before she took the hand he offered. Not only was his smiling face strikingly different from any Lyoza she had ever seen, but a tattoo covered the back of his hand.

"It's all right," he said. "My tattoo won't rub off on you even if you touch me."

Elin started at the sound of his soft voice. "You?"

He nodded. "Yes, pardon me for speaking to you through the curtain yesterday."

Elin blushed. "Oh, no, it's I who should be apologizing. Please pardon my rudeness." She took the hand he held out to her, and he smiled and gently helped her to step up into the room. He guided Elin toward the table, where the couple sat watching her with unconcealed curiosity. "This is my sister and my brother-in-law," the man said.

Elin curtsied deeply. "I am Elin."

"I am Sali, Yohalu Amasulu's daughter, and this is my husband, Muhan," the woman said, then smiled. "And the young man who is still holding your hand and won't let go is my younger brother, Rolan. Now, please have a seat. The food will grow cold. We can explain why my brother looks so different from me while we eat."

With Rolan's support, Elin gingerly lowered herself down and slipped her legs into the hollow beneath the table. She was grateful for his assistance.

Watching her awkward movements, Sali's face clouded. "You're still in quite a bit of pain, aren't you?" she said.

Elin gave a crooked smile. "I'm fine. The medicine has relieved much of the pain, so it's really not that bad." Then her face grew sober. "How is Lord Yohalu?"

"He's fine." Sali laughed. "He's so tough, I'm sure he'll live to be a hundred. But the wound is in his back, which makes it uncomfortable to sit in a chair. That's the only reason he didn't join us here today. There's no need to worry." She gestured for Elin to eat and, picking up a spoon, began sipping her soup.

Looking at the dishes lined up on the table, Elin realized with a start that the food had been prepared to be eaten with one hand. They must have gone out of their way because her arm was still in a sling.

The steaming soup was made with fresh fish and flavored with herbs. Although the broth was clear, it tasted surprisingly rich.

"How do you like it?" Rolan asked from his seat beside her.

Elin rested her spoon on her plate. "Delicious," she said. "It doesn't smell at all like river fish."

"Exactly! This type doesn't have that muddy odor," said Rolan.

Sali's lips twitched. "Don't go praising him now. He already spends all his spare time here fishing."

"And what's wrong with that?" This was the first time Sali's husband had opened his mouth. Muhan had noble features and the sturdy build of a soldier. "He just got back from an important job. Let him enjoy fishing as much as he likes. Besides, we get to enjoy his tasty catch."

Rolan picked a bone out of the soup and sucked on it casually, then licked his fingers. He glanced at Elin and shrugged. "We're an odd family, aren't we? I'm sure you can tell from my face that I'm a foster child. I was born far away on the eastern plains. I'm from Asheh. When I was nine, I was orphaned by the war. Father adopted me."

At a loss for words, Elin simply gazed at him. He had short-cropped brown hair and big dark eyes. Not just his voice, but his looks were strangely attractive. His face still had the innocence of youth, but his eyes were far older.

"I had an elder brother," said Sali, "but he died of an illness when he was nine and I was four."

Rolan nodded. "That's probably why Father felt he couldn't abandon me when he found me. I still remember how he looked in his shining black armor. I was covered in mud and tears. He plucked me up in his great big arms and gave me a home and a family."

He grinned suddenly. "But I didn't turn out quite the way he wanted."

Sali laughed and shrugged her shoulders. "You hated sword practice, and you loved fishing, playing the lakkalu, and singing. Whenever Father wasn't looking, you'd sneak out of the house to tag along after the musicians. I thought he'd brought home a pretty weird little brother, I must admit." Although she spoke in a mocking tone, Elin could see that she loved him dearly, even though he was not blood kin.

Beside her, Muhan smiled for the first time. "It's very fortunate for me that Rolan is the kind of man he is. If not, I'd have no hope of becoming the next ruler of Amasulu."

Rolan laughed. "It's fortunate for me that you joined our family. Thanks to you, Father finally let me go. Ah, the relief when I knew I could spend the rest of my life playing my beloved lakkalu! I shall forever be in both your debts."

From there, they launched into memories of the past, many of them so funny that Elin couldn't stop laughing. No one mentioned what had happened in Oohan, nor did they ask Elin anything about herself. Perhaps Yohalu had ordered them not to. Or maybe they were trying to make her comfortable. Whatever the reason, by the end of the meal, Elin found that she liked Yohalu's strange children very much.

6

KURIU

When they finished their meal, Muhan left to join the men in the great hall, while Sali stepped outside to enjoy a glass of wine in the garden.

Rolan turned to Elin. "How are you feeling?" he asked. "The color has returned to your cheeks, but if you're tired, I'd be happy to guide you back to your room."

Elin shook her head. "I'm fine," she said. "I've slept for two whole days already."

"I'm glad to hear that. If so, then let's enjoy some fruit and conversation together."

Elin nodded. It occurred to her that most young women would probably agree just as readily if invited by this young man. Although there was no romantic attraction, something about him made her want to see him smile.

He led her a short distance down the wide corridor. Stopping in front of a door embossed with sasha leaves, he opened it and ushered her inside. The room was small. No lights had been lit yet, and the interior was sunk in shadow, but the large window opening onto the garden had been flung wide, imparting a sense of spaciousness. Small lanterns shone like fireflies in the blue dusk of the garden, and people enjoying a quiet after-dinner stroll drifted along the paths like vague shadows.

Rolan lit the candles. A soft glow filled the space, illuminating what appeared to be a huge tapestry covering one wall. Drawn toward it, Elin saw that it was a finely detailed map, and her eyes grew round.

A sudden sound startled her, and she turned. A woman was sitting in an armchair in a dark corner. She stretched and leaned forward, blinking against the light. Looking at the woman's face, Elin guessed she was in her sixties. Despite her age, she was beautiful—tall with large eyes and well-defined eyebrows in a slender face, and a long, graceful neck. She had a shadow on her upper lip, like a faint mustache, but Elin quickly realized it was a fine-drawn tattoo.

Running a hand through her hair, the woman looked up at Elin and Rolan. "Oh dear. I must have dozed off." She spoke with an odd intonation.

Rolan deftly caught the book that was slipping from her knees. He handed it to her with a smile. "It's quite late, you know. Did you fall asleep without eating dinner?"

The woman shrugged. "I've been up late these last few nights." A violent fit of coughing seized her. Rolan reached out a hand to rub her back but she waved him away and took a sip of tea from the cup on the side table.

"You need to get proper rest," Rolan said with a frown.

The woman snorted. "As a musician, you should talk. No need to worry about me. Time is what you make of it. I'm just using my time the way I want. That's better for my health anyway."

She poked her head around Rolan and smiled at Elin. "Good evening," she said.

Elin bowed. "Good evening. I'm Elin."

The woman nodded. "I thought as much. Pleased to meet you. I'm Kuriu." The foreign-sounding name confirmed Elin's guess that she must be from another country.

Rolan leaned out the window and hailed a servant, asking her to bring some food for Kuriu. "And while you're at it, bring three servings of fruit."

Kuriu glanced at him, then beckoned to Elin. "Come a little closer. That's it. Have a seat in that chair."

She indicated a chair beside the window and, when Elin sat down, scrutinized her face. "Your eyes really are green. That's a color I've never seen, not even in Imeelu. I've seen brown and blue, but not green."

"Imeelu?"

Kuriu raised her brows. "You haven't heard of it?"

"No. I'm sorry."

Kuriu laughed. "No need to apologize. So even teachers like you don't know it exists."

Elin blinked. This woman seemed to know a lot about her. Perhaps she'd heard that from Yohalu.

"Elin lives in Yojeh territory, that's why," said Rolan. "They don't get many foreign merchants there. Not like here." He stepped away from the window and rested his hand on the back of Elin's chair. "Imeelu is a large caravan city on a great river that runs through the eastern plains." Strolling toward the wall, he pointed at the map. His finger was long and slender, befitting a musician. "That's Imeelu."

Elin rose and went to stand beside him. Rolan touched a spot on the map. "This is Amasulu territory, where we are now." He traced a line back to the other spot. "And this is Imeelu."

As Elin gazed at the places he had pointed out, the picture presented by the map gradually revealed itself to her. When she deciphered the shape of her own country, goosebumps rose on her skin.

It's so small . . .

The kingdom of Lyoza, which lay along the southeast side of the Afon Noah, took up only an eighth of the map. Between Lyoza and the sea lay a single country, which she recognized as the kingdom of Tolah. But to the east spread many countries, only a few of which she knew. It had never occurred to her that there could be so many. As she stared at the map, shock numbed her brain. She had spent her life oblivious of the world in which she lived . . .

"It's a pretty big world, isn't it? In fact, probably even bigger than what you see here." Rolan swept his finger across the southwest and southeast parts of the map. "There could be more countries in these areas that we haven't heard of yet," he said.

He moved his finger to a point in the eastern plain. "This is Asheh," he said, "Where I was born."

Elin narrowed her eyes and stared at the spot. Some words had been written over it in a script she couldn't read. "What language is that?" she asked.

"Shalamu. My mother tongue," Kuriu said from behind her. "Beautiful, isn't it? It's lovely both to look at and to listen to."

"Shalamu." Elin repeated. Even the name was new to her.

Kuriu rose and walked slowly over. Elin was tall for a woman, but Kuriu was almost the same height. A floral fragrance wafted from her robe, and Elin guessed that it had been scented with incense.

"This map tells many stories," Kuriu murmured. "It traversed a strange path before it ended up on this wall." She stopped without elaborating, and the three of them stood gazing at the map for some time, lost in their own thoughts.

What kind of lives had this tall woman and this foreign-featured youth led, Elin wondered. She thought about the days of which they would never speak and which she would never know. A breeze stole through the garden, carrying with it the moist chill of evening. The last glow of twilight had vanished, along with the murmur of people in the garden.

"We call Imeelu the white city," Kuriu said abruptly. "It's dazzlingly white and sits on a great river that intersects many roads leading from other countries. Although it's surrounded by grasslands and desert, our ancestors who built it came from across the seas. At least, that's what our legends say."

She stretched out her hand and pointed one by one to several other towns. "These were once under the rule of the kingdom of Hajan. When Lyoza defeated Hajan, these caravan cities, including Imeelu, became your protectorates."

"Protectorates? Not domains?" Elin asked.

Kuriu cocked an eyebrow. "Yes. Can you guess why?"

Elin stared at the towns on the map, taking in the grasslands and desert that surrounded them and their distance from Aluhan territory. "To stretch the border this far would be difficult and expensive," she said finally. "It would take a huge army to protect such a broad expanse of land."

Kuriu's eyebrows shot up, and her smile deepened. "I can see why you caught Yohalu's attention. You're an interesting woman."

Kuriu walked over to the side table and picked up a book that was lying facedown. Bringing it over to Elin, she said, "The caravan cities are prosperous centers that attract people and goods. But they're small, with little capacity to protect themselves. If the safety of the roads isn't guaranteed, merchants will take their trade elsewhere, leaving the cities to wither. What they need is a country with a strong army to shelter them.

"When the Hajan ruled, we paid them high taxes. And when Lyoza defeated Hajan and seized control over this area, we cozied up to you. No matter who rules, we live on, resilient. That's the way we've chosen."

Kuriu opened the book and flipped through the pages. "This is my work. I'm writing a comparative history on three of the caravan cities. It's quite fascinating and gives me a much clearer picture of what moves a city or kingdom. When I study the choices and foolish actions people have repeated for centuries, I can see how diverse and yet how similar we humans are."

As she listened, Elin felt something stirring in her breast, a burning urge she had often felt as a child—a sense that something connected to the invisible threads that moved this world was almost within reach. Impulsively, she said, "I study the laws of nature that govern living creatures. Because I want to know why they're the way they are, in all their amazing diversity."

She reached out and softly touched Kuriu's book. "What you just said you're doing, it's the same thing, isn't it? But for those creatures we call humans?"

Kuriu's eyes shone. "Yes! Exactly!" Beaming, she turned to Rolan. "Remember what you said? 'Even if people are pursuing different fields, they still share common ground'?"

She turned her eyes back to Elin. "I want to know why humans fight one another. But to find out, I have to examine and explore an enormous volume of cases. I'm sure you understand the incredible amount of work that involves."

Elin nodded.

"Even though you're a teacher, you know nothing about the caravan cities, despite their importance to this kingdom. Many people have no idea of the shape of the world in which they live. It doesn't even occur to them to look at the way cities or countries interact with one another. But I was born into the house of the pathfinders. I had the good fortune to meet many different people, and was exposed to many books."

She ran a finger over her tattoo. "This is the mark of the pathfinder. I'm sure you can't imagine the power invested in the one who bears it. The words of the pathfinder steer the city of Imeelu."

Kuriu's eyes, which were so rich with expression, suddenly darkened with a mixture of impatience and sorrow. She shrugged her slender shoulders and, moving away from the map, sank into a chair. "To know, and to tell. To know, and to tell," she muttered as though chanting, then shook her head. "For centuries, generations of pathfinders have searched for the way, but no matter how deftly they have dodged and squirmed, they've never been able to avert war. The lives of humans are too short. They're always snuffed out before their ideas have sufficient time to mature."

As her voice died away, a note plucked from a string trembled on the air, then swelled into a rich and undulating melody. While they were talking, Rolan had picked up his lakkalu. He stroked the strings, head bent, then looked up and raised his voice in song.

Day breaks, men awake, hold your swords to the red sun.
Hark to the thunder of hooves rolling like a storm across the plain.

The song resonated in the pit of Elin's stomach. For a moment, she saw countless men charging across a field on horseback. Her blood stirred in response to the violent twanging of the strings. There was something tragic about the sound, yet it made her heart beat wildly.

Day breaks, children awake. The morn of your father's death has come. The melody changed to a slender thread of sorrow, a song of mourning for dead fathers and brothers, for torched homes and gutted villages.

Day breaks, people awake. Behold. Night gives way to dawn. This last refrain was repeated several times, like a wave crashing against the shore and receding, only to rush back again before finally fading away. Even when the last reverberation had ceased, Elin remained motionless for some time. She felt as if something enormous had passed through her.

Casting her a faint smile, Kuriu flicked her eyes toward Rolan. "He's always like that," she said. "He seems to see right through your mind, weaving what he finds there into song."

She sighed and rested her head against the back of her chair. "You're right, Rolan. War makes people's hearts throb. Even though they know the cruelty and the misery of it, still they sing of battle."

Rolan didn't respond, but only smiled with his arms wrapped around his lakkalu.

"You're right about one other thing, too," Kuriu said, gazing up at the ceiling. "People will keep searching, endlessly. Like ants whose path has been blocked, they'll pace back and forth looking for a way through."

"Interesting, isn't she?" Rolan said as he guided Elin back to her room. "Quite amazing really. She gave up her position as pathfinder, passing that mantle on to her nephew. But even now her words carry weight; not only in Imeelu, but in many other caravan cities. And her nephew still comes to her for advice."

Elin cocked her head. "Then why is she here? It seems so far from her home."

"She's an old friend of my father's. A very good friend. It's her custom to come here every year in late fall to spend the winter. Because she has asthma. Imeelu's too dry in winter, which makes her condition worse." Rolan smiled briefly. "But maybe that's just an excuse. Perhaps she wants to spend the winter with Father."

I see, Elin thought. With a pair like Kuriu and Yohalu, that was certainly a possibility. She smiled suddenly and gave a slight sigh.

Rolan cast her a quizzical look. "What?"

Elin shook her head. "I was just thinking how small my world is."

"Small?"

"Yes. At this very moment, people like Kuriu are living in distant lands, yet I'd never even stopped to think about it. But here, you're so closely connected to other countries that I suppose it's quite normal to be broad-minded."

Rolan smiled. "Indeed, it is. Amasulu is very small, but it's an important intersection."

"Intersection?"

"A place where many people come together." A grim look displaced Rolan's smile. "But there are far too few gathering points like this in Lyoza." Seeing Elin's gaze, he shrugged lightly. "Here's your room. My apologies for keeping you up so late. I just hope that I didn't tire you out."

Elin shook her head. "It was a wonderful evening. Thank you."

As she entered the room, Rolan kept his hand on the door. "My father wishes to speak with you," he said quietly. "May I take you to his room tomorrow evening?"

Elin inclined her head. Although her heart grew heavy just thinking of what Yohalu would ask when they met, there was no escape.

Rolan's expression relaxed. "Good. Please rest well."

7

YOHALU'S SECRET

The next day dawned cloudy, and by evening, rain was pelting down. Perhaps because of the weather, or maybe simply because she was not fully recovered, Elin felt heavy and listless all day and spent much of her time napping. After the evening meal, however, her strength returned. By the time Rolan came to fetch her, she had dressed and steeled herself as best she could for her meeting with Yohalu.

Rolan led her slowly along a dimly lit, high-ceilinged corridor until they came to a large oak door. He stopped and called out, "Father, I have brought Lady Elin."

Through the thick wood, they heard the muffled sound of Yohalu bidding her to enter. Rolan pushed down on the handle and opened the door. He ushered Elin inside and then left.

The moment she stepped inside, Elin's eyes were drawn to a large bookcase. Sturdily built, it was jammed with books.

"Elin."

At the sound of her name, she recollected where she was with a start and blushed. "I beg your pardon. You have such an impressive book collection that I couldn't help myself."

Yohalu smiled. "How like you to notice my books before anything else."

Elin walked over to the large armchair in which Yohalu was sitting. He sat on the edge leaning forward rather than resting against the back.

"How are you feeling?" she asked.

"Fine. It's not the first time I've been shot, and the wound wasn't that deep. How about you? Your ear will be scarred, I'm afraid."

Seeing the concern in his face, Elin smiled. "Thank you," she said. "But I'll be fine. The scar might even give me a little prestige and make cheeky students pay more attention when I glare at them."

Yohalu laughed. "I see. I forgot you were a teacher of unruly rascals."

"Yes. Although I can't show them the mark of the arrow on my back, the one on my ear will be in plain sight. Besides, I've been scarred by Leelan already. I can add this to my collection."

Her face grew sober. "What happened to the Toda that carried us?"

"Ah. It was given a feast of fish and taken to the Amasulu where it was set free. The poor thing suffered a lot to save us. Toda raised by the Stewards can swim for a night and a day with two men on their back. But not wild Toda. Now that I've ridden one, I realize how useless they'd be in battle."

He paused with his eyes fixed on Elin. "You can control wild Toda, can't you?" he said finally.

Elin gazed back at him wordlessly. From the moment she had used the finger whistle, she had known that he would ask this question. Even now, in a forest somewhere, warned by their ancestors' souls animating the Spirit Beast, the Ahlyo would be lamenting that Elin had committed an irreversible sin. But she'd had no choice. If she hadn't used the finger whistle, Yohalu would have been killed, and she herself abducted.

For the last two days, as she had lain in bed, a thought had taken shape in her mind—she could not choose death to guard the secret of the Toda. She could not do what her mother had done, even if revealing what she knew should lead to multiplying and strengthening the Toda forces.

She could understand why the Ahlyo wanted to prevent another catastrophe. But the way they sought to achieve that goal seemed wrong. She wasn't sure why it was wrong, but she couldn't bring herself to tread the same path. Maybe it was because the Law of the Ahlyo had driven her mother to her death. Yet she sensed it was more than that. Something told her that it was wrong to conceal knowledge, even to avert disaster.

And if that's how I feel . . .

She must choose the path that felt right, even if it meant groping her way along.

"It was a gamble," Elin said finally.

Yohalu's eyebrows shot up. "A gamble?"

"Yes. To be quite honest, I wasn't at all sure those wild Toda would respond. The tune was the same one my mother blew for me. To save me from the Toda . . ."

Her voice shook, and she paused for a moment to steady her breath. "The sound of my mother's finger flute, which she played just before she died, has been seared on my memory ever since. I often try playing it when no one is around. But the finger flute is difficult. At first, I couldn't reproduce the notes I remembered. With practice, I gradually learned how."

Yohalu blinked. "You mean it's one of the Ahlyo's secret skills?"

With her eyes fixed on his, Elin nodded. "I think so. Because before she blew it, my mother told me that I should never do what she was going to do, because it was a mortal sin."

Silence enveloped the room. Finally, Yohalu rose, steadying his shoulder with one hand. A strong light gleamed in his eyes. "I thank you from the depths of my heart for using that finger flute to save my life," he said. "Please accept my deepest apologies for placing your life in danger. I offered myself as your bodyguard but instead I have caused you great pain. Forgive me." He bowed deeply.

"Please raise your head," Elin said hastily. "There was no way you could've known that man would attack us."

Standing erect, Yohalu shook his head. "It's true I never expected Aoolu to attack us. However . . ." He paused and gestured with his eyes toward a chair beside the bookcase. He waited for Elin to sit before lowering himself into his own chair. "I knew that your life was in danger."

Yohalu's study was located deep inside the building. The bustle of the soldiers rushing along the large corridor didn't penetrate this far. The only sound was the occasional scraping of branches against the windows when the breeze ruffled the trees. In that silence, Elin frowned slightly, staring at Yohalu.

Yohalu pressed his right hand against his left shoulder, then coughed slightly. Picking up a flask on the side table, he poured himself some water and took a sip, then placed the cup down with a small click. "I knew that someone was planning to attack you. Not Aoolu, but the Sai Gamulu."

Elin's mind went numb. "The Sai Gamulu?" she blurted out. "They want to kill me? But why on earth?"

The Sai Gamulu, which literally meant "blood and filth," was a secret society. Its members blamed the Yojeh for the cracks in the kingdom's system. For generations, they had sought to assassinate her and make the Aluhan the sole ruler of the country. Bound by strict rules, they swore themselves to silence, never revealing their identity as members even when faced with death. Not even the Aluhan knew who they were. After Shunan married Seimiya, however, rumors of such plots had faded away.

The Sai Gamulu's wish that the Aluhan rule the kingdom had been fulfilled, and Elin had assumed they no longer had any reason to assassinate the Yojeh.

"For the Sai Gamulu," Yohalu said in a low voice, "you are the one piece in this game that could overturn all the others on the board."

The candle flame wavered, sending Yohalu's shadow dancing across the wall. "Although more than a decade has passed since Lord Shunan married the Yojeh, this country remains in a state of confusion, like an ant nest that's been stepped on. Nobles, soldiers, and commoners alike are bewildered, not knowing to whom they should turn for guidance—the Aluhan or the Yojeh."

"But—"

Yohalu raised a finger, cutting off Elin's protest. "Yes, it's true Lord Shunan and Lady Seimiya have joined hands to rule this nation. But we want to know whose will it is that governs our affairs. Which one moves this country, the Aluhan or the Yojeh? If this were obvious, we could follow wholeheartedly. But for some reason, the answer remains unclear."

Yohalu sighed. "Her Highness, the Yojeh, is the cause. For the last few years, she's rarely shown herself, and that makes those who see her as this country's soul unbearably anxious. They worry she conceals herself from shame, that she believes her union with the Aluhan has defiled her and caused disease to spread.

"For those of us who revere the Aluhan as our lord, on the other hand, her attitude's exasperating. She ought to be supporting the wise decisions of Lord Shunan and guiding her people in a beneficial direction, but instead, she's torn by indecision. That's destabilizing political affairs in this country, which outrages quite a few people. She's supposed to be the Yojeh, they say. They can't help but wonder what on earth she's thinking!"

Anger flared in his eyes. He fixed them on the candle beside him and took a deep breath, then shifted his gaze back to Elin. "It's terrifying not to know what Lady Seimiya is thinking. What if she's regretting her decision to marry the Aluhan or prefers the old way of doing things, with the

Yojeh ruling alone by divine right? That would tear our people apart. Even though she married the Aluhan, the majority still revere her as a god. If she should decide to dissolve her marriage and stand as the sole ruler of this country—"

"But that's ridiculous!" Elin shook her head. "That could never happen. Even if she wanted to, it's impossible." A chill ran up her spine as she said this. Suddenly, she saw why the Sai Gamulu had chosen her as their target.

She said no more, and Yohalu nodded. "You're an intelligent woman. I'm sure you can see that you're the one piece that would allow the Yojeh to fulfill such a wish. The vision of you and that mighty Royal Beast, symbol of the noble Yojeh, scattering the Toda army is branded on all our memories. If, at her bidding, you should arise to fly the Royal Beasts—"

Elin shook her head violently. Seeing her expression, Yohalu grimaced. "I know. You'd never do that. Nor would Lady Seimiya ask it of you. But as long as you live, that possibility will never vanish from our minds. Nor, I suspect, from hers.

"That's why the Sai Gamulu decided to kill you. Without you, Lady Seimiya has no card left to play. They wish to make it crystal clear that she has no hope."

Elin stared at him, robbed of speech. His brow furrowed slightly. "But I didn't want you to be killed."

Elin frowned. "Why?"

He stared at her calmly, not answering. The expression in his eyes made her uneasy. "When I heard that all the Kiba in Tokala village had died," he said finally, "I saw it as an opportunity—an excuse to place you under my protection. Fortunately, Lord Shunan was interested. He probably thought my proposal to disguise myself as your bodyguard was just a whim, sparked by an old man's desire to retire and leave things in the hands of his son-in-law. He smiled indulgently when he gave me permission."

Elin wrinkled her forehead. "You mean you didn't accompany me at the behest of the Aluhan? It was your idea?"

Yohalu nodded. "Yes. Lord Shunan doesn't know that you've been targeted by the Sai Gamulu. I used the investigation of the Kiba as an excuse to get his consent for me to guard you."

Elin's heart pounded sickeningly in her chest. Grasping her knees with icy fingers, she said unsteadily, "But how? How could you know that the Sai Gamulu wished to kill me when the Aluhan did not?"

Yohalu kept his eyes fixed on hers. "I know what the Sai Gamulu plan before they act. Because the man who started it was my great-grandfather."

The silence that covered the room hurt Elin's ears. The faint sputtering of the candles sounded disturbingly loud.

Yohalu rubbed a hand over his face. He looked drained. "Yes, it was my great-grandfather who formed the Sai Gamulu. For a time, I ran it, too. But one day, I realized that such means could never bring peace to this country. I relinquished my role as the leader to a friend. A few called me a traitor and insisted that I should be terminated, but most said nothing and let me go."

The ghost of a smile touched his lips. "They trust me, you see. While they were annoyed that I chose a different path, they didn't try to kill me. Besides, they value the blood that runs in my veins. That's why I believed you'd be safe with me."

He rose abruptly, then winced and moved slowly toward the book-shelves, being careful of his wound. He pulled a thin chain with an old key on it from his neck. Bending low, he inserted the key into a hole in a drawer at the bottom. There was a small click. Yohalu returned the key to his robe, pulled open the drawer, and reached inside. With the utmost care, he took out a bundle wrapped in deep blue brocade and placed it on the large desk, gesturing for Elin to come and see. When she drew near, he unfolded the cloth to reveal a thin book wrapped in oiled paper.

It appeared quite ancient, and the spine and cover were falling apart. Gently, Yohalu opened it to expose the inside cover. The paper was yel-lowed and chewed by insects. "I keep bug repellent with it and air the drawer well, too, but even so, it's impossible to protect something this old from getting damaged. I was planning to transcribe it when I retired. At this rate, though, it may fall apart before I get a chance."

But Elin barely heard him. He glanced at her chalk-white face and murmured, "I thought so. You can read this, can't you?"

Staring at the inside cover, Elin forgot to breathe. The words were written in mirror writing, although the script seemed a bit different from her mother's. She could only read the title without a mirror because part of it was already branded on her memory.

The Diary of the Kalenta Loh

8

ORIGINS

Yohalu leaned forward and grasped Elin's wrist. "Please. Tell me. What does it say?"

His voice was quiet, but a fierce light burned in his eyes, and his hand felt hot where it touched Elin's skin. She didn't try to shake off his grip. "Do you have a mirror?" she asked calmly.

He blinked, then released her. "A mirror?"

"Yes. Or something that reflects like a mirror?"

Yohalu thought for a moment, then went to the desk and pulled a hand mirror from a drawer. He gave this to Elin, and she placed it so that it reflected the book's title. Yohalu drew in a sharp breath. Squinting, he ran his eyes over the letters. "Ka . . . len," he muttered. "I can't read the next one. Is the one after that 'loh'?"

"Yes. Kalenta Loh. It's an ancient script. I think it means 'the people who remain.'"

Still staring at the letters in the mirror, Yohalu rubbed a hand across his brow. "So that's it! It was meant to be read with a mirror." He slumped into his chair, resting his forehead on his palm.

"Yes. It's written in a very loose hand," Elin said. "And because the book is so ancient, it's natural to assume the script is some foreign language."

Yohalu nodded, speechless.

"When I was a child," Elin murmured, looking at the words reflected in the mirror, "my mother used to write every night after dinner, once she'd cleaned up. I liked to wrap myself around her shoulders and watch. She taught me how to read and write like this. It seemed like magic, and I was dying to show my friends. But Mother wouldn't let me. She told me it was a secret, just between the two of us."

She raised her face and looked at Yohalu. Her pulse was beating painfully fast. "Why do you have this book?"

Slowly, Yohalu raised his head. His gaze met hers. "It's the diary of my ancestor seven generations before me. Or at least, that's what I was told. It contains secrets passed down to the firstborn son and direct heir of the ruler of Amasulu. That ancestor was said to have had green eyes."

Elin caught her breath and stared at him.

"Do you remember the story I told you when we were in Oohan?" Yohalu asked. "About the man who built the first Toda village, the one who was clever but loose with women?"

Elin nodded. "That man," Yohalu continued, "was the grandson of the author of this diary and the grandfather of my great-grandfather. There aren't many tales of him left in my family. The stories passed down by the villagers of Oohan may paint a more accurate picture. They say he died young, before my great-grandfather was born.

"My great-grandfather was strong and vigorous. He must have been about eighty-five when he died. I was only eight, and I remember him as having a loud voice and a hot temper. Sometimes he'd explode with anger, and at those times, he was terrifying. But I've heard he was also very intelligent." He paused to take a sip of water.

"Was he the one who started the Sai Gamulu?" Elin asked.

"Yes. And the reason is closely linked to this book." Yohalu gestured to the diary with his chin. "My great-great-grandfather learned many things from his father, the founder of Oohan village, including how to read this book. But he wasn't able to pass on that knowledge to his son, my great-grandfather."

A deep furrow cleft Yohalu's brow as he stared at the ancient book.

"He intended to tell him everything when he reached the age of twelve, but he died when my great-grandfather was only eight. Because the secrets, including how to read this book, were transmitted orally, they died with him. My great-grandfather believed that he was murdered."

Elin leaned forward. "Murdered?"

Yohalu nodded. "Yes. One day, the Yojeh summoned him to her palace, but he came back as ashes in an urn. The family was told that he'd died of an illness while at the palace and that his body had been cremated to purify it."

Yohalu sighed. "It was a long time ago so no one knows the truth. But my great-grandfather believed that the Yojeh had him poisoned. He thought she feared the Aluhan's increasing military might and wanted to stamp out the secret Toda arts before he could pass them on to his son."

Yohalu's mouth crooked in a bitter smile. "I can imagine how my great-grandfather would've reacted once he was old enough to understand the meaning of his father's death. From then on, he was consumed with an implacable, twisted hatred for the Yojeh. As he watched how her reign shaped this kingdom, he came up with the idea of the Sai Gamulu. When the time seemed right, he set this secret society into motion, burning the palace and killing the Yojeh and her heir. The only survivor was the Yojeh's granddaughter. I suppose he wanted to inflict on them the same fate he himself had suffered—the severing of knowledge."

The silence when he finished speaking was disturbed only by the hissing candles. So, Elin thought, hatred had sown the seeds of more hatred, transcending time to entangle those who lived now. She found it hard to breathe, as though something thick and heavy had engulfed her, stifling her breath. Trying to shake off that oppressive weight, she struggled to keep her voice level. "What was your great-great-grandfather's relationship with the Yojeh?" she asked.

Cocking his head, Yohalu urged her to continue.

"It's the Yojeh that puzzles me," Elin explained. "If what your great-grandfather believed is true, then the Yojeh must not only have known that your ancestors possessed skills related to the Toda, but also that they were passed on secretly to the eldest son."

A light kindled in Yohalu's eyes. "You're very sharp. You've already grasped the crux of this story."

Elin shook her head. "I don't know about that, but ever since I met that green-eyed girl in Oohan village, something's been bothering me. It's related to the story you just told me."

Yohalu gazed at her intently. "What is it?" he asked.

"Long ago, when the great hosts of the Hajan attacked this country, the Yojeh's loyal subject Yaman Hasalu begged her to give him the Toda Whistle so that he might save the people. Judging his intentions to be sincere, she gave him that sacred treasure and permitted him to ride the Toda. Yaman Hasalu crossed the Amasulu River and vanquished the Hajan.

"That was the origin of the Aluhan, a legend we've been hearing ever since we were children. Yet, it's simply not possible."

Yohalu's eyes narrowed. "Why?"

Elin moistened her lips to continue, when caution suddenly overtook her. She paused. "Have you heard the tale of what happened on the other side of the Afon Noah?"

Yohalu shook his head. "No, never. All I know is that the Yojeh is not a god." He grinned. "That's what I consider to be the crux of this story, the point I really wanted to convey to you. But it appears you knew that already."

Although Elin didn't respond, Yohalu continued unperturbed. "The grandfather of the founder of Oohan village was secretly summoned from the Afon Noah, along with his family, by the Yojeh of that time. In other words, if the Royal Ancestor Jeh was a god, then the blood of the gods must run in my veins, too. But that can't be, because I know for sure that I'm a very ordinary man."

Scratching his chin, he said, "According to what I was told, when our ancestors came from the Afon Noah, they were kept hidden in the palace. They were called Friends of the Yojeh and met secretly with Yaman Hasalu to teach him how to control the Toda. Even after the victory of Amasulu, their existence was kept strictly confidential. After Yaman Hasalu became the Aluhan, they supported him from behind the scenes and married into his family. It wasn't until the next generation that they appeared openly on the political stage of this country. The next generation all had dark brown eyes, but in the one after that, a green-eyed child was born. That was my ancestor, the founder of Oohan village. He was raised in secret within this very place. Eventually, the Aluhan ordered him to establish a Toda village deep in the mountains where not even the birds passed. Green-eyed children are still born in Oohan because it's so remote that close kin often intermarry. In my own family line, no other green-eyed children have been born."

The smile in Yohalu's eyes deepened. "Your ancestors had green eyes, too. If we traced our ancestry back, we might find that we're relatives."

Wordlessly, Elin gazed at this affable yet fathomless man. Long ago, his ancestors had crossed the Afon Noah to settle here, just like hers. The thought filled her with awe, as if she had touched upon something incredibly vast.

"Well, what do you think? Does that solve your riddle?" Yohalu asked.

Elin shook her head with a rueful laugh. "It's only compounded it." She shared with him the tale she'd heard from the Ahlyo about the tragedy on the other side of the Afon Noah. As she did so, she remembered how she'd shared it with Seimiya just after she became the Yojeh. She recalled the astonishment on Seimiya's porcelain features as she had sat wrapped in the steam that rose from the bath. She'd looked so very young.

"So." Yohalu whispered, staring at her with a look of astonishment. "Far from being friends, the Royal Ancestor Jeh and her people were sworn enemies of the Toga mi Lyo."

Elin nodded. "At least, according to the tale passed down among the Ahlyo. Or the Ao-Loh—the People of the Law—as they call themselves. Jeh's people must have been Royal Beast handlers who lived in the valleys of the Afon Noah. The Toga mi Lyo came from across the sea where they had fled their homeland. They took refuge in a prosperous country at the foot of the same mountains."

"And you're saying those two peoples, one mounted on Toda and the other on Royal Beasts, launched a war so disastrous that it wiped out both their armies and even the creatures they rode, and destroyed their nations?" asked Yohalu.

"Yes."

Yohalu took a deep breath and rubbed a hand over his face. "Well. Of all the . . ." He shook his head and sighed. Looking at Elin, he smiled wryly. "Now I understand why you've stubbornly refused to wield the Royal Beasts."

Elin remained silent. Her reasons for not wanting to control the Beasts were far more complex than what Yohalu imagined, but she didn't think he would understand even if she tried to explain. Suddenly she felt terribly tired, as if she had traveled the space of centuries in this short time.

"There's so much that we simply don't know," she said quietly. "Far too much. What did those people who lived and died so long ago do? And why? What were they thinking and feeling?" She wiped her brow. "I wonder what really happened on the other side of the Afon Noah. Were our ancestors—the Toga mi Lyo—really enemies of Jeh and her people? Why did Jeh come here and why did she choose to become the ruler of this country? Why did she summon your ancestor and ask him to use the Toda?"

Yohalu nodded. His face was ashen. He fastened his eyes on the diary, which looked as if it might disintegrate at any moment. "That could tell us some of the answers, don't you think?" He gave a lopsided smile. "But even with a mirror, I doubt I could make much sense of it. How about you? Do you think you could read it?"

Elin pointed at it. "May I take a look?"

"Of course."

The inside cover felt more like rough cloth than paper. She turned it gingerly, revealing a page covered with elegant handwriting. Even with the mirror, she couldn't read the ancient script fluently, but she could still grasp most of the meaning.

Running her eyes over the page, she murmured, *"The letters and words my mother taught me were the language of her people, but I was surprised when one of our professors well versed in the classics read us a poem. It sounded very similar to the words my mother had taught me."*

As she stared at the letters, her eyes blurred with tears. She'd been torn from her mother when she was too young to understand anything. Yet with each step she took along this path, she would probably keep stumbling upon fragments of her mother's life. Just like this.

"Elin," said Yohalu. "That's enough for tonight. I'm a bit tired, and you must be even more so. This diary hasn't been read for more than a century. I'm sure it won't complain if it has to wait one more day."

Elin nodded and gently closed the book. "May I come again tomorrow?" she asked.

"Of course. If you feel up to it. But please be careful not to overdo it."

Elin smiled. "Thank you," she said. She bowed deeply, filled with a quiet affection that she had not felt for him before.

A faint smile touched his lips, and he sketched a bow in return. Then he pulled a string that dangled beside the bookcase. "Please wait a moment. A maidservant will come to fetch you shortly."

Elin nodded, but then her face clouded. There was one other thing she must say, something that couldn't be said once the servant came. "You said that the Sai Gamulu wished to kill me. I assume that that hasn't changed?"

Yohalu's face grew serious. "No, it hasn't. However—and I'm not just saying this to make you feel better—as long as you're with me, you've nothing to fear. As for what comes next, we'll work something out."

"Thank you. But it's my family that I am concerned about. If they can't get at me, isn't there a possibility they'll try to take my family hostage?"

Yohalu shook his head. "I was worried about that myself, but I believe it's highly unlikely as long as you remain under my protection. You see, even if they took your family hostage, they'd still have to go through me if they wished to negotiate."

He frowned. "And I suppose, in a sense, you being with me actually fulfills their purpose."

"Ah, yes. I see," Elin said. As long as she was with Yohalu, she couldn't fly Leelan for the Yojeh. But that also meant she'd have to remain under Yohalu's protection if she didn't want to be murdered by the Sai Gamulu.

"I know," Yohalu said, reading her expression. "You have a life. I won't ask you to stay forever. As I said, we'll think of something."

Before Elin could respond, she heard the voice of a maidservant from the other side of the heavy door. "Please," Elin said quickly. "Take me to them. Let me tell them to their faces that I'll never use the Royal Beasts to reinforce the power of the Yojeh. If they could understand that—"

Yohalu shook his head. "For them, your intention isn't the problem. Still, there must be some solution. Let's keep thinking about it."

He called to the servant and opened the door.

The chilly corridor was dimly lit and smelled faintly of night air. As she gazed down it, Elin felt as if she were looking at the long road that stretched endlessly before her. Once again, she had to walk alone.

At that thought, pain ran through her, as if her breast was being gouged with a sharp pick. How she longed to see Ialu and Jesse, to hold them in her arms. Slowly, she walked down the cold corridor, cradling the feelings that welled up inside her.

9

THE DIARY OF THE KALENTA LOH

"While spring is young and snow remains, then comes the ochiwa." It was with this phrase that the diary began.

The rain of the previous evening had lifted with the dawn, and the sky was now dazzlingly bright. Clear morning light poured through the study's open window. Yohalu sat in his chair listening as Elin read aloud, her finger slowly following the letters on the page.

"How pure its white form as it flies, slender legs together. Oh, noble bird that crosses the steep mountain ridges to our valley, bearing that precious black leg ring.

"Like us, one generation replaces the next, yet still the faithful ochiwa fulfills its mission, winging its flight once a year.

"Letters borne by the ochiwa. A custom begun by my great-great-grandfather

to cheer the spirits of the young maiden who had once again donned that heavy mantle, her heart troubled by the fate of a people in the lowlands far away. Even now, that bond continues in this way.

"Did my great-great-grandfather harbor love in his heart for that maiden? I ask this of Grandfather, but he shrugs and laughs. If that maid won ten million hearts, he says, then it would not be strange if his heart was one of those. An artful dodger is Grandfather."

Without a doubt, the book was a diary. To read it was to hear the voice of a young man who had lived in the distant past and was no longer in this world. He had recorded his travels from the land he called "the valley" to Lyoza. Suddenly impatient, Elin marked the page she was reading with a finger and turned to the last page, skimming its contents.

"Where does it end?" Yohalu asked, craning his neck to peer at the words.

"It leaves off where he begins living in the Yojeh's palace. Do you have any more books like this?" Elin asked.

Yohalu shook his head with a look of regret. "No, none. He may have written more, but this is the only one that was left to me."

Elin returned to the place she'd marked with her finger and resumed reading aloud.

From the pages rose the image of a bold young man filled with curiosity. The ochiwa had come bearing an urgent plea from the Yojeh begging the Toga mi Lyo to aid her beleaguered kingdom. The Hajan, the Yojeh wrote, threatened to invade and overrun the country. After some hesitation, the young man decided to take his family to her aid. His wife and children were also bold by nature. Far from being worried, the prospect of starting a new life in some distant land filled them with a sense of purpose.

Although sad at parting, the young man's grandfather and the people of the valley blessed their journey. From the description of the farewell banquet, it was clear they had no hesitation about sharing the knowledge of the Toda with the Yojeh. Rather, the valley people seemed to accept her request without question, as though they'd anticipated that such a day would come. Unfortunately, the diary did not say why. Nor was there any mention of the battle that had occurred on the far side of the Afon Noah, or the reason the Toga mi Lyo had begun exchanging messages with the Yojeh, the leader of their enemies. The man writing the diary must have considered these things too obvious to require an explanation.

There was, however, an interesting entry about the Toda. The night before the young man's departure he spoke with his grandfather about them.

"*Should the Toda increase in number, the nation will expand and its population increase. That is the beginning of the end, Grandfather says. Every beast in nature knows the right balance. Males fight for females and form packs. Weaker males receive no mate and leave no offspring. Thus is the number of packs perfectly maintained. Should that balance be broken and they grow too large in number, disease will spread, conflicts will arise, and once again catastrophe will strike. This, he says, is the law of nature.*

"'*Man is more intelligent than the beasts,' I say, but Grandfather laughs.*

"'*As yet, man lacks the knowledge to control a pack that has exceeded the size nature intended and so avert disaster. How tragic!*'

"*His words sink into my mind.*

"*The peace of a small impoverished herd. The wealth of a large herd that is constantly fighting. We must always keep the number of Toda within our grasp. These words do I engrave upon my heart.*"

Elin stared at that last sentence. A stillness spread through her. The thought that she had been mulling over for some time had been right, then.

"This fits with what you were telling me last night, doesn't it?" Yohalu murmured. "If they caused a war on the other side of the Afon Noah but managed to survive and settle in the place they called the valley, it makes sense that they would want to hold fast to such a rule."

Their eyes met, and they nodded at each other. This one passage showed that the road followed by their ancestors began at the same place.

"'We must always keep the number of Toda within our grasp.'" Yohalu cocked his head. "It almost sounds like they knew how to do that."

Elin said nothing, but Yohalu's sharp eyes did not miss the subtle change in her expression. He leaned forward. "You mean they did? There is a way?"

Elin's pulse began to race. She had known that if she read this diary, it might mention that fact, and if asked, she had resolved to tell the truth. But now that she was faced with the decision, her heart wavered, torn by an indecision akin to fear. If she told Yohalu how they controlled the Toda, there would be no turning back.

"Elin, please, tell me. I have a right to know. If my ancestor wasn't murdered, that knowledge would have been passed down to me, too."

Elin gripped her knees. "Yes. There is a way," she said. "Your ancestors knew it. I believe that even as they built their villages and began building up the Toda troops, they carefully controlled their number to prevent them from over multiplying."

"How?"

Elin sighed. "With tokujisui."

Yohalu's eyes widened. "What? Tokujisui? Does it have the power to do that?"

Elin nodded. "Do you remember the eggs that killed the Kiba?"

"Yes," Yohalu said hoarsely. "Are you saying that it was tokujisui that caused that?"

"Yes. I believe it wasn't just coincidence or the operation of some natural law. Why is it that only Kiba die en masse? Why don't other females suffer from egg-binding? Why don't Toda raised in the Ponds mate and reproduce? All these things are related to a single factor."

Yohalu stared at her as though dumbfounded. Returning his gaze steadily, Elin said, "The main difference between Toda in the Ponds and wild Toda is tokujisui, the potion that turns Toda into giant Kiba. Although females grow very quickly when given tokujisui, it must cause some kind of deformation. When it's time to lay their eggs, the tokujisui becomes toxic. Although that toxin isn't fatal to the other Toda, which are only given diluted tokujisui, it still seems to stop them from sexually maturing.

"I'm guessing that wild females don't lay eggs unless they mate, but the Kiba, which are fed heavy doses of the solution, produce unfertilized eggs. The tokujisui also causes lumps to form in the fallopian tubes and those lumps block the eggs. This man," Elin said, pointing to the diary, "knew how to make tokujisui and what effect it would have on the Toda. He knew, and yet he still gave it to them."

Yohalu's features twisted with revulsion. Shaking his head, he said, "But the purpose was to make the Toda strong so they'd be suited for battle. Surely, they'd never have done something so hideous? They'd never have intentionally deformed living creatures to prevent them from multiplying."

"It's true that tokujisui increases the size and strength of the Toda. But if that were the reason for using it, why not use it to make all the Toda into Kiba?"

Yohalu opened his mouth and closed it again. His eyes slid away from hers. After a long silence, he whispered, "You're right. Why isn't the same dose given to all the Toda? If all the troops were Kiba, we would have a much stronger army . . ."

Frowning, he looked at Elin. "Why would they make a rule that only Toda hatched from eggs collected every five years could become Kiba?"

Elin sighed. "Because this man knew. He knew that if female Toda were given undiluted tokujisui they would die when it was time to reproduce."

"But if that was the case, then why not select only male Toda as Kiba and—" Yohalu stopped.

Elin nodded. "Exactly. The Stewards couldn't do that. Because the man who made the rules for raising Toda forbade the Stewards from checking their sex. It was more important to him to keep the Toda's sex unknown than to produce a large number of Kiba. If the Stewards started checking the Toda's sex, they'd realize that the Toda in each Pond were either all male or all female."

Elin rubbed her arms, which felt cold and clammy. "I can't say for certain without checking every Pond in all the Toda villages, but I suspect there're no Ponds in which both male and female Toda are raised together. And if my suspicion is true, then that's what caused the mass Kiba deaths."

Yohalu cast her a puzzled frown. "What do you mean?"

"I once read a report about the galyo, a poisonous, water-dwelling lizard inhabiting the wetlands in the southern part of this country. Their sex is determined by the water temperature in the year they hatch. In years when the water temperature during the egg-laying season is high, horned males are born, while in cold springs, hornless females are born. Do you remember the eggs we saw in the wild Toda nests? Before we were attacked?"

"Yes."

"In Oohan, we were told that eggs from nests in the same basin are always raised in the same Pond. When Kolu said they never pick eggs from nests in the upper basin for Kiba because they don't grow as well, I thought that water temperature might have something to do with sex. That's why I went to check out the nests in each basin."

"And?"

"The water in the nest in the upper basin, which they avoid when choosing Kiba eggs, was much colder than the water in the one below. I'm guessing it's because of this custom that females have never been chosen as Kiba in Oohan."

"I see," said Yohalu. "The other villages don't have the same topography, so they never passed on the custom of picking eggs from the lower instead of the upper basin."

Elin nodded. "Are there any other villages with a river like the one in Oohan?"

"No. None are as high in the mountains or on such a steep incline. They're all in places with enough room to make large ponds and a training ground. I doubt there's any difference in water temperature where the wild Toda nest."

"Which means," Elin said, "that the Toda Stewards just gave tokujisui to those Toda hatched every fifth year. If it was a cool spring that year, all the Kiba would have been females. And they would've died of egg-binding when they reached maturity. In the report you showed me, mass Kiba deaths occurred in several villages at once. If those villages were established in the same year and have similar climates, then it would be a strong indication that this hypothesis is correct."

Yohalu stared at her. "You mean, our ancestors went to such extreme lengths to . . ." His words died away.

Elin glanced down at the diary. For a long time, neither of them spoke. At last, Yohalu's chair creaked as he turned to stare blankly out the window. His face twisted. "How ironic. For years, my father and I pondered how to raise more Toda and build a stronger army. To think that it was my own ancestor who obstructed this dream—one cherished by every Toda Rider!"

Returning his gaze to Elin, he said slowly and deliberately, "Elin, I thank you. We have perpetuated this monstrous waste for far too long. Because our family's oral tradition was severed. Thanks to you, we can fix that. This will probably be my last and greatest undertaking." He rapped the side table with his knuckles. "I must inform the Aluhan immediately and have the Stewards' regulations revised. I'll also get the Stewards to determine the sex of every Toda. We must figure out how to multiply the Toda and start doing so right away."

As she stared at his stern, warrior-like features, something cold spread from Elin's shoulders down through her chest. She laid her fingers on the diary. "Are you sure that what this man did was a mistake?" she whispered.

A faint smile lifted the corners of Yohalu's mouth. "I know without even asking what you're thinking, what you fear. You worry that if the Toda army swells, it will bring another disaster like the one that occurred beyond the Afon Noah. But, Elin, think. Time changes things. The conditions in this kingdom today are completely different from those several centuries ago. This man's grandfather said they lacked the knowledge to control a pack that exceeds the size nature intended and avert disaster. Those words may have been true then, but not anymore."

Elin stared at him. "You think we can control hordes of Toda without causing a disaster?"

Yohalu let out a breath and shook his head slightly. "I'm saying we should look at it from the other way around. To refrain from trying because we might not be able to prevent a disaster is to take a step backward. Don't you see? Time moves on and things change with each passing minute. I'm saying we should move with it. We should examine the situation carefully so we can choose the best strategy."

Fixing his eyes on hers, he said, "When we stood on the hill overlooking the Amasulu River, you asked me why the Lahza attack our country. Do you know why I didn't answer you?"

"No."

Yohalu nodded. "You see? Even you, who're so clever, can't guess. That's exactly why I didn't answer you. Because I couldn't." He turned his face toward the window and gazed outside. The white light of morning that had poured through the window earlier had deepened to the color of noon. "If you were just a commoner, I probably would've told you the Lahza are greedy barbarians who love to conquer other lands, that they've swallowed up many smaller countries to swell their own. And now that they've gained great military strength, they wish to conquer this land, which is not only wealthy but serves as a passage to countries that lie along the sea."

Slowly, he shifted his gaze back to her. "And if you knew the situation of this country and of the eastern plains as well as I do, you wouldn't even have asked that question, because you would've known that even if you asked, you could never get a correct answer."

A bitter smile touched his lips. "Why do the Lahza invade this country? Neither I nor the Aluhan know the real reason. Many different theories come to our ears, and we can make some assumptions from those. But at this time, no one in this country has seen with their own eyes or heard with their own ears what kind of people the Lahza are or how they govern their affairs. The capital of Lahza lies far across the great plains. Not even my son Rolan travels that far."

He rubbed his jaw. "You can't question whether it's right to increase and strengthen the Toda forces. Because you know absolutely nothing about the military affairs of this country." He smiled quietly. "So, you see, there's no need for you to bear the burden of that decision. The burden is mine. I, the descendent of the man who made the Toda troops, will create a new Toda army that suits this day and age."

The birds flitting among the trees outside the window warbled cheerfully. Elin kept her head bowed, unable to find any words. A feeling of impotence spread through her, as though her bones had turned to dust.

Yohalu rose from his chair and placed a hand gently on her shoulder.

At that moment they heard a commotion outside the room. A deep voice penetrated the closed door.

"Father. It's Muhan."

"Come in!" Yohalu called out. His son-in-law opened the door and walked in accompanied by a soldier.

"Father, I have just received an important report from this man here. I brought him with me so that you could hear it for yourself."

The soldier, who was standing rigidly at attention, bowed and then glanced at Elin.

"It's fine. You may proceed," said Yohalu.

The man nodded. "We captured the men who attacked you, my lord. Captain Aoolu was discovered with two foreign bandits trying to sneak across a tributary of the Amasulu; they were apprehended."

"Well done. Were you there yourself?"

"Yes, sir. The captives were taken away but rather than accompanying them, I came here instead. One of the foreigners divulged valuable information, and I thought it should be conveyed as soon as possible."

Yohalu frowned. "What is it?"

"The foreigner was from Asheh. Fearing that he'd be executed, he offered us information in exchange for his life."

Asheh . . . The same country as Rolan, Elin thought. In her mind, she saw the spot on the eastern plain to which he had pointed on the map.

Standing rigidly at attention, his face tense, the soldier plowed on. "According to him, their plan was to kidnap a Toda Steward and sell him in Lahza. They'd be rewarded so well, they'd never have to work again."

The meaning of his words seeped into Elin's brain, and a shudder ran down her spine as though a lump of ice had been pressed against the nape of her neck. Her eyes swung to Yohalu's face, but it registered no surprise. With a stern expression, he asked, "You mean they were after Stewards, not Toda eggs?"

"Yes, that's what the man said. It seems that Lahza has been sending out bandits like these for over a decade with the same mission. The Toda villages are so well concealed that almost no one has managed to abduct a

Steward. But eight years ago, it seems that someone did succeed, and the rumor of the fortune he received has been the envy of the others."

Yohalu's jaw tightened. "Someone succeeded? Eight years ago, you said?"

"Yes. The man from Asheh said he found out that it was Aoolu who had assisted the successful bandit. That's why he made contact with him."

Yohalu's clenched fists shook.

Eight years ago . . . Elin recalled the tale she had heard in Oohan. The younger brother of the chief; the great-uncle of the green-eyed girl. They'd assumed he drowned in the river, but his body had never been found.

Yohalu stood as motionless as a statue. His eyes were focused on a single point, and he seemed lost in thought. No one spoke, and a heavy tension pervaded the room. At last, he shifted his gaze to his son-in-law and said, "Send soldiers to every Toda village immediately and strengthen their guard. Recall the sentries posted in each village and replace them with new ones."

"Yes, sir!"

"Interrogate each sentry you recall and find out if any of them have had contact with foreign bandits. Aoolu should be thoroughly cross-examined. Make him cough up every detail about who was abducted and how, and also about how he became connected to foreign thieves."

Muhan nodded, his face grim. "As you wish, sir." Briskly, he repeated Yohalu's orders for confirmation.

"Right, then," Yohalu said. "Carry out those orders as you see fit. And make sure you amply reward this good man here and the others who captured them."

"Yes, sir!" Muhan saluted, then turned and led the soldier from the room. When the door closed, Yohalu looked at Elin. "What I feared most has finally happened," he said as if to himself.

"Was it the chief's younger brother who was taken?" Elin asked.

"Probably. I can only pray he killed himself, as a good Steward should." His words were cruel, but Elin understood what he meant. If the man had shared his knowledge with the Lahza to save his own life, those eight years would take on a terrible significance. Stewards and Riders often said, "Three years do a Toda make." It took three years to raise and train a newly hatched Toda to bear a warrior into battle. If they had started eight years ago, then the Lahza might already have a considerable number ready for battle.

Yohalu took a deep breath. With a slight shake of his head, he said, "I apologize for the rush, but we can't allow ourselves to be put on the defensive again. Tomorrow morning, I'll leave for the palace and take you with me."

Wordlessly, Elin gazed up into his face. The fierce warrior before her seemed a different man. What he saw in her expression she didn't know, but something like sorrow flickered in his eyes. In a soft voice, he said, "Considering the circumstances, it's no longer possible for this old man to protect you on his own. I know this will be hard on you, but please be patient."

Gripping her icy hands together, Elin whispered, "So you mean to place me under the supervision of the palace?"

Yohalu nodded. "And not just you, but anyone who has the ability to influence you. They must all be placed under our complete protection."

Elin stood staring at him silently while the room and everything in it seemed to fade away.

FOUR

FATHER AND SON

I

THE BATHHOUSE

Kokari wood felt as smooth as satin when properly polished. As Ialu ran his fingers over the white surface, his thoughts drifted to Elin. Images of her popped into his head—a casual gesture or expression. He let his mind follow these traces while keeping his hands and eyes focused on planing wood and assembling cabinet pieces, never pausing in his work.

Perhaps because Elin wasn't there, most of the memories that floated through Ialu's brain were from their early days before they married. The way she had looked on the day he first saw her, when he was still a Se Zan. The uncertainty on her face as she stood unannounced outside the door of his dingy little house in the capital. Scattered fragments from the time when, despite their efforts, it became increasingly difficult to keep their distance.

A shrill clanging startled Ialu from his reverie—the evening bell. It's that late already?

For some time, the light had been too dim to see his hands clearly. The late afternoon sun that had shone through the latticed window had faded, and the room was sunk in blue shadow.

Brushing the wood shavings from his knees, he stood up. No flame burned in the lamp in the corner of the room or in the clay oven in the dirt-floored kitchen. Recently, Jesse had become obsessed with striking the flint, reporting eagerly how many strikes it had taken to ignite the fire. But today he was nowhere to be seen. Ialu slipped his feet into his sandals and walked to the clay oven. Children's shouts came through the open door. There must be a fight going on somewhere, he thought. He could hear jeers and hoots mingled with voices pleading for someone to stop; his son's shrill voice was among them.

Ialu knelt in front of the oven and swiftly lit a fire. A neighbor had given them some fahko yesterday. With stewed fish and tsupa, vegetable soup, Ialu figured it would be enough for their supper. But when he looked in the basket where he'd left the fahko, he scowled. There was only half left, hardly enough for their supper, let alone breakfast tomorrow.

Jesse . . . He had probably found another pup. Whenever Jesse snuck off with some fahko, it usually meant he'd taken a stray under his wing and hidden it somewhere.

Banking the ashes around the fire, Ialu pulled a few coins from a pouch that hung above the oven and went outside. Though fairly wide, the lane in front of his house was cluttered with potted plants, laundry racks, and other paraphernalia the neighborhood women left out. The aroma of roasting meat and freshly baked fahko wafted through the air, borne on a thin haze of smoke from the cooking fires.

A short distance down the lane was a major thoroughfare. Just before it was another lane that led to a grocer's backyard. A gang of boys were gathered there, shrieking and shouting. No doubt the grocer would come out shortly and douse them with a bucket of water to shoo them away. A single glance told Ialu that Jesse was one of the two boys grappling in the middle, but he continued on without turning aside.

The lanterns hanging over the shops on both sides of the main road had already been lit. The exhausted faces of the lower-ranked artisans hurrying home glowed briefly in the faint lamplight, only to vanish once again into the blue dusk. Ialu bought a round of fahko, the flatbread still warm and steaming from the oven. Folding it in half, he slipped it under his arm and headed home. Lamplight spilled from the doorways, casting bright stripes across the darkness that lay over the road. Ialu made out a shadowy figure standing in front of his house. The figure's eyes were on the doorway, avoiding the light. A dark puddle spread around its feet.

"Jesse," he said. The shadow jumped. Even in the darkness, Ialu could see the boy's sorry face and bloodied nose. He was sopping from head to toe and looked as miserable as a drenched pup. But he kept his lips pressed firmly together, and his whole body seemed to shout, "It wasn't my fault!"

"Stay there," Ialu said. "Don't go in like that." Stepping inside, he grabbed a towel and handed it to Jesse. "Here. Dry yourself off first."

Jesse rubbed his face with the towel, then winced at his father. "My tooth's loose," he said.

"Good thing it's one of your baby teeth," Ialu said.

Jesse scowled. "That's not what a father should say. You're supposed to say things like, 'Here, let me see.'"

Ialu grinned. "Is that right?"

"Yup. See. It's wiggling!" Jesse pointed earnestly at his tooth.

The look on his son's face wrenched Ialu back to a memory of his own tooth breaking from a punch. He remembered how forlorn he'd felt as he gazed helplessly at his teacher, probing the root of the waggling tooth with his tongue and strangling the sobs in his throat. I guess I still had some baby teeth then, too.

Ialu took a deep breath. Shoving aside his memories, he placed a hand on Jesse's shoulder. His skin was cold to the touch. "Maybe we should go to the bath before we eat."

Jesse's face twisted. "Aw! No! I'm so hungry I'm just gonna float away when I get in that pool!"

Ialu gripped Jesse's shirt collar and raised him up like a puppy, silencing any further protests. The boy was pitifully light. With such scrawny arms, it was no wonder that he walked away from every fight with a bloody nose.

"Put your clothes in a bucket of water to soak while I get you some new ones, will you?" Ialu said gruffly. He left Jesse grumbling behind him and went inside. Once he'd taken a set of clothes from the chest of drawers, there was only one clean set left.

Guess I'll have to do the laundry tomorrow. It was a bother but he had no choice. I wonder when Elin will be back. The anxiety of not knowing where she was or when she'd be home swelled like a dark cloud, filling his chest.

"Dad! I'm freezing!" Jesse shouted. Stripped down to just a pair of knee-length cotton shorts, he was hopping from one foot to another in the dirt-floored kitchen. With a sigh, Ialu bundled Jesse's change of clothes in a towel and handed them to him.

When they reached the bathhouse, it was full of tradesmen. The men stopped by to wash off the grime of a hard day's work before going home refreshed and ready for a nice hot meal. Jesse took off his shorts clumsily, scowling when the burly men jostled him. He didn't like this big public bathhouse much. It was always crowded and so dimly lit he couldn't see people's faces clearly. Besides, sharing the tub with all these men meant that he couldn't swim. If he played around even a little, they'd yell at him to be quiet.

When Jesse went with his mother, he was allowed into the women's bath. He liked it much better, although he'd never admit that to his friends. In the women's bath, he could play with the younger kids, and nobody scolded him. But best of all was the large bath at Kazalumu School.

He had spent most of his life at the school. As a baby, his mother had carried him on her back while she worked in the Royal Beast stables. The sounds of the Beasts had served as a lullaby. Once he was old enough, he helped the men who worked there and played with the older students, sticking around until his mother was done with her work. When she finished late, they would stop at the school bath on their way home. They got the big pool all to themselves, and his mother would place him on her lap. He would chatter away about everything he'd done that day, and about the Royal Beasts, enjoying the feel of her silky skin. His mother, who was usually too busy to pay attention, would listen patiently. That's why he liked the bath at Kazalumu the best.

Jesse's father stripped and stepped into the bath area. Watching him, Jesse sighed. He was about to ask when his mother was coming home, but stopped himself. He couldn't ask. His father would just look sad and troubled. That look always made Jesse's stomach tighten and tears sting his eyes.

His face hurt where he'd been punched, and his lip was swollen. His lower back was really sore, too, throbbing with each step he took. That was really why he hadn't wanted to come. He felt like crying, but shoved his tears back down. Nudging his wobbly tooth with his tongue, Jesse trotted after his father into the dimly lit bath area.

The place where fresh hot water poured into the bath was crowded. He looked around for a space to wash himself, but couldn't find any. Catching sight of him, his father waved him over. Jesse made his way to his side. His father sat him down between his knees, scooped up a basinful of hot water, and dipped a washcloth into it. "Here," he said. "Wash yourself with this."

Jesse dabbed at his body, leaving a wide berth around the places that hurt.

"Hey!" His father gave him a slap on the head.

"Ow!" Jesse scowled.

"That's no way to wash! You're filthy. Scrub yourself properly."

"But it hurts!" Jesse protested. "A little dirt won't kill me. But if any of that hot water hits my sore spots, I'm gonna jump out of my skin. Then I might slip and fall, which really could kill me."

His father chuckled. "Honestly! You haven't lost the gift of gab at least. Give me that." He took the washcloth from Jesse and began to scrub him down.

"Ow! No! Not there! It hurts!" Jesse twisted away when the washcloth reached his lower back. His father's hand stopped, and Jesse glanced up to see why. He was peering at a point near Jesse's waist.

"Someone kicked you here, didn't they?" he said.

Jesse nodded. That spot hurt the worst. His face felt bruised and sore, too, but the pain in his back was a heavy, jarring ache.

"Who did this?"

"Oguran."

A stout man sitting beside them turned and said, "Oguran?"

"Do you know him?" Jesse's father asked.

The man snorted. After glancing around to see who was sitting nearby, he lowered his voice and said, "His father's a real ruffian, and the boy's just like him. A good-for-nothing. Doesn't work, even though he's already thirteen. Rotten to the core. He picks on my boy, too. Seems like his father's been teaching him how to fight. When boys get into a scrap with him, they come home with injuries you'd never expect from a kids' fight." He flicked his eyes to Jesse. "If you see him, run. He could kill you if he kicks you in the wrong place." He poured a basinful of water over himself, then stood up and left the room.

Gently, Jesse's father touched the spot where Jesse had been kicked. "Jesse," he said. "Right next to this spot is your kidney. It's dangerous to kick someone there. Don't fight with anyone who'd do that to you. Do what the man said. If Oguran comes near you again, run."

Jesse frowned. To be honest, Oguran scared him. The thought of being hit or kicked by him again made him feel like crying. But being told to run made him angry. Looking down at his son's scowling face, Ialu smiled faintly. When he wore this expression, there was no budging Jesse. That's just who he was. He talked big but was too little to win any fights. Yet if someone tried to hold him down, he'd rebel. He wouldn't back down from his convictions for anyone. He would probably mellow when he grew up, but until then, he was going to keep fighting back against people much stronger than him . . . And he'd keep getting beaten.

"If you don't want to run away," Ialu said quietly, "learn how to protect your vital points."

"How?"

"I'll show you when we get home." Although he hadn't seen the actual fight, Ialu could tell just by looking at Jesse's body how he'd been hit, and how he'd tried to fight back. Ialu scrubbed him down, keeping an eye out for any cuts and bruises that could become serious later.

This is my son.

For a moment, he felt as if he were dreaming. Although eight years had passed since Jesse was born, this strange feeling still hit him at times. The fact that he had a wife and son made him uneasy, like he was wearing unfamiliar clothes or was in the midst of a forbidden dream from which he might wake up to find Elin and Jesse gone.

Casting off such foolish thoughts, he took a deep breath and slapped Jesse on the bottom. "Right, then. Fetch some water," he said. He watched his son heave an exaggerated sigh and walk away to fill a basin with hot water.

2

AMBUSH IN THE ALLEYWAY

By the time they reached the lane where their house was, even the faint light of dusk had vanished, and night had cast its mantle over the town. People had closed their doors, perhaps against the evening chill, and the alleyway was sunk in darkness. Light seeping through window lattices and cracks in the doorways cast a faint glow on the shapes in the darkness, but potted plants and drying racks were just black shadows.

As he was about to turn into the lane, Ialu stopped. Jesse looked up, but before he could speak, Ialu clapped a hand over Jesse's mouth and peered into the darkness. He could feel their presence—one man behind the drying rack, another near the other end of the lane. Their motionless forms merged with the blackness.

A tingling sensation swept over Ialu's skin, and he frowned. With his hand still clamped over Jesse's mouth, he picked him up and walked back far enough along the main road that they couldn't be seen from the lane. Only then did he put Jesse down. Taking some coins from his robe, he handed them to Jesse and said, "Go back to the bath and stay in the changing room until they close. If I haven't come to get you by then, give this money to the man in charge and ask him to take you to Kazalumu. When you get there, tell the headmistress what happened."

Jesse looked up at him anxiously, eyes wide. He didn't ask why, but merely stared at his father with those big eyes.

"Do you understand?" Ialu asked, keeping his voice calm. Jesse nodded. Ialu ruffled the boy's hair, then pulled away. As Ialu passed a potted plant on the corner, he reached in and pulled out a thin pole used as a climber and stuck it in his belt behind his back. Then he strode off casually and turned into the lane.

For a moment, Jesse didn't move. His father no longer seemed to be his father. He had become a stranger the instant he had clapped a hand over Jesse's mouth, just like in a child's worst nightmare. Jesse could barely feel his trembling legs, but he forced them to move. He wobbled over to the alleyway entrance and stuck his head around the corner.

Despite the darkness, Jesse could make out the shape of his father walking. He saw him stop in front of the house and reach to open the door. A dark shadow leaped out from behind, waving what looked like a club. In the light spilling from the crack in the doorway, his father crouched and turned, bringing himself up under his attacker. There was a groan, and the assailant staggered. His father smashed his knee into the man's chin, sending the man slumping to the ground.

There was a muffled sound of footsteps. Someone came hurtling along the alley from the other end. Jesse's father flung the door open, reached inside, and grabbed the wooden stick with which they barred the door. Then he turned and ran toward the man, meeting him halfway.

There was a muffled scuffling, but the noise was so faint probably none of the neighbors could hear it. No one opened the door to see what was going on.

Shaking, Jesse swallowed. Dad . . .

The shape that lay sprawled in front of his house didn't budge. Peering down the lane, Jesse thought he saw a movement in the darkness, but he couldn't tell what it was or what had happened to his father.

Blood pounded in his veins, as if he had run a long distance. Gulping for air, he stared into the darkness. Dad! Unable to bear the suspense, Jesse stepped forward. His knees wobbled, and he felt as if he were swimming rather than walking. Fear paralyzed his brain, but still he didn't stop. His legs kept moving as though he were being pulled by an invisible cord. When he reached the house, he saw something sticking up from the inert form. A thin pole. Sprouting from the man's stomach. The same pole his father had stuck into his belt.

Sobs rose in Jesse's throat, and his shoulders heaved. The world began to warp and spin around him. He staggered backward, then turned and fled. Somehow he made it to the main street. Shoving his sobs down his throat, he ran without looking back.

Ialu groaned. A dull pain throbbed in his temple. His ear felt stretched and swollen, and the ground heaved upward. Gritting his teeth, he moved in close to his assailant, dodging the strange weapon that swung toward him.

He'd never seen anything like it. Although it looked like a club, it must have something flexible inside. When Ialu had parried the blow with his stick, the club had curved and hit him in the side of the head. He'd managed to twist aside before it hit the vital point behind his ear, but it was still a powerful blow. If it had hit him straight on, it would have knocked him out cold. His stick had flown from his hands and hit the wall with a clatter.

Damn! That was careless. I must be getting rusty.

Though gasping for breath, Ialu stayed glued to the man, giving him no space to wield his weapon. Then he dropped low and rammed his left fist into the region of the man's liver. A single crushing blow to that spot could stop a man in his tracks. Although Ialu couldn't put his full weight behind it, the man groaned and doubled over.

Ialu followed through with a right-hand jab to the man's solar plexus and swung his right knee into the side of his opponent's knee. The man staggered. Ducking down, Ialu slipped his arm around the man's right leg, twisted his body, and flipped him over. The man fell on his back and hit his head with a dull thud against the wall, sprawling motionless on the ground.

His shoulders heaving, Ialu stared down at him. He looked like a complete thug. Even in the dark, Ialu could make out his thick beard and the sloppy way he'd left his robe undone, exposing his chest.

But why?

One in front of his house and the other at the end of the lane to block his escape. Clearly, they'd positioned themselves to attack him. The fact that they had waited until the light from the door had shone on his face before rushing him from behind was further proof. But he couldn't think of any reason he would be attacked by thugs.

The man was out cold. Ialu slipped the man's arms from his sleeves and tied the sleeves together to immobilize him, then used the man's sash to bind his arms above his elbows and his bootlaces to bind his ankles. Once he was tied up, Ialu slung him over his shoulder, took him inside, and laid him in the dirt-floored kitchen. After dragging the second man inside, Ialu closed the door. With a sturdy rope, he tied their hands behind their backs and their ankles together, then gagged them. He left the thin garden pole in the man's stomach. He had stabbed him in the muscle to avoid injuring his organs, but if he pulled it out, the man would bleed.

Only when he had finished did he go over and scoop water out of an earthenware crock, gulping straight from the ladle. He sighed and gingerly probed the spot where he had been hit. It was quite swollen and painful, and his head was beginning to pound. He winced as he crouched down beside the men and began searching them.

Their clothes were new. He could tell just by the stitching that they must have cost quite a bit. Their daggers were still in their sheaths. He felt a chill run up his spine. The lane in front of his house was narrow. He could see why they would have armed themselves with daggers and not swords, yet they hadn't drawn them. If they had meant to kill him, they would have tried to stab him from behind. Instead, they had both used those strange clubs.

They intended to take me alive.

He bit his lip. When he had seen them lurking in the darkness, he had assumed that they'd been sent to assassinate him. On Tahai Azeh, Ialu had killed Damiya, the previous Yojeh's nephew and the man responsible for her death. And he had killed him in front of the new Yojeh Seimiya, who loved and was betrothed to the man.

When he saw the Royal Beast save Shunan, heir to the Aluhan, and bear him back to safety, Ialu had thought, If I'm to kill Damiya, now is my only chance. If he lives, he'll only do more evil in the future.

But it wasn't just noble thoughts of the future that had driven him. Without a doubt, he had also harbored a deep loathing for the man who had killed the wise old Yojeh, and who had mocked and tried to kill Ialu.

Ialu was a shield. His sole purpose in life was to protect the Yojeh. To fulfill this duty, he had taken many lives. If anyone should sully their hands with Damiya's blood, he had thought, it should be him.

Later he'd heard that the Yojeh despised him not because he had killed Damiya, but because he had seemed to do it with such cold indifference. Regardless of how she might feel, however, he was permitted to remain a Se Zan and even offered a reward for saving her from great peril. But he had refused it all. Leaving the palace, he had submerged himself among the commoners.

When had he first learned that his life was in danger? If he remembered rightly, it was soon after Seimiya married Shunan. Damiya's supporters among the nobles had now fallen from grace, and they blamed Ialu. Kailu had come specifically to warn him that they were seeking revenge. Although Ialu had listened, he hadn't bothered to change his ways. If they attacked and killed him, he had thought, so be it. Although he was attacked once, his assassins had been inept and their attempt failed.

When he recalled that period of his life, all that came to mind was a clammy darkness as black as night. He had killed so many men that his continued existence seemed cowardly and despicable. Yet something within him rebelled angrily at this very thought. It was Elin who had shown him the true nature of the feelings that lurked inside him.

Ialu frowned as he gazed down at his captives. He wished they had been trying to kill him for revenge. But instead they had tried to abduct him. Clearly, he was not their true target. Resting his forehead in his hands, he closed his eyes.

It's Elin they're after.

Were they hoping to force her to do their bidding by taking him hostage? Or were they going to use him as bait to lure her out and kill her? Whichever it was, who was behind this?

Opening his eyes, he resumed his search of the unconscious men. Running his hands over the first, he discovered a chafed spot where the beard met the hairline. His eyes narrowed. Spreading the man's hands, he found not only sword callouses but also a bruise on the back of the left thumb—the kind caused by a bowstring. An archer? That would explain the rubbed hairline. It was probably where the man's headband had chafed the skin.

But neither the soldiers of the Aluhan nor the Se Zan that protected the Yojeh were permitted to grow such thick beards. Judging by the length, they must have left the army at least a month ago. The ambush had been carefully planned and executed. Reaching a hand inside the man's robe, he found a pouch weighed down with coins. When he dumped the contents out, his brows rose, and he stared numbly at two foreign coins which lay among the regular currency.

He stood up and walked over to the oven. Picking up two beans, he slipped them inside a small bag that hung on the soot-blackened wall. With swift strides, he stepped into the back room and pulled a large satchel from a cupboard. The cloth smelled damp and dusty and was cool to the touch. He filled it with the bare minimum of things he would need along with Jesse's last change of clothes and enough money for a long trip. Swinging the sack onto his back, he went to the kitchen and made sure the fire in the oven was out.

Before he left, he stopped in the doorway and looked back at his home, at the half-finished cabinet, at Jesse's clothes soaking in a basin, at the curtains that Elin had sewn. Then, pressing his lips together, he stepped into the dark alleyway.

The public bath was still crowded. The men's changing room was full, but Jesse was not there. Ialu wondered if he was in the women's section, but he couldn't go in to look.

"Have you seen Jesse?" he asked the man at the counter.

The man raised a hand, signaling for him to wait while he continued counting coins, muttering the numbers under his breath. When he finished, he put them into the drawers. Only then did he look up at Ialu. "Jesse you said? I haven't seen him since he left with you a while ago."

Ialu's pulse began to race. "I'm sorry to trouble you, but could you check if he's in the women's bath?"

"Sure," he said, then waved at someone behind Ialu. "Hey, Aina! Have you seen Jesse?"

A woman had just emerged from the changing room and was wringing out her wet hair with a towel. She looked up and shook her head. "Jesse? Nope. He wasn't in there. Good evening, Ialu. How've you been? I haven't seen Elin around for a while. I was worried she might be sick."

Ialu bowed his head slightly. "She's fine, thank you, but she's away for her work right now."

"I see."

Before she could ask any more questions, Ialu bowed and left the bath. His forehead felt cold and tight. The route that led to the bath was crowded, but it was only used by locals. If a stranger had abducted Jesse here, there would have been a commotion.

But if he hadn't been kidnapped, where could he have gone? A few of Jesse's friends popped into Ialu's mind, but he had a feeling he wouldn't find Jesse with them. When Ialu had told him to go to the bath, he had nodded. It was unlike him to break such a promise. In that case, there was only one place he could have gone. The Kazalumu Beast Sanctuary.

Surely he wouldn't have walked . . .

It would take more than an hour for a child of Jesse's size to walk that far. The livery stable where Elin usually hired a horse and buggy would be closed by now, and even if Jesse had gone there, they wouldn't have let him hire one if he was alone. Still, Ialu decided to check it out.

His headache was growing worse, and he had to fight down his nausea. All around he heard the sounds of shopkeepers closing up. The lights went out one by one. Hunching his shoulders, he hurried along the broad street.

When he turned the corner, his eyes widened. The livery stable door was open, and light was streaming onto the street.

Stepping inside, he called out, "Hello! Is anybody here?"

"Coming," a voice replied. It came from behind the large stable where the horse and buggy were usually kept. The stable was empty. A few moments later, the shop master's wife emerged through the door on the opposite side. She appeared to have been washing up, because she was wiping her hands on her apron. Catching sight of Ialu, her eyes grew round. "Ialu! Are you all right? Can you walk?"

"What?"

"Jesse came dashing in here, saying that you'd been badly injured and that you'd told him to go and get the headmistress . . ." Catching sight of the expression on his face, her voice trailed off, and she cocked her head. "Isn't that what happened?"

Ialu wiped the cold sweat from his forehead. "Where's Jesse?"

"My husband took him to the school."

"I see. I'm so sorry to have bothered you when it was past closing time."

The woman frowned and stared at Ialu. "Are you sure you're all right? Your face is white as a sheet. I don't think you should be walking around like that."

Ialu smiled. "I'm fine. I just hit my head. It gave Jesse such an awful fright, he ran off. I thought he might've come here, but I guess I was too late."

At this, the woman's face cleared. "So that's what happened. The boy looked so frightened. Like he was being chased by demons. I was scared you'd been badly injured."

"I'm so sorry to have worried you." Ialu bowed his head.

"Not at all," she said, waving her hand. "Jesse paid my husband properly for driving him there, you know. He's a very capable boy. He was just worried about you, that's all." She urged him to stay and rest, but Ialu thanked her and left.

Honestly . . .

Jesse was such a good talker. Ialu could picture him jabbering away, twisting the kindhearted couple around his finger. Still, if he'd gone by carriage, he must have reached Kazalumu safely by now. As the fear that smoldered in his gut eased a little, Ialu felt his body grow heavy. Pressing a hand against his forehead, he began walking slowly toward Kazalumu.

3

IN LEELAN'S SHADOW

By the time Ialu reached Kazalumu, it was long past the students' bedtime, but the lamps were still shining brightly in the main hall, and everyone seemed to be awake and out of bed. Here and there, he could see lights flickering in the woods and fields.

Hearing voices, he turned toward the sound. Children were leaning out of a dormitory window on the second floor. Below them, a teacher waved up at them and said, "That's enough now. Go to bed."

Ialu hurried over to the gate and reached out to ring the bell. At that moment, the front door opened, and a plump man stepped out. It was Yoshi, the master of the livery stable. He stopped and peered into the darkness when Ialu hailed him.

"Ialu? Is that you?" he exclaimed. He hastened to the gate and pulled it open from the inside. Sweat beaded his forehead beneath his balding pate, and words tumbled from his mouth. "Ialu! What's going on? Jesse said you were badly hurt. But when I brought him here, he disappeared while I was wiping down my horse. Now the place is in an uproar.

"When he ran off, I didn't think anything of it at first. I figured he must be with the headmistress. But when I went to fetch them, the headmistress said she hadn't seen him. I couldn't believe it. Then everyone got involved. They're all out looking for him, the teachers and custodians and everyone. It occurred to me just now that he might be hiding under the buggy so I came out to look."

Ialu bowed low. "I'm so sorry. Please don't worry about us. I've got a pretty good idea where Jesse is. I'll go look for him. Please go on home. It's late, and you have to be up early for work."

Yoshi dabbed his forehead. "You're sure, are you? I'd like to stay and see that he's all right, but I do have a customer at dawn."

"Yes, I'm sure. Really, there's no need for concern. We'll be fine." Ialu took some coins from his jacket and handed them to Yoshi. "Thanks, and please accept my apologies."

Yoshi scratched his head and flashed him an embarrassed smile. With a wave, he began walking toward the carriage. Suddenly he stopped and looked back. "I don't know what happened," Yoshi said, "but don't scold him too harshly. Elin's been gone a long time, so he's probably lonely. No matter what he did, I'm sure he's already regretting it. When he came to our place, he was chalk white and shaking all over. On the way here, he didn't utter a word either. He didn't seem like Jesse at all."

Ialu nodded. "I understand." Yoshi smiled and gave him a short wave, then walked off to his horse and buggy.

Ialu opened the school's front door to see Esalu talking with a group of teachers in the dimly lit corridor. She turned and raised her eyebrows. "Well, here comes his father," she said.

Ialu bowed his head. "I apologize for all the trouble we've caused."

Esalu walked over to him. "Trouble is right," she said with a wry smile. "Elin used to scare the wits out of me, too, but I think Jesse might be even worse." When she saw his eyes, however, her face grew grave. "What is it? You're pale as a ghost."

Ialu lowered his voice. "There's something I have to tell you, but I need to find Jesse first."

Picking up that it was confidential, Esalu just nodded and said, "We've split up to search for him, so I'm sure he'll turn up soon. Although to be honest, we've looked everywhere, even in the storage sheds, and still haven't found him."

"Did you check the Royal Beast stable?"

"Of course. It was the first place we looked, but he wasn't there."

Ialu held her gaze. "Please tell everyone to stop searching," he said quietly. "Then take me to Leelan's stable. I'll thank everyone for their help later."

Esalu's eyebrows shot up. "But I just told you. We already looked in Leelan's stable."

Ialu's lips twitched. "I think he might be copying his mother."

As Esalu led him through the dark forest, she warned him that Leelan was irritable because of her pregnancy. "Don't do anything that might disturb her," she said. "You may enter the stable, but whatever you do, don't go near her cage."

Ialu nodded wordlessly.

"I hope you realize that for me to let you enter the Royal Beast stable and stay there on your own is an extraordinary exception."

"I do. And I promise to be very careful."

Esalu sighed but said nothing more. When they emerged from the woods, everything suddenly seemed much brighter. The moon had risen, and the stable roof glowed a pale silver, as if covered in frost.

Esalu opened the door, and Ialu felt something stir inside. A huge black shadow spread its wings in the darkness. Ialu's unfamiliar scent must have alarmed Leelan, because she began to growl with a low rumbling in her throat. Feeling the hairs rise on his neck, Ialu stared up at the enormous creature. The scent of beast surged toward him, and his eyes stayed glued to the two bright orbs that shone in the darkness.

"Are you sure you'll be okay?" Esalu whispered in his ear.

Recollecting himself, Ialu nodded. "Yes, I'll be fine." As he stepped inside, Leelan's warning growl rose sharply. He pressed his back against the wall beside the door and slowly lowered himself to the floor. With a creak, the door shut, and everything was wrapped in darkness.

Even after Esalu left, Leelan kept her wings spread and continued to growl for some time, but she did not throw herself against the cage bars. Ialu sat still, staring up at the towering black shadow.

Like the ebb and flow of waves against the shore, Leelan's growls rose and fell, eventually subsiding into a murmur and fading away like the receding tide. Slowly she folded her wings, but her eyes never left Ialu.

Exhaling, Ialu whispered, "Do you remember me, Leelan?" At the sound of his voice, Leelan twitched, but she did not unfurl her wings. "You saved my life. A long time ago. Elin hid me behind you. I was so shocked. Who would have thought that a Royal Beast would hide me?"

That distant memory came flooding back, vivid and powerful. He felt again the warmth of Leelan's body. "When Elin was young, she used to hide behind Leelan to avoid a teacher she didn't like . . . Did you know that, Jesse? Your mother once did what you're doing now."

He heard the sound of suppressed sobbing, but he kept his eyes on the Royal Beast without looking toward the noise. "Leelan, our family owes you a lot."

The gleam in Leelan's eyes never wavered. What thoughts passed through the mind behind those eyes? Ialu wondered. Did beasts, like humans, treasure memories of the past? Or did such things have no meaning for them?

His eyes blurred, and he took several slow, measured breaths. "Jesse," he said. "I'm sorry I scared you."

The boy's sobs grew louder, gouging Ialu's heart. On his way to Kazalumu, Ialu had pondered why Jesse had broken his promise and gone to the school alone. Gradually, an image had formed in his mind. He saw Jesse running through the dark, trembling. Fear must have driven him to Kazalumu. He was the type to dive under his mother's covers if he had a bad dream. He must have been so petrified that all he could think of was burrowing under Leelan.

I'm so dense. Especially when it comes to fear.

As a Se Zan who shielded the Yojeh, fear was an emotion that Ialu had learned to rigidly control. When under attack, fear could cost him his life. He had pushed fear aside for so long that he'd failed to see how terrified Jesse must have felt when his father had sent him off on his own like that. Listening to his son's faint sobs in the darkness, Ialu closed his eyes.

The boy was only eight. Just a child. By rights, he should have still been sheltered under his parents' wings, blissfully ignorant. But considering what would probably happen next, it would be far crueler to leave him in the dark. Nothing was more terrifying than the unexpected and the unknown. This would likely be Ialu's only chance to tell Jesse what he and Elin had done and how that was bound to affect him.

Ialu leaned back against the wall, wincing when it touched the place where he had been hit. The pounding in his head was beginning to subside, but there was still a dull ache deep within.

"I first met your mother soon after Alu was born," he began, his voice barely a murmur. "The Yojeh at that time, Her Majesty Halumiya, traveled here to see the miracle cub, the first one ever born in a Beast Sanctuary. At the time, I was a Se Zan, and I accompanied the Yojeh as her bodyguard. That's when I met your mother. Do you know what a Se Zan is?"

Receiving no answer, Ialu continued. "Se Zan means 'impenetrable shield.' They're a band of warriors sworn to protect the Yojeh. If she's attacked, they shield her with their bodies, flinging themselves in front of any arrows that might hit her.

"Even a man who's born a commoner can rise to the rank of a noble and make lots of money if he becomes a Se Zan. But he never knows when he might be killed. Or when he might have to kill someone else. It's that kind of job. Anyone who takes the vow to become a Se Zan has to cut all ties with his family."

Behind his closed eyelids, he could see the light of a hot summer's day. "I was born among the commoners in the capital. My father, who was your grandfather, was a carpenter. He made beautiful furniture. But when I was eight, just your age now, there was a big earthquake, and my father was crushed beneath a building and killed. It was a hot day, with puffy white clouds in a blue sky."

Ialu told him everything about the day that had changed his life. About how his mother had been widowed and left with not just Ialu but also a little baby to feed; about how she had sold him to the Se Zan for a bag of gold coins. He told him what had happened after he had met Elin, the events on Tahai Azeh, and the difficult position Elin was in because she could control the Beasts. It didn't matter if Jesse couldn't understand everything. It would be enough if he could grasp even a little.

A breeze had sprung up. Ialu could hear the faint rustling of leaves in the darkness when he finished speaking. Leelan, who had fallen asleep during his tale, was breathing like a pair of bellows. With her eyes still closed, she stirred, her great wings shifting slightly, and a small face appeared from underneath one of them.

Jesse stared at Ialu. Finally, he said faintly, "Is that story true? All of it?"

Ialu nodded. "Yes, all of it."

Jesse opened his mouth to speak, then stopped. After a long pause, he finally said, "Are you really still you, Dad? The same person as before?"

For a moment, Ialu was at a loss for words. He supposed it was only natural. "Do I seem like a different person?"

"Yeah."

"Because of what I told you just now?"

"No. Before that. You changed all of a sudden." There was a tremor in his voice. "I never dreamed you'd do anything like that. Did you do it because you used to be a Se Zan?"

Ialu sighed. "So you saw, did you?"

Jesse's little head bobbed once.

"And that's why you were afraid?"

"Yeah."

"I see." Ialu searched for words, but found he didn't know what to say. "You must've been terrified," he began. "But I couldn't let them kill me." He stopped and shook his head. Taking a deep breath, he said flatly, "Jesse, that man is me. The carpenter you know as your father, and the man who fights back without mercy when attacked, they're both the real me."

Jesse stared at him. Ialu held his eyes steadily. "I know it's frightening, but listen carefully. Those men were trying to kidnap us. I'm just guessing, but I think they're after your mother."

Jesse caught his breath. "Mom?" he asked shrilly. "Are they going to kill her?"

"No. Hold on and let me finish, Jesse." Ialu spoke slowly and deliberately. "Remember what I said before? Your mother can control the Royal Beasts. There're lots of people who would like to use them as weapons because they're even stronger than Toda. But your mother's the only person who knows how."

Jesse shifted. Ialu paused, thinking his son had something to say, but the boy said nothing. "Your mother, however, will never use them as weapons," Ialu finished.

"Oh!" Jesse exclaimed. "I get it! If they catch us, they can make Mom do what they want."

Ialu stared at Jesse in surprise. "That's right. Smart thinking."

"That's what Oguran always does," Jesse said breathlessly. "He'll say, 'Tell me where Choi is. If you don't, I'll catch Atchan and beat him up.'"

"Choi?"

"Yeah. The pup I found. He's got the most beautiful eyes. He's a mutt, but I'm sure he's got wolf blood in him!"

Perhaps startled by the excitement in Jesse's voice, Leelan's eyes popped open, and she began to growl.

Ialu and Jesse froze. Cold sweat trickled down Ialu's temples, and his heart pounded. In his mind's eye, he saw the deep scars on Elin's shoulder and ear, and her left hand with only two fingers. If Leelan began stomping her feet in irritation, she would tear Jesse's little body to shreds in an instant.

Why was it, he wondered, that even though she was such a huge and fearsome beast, until this instant, both he and Jesse had been lulled into thinking that she would never hurt them? Because she was Leelan.

Don't move, Jesse, he begged silently.

They both held their breath, waiting for the growling to subside. Even when Leelan stopped and closed her eyes, they still didn't move. Annoyance radiated from her. They could practically feel it on their skin. Gradually, this too faded, and Leelan's jaw sank onto her chest. Once again, she began breathing with the low rumble of a bellows.

After making sure that no trace of Leelan's anger lingered in the air, Ialu gestured for his son to come.

Jesse moved slowly through the cage. Being careful not to disturb Leelan, he slipped through the bars and tiptoed over to his father. Rolling his eyes, he mouthed, "That was close!"

Ialu gave his son a light swat on the head, then picked him up and hugged him. He smelled like beast and straw; his body was so slight, it seemed like it might break.

"Ow! That hurts." Jesse squirmed. His father had touched the spot where Jesse had been kicked.

"Sorry," Ialu said. "I forgot." He lifted Jesse higher and adjusted his grip. With his son's warm body wrapped in his arms, he left the stable.

4

HARD SHELL

Esalu had stayed up waiting for them. Before Ialu could say a word, Jesse dropped to his knees and prostrated himself on the floor, begging forgiveness. Esalu fixed him with a ferocious glare, but then sighed and told him to raise his head.

"Your scolding can wait until tomorrow," she said. "The horse and buggy has already left, so you and your father might as well stay the night."

Still kneeling on the floor, Jesse answered weakly, "Yes, ma'am."

"Just look at you! You're covered in straw and fur. Make sure to brush all that off before you get into bed. Change your clothes and comb your hair, too."

"Uh-huh."

"Answer properly, young man! With feeling!"

"Yes, ma'am," Jesse answered hastily.

Ialu bowed his head. "Please forgive us for causing such a commotion."

With her arms still folded across her chest, Esalu shook her head and said, "Never mind that now. You'd better tell me what's going on. I'll take you to your room first. We can talk after you've put Jesse to bed."

Ialu shook his head. "No. If you don't mind, I'd like to keep him with me until I'm done."

Esalu frowned. "That's fine with me, but are you sure? I thought you wanted to tell me something confidential."

"I do, but there's a reason I want to keep him in my sight."

It was long past Jesse's bedtime. His eyelids drooped, and he looked up at Ialu with a blank expression. He'd been through quite an ordeal and had just had a big cry. Ialu guessed he must have been so tired he could barely stay awake.

Esalu seemed to have realized this as well. "There're some cushions over in the corner, Jesse," she said gently. "Go lie on those."

Jesse stood up slowly, wincing slightly. By morning, he was going to be very stiff. Completely forgetting Esalu's admonition to brush off the fur and straw, he laid his head on a cushion and curled up with a sigh. Within moments, he was fast asleep.

Esalu gazed at the boy's tear-streaked face, then shifted her eyes to Ialu. "Let's have some tea while we talk."

She gestured for Ialu to sit by the hearth. Taking the kettle from the hook, she poured hot water into a teapot.

"So," she began, fixing him with a piercing gaze, "I was right. You've been hurt, haven't you? Raise that lock of hair over your ear and let me see."

Her eyes were keen. Even in the firelight, she had noticed the swelling above his temple. She knelt beside him and examined the spot where the strange weapon had connected with his skull.

"Were you hit with something?" she asked.

Ialu nodded. "Some kind of club. I caught the blow with the stick I use to bar the door, but the end of the club bent around it and hit me here. It wasn't that strong a blow."

Esalu rested her hands on her knees and rose slowly to her feet. Taking a candle from a cupboard and returning to the hearth, she lit the wick in the fire and placed the candle in a holder. She held this up in front of Ialu's face. "Look at me. Let me see your eyes." After carefully examining the pupil in his right eye and then his left, she blew out the candle.

"At least you seem to have no internal bleeding."

"I think it just shook my brain a little," Ialu said. "The headache and nausea are pretty much gone."

"But you should never take a head wound lightly. Remember Her Majesty Halumiya. Even when there's no initial bleeding, blood can pool later, putting pressure on the brain. If you feel dizziness or nausea within the next few days, tell me immediately."

Ialu gazed at her. She seemed to have aged considerably, perhaps because he hadn't seen her for so long. Her eyes, however, still burned with the same stern light. "Thank you," he said. "But I'm afraid I'll just have to pray that it heals naturally. At dawn, I must take Jesse and leave Kazalumu."

Esalu's face clouded. "But why?"

Ialu explained what had happened. When he finished, Esalu picked up her cup absently, then clicked her tongue. She'd forgotten about the tea. As she poured the now-bitter brew into their cups, she said, "But who would do that? Even if they could force Elin to do what they wanted, what's the point without any Royal Beasts?"

Passing a cup to Ialu, she shook her head. "Only the Yojeh and the Aluhan can actually use the Royal Beasts as weapons. Even if someone in the court wished to wrest power from the Aluhan, it would take years to raise and train enough Royal Beasts. And they could never hide what they were doing. They'd be discovered and executed in no time."

Ialu placed his cup on the edge of the hearth. "Just as you say, such a plot would be meaningless. To anyone from this kingdom, that is."

He pulled out two coins from the pouch at his waist and laid them in his palm. "I found these on one of those thugs."

The coins glinted dully in the hearth's glow. Esalu's face froze. "Lajimu coins . . ." Raising her face, she looked at Ialu and whispered, "You think the Lahza were behind it?"

Ialu nodded. "The Lahza have been spreading across the plains like wind-borne locusts, growing ever stronger as they swallow up caravan cities on their way. Many countries, even ours, use their currency because it's of higher value.

"The bowmen who guard our border are paid only a pittance. Two lajimu coins each would be enough for them to take on any dirty job."

He tilted his palm toward the flame so the light licked the coins, highlighting the shape of a rearing horse. "Eleven years have passed since Elin rode Leelan and scattered the Toda forces on the plain of Tahai Azeh. If the Lahza, who covet this land, have heard about that . . ."

The two fell silent, their eyes resting on the coins. If the eastern horsemen were secretly spreading their net through this kingdom right now while it was shaken by internal unrest . . .

Esalu shuddered and rubbed her arms as though chilled. "What're you going to do?" she asked. "We'd better warn the Yojeh immediately. The country's in danger!" Catching sight of his expression, she faltered. Her mouth hung open for a second, then shut with a snap. She pressed her fingers to her forehead. "Oh, right. If the palace finds out, you and Elin . . ." She could not bring herself to finish the statement.

By order of the Yojeh and the Aluhan, Elin and the Royal Beasts had been surrounded with a gentle wall—a loose supervision that didn't interfere with daily life, just in case a hostile country tried to abduct her. It had been loose precisely because it was "just in case." The threat of kidnapping had been considered remote. But if the palace discovered that Elin was the target of its greatest threat, Elin and her family would be placed under strict surveillance, possibly for life.

"As you said, they can't raise and train Royal Beasts in a night and a day," said Ialu. "And even if they have managed to, which I think is highly unlikely, they obviously don't know how to control them yet. Otherwise, they wouldn't be trying to capture Elin. If so—"

Esalu picked up where he had left off. "They must have raised them with the Silent Whistle. Which means that even if they managed to raise some, they can neither control them nor use them as weapons. In other words, there's no imminent threat, so it won't matter if we wait before informing the palace."

Ialu nodded and glanced at Jesse, who lay with his head pillowed on a cushion. The expression on his face as he gazed at his son wrung

Esalu's heart. "What're you going to do next? Once you leave here?" she whispered.

Ialu shifted his eyes back to Esalu. "Find Elin." His eyes gleamed with a dark light. If they had tried to capture him, it might mean they already had Elin. The thought burned inside him. Raising the cup to his lips, he took a sip of the bitter, tepid brew. Then he turned the cup slowly in both hands. "I still have a few connections from the past. I'll try to find out what Elin has been doing and where she is now. Then I'll think about what to do from there."

"Let's say you find her and you're reunited as a family," Esalu said in a low voice. "Then what?"

Ialu said nothing. Branches scratched against the window, stirred by the night breeze. Esalu gazed into the eyes of this man who looked so much like an artisan. Would he continue to search until he found a way to be just a carpenter and Elin, a beast doctor; for them to live as man and wife? Would such a day ever come for this family?

With a small hiss, a piece of wood crumbled in the fire. A flame flared briefly, illuminating their faces.

"Have you thought about the possibility that you might miss her if you leave now? What if she turns up here after you've gone? What should I tell her?"

"Tell her to go home. If she does, she'll know."

Esalu's brow clouded. They probably had some sign known only to the two of them, she thought. They had lived all this time knowing that one day they might have to flee. It was only natural that they would be prepared. But her chest tightened at his words. She felt excluded.

A memory filled her mind. She had once told Elin it would be safer if anyone could control the Royal Beasts. Elin's face, and her words, came back to her now.

"I would rather that the risk was mine alone," she had said. "If my actions might bring about a disaster, then when it comes, I won't hesitate to lay down my life if I believe that could avert it." She had only been eighteen.

Does she still think that way, Esalu wondered, even now that she has a family? Something about Ialu reminded her of Elin. They're both loners, she thought. They both avoid relying on others—because they don't want to get them into trouble.

Although they were now married, Esalu doubted that marriage would have changed this trait. They would love each other and within that love would guard their son by surrounding him like the hard shell of a walnut. If they had been selfish, she might have felt angry rather than lonely. But Elin and this gruff-sounding man tried so hard not to cause others pain. It was the very thoughtfulness with which they treated her that made Esalu feel excluded.

She sighed and gave her head a little shake. "All right. If Elin makes it back here safely, I'll let her know. But it's time you went to bed. I'll send someone tomorrow to tell the town officer that there was a break-in. In the meantime, you can make your escape. I can lend you a horse."

Ialu bowed his head. Gratitude overwhelmed him, robbing him of the words he needed to express himself. If he tried to pay her, it would only hurt her feelings. Neither he nor Elin had any parents. She was the closest person they had to a mother. In the end, all he could say was "Thank you."

Looking up, his eyes met hers. "I'll do whatever I can to help," she said. Her voice hardened. "So you'd better make sure you come back. Promise me you'll return with your family and let me know you're alive and well."

Ialu lowered his eyes and gazed silently at his hands for some time. Finally, he raised his head and nodded. "I promise."

5

FLIGHT

Ialu's eyes flew open, sleep banished by faint sounds carried on the wind. Day had not quite broken, but in the pale blue darkness he could make out Jesse's small form sleeping beside him. Gently, Ialu pulled back the covers and got up to raise the window. The chill dawn air washed over his face. The noise, which had been faint before, was now quite clear. The sound of hooves pounding turf; a band of horsemen was galloping toward Kazalumu.

Leaning out the window, he could see the road that led up toward the school in the distance. Torchlight danced among the trees. Soon figures came into view. When Ialu caught the glint of armor in the lamp burning by the school gate, he closed the window softly.

"Jesse." He shook the boy, who grunted in response. "Jesse, wake up."

Jesse sat up with a groan, but his eyelids stayed closed. Ialu brought his lips close to Jesse's ear and whispered, "Wake up! We have to go."

Jesse jerked and rubbed his ear as though it tickled. His eyes opened, and he looked up at his father. "What?"

Ialu put a finger to Jesse's lips and gestured for him to pay attention to the sounds. The bell that hung at the gate clanged stridently. It was an old bell, green with age. The visitors rang it urgently and repeatedly, and soon the school began to stir. Footsteps and voices sounded in the hall, as students, startled from their sleep, stumbled from their rooms to see what was going on. The large door at the entrance screeched open, followed immediately by the clatter of boots in the hall. The teacher on night duty called for the headmistress.

Ialu opened the door a crack and peered through it. He saw Esalu stride briskly toward the entrance. When she approached the men standing in the entranceway, she put her hands on her hips. "It's not even dawn!" she exclaimed. "What's all this fuss about?"

Through the murmur of voices rising from the students, a soldier's voice, gruff and overbearing, reached Ialu's ears. "We're here by order of Her Majesty, the Yojeh. Kneel and listen!" The man flourished a document with a seal indicating it was a royal ordinance, and Ialu saw Esalu sink slowly to her knees.

The students quieted, and this time the soldier's voice rang loud and clear. "Her Majesty has commanded us to bring Elin's husband and son to the palace to place them under her protection. Bring us Ialu and Jesse immediately!"

Behind him, Jesse gulped, and Ialu gripped his shoulder to keep him quiet.

"Ialu and Jesse are not here," Esalu said. "They live in town." Her voice was strong and penetrating, and Ialu guessed she was making sure her words reached every listening ear.

"Do you intend to hide them?" the soldier snapped. "You'll be arrested if you dare lie to us. We've already been to their house in town. We know they were ambushed and managed to beat off their attackers. We also know the boy escaped here and was followed by Ialu. We gave up sleep to come here. Surely you realize how critical this situation is. So think carefully before you speak!"

Silence fell over the building, broken only by Esalu's measured voice. "I am speaking the truth. Jesse did indeed come to Kazalumu last night, causing a commotion, but his father, Ialu, came to fetch him. It was very late, so I urged them to stay the night. However, Ialu refused and took his son back with him down the mountain. I believed they had returned home, which is why I answered you thus."

Gently, Ialu closed the door and gestured for Jesse to remain silent. He pushed the window up soundlessly. It was still dark outside, but he saw no other soldiers. They all appeared to be gathered at the entrance. After quickly surveying the surroundings, he pulled his head inside, folded the bedding neatly, and placed it back in the closet. Jesse handed him a pillow, his face tense.

Placing the pillow on top of the bedding, Ialu closed the door, then knelt in front of his son. "Are you scared?" he whispered.

Jesse nodded.

"Put that fear away for now. Just like putting away the bedding in the closet, put it away deep in your mind and forget it's there." Ialu smiled. Jesse gazed at him as though he was looking at something strange and fascinating. Slowly, a faint smile rose to his stiff lips.

Ialu ruffled Jesse's hair. "Let's go," he said. "Do exactly as I say. All right?"

Jesse nodded. Although the boy jumped when he heard a soldier bark commands to search the building, he kept his lips pressed firmly shut, and his eyes never wavered from his father's face.

"I'll jump out the window first. Wait until I signal, then you jump, too."

Jesse's eyes widened. He opened his mouth to speak, but Ialu stopped him with a look. "I'll catch you. Jump straight without waving your arms or legs, just like when you jump into a river. Understand?"

Although he was breathing shallowly, Jesse nodded. Standing up, Ialu grabbed the satchel from the corner and threw it on his back. Then he opened the window and, without a moment's hesitation, leaped like a cat over the sill and landed almost silently on the ground below.

Jesse stared after him, his lips parted, but when Ialu waved for him to jump, his face paled. Leaning out of the window, the height rushed up at him, and his knees began to shake. Ialu looked up, his face fierce, and gestured again. Jesse crouched on the sill, but could not bring himself to let go.

One, two . . . One, two . . .

He counted in his mind and tried to push off with his legs. But each time he failed.

I can't, I can't, I can't . . .

The thud of footsteps rushing up the stairs disturbed his thoughts.

They'll catch me! Closing his eyes, he took a deep breath. Jump as if you were jumping into a river.

He pictured water below him, saw the light sparkling on the surface in his mind's eye, and pushed off with his feet. He clenched his teeth, anticipating the shock of impact, only to find himself in his father's arms.

Holding Jesse close, Ialu ran along the wall and ducked behind a cart parked beside it. There was no horse in sight, just a cart with a large cargo box that was full of sacks stuffed with clothes. The students' laundry, Ialu realized, guessing that it was collected and placed here until the launderer came and took it to town. Lowering Jesse to the ground, he slapped several of the bags with his hands, making dents in their shape.

"Are we going to hide in the cart?" Jesse asked.

"No," Ialu said. He pulled Jesse down lower and pointed to a space under the building. "Crawl in there. As far as you can."

Obediently, Jesse got on all fours and crawled into the space under the dormitory. Feeling the cool, damp earth against his palms, he moved cautiously into the darkness. There was more room than expected, and his head never scraped against the wood above, but still he was afraid. It seemed a likely place to run into mice, bugs, or snakes. He could hear his father crawling in after him, and the darkness grew deeper.

"That's far enough," his father whispered. "Stay there."

Jesse stopped and turned around, still on all fours. In the sliver of the outside world visible from under the floor, he could see the wheels of the cart.

Jesse's father crawled up beside him. "We're going to be here for quite a while. You can sleep if you want, but don't make any noise."

Jesse nodded. He cringed at the thought of pressing his belly against the clammy ground, but his arms and legs were already cramped from crouching. Once he gave up and lay down, it was much easier. Wrapped in the smell of damp earth, he stayed motionless beside his father. Gradually the tension in his body eased.

Perhaps he had nodded off a little. His eyes flicked open at the sound of voices. He could see feet near the cart. Metal gleamed. Soldiers' boots. Tensing himself for flight, he listened intently.

"—here?"

"Could be. The sacks have been disturbed. Someone might have jumped down onto the cart. But it could have been the students playing around."

He couldn't see their faces, but he could tell from their feet and voices what they were doing.

"See anyone inside?"

"No. Just sacks of laundry."

"Right, then. I'll check under the building." One of the men dropped to his hands and knees and peered inside. Jesse froze, staring at the black shape of the man's head backlit by the outside light. He was sure that they had been discovered, but the soldier rose, wiping his hands on his thighs. "Can't see a thing," he said. "But there're no marks of someone crawling underneath."

Jesse's brows rose. He cast a quick glance at his father, but his father just stared ahead without moving a muscle.

They must have left tracks on the ground when they crawled in here. When had they disappeared?

Dad must have erased them while I was sleeping.

Jesse felt as though he were in a dream. His quiet, gentle father, the cabinetmaker, simply didn't fit with this man who flattened thugs with a single blow, sprang like a cat from windows, and fooled their trackers.

A distant memory floated into Jesse's mind. Once, when he had gone to the baths with his father, an older boy had climbed onto the roof on a dare and accidentally broken the skylight. Light had poured through the opening onto Jesse's father. The man beside him had looked at him in surprise. "Quite the body you've got," he had said. "You're a soldier, are you?"

It was the first time Jesse had seen his father in such a bright light. His body was lean and powerful. Here and there Jesse noticed lumps and white lines that looked like scars from old wounds. His father had just laughed and said he'd done a lot of stupid things in his youth. Jesse hadn't paid much attention. Now that he thought about it, though, since then his father only went to the bath after dark.

Jesse glanced at him. Maybe his father sensed it, because he gestured for him to stay still and sleep. Jesse nodded and relaxed. Somewhere along the way, his fear had left him.

Jesse felt someone shaking him and opened his eyes in surprise. For a moment, he wondered where he was, then remembered he was under the school.

"Are you awake?" his father asked.

Jesse nodded.

"Follow me, then. Don't make a sound, no matter what happens." With these words, his father crawled outside. Jesse scrambled after him. For a moment, he was blinded by the light. He felt hands slip under his armpits, and then he was lifted into the air and pressed in between rough cloth. His father climbed in beside him, and after covering Jesse with laundry bags, buried himself under them, too.

Although it was stuffy inside, Jesse smiled, feeling a thrill of excitement. Soon, however, he began to worry. He wondered how long they would have to stay under these dusty bags. Unlike when they were hiding under the building, he was afraid that someone might be able to spot them.

Time dragged on forever. When the lunch bell rang, he heard the sound of approaching hooves. "Whoa, there. That's a girl," a gruff voice called out. The cart tilted, and Jesse clutched the bags. There was a loud rattling noise. Someone had connected the cart to the horse's harness. He waited anxiously, afraid that the extra weight might give them away, but the launderer cracked his whip, and the horse began to plod.

The cart jerked forward, swaying back and forth. Jesse tracked their progress along the wall and felt the cart turn a corner. We're almost at the gate.

At that moment, a voice called out, ordering the driver to stop, and the cart lurched to a halt.

"Let me check inside," the voice said.

Jesse tensed and curled into a tiny ball, squeezing his eyes shut. Don't look! Don't look! he begged silently.

Footsteps approached. Someone began patting the sacks. Hands grasped the one over Jesse.

"Hey!" another voice called out. "I already checked in there. It's all right."

The hands grasping the sack let go. "You did? Okay, then. You can go."

The driver called out to his horse, and the cart began to roll. Jesse let out a long, slow breath. As the tension left his body, he began to tremble and felt a strong urge to pee. The cart lurched, and he knew they had passed through the gate. Then they began the slow descent down the hill.

"Dad," Jesse whispered. "I need to pee."

"Can't you wait?"

"A little bit."

"Then wait. We'll get off at the corner of Takalu Street."

At this, Jesse grimaced. "I can't wait that long."

His father groaned. After a pause, he said, "If you can't hold it, pee in one of the laundry sacks."

"Are you serious?" Jesse scowled.

"Don't worry," his father said. "I'm sure they're used to it. Kids wet their beds sometimes, you know."

Jesse felt his father's hand on his head. The warmth of it made his nose sting, and tears welled in his eyes. He sniffed. "Dad?"

"Yeah?"

"Where're we going?"

His father's face softened. "To see your mother."

6

CAGED

For a long time, Elin sat in the chair by the window and gazed outside.

The Yojeh's palace was located deep in the woods. When Seimiya married Shunan, she had a hall built within the same forest for Shunan to carry out his duties as the Aluhan. This, not the palace, was where his servants lived and worked. Elin and Yohalu had reached the hall the night before. Even though it had been quite late, Yohalu had gone to see the Aluhan as soon as they arrived, and Elin had not seen him since. The servants had given her some supper and then brought her to this room to rest. No one came to see her except the maidservants who brought her breakfast and lunch, and there was nothing for her to do but sit and wait.

She was on the second floor where she could look out at the forest and feel the refreshing breeze from the window. But the scenery brought her no rest, because among the trees, she could see soldiers standing guard.

The rain that had fallen all morning lifted by noon, but heavy clouds still hung low in the sky. A white speck appeared against the clouds. A pigeon, most likely carrying a message. Many pigeons had winged their way to the hall that morning, but this one came from a different direction. Elin's face clouded, and anxiety filled her breast. That way lay Kazalumu. The bird flew through the branches and disappeared into the hall.

Just as dusk began seeping into the room, there came a knock at her door. She opened it to see Yohalu. He glanced around the room, and his brow furrowed. "It's so small. You must feel quite shut in."

Elin's mouth crooked. "I didn't realize it was small."

She stepped aside to let him in, and he sat down in a chair by the fireplace. Fatigue etched his face.

"I told the Aluhan everything," he said. "Including what was in the diary. We've spent hours talking about what to do and have finally reached a conclusion. He'll be here soon to tell you himself. But there's something I wanted to say to you first."

As she listened to him speak, Elin suddenly realized that he had dropped the deferential tone he'd used before. When had he first begun talking to her so familiarly, as though she were his niece?

Rubbing his burly hands together, Yohalu said, "I met with the leader of the Sai Gamulu last night."

"You what?"

"Many men in this hall are members, a few of whom once wanted you killed. After I met with the Aluhan, I went to see the leader. I let him know that a Toda Steward was abducted eight years ago." A bitter smile touched his eyes. "He's sharp. He understood immediately how that would change things. I can't promise anything in the distant future, but for the time being, the Sai Gamulu won't try to harm you or your family."

Elin gazed at him unblinking. She felt neither joy nor relief at this news. Her only thought was that now even the Sai Gamulu saw her as a pawn they needed to keep alive. At least for now. She opened her mouth to speak but at that moment, there was a noise outside the door.

"The Aluhan," Yohalu said. Before he could rise from his chair, Elin moved swiftly to the door and opened it.

Shunan was walking down the hall, flanked by soldiers. He smiled faintly when he saw her. Telling his men to remain outside, he stepped into the room. Elin dropped to one knee and bowed. He nodded, then sat on the chair Yohalu had just vacated.

"Elin, first I must thank you," Shunan said. "You're a clever woman to have solved the mystery of the Kiba deaths so brilliantly."

Head bowed, Elin said nothing. When he finished speaking, silence spread through the room. There was a small sigh, and Elin looked up to find Shunan gazing at her. "It's not possible," he said quietly, "to develop a Toda troop in a short period of time. But if they've had eight whole years, they could have made an army of considerable size."

Kneading the base of his thumb, he sighed again. "It seems we were careless. We thought we had covered every possibility, but we never really believed another country could develop their own Toda force. The Lahza, however, press forward with their plans far more audaciously than we do."

Pain flickered in his eyes. "We received news from our men in Kazalumu a short while ago."

Elin's heart raced, and her face froze as she waited.

"Your husband and son were attacked by robbers."

"What?!"

Her face paled, but Shunan swiftly raised his hand. "It's all right. Trust your husband, the swift-footed Ialu. He beat them off. Despite all those years living as a commoner, it seems he never lost his touch."

Shunan's words, however, did nothing to ease the chill that ran through Elin's body. She gripped her wrist with a trembling hand. "Ialu and Jesse. Are they all right?"

Shunan's mouth crooked. "I don't know. By the time my men went to find them, they'd already escaped."

Elin stared at him blankly.

"The two who attacked him," Shunan continued, "were bowmen discharged from our forces. Considering that it was also one of our soldiers who led the men who attacked you and Yohalu, it seems clear that corruption has taken root among our troops."

His face twisted, and he glanced at Yohalu.

"There will always be some who aren't satisfied with their pay," Yohalu said. "When soldiers are posted far away, such as in the eastern protector-ates, they start mingling with foreign merchants and are more likely to lose their discipline. Lahza must be targeting and recruiting men like that."

Shunan nodded and shifted his gaze to Elin. "They were probably hired with gold to attack Ialu and Jesse. If so, that raises a frightening possibility."

A strong light kindled in his eyes. Elin's breath came shallowly, as if an invisible net was drawing inexorably tighter around her.

"Someone is after you," Shunan said. "If it's the Lahza, it means they already know Royal Beasts can decimate Toda troops. And that you can control them."

The sun had sunk completely, and the light had faded from the room. They could not see each other's faces clearly, but no one moved to light a lamp. "When I think of it," Shunan said huskily, "it was foolish to assume we could keep these secrets. Not when thousands of soldiers witnessed what happened on Tahai Azeh."

Trees brushed against the window. The wind must have picked up because the branches kept grating against the windowpane.

"I won't let them catch me off guard again," Shunan said. He rose slowly. "Just as my ancestor Yaman Hasalu once called upon the Toga mi Lyo, I have called upon Yohalu to help me build the greatest Toda army ever seen. As for you, Elin, I command you to aid Her Majesty, the Yojeh. Like your ancestors who rescued the Yojeh in the past, save our kingdom from this crisis."

Elin kept her eyes fixed on his face. "What is it that you are asking me to do?" she whispered.

Shunan took a step closer. "Breed the Royal Beasts and train them. Create a Royal Beast corps. Royal Beasts are only found in the Afon Noah, the sacred mountains of this kingdom. Our enemies may be able to smuggle Toda eggs out of the country, but they can't possibly steal Royal Beast cubs without being detected. As long as we make sure we're ready, the Lahza can never make their own Royal Beast corps."

A steady light burned in his eyes. "Now I finally see what I failed to understand before. This is what I was meant to do. Seimiya of the Royal

Beasts and I of the Toda. We must join hands and, through the power of these sacred creatures, protect this land. That is the shape this country was meant to take. Just as the Royal Beasts soared through the sky and the Toda opened the way for our Royal Ancestor to descend upon Tahai Azeh."

Elin trembled. The needle of fate, which until now had been wavering, would soon be set. "Her Majesty, the Yojeh," Elin said desperately. "Did she truly say this is what should be done?"

Shunan did not answer right away. Gambling on what slim ray of hope might lie behind his hesitation, Elin plowed on. "I know it is not my place to say such a thing, and I humbly beg your pardon for asking, but would not the creation of a Royal Beast corps itself endanger the political affairs of this country?"

Shunan's brows drew together. "What do you mean?"

"The Royal Beasts are the symbol of Her Majesty, the Yojeh," Elin explained carefully. "The Toda are the symbol of Your Majesty, the Aluhan. If the Royal Beasts, with stunning force, should rescue this kingdom from defeat by a Toda army created and led by our enemies . . ."

The light in Shunan's eyes turned hard. "You are saying that it will seem as if I am merely the Yojeh's lowly subject who must rely upon her power as the True Ruler."

Silence subdued the small room. Feeling that the tension hanging between them would snap at a touch, Elin gazed wordlessly at Shunan.

A wry smile touched his lips. "Elin, you have misjudged me. The fact that I am a subject of Her Majesty, the Yojeh, is something in which I take great pride. No matter what crass conjectures the foolish nobility may dream up, not a single speck of doubt clouds that sentiment. Even though I am her husband, I remain her loyal subject.

"Besides," he added calmly, "you know nothing about the subtleties of politics. A man who grasps these can change a minus into a plus. Thanks to you, we now know the secret of the Toda and can make larger and stronger Toda troops. If the Yojeh should create a corps of Royal Beasts to aid her husband, it will demonstrate the strength of our bond."

The moment he spoke those words, Elin knew. Nothing she could say would change his mind.

Shunan's smile had vanished. For a long time he remained silent, looking at Elin's pale face. "Do you know why the Lahza, who have no hope of ever capturing Royal Beasts, tried to take your family?" he asked suddenly.

Elin said nothing.

"Because they knew we have you in our hands. That's how deeply they have penetrated our midst. But they are not trying to kidnap you and use you like the Toda Steward. To capture you would be meaningless because they can never get any Royal Beasts. There is only one reason they targeted you. Because they want to wipe you from the face of the earth. Before you raise up a Royal Beast corps. Before we can obtain this decisive weapon."

Elin felt as if her chest and throat were being gripped by a vice. Struggling to breathe, she stared at Shunan. He took a step closer and gently placed a hand on her shoulder. "I owe you so much. If I could, I would not ask you to do this. I'm sure you feel trapped within a cage and forced to do what goes against your will. But for me, this is not about what I want to do, but what I must do." His face twisted slightly. "And Her Majesty, the Yojeh, has resolved to sully her own hands, also."

Elin looked at him in surprise. For the first time, she considered what developing a Royal Beast corps would mean for Seimiya. The Yojeh, who for centuries had kept herself pure and stainless, was about to engage in war.

"Is there anyone in this world who is truly free?" Shunan said. His face was only a vague shadow, but his eyes gleamed with a sad light.

"My men are searching for Ialu and Jesse. No matter how fleet-footed Ialu may be, he can't get far with a child. I've warned my men not to hurt them. It won't be long before you're reunited."

The weight of his hand on her shoulder lifted. Shunan turned toward the door, and Yohalu quickly strode over and opened it. Even after the heavy door shut behind them, Elin remained standing, rooted to the spot.

7

DAWN BIRD

The night wore on, yet Elin still sat by the window, staring outside at nothing while her supper grew cold on the side table by the fireplace. No lamp burned in the room, and it was brighter outside, where the clouds had broken and stars twinkled against the ink-black sky.

"I'm thinking of inlaying it with mother-of-pearl." In her mind, she heard the words Ialu had said when spring was still young. "That will look nice on a small, lacquered cabinet like this. Not big pieces, mind you, but small, like stars scattered across the surface. But mother-of-pearl is expensive."

He had still been picking out the wood to build it. Had he finished it? Or had he been forced to leave it half done?

Elin grimaced. So it's finally crumbled. The quiet life they'd built together on that thin layer of ice.

Where are they now? She could almost see Jesse's frightened face. Had Ialu taken the satchel they'd prepared for such a day? Where were they headed under this dark sky?

"Let's be prepared to run when the day comes." The words Ialu had whispered in her ear came back to her now. He had been holding their newborn son, Jesse, in his arms. "Let's give this child a new life," he had said. "No matter where we run to, it will be better than living trapped in the cage of our past."

Does he know?

He must have realized why they had attacked him. He had run because he had guessed what would come next. But even if he managed to elude the soldiers, there would be no end to this flight. If he and Jesse were caught and their family reunited, they would be forever trapped within this cage.

And the Beasts—Leelan, Alu, all of them—would be flown into battle, devouring men and Toda, captive until the day they died.

Elin pictured a distant sky, wide and wind-swept.

There was only one way to free them from this cage. She pressed her head against the cold window frame and gazed absently out the window. It was wide open. Through the branches, she glimpsed the flickering of campfires and the figures of soldiers on guard among the trees.

Far below her lay the ground. She stared at the dark earth, drawn to it like the depths of a pool.

"Elin."

Hearing her name, she searched for the source. At the foot of a mighty tree that stretched its thick branches up to her window, she saw a shadow.

"Rolan?" she murmured. When had he come? She saw him wave.

"I got permission from the soldiers," he called up. "The maidservants insisted that I couldn't go into your room. But if I stand here talking, I'm going to get a stiff neck."

Reaching up, he grasped a branch and began to climb, his lakkalu slung over his back. As Elin watched, Rolan shimmied up the trunk and swung his legs over the large branch that led to her window. He grinned. "That's better," he said. "Much closer."

Elin frowned. "That's dangerous," she said in a hushed voice. "Can you come in?" She moved away from the window but he raised a hand and stopped her.

"It's no problem. I'm quite used to climbing trees and serenading young maidens through the window." With a wink, he swung his instrument around to the front and ran a hand over the strings.

"When did you come?"

"The day before yesterday. I came by horse so I passed my father's carriage along the way." He began plucking the strings with his thumb and forefinger.

"Why did you come?"

He simply smiled without answering, his fingers moving faster over the strings. "The clouds have broken and the stars look magnificent. How about a few love songs?" Strumming softly, he began to sing. He played one song after another, some she knew and some she didn't, but as those melancholy tunes rode the breeze, Elin felt the blood begin to flow again in her numb and heavy heart.

After the fifth song, Rolan began a sixth. The first notes pierced her heart so keenly, she felt pain spread like warm water through her breast.

Frogs chirrup in the moonlit night, he sang. *In the dawn mist the bird's song flows. Oh, how it flows, disturbing the still night. Don't weep, dawn bird, don't weep, for I'll recall your voice from last night.*

A kind face rimmed by a bushy beard floated into her mind. She remembered every detail, down to the shadows of the leaves dancing along the road where she had walked beside Joeun, who was singing this song. When he realized that she didn't know it was a love song, he burst out laughing.

Joeun.

One after another, distant memories slipped into her mind. Once again, she saw the beloved face and heard the voice of the man who had found and raised her. Twenty years had passed since then.

The memory of another night she had recalled this song came back to her, along with the weight and scent of warm skin. She closed her eyes, feeling the tears slide down her cheeks.

Before she realized it, Rolan had stopped singing. Wiping her face, she opened her eyes. He watched her, his head resting against the tree trunk.

"Elin," he said. "You mustn't die."

Silently, she stared at him where he sat in the shadow of the branches.

"Even if you die, it won't change anything. You will just make your family grieve." With that, he swung his lakkalu over his back and slithered down the trunk. Elin gazed after him as he disappeared among the trees.

Elin woke abruptly at dawn. Lying in bed, she stared at the ceiling, which was just a blur in the blue darkness. All sound had vanished, and silence filled her body, as though the rushing torrent that had swept her up had passed and left her floating on the water's mirrorlike surface.

Within that stillness, a warmth kindled and spread, reaching her fingertips.

To alter the nature of living creatures is wrong, she thought. Her heart felt clear like a sky filled with distant, twinkling stars.

No matter how entangled affairs became, to alter other creatures and pervert their lives was wrong. That point, and that point alone, would never change, no matter what the situation.

Then let me defy any force that tries.

No matter how formidable that power, no matter how enmeshed it was with the wishes of others, she must not let it bend or break her. She must not die.

She had longed to let creatures live as they would in the wild; to share her life with the man she loved and with their son. I took all this on, prepared to accept the consequences. If so, then I must keep looking for a way to achieve it, no matter what may come.

She closed her eyes. She saw Leelan soaring in the heavens, saw her radiating the light of the sun as she flew with Eku and the joy of their mating.

I want to free them from the sanctuary.

If that day should ever come, she and her family would finally be free.

She opened her eyes. Something had brushed against her thoughts. What was it? Pressing her fingers to her brow, she followed the trail. The mating flight of Leelan and Eku had reminded her of something else.

Ah! Her eyes widened. That was it. Alu, Leelan's first cub. A white light flashed through her brain, and she sat up. Like a magnet, the first thought drew another and then another, linking all the questions in her mind.

The world outside her window had grown brighter, and she heard birds warbling. She gazed at the morning light gilding the edges of the clouds.

8

SEIMIYA'S GARDEN

The day after Elin met with Shunan, the Yojeh summoned her. The invitation was so unexpected that Elin had no time to bathe. She hastily changed into the clothes provided and headed to the palace.

As she walked down the corridor, a door opened, and Yohalu stepped out. His brow furrowed. "Elin," he said. "I heard that Her Majesty has summoned you."

When she nodded, his face grew stern. "The Aluhan left for his castle this morning and hasn't returned." He said nothing more, but Elin guessed it was only because the maidservant would hear. Clearly, it made him very anxious that the Yojeh had waited until the Aluhan was gone to summon her. Elin could feel his eyes boring into her back as she left the hall.

Her feet crunched softly on the white sand that paved the road through the deep forest. After some time, she glimpsed the wooden buildings of the Yojeh's palace through the trees. The blue roof tiles that covered the connecting passageways glinted in the sun. The servant guided Elin along these passageways, leading her deep behind the palace complex. It was very quiet, and they passed few people on their way. At length, they came to a garden bordered by a high hedge with a narrow gate. A single soldier stood before it—a Se Zan, one of the Yojeh's bodyguards. As she walked toward the gate, Elin felt a spark of hope that it might be Ialu's friend Kailu, but the man was a stranger.

Passing through the gate in the hedge, Elin stepped into an inner garden bathed in soft light. Flowers bloomed in a riot of colors, emitting a sweet fragrance in the warmth of the early afternoon sun. Honeybees buzzed among the blooms, and little birds hovered, sucking nectar from yellow ivy blossoms entwined with the hedge.

On the other side of the garden was a building, and a chair had been placed outside beneath one of its open windows. In it sat a woman, her eyes fixed blankly on the flowers. Elin halted in surprise. The woman, who now turned her head and inclined it slowly as though even that were too much effort, was the Yojeh. She looked shockingly gaunt. Her cheeks were drained of color, and her eyes were puffy. Elin couldn't believe this was the same woman who had once reminded her of a delicate, porcelain doll. Although she had heard that the Yojeh's third pregnancy was taking its toll, Seimiya looked far too thin.

"Come," Seimiya said.

Elin jerked at the sound of her voice and blushed with the realization that she had been staring at the Yojeh. She bowed her head and walked a few steps nearer. Kneeling on the grass, she placed both hands on the ground and bowed low, feeling a twinge in her injured elbow.

"Come closer," the Yojeh said weakly. "It tires me to raise my voice."

Elin rose and came close enough to hear Seimiya even if she murmured. The maidservant brought over a small chair so Elin could sit, then bowed low and moved to a corner of the garden where she couldn't overhear what they were saying.

I see, Elin thought. Seimiya had summoned her here so there would be no fear of eavesdropping.

"Raise your head, Elin."

She looked up to see Seimiya staring at the bandage over her ear. "They told me you'd been injured," Seimiya said. "I see it hasn't healed yet. Does it hurt?"

"No, there is almost no pain now. Thank you for your concern."

Seimiya nodded and then said languidly, "It's been a long time, hasn't it? Is it ten years since we last met?"

"Eleven, Your Majesty."

"We've both aged, then, haven't we?" Seimiya said, and the corners of her mouth lifted slightly. "Although I think I've aged a little faster than you."

Elin hesitated, then asked in a small voice, "Please pardon my impertinence, but you seem very tired."

Seimiya's smile deepened. "Recently, I've forgotten what it's like not to be tired. Especially since I became heavy with child." She stroked her belly. The smile faded from her face. "But never mind that. Let's get down to business."

Sitting up straight, she looked Elin in the eye. "I am sure you remember the promise I once made to you. I vowed that if you saved Shunan, I would free the Royal Beasts and never use them as weapons again."

"Yes."

"I must break that promise." Her voice cracked slightly. "To break a vow is the vilest of acts. I do not wish to do this to you, Elin. You risked your life to save Shunan. When I consider how this happened because you flew Leelan to his aid—"

Her voice caught, and she pressed her fingers against her pale throat. Closing her eyes, she bowed her head for a moment, then drew a deep breath and raised her face. "I would never break this vow if it were just to protect my power as the Yojeh. I would rather kill myself. But I cannot let foreign hordes lay waste to our kingdom. I must protect this land no matter the cost."

Sunlight illumined Seimiya's pale face. Even when careworn and thin, she retained a dignity that made her seem larger than she really was. "When Hajan threatened this kingdom," she continued, "my ancestor chose to have Yaman Hasalu defend this land with the Toda, knowing full well that this would jeopardize the purity with which her kingdom had been ruled. But I have no intention of doing as she did. I will not make my subjects bear defilement on my behalf just so I can remain unsullied."

Gazing at Elin, she said, "I, the Yojeh, order you to raise up a Royal Beast corps and defend this country from invasion."

Elin rose from her chair and knelt on the grass. Gazing up at Seimiya, she said quietly, "Forgive me, Your Majesty, but I cannot obey this command."

Seimiya's face grew stern. "You think your wish is more important than the lives of the masses?"

Elin shook her head. "No. I cannot obey because I do not know if creating a Royal Beast corps is truly best for this land. In the past—" She stopped, arrested by the look of loathing that crossed Seimiya's face.

The Yojeh's lips curled, and her voice was cold. "You need not repeat that tale to me ever again. It will stay branded on my mind forever. But you also said that Royal Beasts suffer neither pain nor regret when they devour men and Toda. It is you, you told me, who suffers."

Elin was stunned. She had no idea Seimiya remembered her words so clearly. The Yojeh raised a slender finger and pointed it at Elin. It trembled slightly. "That's what I'm talking about. I am asking if you would sacrifice the lives of millions just because using the Royal Beasts as weapons causes you pain."

"Your Majesty," Elin began. Exposed to the unexpected disdain in Seimiya's tone, she struggled to control her voice and subdue her urge to respond in anger. "I beg you to hear me out. Even if I were to bend my will and obey your command, I am incapable of making you a Royal Beast corps."

Seimiya frowned. "Incapable? Why?"

"Because the Royal Beasts in the sanctuary do not multiply."

"What do you mean? Leelan has given birth to all those cubs . . ." Seimiya's voice trailed off as understanding dawned in her eyes. "You mean Alu and Kalu."

"Yes. As you know, Alu was born while Her Majesty Halumiya was still alive. She should have matured long ago. And Kalu is now older than Leelan when she matured. Yet neither of them shows any interest in mating."

Seimiya's eyes bored into Elin. "You aren't doing anything to prevent them from maturing, are you?"

Elin shook her head emphatically. Catching a ray of the afternoon sun, Seimiya's light brown eyes gleamed golden. For a long moment, she gazed silently at Elin, who stood motionless, waiting.

"No," Seimiya said at last. "You would never do that." Her eyes darkened, like the sun obscured by a cloud. "I suppose you're relieved to have a good reason for refusing my command. But you do realize this could have terrible consequences for our kingdom, don't you?"

Elin gazed into her eyes, wondering whether she should say the words that hovered on her tongue. Seimiya seemed unstable. Her emotions rose and fell so rapidly that Elin couldn't follow. Elin feared that if she touched the wrong nerve, Seimiya might explode. Hesitantly, Elin spoke. "Your Majesty, is there truly no other way to protect this country than to create a Royal Beast corps?"

Seimiya brushed a lock of hair from her forehead and secured it behind her ear. Head bowed, she remained silent for a long time. "There's no solution as failproof as this," she said finally. A deep fatigue crossed her face. "Although I'm sure inwardly you must reproach me for sending the Royal Beasts to the battlefield," she added.

Her eyes burned with a fierce light as she fixed them on Elin's. "You aren't the only one who wishes to solve this without a fight, you know. You will never understand how much I abhor this decision, how I wish it didn't have to be made at all.

"To the Yojeh, war has always been an abomination. The blood of the gods may never have run in our veins, yet we still strove to live sincerely in accordance with this belief. In that regard, there was no deception on our part. And because that's who the Yojeh was, this kingdom never took the path of a greedy aggressor. We never sought to expand our territory by invading other lands. Even though we possessed the mighty Toda."

Her face twisted. "Perhaps my ancestor should have tried harder to quench Oshiku Hasalu's ambition when he sought to increase our territory. By attacking and destroying the Hajan, we took the caravan cities. As a result, our country prospered. But prosperity is a two-faced demon.

"When a kingdom prospers, its population increases, and it needs more wealth to support its people. For this reason, we must protect the source of that wealth. We can't afford to lose the caravan cities, which means we have to continue this unending fight with the Lahza who covet them."

Closing her eyes, she clenched her pearl-white teeth and gave her head a little shake. "The moment I utter the command to increase our forces and lead them to war, I am no longer the Yojeh," she said in a strangled voice. "Unable to bring this war to a halt, I'm just an ordinary ruler like any other."

She opened her eyes. They were filled with tears. "Yet I have decided to make a Royal Beast corps." Her expression turned fierce. "Elin," she said.

"Yes."

"What do you think we should do to end this war with Lahza?"

Elin gazed at Seimiya. "I do not understand politics," she said, "but is there no way to negotiate for terms that both sides can accept?"

Seimiya's expression softened. "You're right," she said quietly. "That would be the best way. But, Elin, we can't simply resolve our differences by extending our hand to the other. The Lahza have attacked us for years. If they believe they can win and gain more wealth, they'll never give up. The only time such a country will even consider sitting down to negotiate is when they realize they have no chance of winning; that to keep on fighting would be a waste of resources."

A cool serenity suffused her face. "If the Lahza already have their own Toda army, they'll be eager to fight because they believe they have a much greater chance of winning. The whole country will be urging its leaders to strike soon. If we reach out and try to make peace, they'll merely assume we're desperate to make a deal because we've lost the advantage."

A bitter smile touched Seimiya's lips. "Unless we can show them that their possession of a Toda army makes no difference because we have something even more powerful, they'll never agree to negotiate. Or if they did, it would be as a victor making excessive demands out of contempt for the loser."

She looked at Elin, a sad resignation in her eyes. "If we want to negotiate an end to war, then we need the unsurpassed power of the Royal Beasts."

A wind rustled through the leaves on the trees and brushed Elin's cheek just as a cloud covered the sun, hiding its light.

Seimiya sighed, and her shoulders relaxed. The expression on her face seemed a little calmer. "Still, I wonder why Alu hasn't borne any young yet."

"I wonder, too. Alu and Kalu were raised just like Leelan without toku-jisui or the Silent Whistle. The only difference is that Leelan was born in the wild, while her young were born in the sanctuary."

Seimiya's eyes brightened. "But that's it, Elin! You see! There is a way to increase their number. If we bring wild male and female cubs to Kazalumu, we could build up a corps in just four or five years."

Her face shone like that of an excited little girl. Elin regarded her silently. Noticing her expression, Seimiya's face clouded. "Is there some reason we can't?"

Elin nodded. "Wild Royal Beasts bear few offspring, so it would be hard to get enough. And there is another concern."

"What's that?"

"When I rode Leelan and subdued the Toda troops, didn't something about that strike you as strange?"

"Strange? Why?"

"I didn't notice at first, either, but later I realized it was quite odd. You said the tale I told you was branded on your memory. In that tale, the battle between two thousand Royal Beasts and tens of thousands of Toda wiped out not just the entire Toda army but the Royal Beasts and their Riders as well."

Seimiya's nose wrinkled, as if at a foul odor, but Elin ignored this and pressed on. "It was because I actually flew Leelan against the Toda troops that I began to wonder about the story."

At this, Seimiya's expression changed. "Wonder about what?"

"Leelan showed no trace of fear or hesitation when she swooped down on the Toda, despite the number gathered there. And she slaughtered dozens of them in a matter of minutes. If I hadn't stopped her, she would have killed a hundred."

Seimiya nodded as she listened.

"I was raised in a Toda village. From a very early age, I saw how much training goes into preparing Toda as steeds for battle. But Leelan, who had no military training whatsoever, destroyed those well-trained Toda with ease. If two thousand trained Royal Beasts flew to battle, then even if they were met by tens of thousands of Toda troops, the Toda wouldn't have stood a chance. It should have been an overwhelming victory for the Royal Beasts, not a disaster that wiped out both sides."

Lips slightly parted, Seimiya looked taken aback. "You're right," she said hoarsely. "I suppose their Riders might have been picked off by archers, but even so, the Royal Beasts would still have had the advantage because they were attacking from above. It's much easier to hit your target when shooting downward than when aiming at the sky."

"Yes. The Toda Riders shot many arrows at me and Leelan, but Leelan's body repelled them. None of them hit me. I was shot while on the ground helping Shunan to climb onto Leelan's back."

Seimiya bowed her head and nodded. Elin guessed she was remembering the events of that day.

"Even when Leelan was right among the Toda, attacking them," Elin continued, "the Toda were milling about in confusion or rolling over onto their backs, so the Toda Riders had little chance to shoot. And that was just one Beast against several thousand Toda. If two thousand Royal Beasts descended, then—"

Seimiya raised her face and leaned slowly back against the chair. "Then the tale might not be true," she whispered. A fierce longing crossed her face.

"It may not be true," Elin said. "Or there may be something that we haven't been told."

Seimiya's eyes narrowed. "Something we haven't been told. Yes, you're right. That's a possibility, too. After all, many centuries have passed."

Watching her expression, Elin asked hesitantly, "My Lady, do you know who the lord of Amasulu's ancestors were?"

Seimiya blinked. "The lord of Amasulu? You mean Yohalu Amasulu? What about them?"

So she doesn't know, Elin thought. It was just as the previous Yojeh, Halumiya, had told her many years ago. The fire set by the Sai Gamulu had completely severed the Yojeh's link with the past. Spurred on by hatred, Yohalu's great-grandfather had exacted a fitting revenge. But in the process, something infinitely precious had been lost.

Elin's knees ached. She rose and sat in the chair. The sun was already tilting in the sky, dyeing the plain wooden walls a warm amber. Taking a short breath, Elin said, "Like mine, Yohalu Amasulu's ancestors had green eyes."

Seimiya's eyebrows rose. "They did?"

"Yes. When Hajan attacked Lyoza, the Yojeh of that time sent a message to the Toga mi Lyo, the Green-Eyed Ones who lived in a valley in the Afon Noah, and asked them for help."

Seimiya's eyes widened. "I had no idea. And you're saying they were Yohalu's ancestors?"

"Yes. According to the legend, the Toga mi Lyo were skilled in raising and training the Toda for war. Your ancestor Jeh, on the other hand, was a Royal Beast handler. She would not have known as much as the Toga mi Lyo about training Toda."

"So at the time of Yaman Hasalu, Jeh's descendant summoned the Toga mi Lyo to teach him," Seimiya whispered. She pressed her fingers to her temples. "But weren't the Toga mi Lyo and Jeh bitter enemies? I thought it was against the Toga mi Lyo that she fought that disastrous battle."

Elin nodded. "I was shocked when Yohalu told me this story, too. But when I thought about it, a Toda army could never have been developed in this land without the Toga mi Lyo's aid."

Seimiya heaved a sigh. "Incredible. The things you say always throw me into confusion." She shook her head slowly. "If only we could peek into the past and see what really happened."

Elin's pulse beat faster. They had reached the critical point. But would Seimiya understand? Elin took a deep breath. "I wish we could, too," she said quietly. "Your Majesty, why do you think the Yojeh in Yaman Hasalu's time did not arm this country with the Royal Beasts, which she could control? Why did she choose instead to write to the Jeh's enemies and introduce their weapon, the Toda, to protect this land?"

Seimiya's mouth crooked in a bitter smile. "To preserve the purity of her reign by foisting the defilement of war onto the Aluhan and the Toda."

"Yes, I also suspect that was an important reason. But what if it was not the only one? What if there was some reason why the Royal Beasts shouldn't be used as weapons?"

Elin lowered her gaze, and her voice dropped to a whisper. "What could have happened on that battlefield so long ago? How on earth could two thousand Royal Beasts have been destroyed while attacking Toda?"

She gripped her wrist with her hand. "Your Majesty," she said, forcing out the words. "I'm afraid. There is still so much I don't know. What if that tale is true? What if flying two thousand Royal Beasts to war caused some unforeseen disaster? If I breed and train a fighting corps before finding out, I'll end up repeating the same mistake the Royal Ancestor Jeh made, a mistake that can never be undone."

A hush fell over the garden. Elin could hear the birds flitting among the branches above.

Seimiya gazed at the hedge, a faint crease between her brows. "You think that we're standing on the brink? Just as we were at that time?"

"Yes," Elin said hoarsely. "If we take one step further, we might plunge ourselves into a catastrophe that could reduce this land to ashes."

She rested her hands on her knees. "Lady Seimiya, would you give me a little more time?"

Seimiya drew her gaze from the hedge and fastened it on Elin. "Time? To think?"

Elin shook her head. "No. To find out the truth about what happened in the past."

Seimiya's eyes widened. "Is there really a way you can do that?"

Elin nodded and told her about the references to the Kalenta Loh in the diaries of her mother and Yohalu's ancestor.

"If the Kalenta Loh still live somewhere in the Afon Noah, and if I can find them, I believe they can help us solve the riddle of what happened in the past. And answer such questions as why Jeh's enemies, the Toga mi Lyo, later agreed to help, why Royal Beasts shouldn't be bred by man, and why those born in the sanctuary don't mate."

Seimiya frowned, looking perplexed. "Do you intend to go to the Afon Noah to find out?"

Looking her straight in the eyes, Elin nodded. Seimiya smiled and shook her head. "But that's like grasping at clouds."

"I think I can find their valley," Elin said quietly. "When I read the diary of the Kalenta Loh, it described several places that sounded familiar."

Seimiya's smile faded, and she stared at Elin.

"I was raised by a beekeeper," Elin explained. "We used to move from one place to the next, following the flowers in the mountains very close to the Afon Noah. If I trace the places written in the diary and search for valleys with the right topography for Royal Beasts, I should be able to find it."

"Are you serious?" Seimiya said, her voice faint. "You would attempt such a journey?"

Elin nodded. "Perhaps this seems like an unnecessary detour, especially when we may be threatened by invasion. Still, I don't think it will be a waste. If time is of the essence, then please begin gathering wild cubs at the sanctuary. That can be done even if I am not there. But"—she looked straight at Seimiya—"if my investigation makes it clear that we should not use the Royal Beasts as weapons, please revoke your command."

Seimiya stared at her incredulously. "But the Afon Noah are steep and rugged. Do you intend to travel alone? What about your husband and your son? If you fail to return, you'll never see them again. Would you really go despite that?"

Elin's face twisted. "Yes. Because this is our only hope."

"What do you mean?"

"Making an irreversible mistake is not my only fear." Tears welled in her eyes, and she struggled to keep her voice steady. "If I obey your command and develop a Royal Beast corps, my family and I will spend the rest of our lives under guard. The same is true for anyone else I might train to control the Beasts. This is our only hope for avoiding such a fate."

Seimiya cocked her head, watching the tears roll down Elin's cheeks. "You are so strong," she murmured.

But Elin shook her head. "A cornered mouse is neither strong nor weak."

Seimiya frowned, repeating Elin's words to herself. A bitter smile touched her lips. "You're right. It is neither strong nor weak to search for the best path under the circumstances you find yourself." She stared at the dusk creeping across the sky. Then, as if to shift her mood, she sighed and returned her gaze to Elin. "I can't believe that traveling to the Afon Noah is a sane choice. And I don't think you can possibly succeed. Are you telling me to gamble and risk losing you, even though you're irreplaceable?"

Elin didn't answer. She couldn't. Her throat was so swollen with tears that her voice found no way out. She bowed her head and let the tears stream down her cheeks.

The sun had set, and a cool breeze touched her face. Watchfires had been lit at each corner of the hedge, and the flames wavered in the evening breeze. After a long silence, Seimiya said, "Tonight the Sick Ones will come."

Elin frowned, wondering what she meant. The Sick Ones were people who came to the palace, robed in white, to pray for healing on behalf of the many ailing people in the country and to touch the hands of the Yojeh and receive her healing power.

"Elin," Seimiya murmured. "Stay here a while. And when the Sick Ones leave, go with them." In the darkness, her face floated like a white mask.

FIVE

A NEW ROAD

I

ELIN'S WHEREABOUTS

A blast of hot, humid air bearing the aroma of deep-fried food enveloped Jesse and Ialu as they turned into the alleyway. Jesse's stomach growled. He blushed and looked up at his father, wondering if he'd heard. His father, however, strode on without even a glance.

In the early afternoon sun, wisps of cooking smoke drifted on the air. Stalls jammed both sides of the narrow street. Drenched in sweat, merchants fried chunks of meat or sautéed vegetables and chicken on large griddles while calling out their wares to passersby. Here and there, Jesse saw restaurants, each marked by a large lantern hanging out front. But when he peered through the open doors, there were no customers in the dimly lit interiors, just tables and chairs. Maybe the restaurants got crowded in the evening, he thought.

Jesse had been overwhelmed by the size of the capital when they arrived the night before. It had seemed so prim and proper, like a pompous official.

But this part of town reminded him of the alleyways in his neighborhood back home.

A boy about his own age was turning a chicken on a spit. Fat dripped from the crisply browned skin and flared on the coals below. Mmm, that looks good. Jesse turned to ask his father if he could have some, only to see him duck beneath a large lantern and disappear inside a restaurant. Jesse scurried after him. Although it was lunch time, there was not a customer in sight. An elderly woman sat shucking peas in the corner. She rose reluctantly when she saw them.

"I came to meet someone," Ialu said. The woman nodded and pointed toward a reed curtain in the back. There appeared to be a private room behind it. Jesse's father's gaze shifted toward the kitchen. Jesse followed it, wondering what he was looking at, but there was just an open door with people passing in the lane beyond.

Hearing a rustling noise, Jesse turned and saw his father part the curtain and step into the other room. There was the scrape of a chair as someone stood up. Hurrying into the room, Jesse saw a large man with a broad smile on his face. "Hey there!" the man said, giving Ialu a thump on the shoulder. "You haven't changed a bit. I thought you'd look a little older."

Ialu was grinning, too. Jesse's eyes grew round. He'd never seen his father grin like that before. It made him look young.

Wordlessly, his father wrapped an arm around the man's shoulders in a hug, then stepped back. "Sorry to contact you out of the blue," he said.

The man waved a hand. "No need to get all stuffy now." He poked his head around Ialu and cocked an eyebrow at Jesse. "You must be Jesse. You sure have grown!"

Perplexed, Jesse glanced up at his father, who placed a hand on his head and smiled. "This is Kailu, an old friend," Ialu said. "Don't forget your manners. He held you when you were just a baby."

Jesse bowed his head dutifully, wondering how he was supposed to remember if he'd only been a baby.

"How old are you now?" Kailu asked.

"Eight."

At this, Kailu's brows rose again. "Eight! It's been that long has it? Time sure flies." As if it were an afterthought, he added, "You look a lot like your mother." His expression sobered, and he glanced at Ialu as he gestured for them to sit down.

Kailu must have arrived sometime before them, because the table was already laden with dishes. "We can talk while we eat," he said. "I know this place well. No one can hear us from outside, so you can speak freely. Jesse, grab those side plates from the corner over there, would you?"

On a small table in the corner, Jesse found little plates as well as seasonings. He thought for a moment, then picked up six plates and placed two in front of each person.

"Oh-ho! That was good thinking," Kailu exclaimed.

"I thought it might be better to have two each, you see, because some of these dishes are spicy and others are sweet," Jesse explained, his cheeks flushed. "They'll taste nicer if the flavors are kept separate."

Kailu laughed and looked at Ialu. "Considering he's your son, he sure can talk. I wonder who he took after. Elin's not much of a talker either."

Ialu picked up his chopsticks and flashed Kailu a crooked grin. "I haven't figured that out yet."

Jesse picked up his chopsticks and looked at his father. Sensing his glance, Ialu nodded. "Go ahead. Eat."

"All right!" Jesse said loudly, helping himself to chunks of beef tenderly stewed in a sweet-and-sour fruit sauce. He also took a piece of deep-fried chicken coated in finely chopped nuts. Placing the stewed meat between two pieces of fahko, he took a large bite. Juice from the meat trickled down his chin. The inn they'd stayed at the night before was a grungy place that hadn't served breakfast, and Jesse was starving. But even while he devoured the food, he kept his ears on the men's conversation.

"What's going on?" Kailu demanded in a low voice. The cheerfulness had left his face.

Ialu shook his head. "All I know is that whatever's happening, it's got something to do with Elin. And we've been targeted as pawns to be used as leverage."

Kailu opened his mouth, but then glanced at Jesse. Ialu smiled wryly. "It's all right. He may talk a lot, but he can keep a secret. He won't tell anyone something he shouldn't, even if they beat him."

Jesse kept his head down, focusing on his food. His face was burning all the way to his ears, but he didn't want them to know.

"After I got your message," Kailu said, "I started looking into it. It seems Elin entered the palace about three days ago."

Startled, Jesse raised his head. The thought that his mother was close by made his pulse race so fast it hurt.

Ialu leaned forward. "Is she still there?"

"Strangely enough, it seems that she isn't."

Ialu frowned. "What do you mean?"

Kailu looked as though he didn't know how to explain. "Well, you know," he began, "I'm one of the older Se Zan. That means I'm not often posted to guard the Yojeh. I spend most of my time training new recruits. I didn't see or hear anything myself, but one of the younger Se Zan, Lagimu, says he saw Elin yesterday."

Kailu tapped the table with his chopsticks as he spoke. "He saw her enter the Yojeh's inner garden yesterday afternoon. 'So that's Elin,' he said to himself. But he never saw her leave."

"You mean she hadn't left by the time he was relieved from duty?"

"No, because he was on duty from yesterday afternoon until this morning. He stayed outside the Yojeh's room after she retired from the garden, yet Elin left neither the garden nor the room." Kailu lowered his voice. "But since yesterday evening the Aluhan's hall has been in an uproar with soldiers and carrier pigeons rushing in and out."

Ialu's face turned grim. "What about the garden or the Yojeh's room? Did anyone leave or enter after Elin went into the garden?"

"The Aluhan wasn't there, so other than the children and the maidservants, no one else came. In the evening, however, the Sick Ones were invited inside the garden."

"The garden? Not the audience room?"

"Yes, the garden. These days, that's not so unusual. Ever since the Yojeh became heavy with child, she almost never leaves her private quarters. Rather than going to the audience room, she receives people in the garden."

As Ialu listened, he seemed lost in thought. "Lagimu would have counted the number of Sick Ones who entered and left the garden, right?" he asked.

The corners of Kailu's mouth lifted. "That's exactly it. According to Lagimu, just as he was counting the Sick Ones passing through the gate, the Yojeh called him. She said she'd heard a strange noise in the hedge on the west side of the garden. Lagimu asked one of the maidservants to finish counting while he went to investigate."

Ialu stared at Kailu. A chunk of meat from Jesse's sandwich fell with a plop, and he jumped, apologizing in a small voice. But his father didn't even glance at him.

"You think the Yojeh let Elin escape?" Ialu asked. "But why would she do that?"

Kailu shook his head. "I don't know. You know yourself that the Se Zan and the Aluhan's men have nothing to do with one another. We get very little information from them. As for the Yojeh . . ." He stopped and sighed. "She's not like her grandmother. Lady Halumiya kept us informed of everything to make sure we had an accurate grasp of the situation."

Chewing diligently, Jesse snuck a peek at his father, who seemed so wrapped up in his thoughts that he hadn't touched the food.

Kailu grabbed a piece of chicken with his chopsticks and popped it into his mouth. Then, as if he suddenly remembered Jesse was there, he poured some tea into Jesse's cup.

Ialu raised his eyes and looked at Kailu. "You say that Elin entered the palace three days ago?"

"Yes."

"What about before that? She left Kazalumu over a month ago. What was she doing all that time? Do you know?"

Kailu shook his head. "No, I know nothing. Except that she wasn't at the palace until three days ago. She arrived in the lord of Amasulu's carriage, so she must have been away on some mission for the Aluhan."

"The lord of Amasulu? You mean Yohalu Amasulu? Of the Black Armor?"

"That's what I heard."

Frowning, Ialu remained silent for some time. "How's security at the checkpoints?" he asked finally.

Kailu made a sour face. "Again, that's not our job so I don't know. I can tell you that there're a lot of soldiers on the move. But that was true even before Elin got here, so not all of them are after her."

Ialu shook his head. "Even so, the checkpoints are probably at maximum security." He flicked his eyes at Jesse, which made Jesse jump. "Hurry up and eat," he said. "We don't know when our next meal will be, so fill yourself up." His voice was gentle, but somehow that made Jesse so nervous that he lost his appetite.

Ialu picked up his chopsticks, but after only a few bites of food, he drew some coins from his robe and placed them beside his plate. "Kailu, you've really done us a great favor."

"Don't mention it," Kailu said with a worried frown. He blinked. "Oh," he said, "I forgot to tell you something. Elin was injured."

Ialu's face clouded. Jesse bit his lip, feeling his scalp grow cold.

"It's nothing serious, though," Kailu added hastily. "Lagimu said she wore a bandage around her ear and her left arm was in a sling, but she seemed fine."

His words, however, couldn't chase away the anxiety that nestled in Jesse's chest. In the end, he didn't touch the chicken he had taken, pushing his plate away with a quiet "Thank you." When his father stood up, Jesse stood, too.

Kailu reached out a hand and grabbed Ialu by the arm. "You take care, you hear? I'll do anything you ask, so stay in touch."

Ialu nodded and gripped Kailu's hand in return, then gently let it go.

When they stepped outside, Jesse squinted against the blinding sun. Trotting after his father, he asked, "What're we going to do now?"

Ialu turned and looked at Jesse, narrowing his eyes against the glare. "I know a place your mother might've gone," he said. "We'll go there first."

2

HOUSE FOR TWO

Jesse felt the air cool as soon as they turned into the street. His father had been walking so quickly that he had to trot to keep up, and he was now drenched with sweat. It had been a very hot day, and the humid midday heat lingered even now that the sun was lower in the sky. A welcome breeze flowed along the street, caressing Jesse's sweat-beaded skin. The houses lining both sides had bigger eaves and were surrounded by hedges that muted the sound of voices. Dainty flowers blooming in the hedges fluttered in the breeze.

A shadow fell over them. Clouds had billowed up in the dazzling blue sky and were spreading quickly across it. Ialu stopped in front of a small house partway down the street. It looked quite old and deserted. As if it were his own home, Ialu pushed open the wooden gate and walked up to the door. Then he looked up at the eaves trough. His expression shifted slightly. "What?" Jesse whispered.

Ialu reached up and pulled a key from the eaves trough. "Your mother's been here," he said.

"Really?" Jesse blurted out, then quickly clapped a hand over his mouth. Ialu pointed. "Can you see?"

On the dusty eaves trough, Jesse noticed a spot that looked as if someone had wiped their fingers across it. "Are those Mom's fingerprints?"

"I'm pretty sure they are. They weren't made by a man." Ialu turned the key in the lock and opened the door.

Inside, the house was bare. Beyond a dirt-floored area was a large room floored with wood. Dust floated lazily in the afternoon light that slanted through the window. Before he set foot inside, Jesse's father let his eyes run swiftly around the interior and then up at the ceiling. Jesse did the same. "Whose house is this?" he asked.

His father gave him a swift smile. "Mine," he said.

"Really?"

"This is where I used to live. I thought about selling it when we moved to Kazalumu," he said, taking off his shoes before stepping into the wood-floored room. "But I decided to keep it in case something like this happened." He stared at the room for a moment, as though lost in a memory.

The wooden floorboards felt cool against the soles of Jesse's tired feet. He walked over to stand by his father, who glanced down at him. "You've been here before," he said. "When you were still inside your mother's tummy."

Jesse raised his eyebrows. "Mom lived here, too?"

"Yes, for about a year. We decided to move to Kazalumu after she got pregnant."

Ialu could almost see Elin standing by the window. She loved to open it wide and let the breeze flow through. He had rarely opened the window when he lived on his own. But when she began living with him, they often opened both the window and the front door to air the house.

Memories washed over him in waves, and for a moment, he gave himself up to them.

Why did she decide to come to me?

He had thought about this many times. It couldn't have been easy for her to find this house. Only Kailu and his foster brother Yantoku knew where he lived. She'd said that Kailu had told her where to find him. According to Kailu, she'd approached him at dawn as he left the woods around the palace at the end of the night shift. What had she been thinking as she stood at the edge of the forest waiting for him?

Living in the capital, away from her friends and Esalu, she was under great pressure. The Royal Beasts at the Lazalu Sanctuary had all gone into convulsions. Elin had been summoned to find out why and treat them. In the end, she found that their handlers had caused the convulsions; trying to copy Elin's methods, they'd stopped giving the Beasts tokujisui.

The Lazalu Sanctuary was home to the handler whose lips and nose had been bitten off by Leelan. It must have been agony for Elin to have to expose the handlers' mistakes in that place. Had she come to Ialu because he was the only one she could talk to about those things? He could still see her face from when she'd stood at his door. Her expression had been a mixture of confusion and defiance.

He took a deep breath. Stifling the memories that welled up inside, he looked down at his son. "Jesse," he said. "There's money hidden in this room. Can you guess where?"

Jesse's eyes shone. His first thought was the closet or the cupboard, but he quickly discarded these options. Those would be the first places a thief would look. His eyes swept the room and fastened on something that seemed different. "Oh! I know!" he exclaimed. "Under the floor!"

Ialu looked surprised. "What made you think that?"

"Because everywhere else is dusty except the floor. If Mom had cleaned the house, she wouldn't have left any dust. She likes cleaning."

A smile spread across his father's face. "You've got sharp eyes. But you're only half right. Bring me that stool, will you?"

Jesse walked over to the corner and picked up the stool. As soon as he saw it, he clicked his tongue. "Rats. I missed this. There's no dust on this stool either."

Ialu's smile deepened. "Your mother wiped the floor so that thieves wouldn't notice that she'd used this stool." Taking it from Jesse, he stood on it and hit the ceiling with his palm. A small board popped out with a click. He passed it down to Jesse. "Stick that piece of wood in the bottom of the cupboard over there," he said.

Jesse turned the piece of wood in his hands. There were several grooves in the flat tip. It's a key, he thought. He ran over to the cupboard. There were three slots in the base that looked like part of the design. One was the same width as the piece of wood in his hand. He slipped it into the slot and felt something move inside. There was a small noise above him, and the top of the cupboard popped outward. His father walked over and removed the top board to take out a hidden drawer. When he placed this on the floor, Jesse's eyes grew round. There was a bag of gold nuggets and a dagger, clearly old and well used because the leather of the scabbard and the hilt was amber-colored with use.

"Didn't Mom take any money?"

"There were two bags. She took one and left this one for us," his father said. As he picked up the bag of gold and the dagger, he frowned.

Following his gaze, Jesse gasped. There was writing on the bottom of the drawer. Ialu tilted the drawer so he couldn't see. He grabbed his father's hand. "Wait! What did it say? Is it from Mom? Did she say anything about me?"

Ialu put the drawer back on the floor so that Jesse could see the thin letters, which Elin had likely carved into the wood with a sharp object. Jesse read them aloud. "I'm going to the place where my mother and Jeh came from. I promise to come back. Please tell Jesse to be a good boy."

Jesse's eyes blurred with tears. He rubbed his fists into his sockets and sniffed, trying to keep the tears at bay. But he couldn't.

"Why?" he cried. Why had she gone away? Why hadn't she waited for them?

Ialu cradled Jesse's head in his hands and pulled him close. Pressing his face into his father's chest, Jesse clung to him and wept.

The sound of the boy's sobs tore Ialu's heart. Holding him tight, he closed his eyes.

A searing light flashed inside the dimly lit room, and seconds later Ialu heard the rumble of thunder. After two more flashes, rain began to pelt the roof. Jesse, who hated thunder, squeezed his arms tighter around his father. Feeling the strength of that grasp, Ialu looked out the window and frowned.

Where Elin's mother and Jeh came from . . .

There was only one place that could be. He found it hard to believe that she would attempt the journey. Still, if that's where she was headed, she would be going west, which meant that she would need to cross the river to leave the capital.

Ialu's face froze. They had planned different escape routes together. If she was planning to take that route, this was the worst possible weather for it. Elin hadn't grown up in the capital. She wouldn't know how dangerous the river could be in weather like this.

A chill spread deep inside his chest. Fear seized him. They might never see her alive again. He took a deep breath, trying to shake off his foreboding.

"Jesse. Stop crying," he said. "We're leaving."

Jesse wiped his tears and looked up. "Where're we going?"

"To the river." Ialu stood up and stuck the dagger in his belt.

3

RAGING RIVER

Lightning flickered across the undersides of the clouds. Elin glanced at the sky, then lowered her head. A warm, dank wind rippled across the river's surface and whipped her face, bringing with it the smell of water and the stifling odor of grass. Large circles appeared on the water. Almost instantly the river disappeared behind a gray curtain of pounding rain.

Sheltered beneath the bridge, Elin was untouched by the worst of the rain, but gusts of wind sprayed her with a fine mist. She gripped the collar of her loose cotton jacket tightly. Moments before, it had been so hot that she'd wanted to take it off, but now she was grateful for it. It smelled faintly of moth repellent and had been so long in the cupboard that the pattern was noticeably out of date. She'd worried that she might stand out if she wore it in town, but she'd had no choice. She needed to hide the bandage covering her elbow.

In addition to the checkpoints set up on all the roads and bridges leading out of the capital, there were soldiers posted throughout the city. They had never seen Elin. That meant they would be seeking someone with green eyes and a wounded arm and ear. Elin had hidden those features under the half-coat and a broad straw hat. She'd removed the bandage over her ear because it would have shown beneath the hat. But the stitches in her elbow hadn't been taken out yet, and she wanted to leave the bandage on if possible. Especially considering what she would have to do next.

An elderly woman sitting nearby squashed a mosquito on her arm with a loud slap. "Honestly! What's taking him so long?" she muttered. A mosquito buzzed near Elin, and she waved it away, listening absently to the woman grumbling about her husband under her breath.

This was where peddlers waited for their husbands' boats. They set out from nearby villages early in the morning with fresh vegetables, small fish, and other wares to sell, then got a ride home from here in the evening. There were five women sitting in the grass under the bridge talking quietly while they waited for their husbands.

This broad, slow-moving river served as a moat guarding the capital. On this side spread the city, while on the other spread farm fields.

"I wonder what's going on," one of the women said with a frown.

"You said there's one on Mugo Bridge, too?" another asked. "Really? That means anyone going in or out of the city's being checked."

"Looks like it. Even on the main street, they're making people take off their hats and show their faces. That's what I heard."

"Perhaps they're checking everyone at the landing on the other side of the river, too. Maybe that's why the men are so late."

"I bet you're right! Just like they did here."

From the shadow of a street stall on the bank, Elin had watched soldiers climb down under the bridge and examine the women's faces. She had only joined them after she'd seen the soldiers leave.

The old woman beside her suddenly turned to Elin. "I've never seen you here before," she said. "What're you doing here?" She had probably been wondering about her for some time because Elin carried no basket and didn't look like a farmer's wife.

Dusk had already fallen. Although Elin couldn't see the woman's face, she could feel the suspicion in her eyes. "I'm waiting for my nephew," Elin murmured. "I'm going home to my parents' house."

The woman snorted, apparently satisfied that Elin must have left her husband and was going back to live with her parents.

The drumming of the rain intensified, and lightning flashed incessantly. The women huddled together under the bridge, staring at the river. "At this rate, we may be spending the night at an inn," one of them grumbled.

It grew so dark they couldn't see each other. With each flash of lightning, their anxious faces glowed white and then disappeared.

"Wait a minute. I think I hear them!" Picking up the sound of oars through the pounding rain, the women stood up. Several lights appeared in the darkness—lanterns borne by the women's sons who sat in the prows. When the boats landed, each woman climbed into one. Snatches of conversation drifted through the darkness.

"I thought you'd never come."

"Any longer and we wouldn't have made it home."

Elin remained seated, listening as the boats pulled away and the women's voices, shrill with excitement and relief, faded along with the sound of oars. Once they were gone, the darkness deepened. Even in the pouring rain, however, she could see the watchfires burning brightly in sheltered stands on the bridge and at the landing on the far side of the river. They warned her that soldiers waited there.

Why had Seimiya let her go? And how had Yohalu and the Aluhan reacted?

Was she making the right decision to cross this river without seeing Ialu or Jesse? She guessed they were on their way to the capital. Should she have hidden herself in the city and waited for them?

Jesse . . . His worried face rose into her mind. Maybe he's plodding through this rain toward the capital right now, driven by the hope that he can see me again . . .

So many thoughts clamored in her mind that it ached. If she listened to them now, they would twist themselves around her heart like vines, making it hard to move. She stood up abruptly and removed her jacket. Pressing her lips firmly together, she took off her top and tied it around her waist. She removed her sandals and tied them together by their laces, then shoved them firmly inside her sash at the back. She also tied the pouch of gold nuggets to her sash and tucked it inside against her stomach so that she wouldn't lose it.

Taking a deep breath, she walked across the sodden grass and down to the landing. Her plan was to ride the river downstream to a sandbar at the mouth of a small tributary. A boat might be distinguishable in this darkness, but a person would just look like a log drifting on the water.

The rain was still falling hard, but fortunately the lightning seemed to be less frequent. The river did not appear to be flowing much faster than before, either. Elin, who used to swim with her friends in the swift mountain river below the school at Kazalumu, knew how to let her body glide on the current. But when she slipped off the simple dock of rough planks into the water, she felt the river tug at her with unexpected force. She'd intended to grab the post of the pier and get her bearings before swimming off, but the water swept her away before she could even touch it.

Fear gripped her chest. The current was much faster than anticipated. She squirmed, trying to get into position to swim, but her body couldn't do what she wanted. Pain shot through her left elbow when she moved it. Water surged over her face, and she couldn't breathe.

Thrashing and kicking, she thrust her face above the water and gasped for breath. She glimpsed a light behind her and shuddered at the speed with which it receded. When she tried to take another breath, something huge seemed to swell and rear up beneath her legs. In the next instant, she felt herself propelled forward at breakneck speed.

There was no hope of swimming. She was swept along like a piece of wood, jostled and battered by the roiling water.

Her lungs writhed, desperate for air. She knew with sudden clarity that she was dying.

The water level's rising.

Ialu bit his lip, his body pummeled by the heavy rain. For a long time, he and Jesse had been standing in the shallows where the current slowed, scanning the river. They could see the watchfires burning far upstream.

Before sunset, they had crossed the bridge, one at a time, waiting a little between each passage before finding their way to this spot. Although the soldiers examined all the women's faces carefully, they didn't stop any men or children, and Ialu and Jesse made it through almost too easily.

Still, Ialu was impatient. The fact that it was growing darker and harder to distinguish people's faces meant Elin might try to cross the river at any time. It had taken him much longer to get a sturdy rope than he had expected, and that time loss could be critical.

The water level was much higher than before. Although it didn't look so fast, the river was fed by many tributaries and could suddenly swell with water in a heavy rain.

"Dad." Although Ialu had told him to keep quiet, Jesse couldn't help himself. "It's dark already. Are you sure you can see her?"

With each flash of lightning, Ialu's figure blazed out in the darkness. He had tied one end of a long rope to a nearby tree and the other around his waist. Stripped down to his underwear, he stood staring into the blackness like a beast hunting its prey.

"Stop worrying," Ialu answered. "I've got good night vision." For a second, he recalled the years he had spent searching the darkness on rainy and moonless nights, determined not to miss anything that moved. He reeled his thoughts back to the present. "Quiet now, Jesse," he said. "Don't distract me."

Slowing his breathing, he extended his awareness to embrace everything around him. With his mind stretched evenly across his surroundings like a tautly strung net, the bottom of the darkness brightened. Each sound—the raindrops, the churning water—registered separately in his ears. He could even distinguish the noise of each log rushing past. Something pricked his sharpened senses like a needle. He peered upstream. For a moment, he thought it must be a log. Then a slender hand reached above the water, only to vanish again.

Elin!

With an earth-shaking roar, the river heaved and swelled. Ialu dashed forward and flung himself into the water. The force of it hit him like a board. He gritted his teeth and parted the water with his arms. Although blinded by the dark, he kept his position fixed in his mind along with that of Elin's path down the river. He didn't swim, but instead let the river carry him while he strained every muscle to steer himself toward the place where Elin would pass.

Something touched his outstretched hand, then slipped away. He was about to despair, when he felt a tug on his fingertips. He closed his fist and pulled. Catching the limp body in his arms, he felt the rope yank at his waist. Pain seared through his abdomen. It seemed like he was being torn in half, but he didn't let go.

He clenched his jaw. Clutching the body with all his strength, he let the water carry him, using the tree to which the rope was tied as a pivot. He kicked his legs feebly and felt something brush against him. Weeds. Something grated against his skin, and he grimaced with pain. He was stuck in a field of reeds on the sandbar.

For a few moments, he lay gasping, unable to move. Gradually, however, he became aware of the cold, lifeless body embraced in his arms. When he placed his cheek close to its mouth, no breath touched his skin.

Elin!

He was too weak to lift her. On shaking knees, he dragged her through the reeds and onto the shoal.

He heard Jesse's shrill voice. "Dad! Did you save her?" The boy ran up beside him, but Ialu didn't answer. Laying Elin faceup, he lifted her jaw, pinched her nostrils shut, and, placing his mouth against her frigid lips, breathed into her mouth. He put his hands on her chest, one on top of the other, and pressed sharply and repeatedly. Elin's arms flopped limply with each press, but she showed no sign of coming back to life.

"Mom! Mom!" Kneeling beside his father, Jesse rubbed his mother's arm and wailed in a thin voice. Her flesh was shockingly cold. In the occasional flash of lightning, her pale skin glowed in the dark.

Ialu pressed on her chest. Again and again he pressed, then blew into her mouth.

She's not breathing! Jesse began to sob. She'll die! She'll die! Without even knowing what he was doing, he rubbed her arm frantically, then grabbed her hand and tugged on it, calling her repeatedly. But his voice was drowned by the whistling wind, the rolling thunder, the pounding rain.

How long this went on, Jesse didn't know. Ialu pressed once more, and Elin suddenly twisted and coughed, spitting up water.

"Elin!" Ialu turned her on her side and pounded on her back. She coughed violently, then inhaled with a whistling sound. After drawing several rattling breaths, she opened her eyes and stared blankly into space.

Jesse gazed dumbly at his father as he scooped Elin into his arms and hugged her tightly.

4

A SERIES OF NOTES

Water dripped from the eaves of the stable. Rolan pushed away the head of his beloved steed, Guloh, who kept nuzzling his chest. Sensing someone behind him, Rolan turned and glanced outside. The previous night's storm had blown all the clouds away, and the day was dazzlingly clear. Rolan's brows rose when he saw who was standing in the white sunshine.

"Oli." How like her to have come alone, he thought, even though she was the Aluhan's sister.

Picking up the hem of her skirt, Oli sauntered into the stable. "Morning, Guloh," she said, reaching up to give him a friendly pat.

"What's this? My horse gets greeted before me?"

Oli cast Rolan a piercing glance. "And why should I greet someone who doesn't even have the courtesy to say goodbye before he leaves?"

Rolan's mouth twitched. "I'm sorry. I was just tired of all the commotion these last couple of days. I wanted to get away as soon as possible."

Oli gave him a searching look. "Are you attracted to her?"

Rolan's eyes widened. "To whom? You mean Elin?" He grinned and shook his head. "Well, I guess I was quite taken with her. Or rather, I still am. But it's not like I want to hold her or anything. Well, okay, maybe that, too. A bit. But more than that . . ." His gaze wavered as though he were searching for words. "I want her to be happy. It may sound strange, but I've thought that ever since Father told us about her."

Wrinkling his nose as though embarrassed, he added, "Because she's a musician, you see."

Oli blinked, then understanding dawned in her eyes. "Ah, I see." Stroking Guloh's nose as he nudged her with his muzzle, she nodded. "You're right. She's a musician, too."

Rolan leaned against the stall gate. Narrowing his eyes, he gazed absently at the sunlit pasture. "She's an interesting woman, don't you think? To come up with the idea of using a harp to communicate with those fearsome Beasts. And not just to come up with it, but to actually do it. I like that."

Shifting his eyes back to Oli, he smiled slightly. The pain Oli glimpsed beneath his smile hurt. "Isn't it beautiful how a series of notes, a melody plucked on the strings of an instrument, can move the heart?" Rolan said. "Where we come from and what we are—all those things disappear into the music, and everyone who listens is moved. At moments like that, I see light. It's those moments that keep me playing my lakkalu."

There was something fragile about Rolan. Having lost his family to the flames of war, he now roamed through different lands, placing himself in the midst of conflict. Oli knew all too well the nihilism that lurked behind his cheerful, carefree façade. And he had just explained why, despite all this, he could still keep his head up.

Once again, Rolan gazed out at the pasture. "I think that Father and the Aluhan are too smitten with the Toda and the Royal Beasts. Other countries can never succeed in raising Royal Beasts? Even though the secrets of the Toda have already been stolen?" His voice dripped with sarcasm, and he shook his head slowly. "There's no such thing as 'never,' is there? Right now, Elin's the only one who can control the Royal Beasts. But if she's going to make a whole troop, more people will have to get involved, and her methods are bound to find their way to other countries. We shouldn't be so heavily dependent on one weapon. Nothing is absolute. Things change all the time. We have to keep adapting and trying out new approaches."

He turned toward Oli and placed a hand gently on her shoulder. "I'll probably spend my whole life searching for new ways. I'm just a messenger who seeks to witness and convey what the people of this land refuse to see."

Pressing her lips together, Oli stared at him for some time. Finally, she asked, "Where will you go next?"

His face softened. "I'll drop by Amasulu and take Kuriu to Imeelu. That city's full of people with interesting connections. If I can find someone with the right ones . . ." He paused for a moment, then said, "I'm thinking of going to Lahza."

Oli paled. "Are you serious?"

Rolan nodded. "We can never find a way forward until we learn more about the Lahza and how they think. If we want to reach a solution through negotiation rather than war, we need to know them."

A light gleamed in his eyes. "And if there's anyone in this country capable of finding that out, it's me, don't you think? I look like an Asheh of the plains but have the heart and mind of a man from Lyoza."

Oli's face twisted. "You'll come back, though, won't you? Promise me you'll return safe and sound."

Rolan gazed at her, his jaw set firmly. "I promise, Omli," he said quietly. "I'll come back."

5

TWO PATHS

Birds chirped. The shed door was open a crack, and little bird shadows flitted across the shaft of light that fell through it. Jesse had woken a few minutes earlier when his father had gone outside, but he stayed in bed. He didn't want to lose the comfort of pressing his face against his mother's side, of being enveloped by her scent. Her blouse touched his nose each time she inhaled, then fluttered away when she exhaled. He loved the feel of the cloth caressing his skin. She was still asleep.

Last night had been terrible. They'd searched frantically for a farmhouse that would take them in. His father had carried his mother while Jesse had hauled all their stuff through the pouring rain. How relieved he'd been to see a light shining through the darkness.

The elderly couple that answered the door reminded Jesse of the people back home. They looked shocked to see a family standing drenched in the rain. Ialu told them their boat had capsized in the storm, and the couple quickly let them in to warm themselves at the hearth. Mother was listless and exhausted, and the old man and his wife fretted over her, urging all three of them to sleep in the house. But his father had refused and asked the couple to lend them the shed.

Jesse had wished they could have stayed in the house, which he believed would have been much nicer. But once he'd eaten the hot supper the couple had shared, it didn't matter. His full stomach warmed his frozen body, and he was amused to see steam rising from his and his parents' clothes when they sat around the hearth. Elin lay down beside the fire and fell fast asleep. She didn't wake even when Ialu picked her up and carried her to the shed. Still, gladness filled Jesse's chest like warm coals.

The shed was much colder than the main house, but the old man had spread a blanket over a pile of the hay that he kept as fodder for his livestock. With another blanket on top of them, they were soon warm. Ialu turned his back to the door and cradled Elin in his arms, while Jesse buried his face in his mother's chest and was soon sound asleep.

In the middle of the night, Elin groaned and thrashed about as though in pain. Jesse opened his eyes in surprise. "It's all right, Jesse," his father whispered. "She's just got a little fever. I'll watch over her. You go back to sleep."

Worried, Jesse had tried to stay awake, but his eyelids felt so heavy, he couldn't keep them open. As soon as they closed, he'd dropped off again.

Elin muttered and jerked.

Jesse sat up and peered into her face. "Mom?" he said.

Slowly she opened her eyes. "Mom! Can you see me?" He waved his hand in front of her face. Her eyebrows drew together. "Jesse?" she murmured in a puzzled tone.

Throwing himself across her chest, Jesse wrapped his arms around her neck and rubbed his cheek against her face. "Mom . . ." Tears choked his voice; he sniffed and squeezed her tightly.

His mother's hand stroked his back. He clung to her, feeling the warmth from her hand and from her cheek where his face touched hers.

At first, her touch was hesitant, but then it grew stronger. "Jesse?" she said. "Is it really you?" She pulled him close. For a long time they hugged each other.

When Jesse finally released his arms from around her neck, it was only because he was in such an awkward position that his knees and back were starting to hurt.

"Jesse." Elin was looking straight at him. Not like last night, when she had stared blankly, seeing nothing. "Where are we?" she asked. "And where's your father?"

"We're in a farmer's shed. Dad just went outside. Probably to wash his face."

Elin furrowed her brow and raised her eyes to the ceiling. "But why are we here?"

"Don't you remember?" Jesse grimaced. "It was so awful, Mom! Why'd you try and swim that river? If Dad hadn't jumped in to save you, you would've been swept all the way to the sea! It was pouring, and freezing, too. Father carried you, so I had to carry all our heavy luggage until we found this place!" The words were still spilling out of his mouth when he heard the door open behind him.

"Jesse, lower your voice. I can hear you even outside."

Jesse turned to see his father holding a tray laden with wooden dishes. The aroma of freshly baked fahko and warm milk reached Jesse's nostrils.

"Ialu," Elin whispered. Ialu nodded, then placed the tray on the floor.

"How're you feeling?" he asked. Elin just stared at him without answering.

"Can I eat now?" Jesse said, unable to wait any longer. Ialu nodded.

The fahko had been drizzled with honey and soaked in warm milk.

Jesse took a bite, and the sweet taste of milk and honey spread through his mouth.

Ialu handed Elin a bowl, and she took it without a word. The two of them began to eat in silence. Jesse was dying to know what they were thinking, but sensing that he shouldn't say anything, he focused on his breakfast instead.

When they had eaten the last crumb of fahko and drunk the last drop of milk, Ialu stacked the bowls quickly on the tray and slid the door open. Sunlight poured into the room. It was a lovely day.

Elin blinked in the light as though waking from a long dream. Then she stood up suddenly.

"Mom?" Jesse said in surprise.

"Stay here," she told him absently and followed after Ialu.

"Stay here?" Jesse grumbled to himself. "She's got to be kidding!" He tiptoed to the door. His parents were on the other side. Their voices were too low for him to hear, but he caught the words "Yojeh" and "Toda" and "Royal Beasts." They talked tensely for a long time. Then his father said something in a harsh tone, and his mother's voice broke off. Neither of them spoke after that, and his father's footsteps receded into the distance.

It was quite some time before he heard his mother move. He scuttled away from the door just as she opened it. He looked up at her, red-faced, ashamed to have been caught eavesdropping, but she didn't seem to see him.

"Where's Dad?" he asked. "Did he go to take the dishes?"

His mother blinked, as if his voice had jolted her back to the present. "Yes," she said. Then she took a breath and shook her head. "He went to the capital to do some shopping."

Shocked, Jesse frowned. "But we just went to all that trouble to escape from there. Why would he go back? That's so dangerous! The soldiers are looking for us, aren't they?"

His mother placed a warning finger to her lips. "It's all right," she said quietly. "The soldiers won't catch him."

Jesse raised his brows doubtfully. "Why? Because he was a Se Zan?"

His mother's eyes grew round. "Who told you that?"

Jesse sighed, exasperated. "Mother, I'm eight years old, you know. I'm not a child anymore. Dad told me everything. Everything! Like how he met you. And how some bad guys are trying to make you use the Royal Beasts. And that they tried to catch us so they could make you do what they say." He wanted to show her he knew everything so that she wouldn't leave him out of the conversation anymore.

A mixture of emotions crossed her face as she gazed at him. Neither of them spoke for a long time. Finally Jesse couldn't stand it anymore. He grabbed her hands and swung them back and forth. "Mom, why were you gone so long? Where were you? What were you doing?"

She pushed the door open and leaned against the doorframe. In the garden of the main house, hens bathed in the warm sunlight and scratched lazily at the earth, pecking at the ground. Far in the distance, a lone figure worked the fields.

"I was visiting different Toda villages," Elin said. She pulled Jesse to her and ruffled his hair. "I'm sorry I was gone so long. I know you must've missed me. The Aluhan commanded me to go. I couldn't tell anyone because my work involved the Toda."

"The Toda? Can you heal sick Toda, too?"

"If it's not serious, yes, I can." She paused, then added, "My mother was a Toda doctor."

"She was?" Jesse gaped at her.

Gazing down at her son, Elin felt a pang in her heart. She and Ialu had hidden their pasts from Jesse all these years, telling him nothing about themselves. She was wondering where to begin when the door of the main house slid open. The farmer's wife stepped out, bearing a bamboo basket. It was packed so full of potatoes that Elin was sure they would start rolling off the top. At that moment, a chicken darted past, squawking loudly as it ran between the woman's feet. Startled, she lost her balance, and the basket tilted. She gave a little shriek as the potatoes rolled and bounded every which way. Before Elin could move, however, Jesse had run to her side and begun picking them up, using the hem of his shirt to hold them.

"Why thank you, dear," the woman said. Jesse dumped the potatoes he'd collected into the basket, and Elin hurried over to help.

"Are you feeling better?" the woman asked, peering into her face.

Elin bowed. "Yes. Thank you so much for all your kindness."

The woman shook her head. "Not at all. We didn't do anything. My, but you gave us such a fright! You looked so pale and weak. We worried about you all night."

"I'm so sorry to have troubled you. Would you mind if we waited here until my husband comes back?"

"No, of course not. Please stay. Your husband kindly gave us a small gold piece before he went off. He said he'd be back by evening." She glanced at Jesse, who came running up with a potato retrieved from some distance away. He looked in high spirits. "Thank you, boy. Guess I'd better get on with this now."

As she started to walk away, Elin called out, "Are you going to peel them?"

The woman nodded. "That's right. See that little pool by the spring? I'm going to peel them over there."

"Then let me give you a hand. And I'm sure my son can at least help wash them."

"Are you sure? That would be a real help."

The spring water was cold, and the surface of the pool was littered with green leaves torn off in the storm. While Jesse scooped them out, Elin began helping with the potatoes. The woman washed them deftly, chattering all the while about how she was going to boil and mash them to make potato dumplings that she would sell in the city. Elin listened with one ear, making appropriate responses here and there, but her thoughts were focused on her conversation with Ialu.

After they had brought each other up to date, she had told him what she planned to do. All expression had vanished from his face. He didn't move a muscle, even when she explained her promise to Seimiya. She had guessed how he'd react if she told him that she was going to the Afon Noah. That was why she'd decided not to wait for them at the house in the capital.

"Are you planning to leave Jesse motherless?" he said. His voice was calm, but she could tell he was furious without even looking at his eyes. "What do you really care about?" he asked. Then he had turned his back on her.

She grimaced. He knows full well what I really care about. But he just couldn't accept her decision.

Jesse had climbed into the pool of water, tucking the hem of his long shirt into his sash at the front and back to keep it dry. Elin looked at his slender limbs. He was still so young. She couldn't take him with her into the mountains. Even in spring, it would be a rough journey, and she might be traveling where there was no trail. As Ialu feared, there was a good chance she might not come back alive. But if she was going to go to the Afon Noah, if she was ever going to find the Valley of the Kalenta Loh, now was her only chance.

As things stand, Ialu, these fetters that bind me will trap you and Jesse both, for life. I can't do that to Jesse. Even if I die on the way, at least you and Jesse will be freed.

She bit her lip. If she was going to go, she had to go now. Ialu wouldn't be back until evening. It was time.

She breathed shallowly, watching Jesse. He was so engrossed in gathering leaves that he'd forgotten about washing potatoes. She tried to stand, but her legs refused to budge. She felt again the warmth of Jesse's arms around her neck and his cheek pressed against her face. How would he feel when he realized that she'd left him?

She stared at her hands, unable to move.

At sunset, Ialu still hadn't returned. Elin smiled reassuringly at her anxious son and told him his father would be fine. But when he failed to show up by the time they went back to the shed after supper, she worried something had happened.

It was close to midnight when she finally heard the *clip-clop* of hooves and the creak of wagon wheels. She slid gently out from under the blanket so as not to wake Jesse and opened the door. The moon had set, and the sky was lit only by the stars. A lantern hung from the roof of a large covered wagon, and in its light, she saw Ialu climb down from the driver's seat.

The night wind was chilly, making the heat of the day seem like a dream. Pulling her collar close, Elin walked over to Ialu, who was tying the reins to a large tree. He raised his head when she reached his side. "It's a big wagon, but Yantoku wouldn't hear of me refusing. He sold it to me for half its value, saying it was his gift to us."

"How is he?" asked Elin, recalling the kind face of Ialu's childhood foster brother and fellow carpenter.

"Good. They have a child now." He went behind the wagon and pulled out a fodder pouch. Seeing this, Elin went over to the pool by the spring, filled a large bucket with water, and brought it to the horse. Judging by its muscled body, it had probably been a workhorse. It seemed sturdy and good-tempered. When she placed the bucket beside it, it snorted and slurped the water thirstily. Once the horse was done, Ialu placed the fodder bag over its neck.

Something about his movements made Elin pause and look at him closely. The horse shifted slightly, exposing Ialu's face to the lantern light. "Ialu!" she exclaimed. She placed a hand on his forehead. It was beaded with sweat and burning hot.

"The fever's not that bad," he said, shaking his head listlessly.

"Because you jumped into the river—"

He shook his head again. With a grimace, he loosened his sash and exposed his midriff. "It would help if there was some clean water to wash this with," he said.

Looking at his skin, Elin gasped. A dark red line circled his abdomen, as though something had dug into his flesh. The bruising spread all the way up to his ribcage.

"It looks like it was made by a rope," Elin breathed. With a shock, she realized what must have caused it.

"Come into the light," she said, pulling him toward the lantern. She probed the wound, and he winced when she pressed her palm against his ribs. Frowning, she chewed her lip. The wound was already festering in places, and his ribs might be cracked. "Did you buy some medicine?" she asked.

"It's in the back."

Elin climbed up into the wagon. Opening a wooden box filled with medicine, she scanned the labels and picked out some ointment and cloths. She handed these to Ialu and jumped down. "There's a well behind the shed," she told him. "Sit here while I go and get some water."

With a nod, Ialu rolled up his sweat-drenched top and threw it into the wagon. When Elin returned, he was sitting on the ground with his back against a wheel. Elin took down the lantern and placed it nearby. Kneeling down beside him, she soaked the cloth in water and gently washed the wound.

In one spot, the weave of the rope stood out starkly on his flesh. Tears filled her eyes, blinding her. She brushed them away with the back of her hand, but still they fell as she washed his wound.

"I was thinking the whole time," Ialu said hoarsely. "Trying to see if there wasn't some way the three of us could live together in peace."

His voice was the only sound in the blackness of the damp night. "I was thinking that when we met up, the three of us could escape somewhere far away. I thought we might make it if we could disappear into a town where no one knows us."

His voice faded, and a hush fell over Elin's skin. After some time, Ialu spoke again. "Elin, today the palace issued a proclamation to the rulers of every domain in this kingdom." His voice was barely a whisper. "It called on them to find us; to take us into custody and bring us to the palace. Whoever succeeds will be generously rewarded. But any domain that fails to notice us hiding there will be held responsible and punished severely."

Elin listened with her head bowed.

The net that surrounded them was closing in. No matter where they fled, no matter where they might try to hide, the relentless gaze of the people would seek them out. She put a hand to her face and closed her eyes.

They could never escape, not unless she gouged out these green eyes of hers.

"I thought of living deep in the mountains where no one comes," Ialu murmured. "I thought maybe the three of us could stay hidden in some remote mountain stronghold."

If it were just the two of them, maybe they could have, Elin thought. But she couldn't subject Jesse to such loneliness. Slowly, she shook her head.

Ialu sighed. "Yes, you're right. We can't do that. It would be too hard on Jesse. And too dangerous. We're being hunted by the Lahza as well. If they attacked us in the mountains, no one could help us."

Somewhere in the distance Elin heard the call of a bird, thin and shrill. Then it died away. Feeling Ialu's hand on her arm, she looked up. His calm eyes held her own. "Do you think by going to the Afon Noah you can change this?"

Trembling, Elin drew a breath. "I don't know. Even if I find the Valley of the Kalenta Loh, who knows if they've followed the same lifestyle for centuries or kept the old records? And even if they have, there's no guarantee I can find anything that will convince the Yojeh and the Aluhan to give up their plan."

She closed her eyes tightly. "It's just that it seemed the only way left. The only way I could free us from this hopeless situation. And the only way I could . . ."

She swallowed the words, unable to continue, but Ialu murmured, "The only way you could avoid using the Royal Beasts as weapons?"

She nodded. Tears welled behind her closed lids and slid down her cheeks. For a long time, neither of them said anything. In the quiet darkness, Elin felt reality sink slowly to the bottom of her chest, like dust settling to the ground after being stirred up into the air. She had tried to race forward, shutting her eyes to all the impossibilities. Having lost her momentum, she now saw clearly that it was an impossible dream.

"You can't go to the Afon Noah alone. You know that," Ialu said quietly. "There are checkpoints set up along all the main roads. And who knows what traps have been laid by those who work for the Lahza. They were able to find our house and attack me. If they've infiltrated our troops, some of their agents might be posing as soldiers."

Elin nodded. A shudder ran through her as she recalled how they had abducted the Toda Steward without anyone suspecting. The net laid by the Aluhan was in plain view. But she had no way of knowing the extent, or even the nature, of the one laid by the Lahza.

"I could go with you, but we can't take Jesse. We would have to leave him with Miss Esalu. Shall we do that?"

Elin raised her face, then shook her head. "No. I can't." A quietness filled her breast. The shining white path that had stretched into the distance vanished. In its stead, she saw before her, clear and distinct, the dirt-colored road that she had to take.

"I guess this is as far as it goes," she said. The figure of a Royal Beast soaring in the heavens flashed through her mind and was gone.

"Yes. This is as far as we can go," Ialu said. He moved his hand from her arm to her head and pulled her toward him. Elin pressed her cheek against his chest. His voice came to her, muffled by his body. "In my life, I'm so grateful for these last ten years."

Tears flowed from Elin's eyes. She couldn't speak.

These last ten years. Yes, how glad she was to have had them. Somewhere inside she'd always known that it couldn't last, yet still she'd been happy.

And now those days had come to an end. A new life would begin. Listening to the beating of Ialu's heart, she closed her eyes. Gradually, something filled her, like the tide flooding in. She must do what she had vowed never to do. This was the path that lay before her. But she would have had to confront it sometime anyway.

Behind her closed lids, she saw snow-tipped peaks. Whatever had happened beyond those mountains long ago had changed the lives of every generation—the lives of her and her mother, of Seimiya and Yohalu. The catastrophe that had started all this—what had it really been? What would happen when Royal Beasts covered the skies and swooped down upon the Toda hordes?

Concealed by her mother's people and the Yojeh's ancestors, the answer now lay buried beneath the sands of time. If she couldn't ask the Kalenta Loh to tell her what that was, then she had only one choice.

Slowly, she opened her eyes. I must find the truth for myself. She must unravel the secrets of the Royal Beasts and the Toda with her own hands, using everything she had learned so far.

In the depths of her nostrils, Elin smelled once again the Kiba she had dissected in that cold, clammy cave; saw the fallopian tubes, deformed by the tokujisui, and the unfertilized eggs that had taken the life of their mother without bringing forth new life.

At the end of this search, maybe all she would find would be the cruelty of the human herd. But if she never found out and simply let the flow sweep her along, when the battle raged, she and her family would die just like those Kiba with the mistakes of the past buried inside them. Many people—and many beasts—would die, without ever knowing the reason.

She couldn't let that happen.

A breeze seemed to flow through her body, whipping away her murky doubts and filling her instead with a quiet thought.

With my own hands, let me break asunder the chains that Jeh and my mother's people made to bind the beasts. With my own eyes, let me find the truth that was hidden.

If there was any path that could free both the beasts and her family, it could only be found at the end of that road, when all was revealed. Her work was just beginning.

6

AUDIENCE

Jesse tugged at his mother's sleeve and whispered in her ear. "I need to pee."

Sunlight poured into the large, bright room. On one wall hung a tapestry of charging Toda scattering men on horseback. Jesse had tried to distract himself by examining every detail, but the chair on which he sat was so big his legs dangled, and he sank into the upholstery. Worst of all, the thought of facing the Yojeh and the Aluhan made his heart pound so hard he could barely stand it.

He had waited as long as he could before telling his mother. Dressed in their finest clothes and lost in thought, she and his father seemed like strangers. But when he pulled on her sleeve, she moved into action. Rising, she spoke to the pretty young woman in the corner of the room. "Excuse me, but my son wishes to use the lavatory."

The woman glided over. "Allow me to take him there for you." She smiled at Jesse, but he tightened his grip on Elin's sleeve.

Perhaps she felt it, because Elin said, "Thank you. I'll go with you. Please lead the way."

The air was much cooler in the corridor. The high-ceilinged passageway was so broad, they could have raced down it four abreast. But we'd probably slip and fall, Jesse thought. He sighed as they walked along the shiny wooden floor.

Elin squeezed his hand. "There's nothing to worry about, Jesse. The Yojeh and the Aluhan are very kind."

Jesse pursed his lips. "That's all very well for you to say," he said. His voice came out much louder than he'd intended. Glancing at the woman walking in front, he whispered, "I just don't get it, that's all."

His mother had escaped from the palace, only to announce suddenly that they were going back. And now, here they were, but she wouldn't tell him why. Instead, she kept telling him to behave himself and that she'd explain later. He glared up at her to make sure she knew he was mad, but she just smiled.

"Yes, I know," she said. "But be patient a little longer. I'll tell you all about it later." Then she gazed off into space as though she were somewhere else.

Even the lavatory was large. It smelled of flowers. The water jug and the basin for washing his hands were both made of white ceramic with a pattern of little birds.

Once Jesse had peed, he felt more relaxed, and memories of the last few days filled his mind.

I liked staying in that shed.

The farmers had let them stay two more nights because his father had come down with a fever. They were really kind, bringing slices of freshly picked melon. They had chilled the melon in well water first, and, sprinkled with a little salt, it tasted delicious.

Jesse's mother spent most of her time sitting beside his father, writing a letter. Once Ialu was better, she gave him the letter to take to the capital. After that, everything had happened very quickly.

They said goodbye to the farmers and headed toward the bridge to the capital. While on their way, soldiers rode up and surrounded them. Jesse was petrified, but his parents patted his head and told him not to worry. From there, they were led to this hall.

A tall, middle-aged warrior was standing in the entranceway, waiting. To Jesse's surprise, as soon as his mother saw him, she dropped to her knees and pressed her forehead to the ground. At his father's urging, Jesse had knelt, too, bowing low as though he were sorry, even though he had no idea what he was supposed to be sorry for. Instead of scolding Mother, the man had reached out his hand and helped her to her feet, then led them inside.

Waiting for dinner had been especially hard. Jesse was starving but his parents had made him sit in a big room all by himself while they talked with that man in the room next door. All he could do was watch them through the crack in the doorway.

When he finally did get to eat, however, the meal had been fit for a king. And afterward, he'd been thrilled to have the big bath all to himself and Mother. It had been a long time since they'd been in the bath together. They got to sleep in the same room, too, on soft, comfy bedding that smelled heavenly. Although he hadn't a clue what was going on, his parents didn't seem to be worried. He felt pretty sure the bad things were over.

"So you're Jesse, are you?"

Jesse drew in his breath. Two armchairs sat on a dais at the far end of the enormous room. On one sat the Aluhan, while on the other sat a woman dressed all in white. She was smiling at him. Her long luxuriant hair fell down her back, and her eyes looked golden.

The thought that this was the Yojeh made his throat constrict so that he could barely talk. His words came out like a high squeak. "Yes, ma'am. I'm Jesse."

"You look so like Elin. Except that your eyes aren't green."

Jesse pouted a little at this. "Yes, ma'am. My mother and father have given me a lot of things. I get my eyes from Dad. But my face is like Mom's. And Miss Esalu tells me that I get my stubbornness from them both."

When he stopped speaking, a strange expression rose on everyone's faces. The first one to start laughing was the Yojeh. She put a hand over her mouth as she struggled to control herself. Glancing at Mother, she said, "Elin, your son is certainly an accomplished orator."

Elin's mouth crooked. "Yes. My apologies. There are times when I wonder who he takes after."

The Yojeh wiped tears from the corners of her eyes and nodded. "That's children for you. Ours are the same. Although they resemble us in some ways, I wonder where they got some of their other characteristics."

The smile faded from her face. "My daughter's eyes are dark, too," she added quietly. "Not golden-brown like mine. The golden eyes of the Yojeh ended with my generation. Whether we like it or not, everything must change."

Elin's smile had faded, too. The Yojeh sighed and said, "So you have decided to obey my command."

"Yes," Elin said. "I thank you for giving me time to make that decision. Please accept my sincere apologies for the trouble I caused you."

A smile touched the Yojeh's lips, but it seemed somehow sad. "What matters is that you're here. And that you are willing to fulfill my wishes."

Elin bowed deeply. "Thank you. I do not know if I actually can, but I will do everything in my power to multiply the Royal Beasts."

"Not just multiply them," the Aluhan interjected, "but train them to fight as a corps."

Elin turned to face him. "Yes, Your Highness. But I have two requests."

The Aluhan frowned slightly. "And what might they be?"

"The first is about how to use the Royal Beasts. Rather than being ridden and controlled by warriors as the Toda are, I would like to train them to fly riderless."

At this the Aluhan's gaze grew sharp. "Why?"

"There are two reasons." She looked the Aluhan squarely in the eye. "One is because riding them is dangerous. Toda can be controlled by gripping their horns, but not the Royal Beasts. When they see Toda, their natural enemies, they respond swiftly and with tremendous force. It takes every ounce of strength just to hang on, which makes it impossible to shoot arrows while riding. In addition"—she flicked her eyes to the Yojeh then back to the Aluhan—"I have absolutely no idea what will happen when a whole pack of Royal Beasts attacks a host of Toda. If the tale passed down by the Ahlyo turns out to be true, at least we can prevent needless deaths if the Royal Beasts fly riderless."

The Aluhan's eyebrows drew together. "But how can we control them, then?"

"I don't know if it will work until I try it, but I'm planning to train them to fly in response to my harp."

"You mean you intend to control all of them on your own?" the Aluhan said incredulously.

"Yes. Which leads me to the second reason I believe they should fly riderless," Elin replied. "The more people who can control the Royal Beasts, the greater the possibility that this secret could be leaked. We may choose people we believe are completely trustworthy, but nothing is absolute when it comes to humans. Just think about how the Toda Steward was abducted. If we train warriors as Riders, the day is bound to come when the secret to controlling them makes its way out of this country."

The Aluhan pondered Elin's words for some time, then looked at the Yojeh. She gazed back at him, then turned and said, "Elin, I understand how you feel. Much of what you say makes sense. But we cannot rest easy if you are the only one who can control the Beasts. What would we do if anything happened to you?"

"Yes, I thought of that, too," Elin replied. "There's a limit to what I can do on my own. I would like to ask the headmistress of Kazalumu, Miss Esalu, to help me."

The Yojeh nodded. "That would be fine. I hear that she knows the Royal Beasts well, so I'm sure she'll make a good assistant. But she's quite elderly, isn't she?"

"Yes. She is. So there is one other person with whom I wish to share this knowledge." She looked straight at the Yojeh. "With all respect, I would like to share what I have learned about the Handler's Art, and what I will learn from here on, with you, Your Highness."

A stunned silence fell over the room. Only the swish of the Yojeh's robe as she jerked could be heard in that frozen moment.

"With me?" she whispered.

"If it had not been lost in the fire," Elin said, "you would have inherited this skill from your ancestors. And what more certain way could there be to safeguard the secret than this?"

The Aluhan had been listening to this exchange with an arrested expression, but now he cast the Yojeh a look of concern. "I think this is a good idea, but the Yojeh is with child."

Jesse's eyes swiveled toward his mother. He saw her nodding calmly. "Yes, of course," she said. "I didn't mean right away. I don't even know yet whether it is possible to breed the Royal Beasts. If I do manage to find a way, it will take at least four years to raise the cubs that are born. So we have the next five or maybe even ten years to think about it."

When she finished speaking, the room was quiet. Jesse watched the Yojeh's face. She looked different somehow. Up until this moment, she had seemed so lofty he had been overcome with awe. But now, with her eyes fixed on his mother, she seemed like an ordinary human.

"I accept your offer, Elin," the Yojeh said finally. Leaning on the arm of her chair, she pushed herself up. The Aluhan rose swiftly and slipped his hand under her elbow. With one hand on her belly, she climbed down the stairs. She drew near and took Elin's hand in her own. "I want to know what my ancestor saw and why she chose to become the Yojeh," she murmured. "Do you think the Royal Beasts will tell us?"

Jesse looked up at his mother. Her face seemed strained, as though she was hiding her pain. "Let us see what the Royal Beasts will teach us," she said, her voice just a whisper.

The Yojeh squeezed her hand then let it go. She looked at Ialu where he stood behind Elin. He kept his head bowed.

"Ialu," the Yojeh said. "It has been a long time."

"Yes, Your Majesty."

The Yojeh's expression turned hard. "Raise your face."

Slowly, Ialu lifted his head. "You haven't changed," the Yojeh said. "Maybe you have aged a little, but that's all." Her face softened. "I hear that you make furniture."

Ialu nodded. "My father was a cabinetmaker," he said.

The Yojeh's eyes widened. "Your father was an artisan? I thought that you were born into a warrior family."

A wry smile touched Ialu's lips. "I was eight when I first gripped a sword. I became a warrior on the training grounds on the outskirts of the palace."

The Yojeh regarded him silently for a moment. "Do you intend to spend the rest of your days wielding a chisel?" she asked.

"No." Ialu returned her gaze. "Yesterday I consulted the lord of Amasulu. If your Majesty and the Aluhan will permit me, I wish to become a Toda Rider."

Jesse caught his breath. He saw his mother spin around to look at his father, her face turning deathly pale.

7

TODA RIDER

Elin stared at Ialu, feeling the blood drain from her face. When he had left the room after supper the night before, she had thought he was stepping out for some fresh air, but he must have gone to consult with Yohalu. And now, he had shared his intention with the Yojeh and the Aluhan, so that even if she protested, there was no turning back.

But why?

She couldn't breathe. The skin from her brow to her cheeks felt taut and numb. Everything around her seemed to recede into the distance, and she broke into a cold sweat. Gripping her hands together, she fought to stay on her feet and betray no sign of the consternation she felt.

Seimiya frowned at Ialu's words, and she turned to Shunan. "Did you know about this?"

Shunan shook his head. "No. This is the first I've heard of it." He fixed his eyes on Ialu. "You were a Se Zan," he said. "Why would you want to become a Toda Rider?"

"Your Highness, it is precisely because of my experience as a Se Zan that I feel the need to do this." Ialu's voice was cool and steady. "I longed to support the union of Your Majesties. To that end, I played my small part. Eleven years have passed since you were wed, yet I hear that the Se Zan and the Aluhan's men still do not communicate."

Seimiya and Shunan looked slightly uncomfortable.

"If my wife is to fly the Royal Beasts with Her Highness, the Yojeh,"

Ialu continued, "then allow me to ride the Toda in service to the Aluhan. Limited though my capacity may be, I long to serve as a link between those who guard you both."

A light kindled in Shunan's eyes. "Is this truly what you wish?"

Ialu nodded. "Yes, Your Highness."

Shunan glanced at Seimiya. Seeing her incline her head, he turned back to Ialu. "You said that you had spoken with the lord of Amasulu. What did he say?"

"He understood. He said that if I could truly bridge the gap between the Toda Riders and the Se Zan, it would be most welcome. But he also voiced one concern."

"What was that?"

Ialu's lips quirked. "I believe that you must share this same concern, Your Highness. It was my age."

Shunan smiled wryly. "Yes, that's true. How old are you?"

"Thirty-nine."

"Almost forty. I see. And what else did he say?"

The smile left Ialu's face. "He was worried for my safety. After all, I have killed many of the Sai Gamulu."

Elin struggled to control the trembling that seized her. Many Sai Gamulu served in the Aluhan's army, driven by their desire to see the Aluhan rule the kingdom. More than a few must hate Ialu for taking the lives of their comrades and their kin. If he joined their ranks, she thought, they could easily get revenge by making it look like a training accident.

Shunan frowned slightly and gave Ialu a measuring look. "Yet even so, you still wish to join my army?"

"Yes."

For a long time, Shunan stared into his unwavering eyes. Finally, he heaved a deep sigh. "As you say, this rift between my army and those who guard the palace is undesirable. The older Se Zan trust you completely. And there are many among my own men who hold you in high esteem. They respect you as a rare and accomplished warrior who aided my marriage to the Yojeh. In that sense, there's no one more suited than you to serve as a bridge between them."

He nodded as if to himself. "All right, then. You shall join my army as a high-ranking officer in the supply troops who make up the rear guard. Your age won't be a problem there. You'll be safer, too."

Ialu shook his head. "I am deeply grateful for your consideration, Your Highness. However, please allow me to serve as a Toda Rider, not as an officer in the rear."

Shunan frowned. "Why?"

"Warriors will never respect someone who isn't prepared to risk his life on the front lines."

PART TWO

THE FINAL CHAPTER

SIX

FAMILY DAYS

I

HOT WATER BOTTLE

Snow clouds streamed in the wind. The Royal Beasts wheeled like dark shadows against the gray sky, turning into dazzling specks each time the sun burst through a break in the clouds. The slow, rhythmic notes of a harp quickened, and the flock of lights swerved in unison, climbing higher in the air.

Batting away the snowflakes that flew like dust into her eyes, Esalu paused to stretch her back and catch her breath from the walk up the hill. She gazed at the Royal Beasts that danced across the heavens.

Two years, Esalu thought. Elin had managed to train them this far in that short a time.

The heat of exertion ebbed, and Esalu felt the air pierce her skin. No matter how thickly she dressed, the bitter cold seeped through her clothes like water. Yet Elin had been working in this icy temperature since early morning and was still standing on the edge of the snow-covered cliff, her face turned upward.

Esalu sighed. Ever since Elin had returned to Kazalumu, she had seemed possessed. She rarely took a day off and spent all her time studying the ecology of the Royal Beasts and training them. It reminded Esalu of when Elin was just a girl and had forgotten to eat and sleep in her longing to cure Leelan.

She must have made up her mind, Esalu thought. For eleven years, Elin had agonized over how to raise the Royal Beasts. Until she had been summoned by the Aluhan. Now she seemed to have no trace of doubt. She knew exactly what she was doing as she broke, one by one, the rules the Royal Ancestor Jeh had made to prevent catastrophe. Elin's eyes were fixed on something that only she could see. Head raised, she deliberately walked into the wind, focused solely on the final outcome of her actions.

Where will her path lead her in the end? Esalu shivered and rubbed her arms.

The dazzling specks began to descend. One at a time, Royal Beasts dropped to the ground. Some landed partway down the cliff, others on the snowy ground at the top. Keeping a fixed distance from each other, they formed a ring with Elin at the center. Although they looked like they were randomly scattered, Esalu, who was used to this sight, knew there was meaning in the order of their descent and in each landing spot.

Leelan alighted first, beside Elin, followed almost immediately by Eku. Next came their children, each landing some distance away and in order of their age. According to Elin, Leelan and her family, who had been living in the sanctuary the longest, had staked out a core territory within the pasture. The Royal Beasts that had been brought to the sanctuary later each made their own territory on the edge of that family circle. They maintained the same hierarchy and physical distance between them wherever they were. Even here in the ravine that served as their training ground, they still stayed the same distance apart when they landed. However, Elin had discovered through many years of observation that the size of each Beast's territory was much smaller than that of wild Royal Beasts.

I suppose in the wild such enormous, meat-eating creatures would need quite a lot of space, Esalu thought. But in the sanctuary, where there's no need to hunt for food, territory probably has a different meaning.

Elin had told Esalu that Royal Beasts were amazingly intelligent and adapted to new conditions very quickly. Through studying the behavior of Beasts newly introduced to the sanctuary, Elin had identified how they maintained an appropriate distance from one another. It seemed they had their own language, communicating with complex combinations of cries, wing movements, and sounds made with their teeth and joints.

Leelan lowered her head and nuzzled Elin in the back making a cooing noise like a cub—*shashasha*.

"Stop that, Leelan. You might push me off the cliff." Smiling, Elin pressed her hands against the enormous Beast's nose. On her breast, a Silent Whistle gleamed.

As Esalu walked toward Elin, she noticed footsteps in the snow. They led not from the direction of Kazalumu but from the edge of the forest to the training ground and back again. She sighed.

Elin turned at the sound. "Oh, I didn't realize you were here." With a worried frown, she strode quickly over to Esalu. "You shouldn't have come all this way in such freezing weather."

Esalu stretched and raised her brows. "I'm not the only one who came all this way in this weather. Did you notice?"

Elin looked to where Esalu was pointing, and her face clouded. The boy must have been hiding in the rock's shadow for some time. The snow was much thinner there. Catching sight of something on the rock, Elin walked over and picked it up.

"What is it?" Esalu called out. Elin turned and waved what looked like a red scarf.

"It's my old scarf," she said as she drew near. She wrapped it around Esalu's neck.

Esalu's eyes widened as she felt its soft warmth. "It's so warm," she exclaimed. "Did he just leave it there now?"

Elin shook her head with a playful smile and placed a small pottery vessel in Esalu's hands.

"Ah! A hot water bottle!" Esalu exclaimed. At this time of year, it was quite common for the elderly to fill a clay jug like this with hot water, wrap it in cloth, and stick it inside their robes. The boy had probably wrapped it in his scarf so the heat wouldn't escape when he left it on the rock for his mother.

"Honestly! That little rascal. It's hard to scold him when he does such sweet things." Esalu sighed again. "I know he misses you, but it's not good to let him sneak in here like this all the time. It's not only the guards I'm thinking of. The forest is much deeper here than around the pastures; he could get into serious trouble along the way."

"I know. I really need to make him stop, but . . ."

Jesse was lonely. His father was no longer here, and his mother spent most of the day with the Royal Beasts. They had gotten rid of their house in the city and moved into a house built for them inside the sanctuary, meaning Jesse couldn't play with his old neighborhood friends anymore.

When school was in session, he could at least play with the students sometimes, which helped him forget his parents' absence. But during the holidays, when the students went home to their families, there was only the housemother, Kalisa, and the custodians. Although they might spend some time with him, he must have been unbearably lonely.

The training grounds were heavily guarded, with many soldiers posted in the forest, and no one was allowed in except Elin and Esalu. But knowing Jesse was Elin's son, the guards turned a blind eye when he snuck through. When Elin thought about how the Aluhan and others would react if they heard that Jesse was watching her train the Royal Beasts, she knew she couldn't let him get away with it. But when she thought of how Jesse must have been feeling, she couldn't bring herself to scold him either.

"Honestly, you and Jesse are hopeless. Your husband, too," Esalu grumbled. She bit her glove and pulled it off, then took a letter wrapped in oiled paper from her cloak.

Elin's heart raced at the sight. Just feeling the weight of the letter in her hands made her happy.

"Do you think he'll come home this winter? Even once?"

Elin smiled and cocked her head. "I wonder."

"He doesn't come because you don't put enough pressure on him," Esalu said. "I bet he'd be happier if you begged him to come home instead of being so understanding."

Elin replied with a vague smile, and Esalu threw up her hands with a snort of disgust.

With the sun sinking lower in the sky, the snow that had been blowing in soft little flurries began to fall thick and fast. "I guess it's time to get back to the stable," Elin said. She tucked Ialu's letter into her cloak and raised her harp. With the first twang of the string, the Royal Beasts turned toward her. Listening to the notes she played, they rose as if drawn by a thread, flying up into the dusky heavens. Their wings beat noisily as they passed overhead and flew off toward the pasture.

"Not a Beast out of place," Esalu whispered as she watched them disappear into the distance.

Esalu left when they reached the stable. Pushing open the door, Elin stepped inside. Having arrived home long before and been fed by Tomura and the senior students, Leelan was grooming her fur with a contented look.

It was warm inside the dimly lit stable. Although the stalls were cleaned daily, the distinctive scent of Beast never left. The smell might have disturbed someone who wasn't used to it, but Elin felt herself relax whenever she entered the stable.

It was completely different in size and shape from the building that had been here when she was a young girl. Carpenters sent from the palace had replaced it with a far larger and grander structure. Now, plenty of fresh meat was delivered daily for the Royal Beasts, so the sanctuary no longer had to mix potatoes into the feed to make it stretch further.

Listening to the Beasts' gentle rustling, Elin knelt in front of the fireplace and stirred the embers in the banked fire. When they began to glow, she added a few sticks of wood. The flames caught, and she sat down by the fire and pulled out the bundle Esalu had given her. Breaking the seal, she tore off the oiled-paper wrapping and unfolded the pages inside to reveal Ialu's handwriting.

Breathlessly, she began to read the tightly packed script. Just like his character, Ialu's words were plain and straightforward. He described different events in his life over the past month. As a former Se Zan who had once guarded the Yojeh, it couldn't have been easy for him to fit in with the Toda Riders, who pledged allegiance to the Aluhan, yet his letter never even touched on this subject.

For the last two years, he had worked patiently and steadily to form a bridge between the Aluhan's men and the Se Zan. With Kailu's help, he had invited a Se Zan and a Toda Rider, both of whom were well liked by their comrades but flexible in their thinking, to join him for a drink. He had started off with just the three of them meeting once or twice a month, but slowly his efforts had borne fruit, and twenty or thirty men now joined this regular gathering. Through their conversations, he identified what was needed and formulated proposals to meet those needs. He had also established a channel through which he could share these proposals with the Yojeh and the Aluhan. He approached this work with the same methodical patience he showed when building cabinets. At the same time, he was working to improve the Toda army and sent Elin detailed descriptions of the new Toda troop he'd helped establish under Yohalu.

Although not a talkative man, Ialu was a surprisingly good writer. When Elin had first begun living with him, she had stumbled upon a bundle of papers while cleaning. Ialu wasn't home. She knew she shouldn't look at them without permission, but she couldn't help herself. Undoing the string that bound them, she began to read.

It was a diary of sorts. The mental anguish Ialu had experienced after quitting the Se Zan came through so vividly, she couldn't put the pages down. It was only when she came to the place where he mentioned her that she finally stopped. Although she was dying to read further, she was afraid she couldn't bring herself to look Ialu in the face if she did. With trembling fingers, she retied the string.

After agonizing over it all night, she'd finally confessed. She'd been ter-rified that it would mean the end of their relationship, but Ialu had seemed neither surprised nor angry. Taken aback by his indifference, she had asked him why he wasn't mad, but he'd only looked puzzled and in the end had never answered her.

She still didn't know why he hadn't gotten mad. They'd been married a long time now, and there were quite a few things she still wondered about. Perhaps it was the same for him, too.

Elin pulled her rambling thoughts back to the present and started reading from where she'd left off. At a certain spot, her eyes widened.

"Yesterday," Ialu wrote, *"a secret envoy arrived bearing a letter from Sir Rolan. Lord Yohalu summoned me to his room and told me what it said. The con-tents were surprising. According to Sir Rolan, Lahza is not the name of a single nation."*

Rolan had traveled deep into the eastern plains, and the country he described was a far cry from what Elin had imagined Lahza to be. According to him, the word "Lahza" meant "we" in the language of a people who called themselves the Oolish. The correct name for their country was Lahza Oma Kaluda, meaning "we who worship Kaluda." Kaluda was the god they worshipped in a shrine far to the east. Furthermore, the Oolish were divided into two large groups of people: the Oolish Oh and the Oolish Yah, mean-ing the Western Oolish and the Eastern Oolish. These two groups vied with each other to see who could bring the most prized offerings to their god.

Once every five years the god sent the Voice of Joy from the heavens to announce which group, the Western or the Eastern Oolish, had most pleased him. For the last fifteen years, the Eastern Oolish had received the most praise for their achievements, and the Western Oolish longed to offer up some dazzling exploit that would win the god's approval.

According to Rolan, this was likely why attacks on the caravan cities, including Imeelu, had increased. He warned his father, however, not to dis-miss the Lahza as mere fanatics. Although their lifestyle and their way of thinking was grounded in their belief in Kaluda, the glory of their cities and the prosperity of their trade were so indescribably great that one would have to see it to believe it.

Their style of government was also extremely efficient. They had succeeded in absorbing so many surrounding tribes and peoples because they treated everyone, even non-Oolish, as equals as long as they accepted the god Kaluda.

As she read, Elin recalled the guestroom in Yohalu's hall; the beautiful woman Kuriu sitting in an arm chair by the window that opened onto the inner garden; the huge map that covered the wall. She remembered Rolan's rich, gentle voice as he had pointed to the caravan city Imeelu on a distant plain, and his homeland, Asheh. From Ialu's letter, she sensed once again the vastness of the world that she'd felt at that time.

She raised her face and gazed at the Royal Beasts. In the half-dark of this winter night their hulking shadows were hunched in sleep, and their muzzles were buried deep in the fur on their chests as they snored contentedly. Something boundless spread through her chest at the thought that in some faraway land, people who worshipped the god Kaluda were also passing this winter night.

How big the world was! And so filled with people of different perspectives.

A quiet thought dropped to the bottom of her chest and fanned outward. Wars will never cease. No matter how hard people might try to prevent conflict, no matter what clever scheme they devised, humans would continue to form packs that fought over territory.

Looking at Leelan's sleeping form, Elin thought of Jeh, who had left this world long ago. Having led two thousand Royal Beasts through the skies to battle, she would have been painfully aware of human nature. Surely, Jeh, you must have felt the same way. Yet you didn't let that stop you. You used the Royal Beasts to safeguard the stability of this country while trying your best to avert another catastrophe.

And now, one piece at a time, Elin was dismantling the clever devices Jeh had created to prevent people from flying or breeding the Beasts. The final outcome to which these actions could lead was always on Elin's mind, yet she no longer felt like stopping.

The system Jeh had so carefully woven was truly masterful—as long as the sole object was to stabilize the country and maintain peace. But time passed. The country grew, its population swelled, and border disputes with other nations became frequent. When Yaman Hasalu was given the Toda as weapons, Jeh's exquisitely woven cage had begun to unravel and had now reached the stage where it could no longer hold its shape.

While the kingdom of Lyoza had been flaunting the power of the Toda to other countries, it had also been sowing the seeds of its own downfall. Countries that lacked Toda and relied on men as weapons naturally wanted a Toda army of their own. As long as people were driven by the desire to win, to have a better life than someone else no matter how small the difference, they would keep looking for ways to conquer. One day, someone was bound to discover a weapon that could overwhelm the Toda forces.

Elin stared at the floor of the dark stable. *In the end, it was I who found that weapon and showed it to those in power.*

As the one who had opened the lid of that box, what should she do? Having thought this question through carefully, she was now walking the only path she'd found.

If we could rid the world of war . . .

This thought crossed her mind at times, and each time she would dismiss it as an impossible dream. Humans, who staked out territories in packs, seemed to have an incurable inclination to wage war. But at the bottom of this dark thought a faint light still gleamed. In her mind, she would see the shadow of a little fish flitting through a stream while the sun played on the water's surface—a fish she had read about in a book long ago.

Known by the name of Iya, the fish fed on algae that grew on rocks in the riverbed. Each Iya claimed several rocks as their territory and would slam into other fish to stop them from eating their algae. The more they ate, the stronger these fish grew, and the better they could protect their territory. The strongest survived.

Strangely, when something in the river's condition changed, they would begin to swim in schools and no longer stake out territory. The fish that swam in such schools weren't particularly small. No longer bound by territories, they could forage in a broader area and had more algae to eat. Sometimes more lya survived this way than on their own. The passage Elin had read kept a clear light alive in her mind. Although faint, it glittered like the sun on the river's surface.

Living things can change, she thought. We can never know people or the world to the point where we can write them off as hopeless. She felt that she could keep moving forward as long as she could think this way. Even if dark and menacing clouds rose above the road that stretched ahead.

Elin bowed her head, the letter still grasped in her hands. Ialu had written in such detail about the Lahza to help her prepare. At the end of last year, Lahza horsemen had repeatedly attacked the kingdom's protectorates, the caravan cities in the east. Ialu was warning her that if they had done so seeking good tidings from their god, they were likely to launch an even larger campaign in another four years.

Thanks to Ialu's detailed reports on the Toda forces, Elin had a solid grasp of what was going on. His letters conveyed the inner thoughts and opinions of each officer and soldier he named, along with the subtleties of what was happening in the field. She suspected that he sent her these long and frequent messages so she would know the people alongside whom she fought when it was time to fly the Royal Beasts into battle.

She longed to be with him. To see his face, to hear his voice. This yearning burned through her chest like fire. She closed her eyes.

Esalu had said she was too understanding, but she was wrong. The night before Ialu left, Elin had wept furiously and berated him. In the end, however, she had been forced to give up because she realized he felt the same as she did.

Once it was clear that the transient peace in which they had lived had come to an end, the dams concealed in their hearts had burst. The walls behind which they had built their protected life crumbled and were swept away; in the wake, a single thought reared its head: Unless they faced their fate, there would be no future for them at all.

Elin had known all along that Ialu was stalked by ghosts. The shades of those he had killed weighed heavily on his mind even after he and Elin began living together as a family. No matter what he did, these memories never left him. She also had longed to find something that would help her confront her past and confirm that it was all right for her to go on living. Nothing anyone said could quench that desire.

But that wasn't the only reason Ialu had decided to become a Toda Rider. Each time she read his detailed letters about the situation the kingdom faced, she sensed another reason, one that he would never say aloud.

He's trying to stand beside me wherever I must put myself. If so . . .

Elin covered her face with her hands. In her heart, she wept for Jesse.

2

YUGULA FIRE ANTS

Snow dusted the banks of the rushing mountain river, the white contrasting starkly with the black of the wet rocks. The water was so cold it cut the fingers, but the Royal Beasts appeared unperturbed, dunking their muzzles in the stream to drink. The day was fair, and the bright sun shone on their fur.

When they'd landed on the rocks during their morning training session, Leelan had slipped on a snow-covered rock. She must have hurt her claw because she was licking it diligently. Elin walked over to her. "Let me see," she said.

Leelan stopped licking her paw and raised her head. There was a small cut where the claw joined the foot pad, but it wasn't serious and was no longer bleeding.

"It's just a tiny cut," Elin said with a smile. Leelan snorted, her breath rising like white steam. Unlike the other Royal Beasts, Leelan had borne several cubs, and two dark red nipples peeped out from the fur on her chest. The fur around Leelan's nipples was always ruffled because whenever she returned to the sanctuary pasture, her youngest cub would snuggle up and tug on them, even though she had weaned long ago and was already eating meat.

Elin moved away, and Leelan immediately resumed licking her paw, as though she had been waiting to do so. Suddenly, however, she raised her head and pricked her ears, her eyes focused on a point in the forest behind Elin. Alu and Eku also lifted their heads and gazed at the trees.

Elin's brows drew together; although she peered in the same direction, she couldn't see any change. "What is it?" she started to ask, but paused before she finished, sensing a sound. Now she could hear it. A child's scream.

"Jesse?" Elin gestured to the Royal Beasts to stay put and set off at a run. It was Jesse's voice. She was certain. Over and over, he screamed.

"Jesse! Jesse!" Elin cried. She raced toward her son's voice, weaving through the trees and leaping over snow-buried shrubs. Branches whipped her face, drawing blood, but she plowed on, pushing through the brush as she dashed through the winter forest.

Jesse's high-pitched screams drew closer, and she stumbled into a small clearing in the trees. At the foot of a tall tree, she saw him. He was writhing on the ground, hands and feet flailing as though he was on fire, and his body was covered in countless reddish-brown specks. Elin screamed at the sight. "Jesse!"

Yugula fire ants! Their bite was excruciating. Too many, and the victim could die.

The soldiers who guarded the forest came crashing through the underbrush, probably hearing Jesse's screams. They froze when they saw him. Fire ants, which nested in tree trunks they gnawed hollow, were pouring forth from holes in the trunk and spreading over the ground like water.

Elin leaped into the swarm. Pain shot through her feet and spread to her thighs, her stomach, then all the way up to her hands and neck, each spot burning as though pressed against hot metal. Gritting her teeth, she scooped Jesse into her arms and dashed toward the river where she had left

Leelan and the others, brushing the ants off his body as she ran. She slipped on the snow and staggered into the water.

"Take a deep breath and hold it!" she yelled into Jesse's ear. Still holding him in her arms, she waded into the middle of the river and squatted in the icy water. She planted her feet firmly on the bottom to keep her balance and kneaded his body all over to remove the ants. Straightening her knees, she brought his head above the surface so he could catch his breath, but he was limp and his eyes remained shut. Angry red lumps were already rising on his face, which had turned bluish from the frigid river.

Elin called his name frantically. Holding him close, she rubbed his body, then brushed a damp lock of hair from his forehead and caressed his cheek. His eyelids were beginning to swell. He opened them a crack, and his lips parted, but the only sound was the whistling of his breath. The agony was so excruciating he couldn't speak.

Gradually, the ants clinging to his clothing began to peel off, swept away by the water. Rage seized Elin, and she slapped at the ones that still clung to him. It was only when she could no longer see his face clearly that she realized her own eyelids had swollen, too. But she was barely aware of the scorching pain that seared her body.

When she had finally gotten rid of most of the ants, she lurched out of the river onto the bank, clutching Jesse to her. She had to get him some medicine as soon as possible. She staggered over to Leelan. Someone spoke. One of the guards, asking her what they should do. But she had no energy to answer. She paused only to shift Jesse higher up in her arms.

Fortunately, she had left Leelan's saddle on. There was no way she could have attached it now with her frozen fingers. She lifted Jesse onto Leelan's back first, then dragged herself up after him and climbed into the saddle. Leelan, who had been craning her neck to look at them and making encouraging noises, launched herself into the air at Elin's command.

Elin draped herself over Jesse's body, trying to warm him. She didn't even bother to check whether the other Royal Beasts were following. The wind roared in her ears. Her fingers, bitten by the fire ants and then plunged into ice-cold water, were so numb she couldn't tell if they gripped the reins.

"Jesse, Jesse, Jesse," she whispered over and over. Cradling his body with her own, she prayed desperately. Don't die. Please, please, don't die!

She was awoken by the sound of Jesse crying. A ray of morning sun fell through the partly open window, casting a faint light into the room. She could barely open her swollen lids. She tried to rise, only to fall back with a groan. Her arms, her legs, every part of her body was throbbing with pain as if she'd been stung by bees. Her skin felt taut and feverish.

Jesse lay beside her, and she placed a hand on his forehead. His fever had come down a bit overnight, but he was still quite hot to the touch. He wept listlessly, his face bright red and puffy.

"You'll be all right, Jesse. The pain will be gone soon. Just a little longer," Elin murmured, stroking his hair and pressing her cheek against his.

"Mom," he croaked. "I'm . . . thirsty . . ."

Elin nodded. "I'll get you a drink." She found two cups with spouts by her pillow, both full. Esalu must have put them there, Elin thought. She picked one up. Slipping her other hand under Jesse's head, she raised it a little and put the spout against his lips. He gulped noisily. The cool water seemed to relieve some of the pain, because when she laid him back on the pillow, he began breathing peacefully.

Elin soaked a cloth in a basin of water by the bed, wrung it out, and gently wiped the sweat from his face. Taking care not to wake him, she loosened the collar of his shirt and slipped out the cloths she had placed under each armpit. The cloths, which had been wet when she'd put them in, were already dry. She cooled them in the water, wrung them out, and tucked them under his armpits once again.

She would have liked to use ice, but that would have been too cold. The fever was his body's defense against the poison. Rather than cooling him down suddenly, it would be better to keep changing the cloths.

After placing a damp cloth on his forehead and another under the nape of his neck, Elin finally relaxed. Esalu had cared for them all night, but she had probably gone back to the school to get more medicine. No one else was there, and the house was very quiet.

When they had moved here two years ago, a small guardhouse had been built onto the front entrance. No one could enter without passing through it, and there were always two guards stationed there. Every morning around this time, Elin could hear them preparing their breakfast, but today there were no sounds. Perhaps they were trying not to disturb the patients.

Elin lifted the second cup to her mouth and took a long gulp of water from the spout. The ice-cold liquid seeped into her parched, swollen throat. The faintly medicinal smell jolted her back to her childhood. Once, she'd been badly stung by bees. Joeun had given her this same medicine and nursed her through the night as she fought a fever. Though she'd been grateful, she remembered vividly how much she had missed her mother.

She stroked Jesse's flushed cheeks with her fingers. Snuggling close enough to feel the heat of his fever, she closed her eyes.

Poor Jesse.

She'd failed him. One of the first things new students at Kazalumu learned was how to steer clear of the poisonous bugs and snakes that lived in the forest. Jesse, who was too young to go to school, had had no way of knowing about Yugula fire ants.

I should have taught him.

Remorse stabbed her heart. She knew that Jesse was lonely and frequently snuck through the forest to watch her on the training grounds, yet she'd been so preoccupied with the Royal Beasts that she'd never stopped to think about the risks. Somewhere in her mind, she'd assumed he would be all right because the guards were always nearby. She'd left most of his care to Esalu, Kalisa, and the others who worked at the school.

She sighed. For the last two years, she'd been so rushed and pressured by the urgency of her work. She could be called up to fight the Lahza at any time. Before that happened, she had to find out why the Royal Beasts could cause a disaster. Even if she couldn't do that in time, she at least wanted to train them so she could prevent the worst. These thoughts had consumed her.

But the time she spent with Jesse was also irreplaceable.

She opened her eyes a crack and watched his sleeping face. She hadn't had much time with her own mother, but the love she'd received, each memory they'd shared together, were precious gems that gave her comfort.

Am I that kind of mother to Jesse?

Elin placed her forehead gently against his ear and closed her eyes once again.

3

THE MYSTERY OF TREES

On a fine spring day when the snow along the banks of the mountain river had melted, Elin left the training of the Royal Beasts in Esalu's hands for half a day and took Jesse on an outing. He walked beside her with the bundle that held his lunch, sometimes balancing it on his head, at other times hugging it close to his chest. He looked up at her. "Are we going to eat outside?" he asked. The ant bites on his face had scabbed over and fallen off, leaving just faint traces on his skin.

"Yes, we are. Let's go down to the field along the river and have lunch there. We can light a little campfire to keep warm."

Jesse's eyebrows rose. "Really? What's going on, Mom?"

"What do you mean?"

"You're always so busy. We never eat lunch together. Are you trying to be nice to me 'cause you're feeling guilty or something?"

Elin grinned. "Well, yeah. I do feel a little guilty, I guess."

"A little?" Jesse snorted. "Well I guess that's better than not at all." His lips were pouting, but his smile gave him away. Clearly, he was bubbling with excitement.

He brought the bundle containing his lunch up to his nose and sniffed. "What's in here? Doesn't smell like fahko."

"It's a surprise," Elin said. "There's a place I want to show you before we have lunch, though. Here, let me hold that. You should keep your hands free when walking in the forest." She reached out to take his lunch, but Jesse refused to let go.

"You've got to be kidding!" he said. "I'm way more used to walking in this forest than you. You should give me your lunch so you can have your hands free. You aren't riding Leelan today, you know."

He popped his bundle on top of his head and, holding it with one hand, set off at a dash. Jumping over a tree root as nimbly as a monkey, he ran into the forest.

"Jesse, stop!" Elin shouted. "Your lunch! You'll spill the sauce!" She chased after him through the trees. Their branches were so thick with new leaves that they turned the sunlight shining through them green and dyed Jesse's hair and body the same color. As he sped down the path, she called out again. "Wait! Not that way."

Jesse stopped and turned, frowning. "Aren't we going to the training ground along the river?"

"Yes, but there's something I want to show you first."

He skipped back toward her, holding his lunch in his hands. She placed her hand on his head. Pointing to the right, she indicated a game trail that was only faintly visible. Jesse's face clouded. "Oh. You want to go that way?"

The forest path they were on was quite wide but there was a steep hill in the middle. The narrow game trail to which Elin had pointed sloped gently. When the snow lay on the ground, it was easier to walk along. This was the trail that Jesse had used all winter to sneak to the training grounds. It also passed close to the fire-ant nest where he had been bitten.

"That's right," Elin said smiling. "Are you scared?"

Jesse pushed out his lower lip. "Nope. Why would I be scared? I've gone this way lots of times."

Elin ruffled his hair and then gave him a light tap on the back. "Off we go, then." Whereas before he had been skipping along, Jesse's feet began to drag. Elin's face softened as she strolled after him. When they were almost at the place where he'd been bitten, his feet faltered and came to a standstill.

"The other day," he said, "when it was still winter, I saw a rabbit. A real beauty, pure white. At first, I thought it was just a clump of snow, but then it jumped. When I saw it was a rabbit, I ran after it." His hands mimicked the movements of the rabbit as it ran, then he turned and looked up at Elin. "I pushed my way through those bushes, but suddenly there was this big open space, and I slipped and bumped into a tree. The one with the nest."

Elin nodded, then turned and began pushing her way through the bushes.

"Mom! No! It's dangerous!" Jesse shrieked, his voice cracking.

Elin shoved aside the bushes to make a path and looked back at her son. "It's all right," she said. "Come over here."

Jesse stared at her for a moment, scowling, then walked over. "Give me your lunch," she said. "Climb over these bushes, but don't rush. Once you get across, stand on the edge of the clearing."

He handed her his lunch obediently and climbed over the bushes to stand on the grass on the other side. Elin followed and stood beside him, resting a hand on his shoulder.

"That's the tree with the ant nest, isn't it?"

Jesse gazed up at a tall tree that rose straight toward the sky and nodded.

"Do you notice anything different about it?" Elin asked. "It's not the same as the others."

Jesse frowned and stared at the tree. The clearing looked very bright, perhaps because he had just emerged from the dim forest. The sunshine fell fully on the tree, making its bark shine white. A crack ran up its trunk, a black line that seemed to run from the top to the bottom, as though it had been cut with a sharp knife.

Jesse looked up at his mother. "It's got a crack."

She smiled at him with a twinkle in her eyes and raised her brows. "Is that all? Some of the other trees have cracks, too."

Jesse pursed his lips and examined it again. How was it different from the others? Maybe it's a different species, he thought. No, that can't be it. But then what?

He stared at the tree with the nest for some time without finding an answer. To say so, however, would be to admit defeat. Thinking hard, he compared it with the other trees nearby. "Hmm. For some reason this tree looks brighter than the others," he muttered.

A smile lit up his mother's face, and she gave his shoulder a little shake. "That's it! Now why do you think it looks brighter than the other trees?"

Jesse cocked his head. "Because it gets lots of sunshine?"

"Exactly! Now why does this tree get so much more sunlight than the others?"

"There aren't any trees around it. It's all alone in the middle of the clearing. All the other trees are crowded together so their branches block the sun."

"Right!" Elin nodded and stepped away from him onto the grass. He called after her in a panic but she said, "It's all right. Follow my footsteps."

Jesse walked cautiously across the grass toward her. She pointed to the branches of the trees closest to the one with the nest. "Take a look at the leaves on those trees. What do you see?"

When Jesse looked up, he gasped. "Amazing! They look like lace. All of them! All the leaves around here have been eaten by bugs."

The leaves on some branches had been gnawed off, even the buds, while those on other branches were so riddled with holes, they were like a fine mesh with sunlight glinting through them.

"Yugula fire ants eat leaves as well as bugs," Elin said. "They've got big appetites, too. That's why the leaves and buds on the trees around their nests are usually all gone. These trees can't live without their leaves, and they can't grow unless they sprout new ones. Eventually, they'll rot and fall. That's what happened to the logs you see here."

Elin tapped her foot against a fallen tree half buried in moss and earth. Her foot thudded dully against it. Jesse grimaced. "Those Yugula fire ants are awful," he said.

Elin shook her head. "Maybe, but I bet that tree in which they built their nest is grateful to them."

"Why?"

"Just think about it. The fire ants ate the trees around it. Because those trees are no longer there, it now gets plenty of sunshine, its branches can reach out as far as they want, and it can grow strong and healthy."

"Ah . . ." Jesse looked up at the tree, his lips slightly parted. Reddish-brown ants scurried in and out of the trunk. With its branches spread wide, the tree seemed to soak up the sun contentedly.

"There're many types of fire ants, but most of them live much farther south in damp jungles with lots of rain. Those forests tend to be very dense. Trees need sunlight to grow, so the amount of light a tree can get is very important. When fire ants pick a tree for their nest, they'll eat all the others around it, letting the one they choose grow strong and healthy."

The dappled sunlight fell on Elin's face, and she squinted against the brightness. "Yugula fire ants are unusual because they live in cold places where snow falls. But they still eat the trees surrounding their nest, making a grassy clearing around it. That must be very pleasant for the ants because it's warm."

Jesse observed the ants swarming around the crack in the trunk. "They're like soldiers, aren't they?" he said. "They're probably attacking everything around their base so they can make it bigger."

Elin's brows shot up. He was still so young; she hadn't expected him to say such things. But perhaps he'd learned something about war tactics while play-fighting with other boys. "I see what you mean," she said. "Yugula ants and people both try to make their lives better by snatching up everything around them."

Jesse nodded. "The best way to win is to get lots of powerful allies. That tree was lucky to have such strong bugs on its side."

Elin smiled. "It wasn't lucky. It drew the luck to it."

"What?"

"That's a kogu tree. Its sap smells sweet. The ants made their nest in it because they were drawn to the smell."

Jesse's eyes grew round. "Oh, I get it. The tree used food to get them on its side, just like Potchi!"

"Potchi?"

"Yeah. His father runs the fahko bakery. Potchi used to get his Mom to make jugu cookies and then tell everyone he'd give them some if they'd join him. That's why he always won. I really wanted to beat him one day, even just once."

Jesse's expression changed suddenly. "But how come only that tree has sweet sap? It's not fair. Why don't the others have some? If one tree can attract fire ants while the rest can't, the winner's already decided from the start. That's not a fair fight." He looked up at Elin. "Why is it that way?"

Elin placed a hand on his head. "I don't know, Jesse. But Yugula fire ants aren't the only things trees depend on to survive. Take this tree here, for instance. Its blossoms will be replaced with sweet little fruit. The birds love them and gobble them up, seeds and all. What do you think happens to those seeds?"

Jesse thought for a moment, then grinned. "They come out in their poop. Plop! Plop! Plop!" He burst into a fit of giggles.

Elin laughed and gave him a gentle rap with her knuckles. "I've never figured out why kids like poop so much. But you're right."

Jesse frowned. "But what's the point of turning them into poop? That doesn't help the tree."

"Oh, but it does! Wrapping a seed in poop is like wrapping it in fertilizer. When it falls to the ground, it's got enough food to make it grow big and strong. This tree lets the birds carry its children so they can set down roots all over."

Jesse's eyes widened. "That's pretty smart!" He fell silent, biting his lip as he stared at the trees around him.

"What're you thinking about?" Elin asked.

Frowning, he said, "It's just kind of creepy. It never occurred to me that trees might have thoughts of their own or do things like that. It's weird, you know."

A breeze passed through the wood, stirring the leaves. Looking up at the branches, Jesse shivered. Elin wrapped her arms around him and gave him a squeeze. "When I was about your age, I thought exactly the same thing."

"Really?"

"Uh-huh. Trees, bugs, birds, beasts. I suddenly realized that maybe they weren't what I'd thought they were. If trees can't think or talk, then why can they attract birds to carry their seeds or bugs to protect them? Is it coincidence? Or do trees do it on purpose, and if so, how?"

When she finished speaking, all that could be heard was the rustling of the leaves, the occasional bird hopping from one branch to another, or a trill of birdsong, and even these sounds seemed to sink into the stillness.

Feeling the warmth of her son against her chest, Elin stared at the sky through the branches. "When I was young," she said finally, "I wanted to know all those things. I thought if I read lots of books and studied hard, one day I'd understand . . ."

She rested her chin on Jesse's hair, warmed by the sun. A smile touched her face. "But you know what? I don't think that day will ever come."

Jesse twisted his head to look at her. "Why not? You don't know that, Mom. It might happen."

There was a note of apprehension in his voice, and Elin tightened her grip. "The world is so huge," she murmured, her chin still resting on his head. "And people are so small. It's impossible for just one person to see the whole picture.

"Still, we have words so we can tell others what we find out. There was a beast doctor named Tokima who died a long time ago. But in one of his books he wrote about the galyo, poisonous water lizards that live in the marshes far to the south. He studied them for many years, hoping to find an antidote for their poison. During that process, he accidentally discovered that water temperature determines whether their eggs will hatch males or females. He only wrote a few lines about that, but because I'd read his book, I was able to figure out that water temperature also determines the sex of Toda when they're in the egg."

Still gazing at the sky, she continued, "The life of one person is short, but there're a lot of us. If we keep recording everything we know, down to the smallest scrap of information, those records can lead others to important discoveries. At least, that's what I think. We're living on the far edge of the lives of many who came before us, people we never even knew. In the same way, others will carry on from the far edge of our lives."

Whether Jesse understood or not, she couldn't tell, but he was listening. It doesn't matter, she thought. She hadn't understood most of what her mother had told her either. But fragments of her words had remained deep inside Elin's mind, surfacing again much later, each time bringing memories of her mother, who was long gone.

"Jesse," she murmured in his ear. "Imagine holding a torch. Its light only reaches the world around your feet. But if many people use the flame from that torch to light their own, it will bring a much wider world out of the darkness." She gazed at the trees waving in the spring breeze. "That's what I want to be," she said. "Someone who can pass on that flame."

4

JESSE'S DREAM

Sitting beside the campfire, Jesse unwrapped the layers of oiled paper containing his lunch and looked inside. His eyes widened. "Mom!" he shouted. "Did you wrap our lunch in leaves?"

"Careful!" Elin said. "You'll spill the sauce. Put it flat on your knees."

Jesse hastily did as he was told, bringing his knees together so that the bundle, wrapped in a big, shiny leaf, rested on his lap. He struggled to untie the string that bound it, but it was slippery with juice, making it difficult to undo.

"Why'd you go and tie it up like this?" he grumbled as he worked on the string. "It just makes more work, doesn't it?" When he finally got the leaf open, however, his jaw dropped. "What's this? Meat! And underneath, is that rice?"

Laughing, Elin passed him a pair of chopsticks. "That's right," she said. "Rice is best eaten hot, but it should still taste good even cold. Go ahead and try some."

She had cut the boar meat into chunks to make it easier to eat. Jesse popped a piece into his mouth.

"Mmm!" Juice trickled down his chin. He wiped it away quickly and seemed about to say something, but Elin stopped him.

"Don't rush," she said. "Wait until you've swallowed your food before you talk."

Nodding, Jesse swallowed, then broke into a broad grin. "Wow! Yum!"

"Say 'delicious,' not 'yum.' You need to work on your manners, Jesse."

"Who cares! Something this good is yummy! The meat's so tender!"

Elin watched him as he grasped another chunk of meat with his chopsticks. Slipping her hands under his leaf, she raised the bundle of food up. "Try eating it with the rice, too."

Jesse shoveled some rice and meat into his mouth. His eyes grew round, and his cheeks bulged like a squirrel's when full of nuts. He nodded emphatically. A warmth spread through Elin's chest at the sight of his face. Still holding his leaf for him, she said, "It's boar meat. I wrapped it in this leaf with spicy miso and sweet lacos fruit and steamed it in the oven. The leaf I cooked it in wilted, so I wrapped it in a new one for carrying."

When Jesse had almost finished and could hold his meal with one hand, Elin took a mouthful of her own. Tender boar meat steeped with lacos and spicy miso, rice well flavored with sauce—it was such a delicious and familiar taste.

"My mother used to make this," she said.

Jesse's brows rose. "You mean the Toda doctor?"

"Yes," Elin said. "People in Aluhan territory eat a lot of rice, you know." She had to force down the flood of words that threatened to follow. He was still too young to hear the story of Elin's mother; too young to understand what it meant to have Ahlyo blood or why her mother would have chosen silence, even though it meant she would be executed.

She removed a grain of rice from Jesse's cheek, then tapped his nose playfully with her finger.

Jesse frowned and shook his head. "Stop that! I'm not a kid anymore, you know!"

Elin laughed and took the empty leaf from his lap before he could spill any of the sauce on his clothes. Though delicious, the dish's one flaw was the stickiness of the sauce.

Together, they walked down to the water and washed their hands. Elin passed Jesse a towel and pointed to a bag she had placed in the river. "There's chuku fruit inside that bag. Can you go get them for me?"

"Why me? You're closer," he grumbled as he nonetheless ran over to take out two dark red and well-ripened chuku from the bag. After trotting back to Elin, he handed her one. They sat down on a rock and peeled the fruit, enjoying the sweet, citrusy aroma. The sunshine pouring down on the field kept them comfortably warm.

"Jesse," Elin said as she removed the peel. "You know I got a letter from your father the other day."

"Yeah."

"He told me to ask you about your future."

Jesse blinked. "My future?"

"Yes. You turn eleven this year. It's time you started thinking about what you want to do next. You have a few more options than kids born to the artisan class. Because your father's a Toda Rider, you could rise up into the warrior class if you wanted." Although she fervently hoped he wouldn't choose that path, Elin strove to keep her voice neutral.

Jesse frowned, as though thinking.

"You could also become a cabinetmaker, like your father when we lived in town. In that case, we'll need to find you a good teacher so you can apprentice. You might feel lonely living away from home, but that's what all artisan children do. The master carpenter will pay your food and board, which means your father and I can save up some money for when you go independent."

Jesse glanced at his mother, wondering if he could tell from her face which she wanted him to choose. But she just smiled gently.

A cabinetmaker . . .

The sharp scent of wood chips that pricked his nostrils rose in his mind. Jesse loved watching his father build his beautiful cabinets, smoothing the wood with rhythmic sweeps of his plane, and he'd often made his own toys from scraps of wood. To grow up to be like his father would be awesome.

It would be great to have his room and meals paid for, too. All his friends in town were already apprentices in some trade or other. He felt ashamed to be the only one who was still being fed and cared for by his parents, as though he were a kid. Although the thought of moving away from his mother made him a little anxious, not being able to live away from home would prove he was still a boy. To apprentice like his friends was the manly thing to do. Yet when he tried to picture himself as a cabinetmaker, it just didn't feel right. Why?

As he was pondering the question, he caught a flicker of motion in the corner of his eye. Turning, he saw a little lizard, a kanachoro, climbing up a nearby rock. Its skin shimmered like a rainbow, and light rippled down its back with each movement. Maybe it wanted to nap in the sun, because as soon as it reached the top, it raised its nose and stopped moving.

"Mom," Jesse said. "Do Toda nap in the sun, too?" Glancing at her, he saw she was also looking at the kanachoro.

"Yes, they do. On a sunny day, they crawl out and sunbathe on the riverbanks." She looked at him. "Unlike humans or Royal Beasts, the body temperature of lizards like that kanachoro changes with the temperature of the surroundings. That's why they move a lot more when it's warm."

"Really? Toda, too?"

"Toda are more affected by the surrounding temperature than humans or Royal Beasts, but not as much as lizards or snakes."

"Hmm." A little bubble rose in Jesse's breast and floated up to form words. "Mom, I want to be like you."

His mother blinked.

"Like me?" she asked. "You mean you want to be a beast doctor?"

Jesse was looking at her as though surprised by what he'd just said.

"A beast doctor? Umm. Yeah, I guess, but . . ." Looking up at her, he whispered, "Can I tell you the truth?"

Elin nodded. He took a deep breath, as if he needed to gather his courage. "I want to be a Beast Handler like you," he said.

Elin stared at him, feeling a deep pain in her heart. A Beast Handler. Where had he learned such an expression? She wondered if that's what the guards or teachers called her. These thoughts were followed rapidly by a complex mix of inexpressible emotions that filled her chest.

The boy had lived with the Royal Beasts from the time he was born. He'd watched her control the huge creatures seemingly with ease, even though everyone else feared them and believed they couldn't be tamed. It was only natural that he would want to try controlling them, too. Just as she had once longed to be like her mother, who had looked so brave and calm when she stroked the Toda that scared everyone else.

Unable to find words, Elin could only stare at her son. Dread seeped through her bones, expanding through her body, and the blood drained from her face.

If he chooses to enter Kazalumu School, he's bound to follow the same path as me . . .

Should she say no? Should she forbid him to even consider it? Because she believed that was best for him? Even as these thoughts ran through her mind, however, she knew that would be wrong.

Jesse's life is his own.

When she remembered what had driven her to connect with the Royal Beasts and the beauty of what she had gained through that connection, she couldn't bring herself to bend him to her will. She wanted to tell him everything—not just the joy of communing with the Royal Beasts but also the terrible burden that came with it—so that he could choose for himself. But he was far too young to understand.

I'll just have to take the time he needs and keep thinking about how to tell him while I watch him grow.

"Jesse," she whispered, then drew a deep breath. "If you wish to be a beast doctor, you must study many things so that you can pass the exams and enter Kazalumu School. It's too far to commute to the school in town, so I'll teach you what you need to know."

Jesse leaned forward. "Mom! I want to be—"

Elin raised her hand. "I don't ever want to hear you talk about being a 'handler' of Royal Beasts again, Jesse."

Jesse flinched and hunched his shoulders. "Why?"

Gazing straight into his eyes, Elin said quietly, "You can't understand why I would say that, can you?"

Jesse shook his head.

"That's exactly why you shouldn't say it." As the words left her mouth, Elin heard her mother's voice in her ear. She had once told Elin the same thing. Elin's mouth twisted. "Jesse," she said huskily, "Remember what I just told you and really think about it. If you do, one day you'll understand how I feel."

He scowled, and she gazed at his face silently for a moment. "Once you've decided what you want to be," she said, "tell me. There's no hurry. Think about it carefully before you decide."

In the evening three days later, Jesse told her. He came over to where she was laying out their bedding and announced, "I've made up my mind. Even if you say no, I want to stay with Alu and the others. I'm going to become a beast doctor like you."

Elin stared at him for a long time. A strong light gleamed in his eyes, and she could tell from his stance that he wouldn't change his mind unless she had a very good reason.

If she let him make this choice, she knew that one day he was sure to tread the path she now walked. Yet she longed to let him do what he wished. All this time, she had worked to burn away the thick mist that covered the way ahead. Those efforts would help clear the path for him, too. She would keep trying to chase that mist away, so that when it came time for him to set foot on this road, he could see where it led.

Jesse loved the Royal Beasts from the depths of his being. With that love as his core, he would grow and mature. Once he understood more, he'd be able to grasp unerringly what she had meant before. Then they could talk, as fellow travelers, their eyes fixed on the same destination.

She looked at Jesse and smiled. "In that case, write to your father and tell him what you've decided."

Jesse's eyes brightened. "All right!"

Elin schooled her face into a stern expression. "From tomorrow," she said, "I'll help you with your studies. But Jesse, the entrance exam isn't easy. Children come from all over Lyoza determined to enter Kazalumu School. Whether you get in depends on you. If you fail, you'll have to apprentice. So be prepared."

Jesse pressed his lips together and nodded.

5

SOUNDLESS SOUND

Something hard smacked Elin's forehead, and she opened her eyes with a start. The wind whipped her hair and ruffled the fur on Leelan's neck. Far below she could see the green forest spreading across the land. A chill seized her gut, chasing away all trace of drowsiness. She rubbed the lump that was beginning to swell on her forehead and checked to make sure that the other Beasts were still flying in formation.

She couldn't believe she'd dozed off in the middle of a training flight. It showed how tired she was. For more than a year, she'd not only been training and studying the Royal Beasts, but also teaching Jesse. Fitting Jesse's lessons into an already busy schedule was hard, and at times she had felt sleep sucking her into its embrace. But to fall asleep while in the air!

I've got to get a little more rest.

She'd have to find a way to adjust her schedule. If she got sick, her efforts would have been for nothing. Although physically demanding, the hours she spent with Jesse in the evening were precious. She learned so much about him as she sat by his side and instructed him. He wasn't an easy pupil. For one thing, he didn't accept anything without question. He seemed to have his own unusual perspective and stubbornly resisted memorizing what she taught him until it made sense according to his own logic.

Even if he gets in to Kazalumu School, his teachers are going to be in for a challenge. And the other kids may get fed up with him, too.

Although this was a concern, Elin knew she had the same stubborn streak, and seeing it in him gave her a strange feeling. Recalling Jesse's frowning face as he demanded to know why, she realized how incredibly patient her mentor Joeun had been.

She glanced at Leelan. Unlike Jesse, the Royal Beast memorized every command and did what she was told without question. If Elin tried to make her do something she didn't want, she'd resist. But she never asked why. Although sometimes the Royal Beasts would gesture or cry out, as if checking whether they were doing what Elin wanted, they didn't ask for explanations.

If only Leelan would, she thought. If only we could talk about such things together.

She'd thought this many times and tried to find ways to make it happen. But she had yet to achieve such a complex conversation. As she flew along lost in thought, Elin suddenly realized it was getting harder to see ahead. Thick clouds covered the sky, blocking the sun. It had started growing darker a while back, and the air had felt chilly against her skin. Now, however, the clouds seemed to disintegrate, wrapping the world in white mist.

Elin frowned. What should I do? We're almost there.

She was headed toward the Stone Colonnade, a valley studded with great rock pillars that rose up to pierce the heavens. She'd been planning to fly the Royal Beasts through the pillars without breaking formation, but it would be too dangerous to fly through the rocks in the mist.

As she pondered what to do, the mist thickened rapidly, wrapping itself around Leelan's body as she flew. The way forward was veiled by white clouds. When Elin glanced to the side, she could no longer see Eku or the others.

We'd better go back, she thought, and raised her harp. At that moment, Leelan flapped her wings and swerved suddenly.

"Whoa!" Elin was jerked sideways. The harp flew from her hand, hitting the saddle before it bounced off. If it hadn't been tied to her with a rope, it would have plunged to the ground far below. She grabbed the saddle with one hand and fumbled for her harp with the other. A chill ran along her back as her eyes followed Leelan's wings slicing through the wind.

Something stroked her face, like a ripple running across it, and Leelan swerved once again. The mist swirled, caught by the gust from Leelan's wings. A huge shadow loomed through the break, and Elin caught her breath.

The stone columns!

They'd already reached the Stone Colonnade! And were flying blind right through those pillars! It was only a matter of time before they crashed into them.

"Leelan!" Elin screamed, her lips trembling. "Up! Fly up!"

They had to get up above the rocks. But the moment she stroked the harp to tell the other Beasts to rise, she was thrown so violently to one side she thought her shoulder would dislocate. Something skimmed the tip of her head. Looking up, her eyes widened. Right above her was damp black stone. Leelan had been flying underneath a rock outcrop.

Fear seized Elin, and she froze, not knowing what to tell the Beasts. All she could do was cling to the saddle so that she wouldn't fall off.

Leelan appeared to be following Elin's last command to move up because she was rising higher. Rock pillars appeared from the mist but Leelan never hit one. With powerful strokes she twisted and turned, slipping through them with ease.

As Elin gave herself up to the flight, she noticed something strange. Leelan was avoiding the stones before they came into view. It was only after Leelan swerved that Elin saw each pillar. The Royal Beast seemed to be keeping a fixed distance between herself and the stones, as though she could feel their location without having to see them. Although she had no idea where the other Beasts were, Elin heard no thud of impact or screams of pain, so she assumed they must be evading the columns as well.

But how?

Straining every nerve to feel what Leelan was doing, she realized that a split second before Leelan's muscles rippled for a swerve, her ears pricked. And just before that, Elin felt something—a ripple of air—caress her face. That's when Leelan's ears twitched.

Wind? Was Leelan reading the movement of the wind? No. It seemed more like she was listening to something. But what? Elin could hear nothing.

A soundless sound, she thought.

At that moment, the world around her brightened, and Leelan burst above the mist. Gazing down, Elin felt goosebumps rise on her skin. Below her, the other Beasts flew in perfect formation, keeping a fixed distance between each one.

Royal Beasts weren't like humans. Perhaps they could measure distance with something other than their eyes. Speechless, Elin stared at their radiant forms.

6

JESSE ENROLLS

The entrance exam for Kazalumu School took place on the morning of a very hot summer day. Those who passed would return to Kazalumu in the fall when school started.

As she did every morning, Elin sent the Royal Beasts into the pasture so she could clean the stables. But she couldn't stop thinking about Jesse, who would be sitting in a classroom, taking the exam. One after another, his weak points popped into her mind, and she felt her chest tighten. If he failed the test and had to leave the Royal Beasts behind to become an artisan, he would probably have a more peaceful life. But having seen how diligently he'd studied, driven solely by his desire to be with the Beasts, she couldn't help but hope that he passed.

The school bell sounded, and Elin paused in the middle of wiping the floor. The bell marked the end of the exam. The teachers would now gather to mark the papers. She'd done it herself every year until a few years ago; she could picture in her mind exactly what was going on.

She had planned to keep on with her chores until Jesse came to tell her the results, but when she heard the bell that signaled the marks were in, she couldn't stand it any longer. She dashed from the stable and headed toward the school. When she reached the familiar dark hallway and took off her dirty boots, her heart pounded and her knees shook.

Shafts of sunlight slanted through the windows onto the wide corridor. As she walked along it, a group of teachers at the other end turned and saw her. Tomura raised his brows and smiled, but she was too anxious to respond in kind. She bowed her head slightly, then stared rigidly at the room where the children were awaiting the verdict.

Because the day was hot, all the doors leading into the corridor, as well as all the windows, were open wide. Bathed in bright summer sunshine, the room was filled with twelve-year-olds sitting tensely as they were handed their papers. Elin saw Jesse sitting second from the back by the window.

Once every child had their test, Esalu spoke, her face stern. "Look at your marks," she said. "Those who received eighty-seven points or above have passed."

A murmur rose from the children. Joy suffused the faces of some who could barely keep from jumping out of their seats. Others, however, put their heads on their desks and buried their faces in their arms. This was a scene Elin had witnessed many times, but she still found it difficult to watch the children who had failed. She kept her eyes on Jesse. He was biting his lip, his eyes on a girl weeping bitterly in front of him. Elin gripped her hands, unable to tell from his face if he'd passed or failed.

Jesse tore his eyes away from the girl and looked around the classroom. When he caught sight of Elin, his eyes widened, then he grinned.

He passed.

Relief drained the strength from Elin's body, and she leaned against the wall. She was trembling so much, she was embarrassed.

She felt a hand on her shoulder and raised her head. "Congratulations,"

Tomura said, an odd smile on his face. "Jesse's test was quite something. I burst out laughing when I was marking it."

"You did?" Elin said.

The other teachers smiled among themselves as Tomura continued. "He had you as his teacher, so he placed third overall in every subject. Otherwise he might have had a hard time passing with that answer."

"What answer?" Elin asked nervously, and Tomura's grin widened.

"His answer to the essay question on why he wanted to enter the school. I've been a teacher here a long time, but I've never seen anything quite like it. He wrote in big black letters, *I love the Royal Beasts! So I want to be like my mother!*"

Elin blushed bright red. She didn't know if she should laugh or feel embarrassed, so she kept her head down. Still chuckling, Tomura patted her on the shoulder. "Just proves he's your son, doesn't it?"

After that, Jesse played like he'd forgotten what studying meant, reaching the day of the entrance ceremony in high spirits around the time the autumn winds began to blow. On the morning of the ceremony, he changed into his new clothes. As he tied his belt, he said suddenly, "I guess Dad won't be coming, will he?"

Elin had just reached out to straighten his collar. She paused and looked at him. "I did write and tell him the date of the ceremony, but there've been quite a few skirmishes lately. It was probably difficult for him to get leave to come. I'm sorry, but you'll have to be patient. The fathers of many other students won't be able to make it either."

She adjusted his collar and stood up. "Let's go, then. We live really close. We wouldn't want that to end up making us late, would we?"

Though his face was still clouded, Jesse nodded and grasped his brand-new schoolbooks under his arm.

On sunny days, the entrance ceremony was held outside, but on rainy days, it was held in the dining hall. The day was cloudy with a light drizzle, and so the new students, who came from all over the kingdom, marched down the corridor toward the hall. As they stepped, tense-faced, through the door, applause erupted, and they stopped in surprise. The students from the higher grades stood in two rows, from the youngest to the eldest, welcoming the newcomers with smiles and waves.

"Line up!" Esalu's powerful voice carried through the room. "That's it. Line up in single file and pass between the other students."

The boy at the front of the line stepped forward hesitantly, glancing behind him occasionally. The older students clasped hands and raised their arms above their heads to make an arch. Ducking, the new students began walking through the tunnel. They moved shyly at first, but gradually relaxed as the other students called out encouragingly. Their backs straightened, and by the end, they were skipping through.

Watching Jesse hop along, Elin remembered how she and Yuyan used to hold hands like this to welcome younger students. Beside her, a youthful father stretched to see his child, and his shoulder touched Elin's. "Pardon me," he said.

"Not at all," Elin said with a smile. Looking at his happy face, she sighed inwardly. I wonder what Ialu's doing, she thought. She wished he could have seen Jesse in his hour of triumph.

Esalu clapped her hands sharply, and the hall fell silent. "Attention, everyone!" she called out. "The entrance ceremony will now begin!"

At that moment, the door behind the parents opened with a click. Turning to look, Elin saw several parents who had arrived late step apologetically into the room. Catching sight of the figure in the rear, she blinked, unable to believe her eyes.

"Ialu!" she exclaimed, then clapped a hand to her mouth. Bowing in apology for disturbing the silence, Ialu walked over and stood beside her. He smelled of the cool autumn breeze and, very faintly, of Toda. Elin gaped at him. He flashed her a quick smile, then touched her shoulder, gesturing for her to look forward.

The children were all craning their necks to see what was going on, when suddenly Jesse jumped out of his seat with a shout. "Dad!" he cried. Turning to the others, he pointed. "That's my father!" The other parents grinned.

With a bang, Esalu slammed her hand on her desk. "Jesse! Quiet, please!"

Jesse snapped to attention and bowed his head. "I'm sorry," he said, and sat down.

"Once again, the ceremony will now begin," Esalu said. She gestured with her right hand, and a row of students in the front lifted wooden flutes to their lips. As soon as they began playing, the other students and teachers raised their voices in the school's song of welcome. Singing the familiar tune, Elin felt her eyes blur.

Ialu was supposed to be off guarding distant caravan cities. He must have ridden for days, changing horses along the way, she thought. Knowing what feeling had driven him to make such an effort, a warmth spread from her chest to the tips of her fingers. Beside her stood her husband. Before her was her son, who had just become a student of Kazalumu. Although she couldn't stop time from moving on, this moment of happiness was right here, right now.

SEVEN

SPRING FLIGHT

I

ALU AND JESSE

Winter was more than half over when a message reached Kazalumu from the Yojeh. The snow that had been falling for days finally lifted after lunch, and the winter sky showed itself for the first time in a long while. It was then that the palace messenger, who had been stopped by the snow in the town below, was able to deliver her letter.

Esalu led the messenger to the guest room to wait in case an answer was required. She then put on her snow boots and, taking the letter, went to the training grounds to find Elin. As she trudged along the snowy road, she was conscious of her aching knees, and by the time she had trekked through the forest, she was gasping for breath. When she stepped onto the snowy plain, which seemed to stretch forever, the sun was beginning to tilt in the sky, tinting the snow pale pink. Royal Beasts stood scattered over the field.

"Elin!" she called.

Elin was standing beside Alu. She turned and, seeing Esalu, hurried across the snow, taking care not to slip.

"What is it?" she asked.

"There's a message for you from the Yojeh," Esalu said, rubbing her knees. "I assume it isn't urgent because it wasn't sent by horse, but as the messenger was delayed for some time by the snow, I thought you should probably look at it right away." She took the letter from inside her cloak and handed it to Elin.

Elin pulled off her gloves with her teeth and broke the seal. The letter was written partly in code so that only those who knew it could understand the content. As she read, Elin's face clouded slightly.

"What's it say?" Esalu asked.

Elin looked up and handed her the letter. "She's asking about our progress here. It's not urgent, but . . ."

Esalu's eyes swept across the page. When she finished, she sighed. "I see. The Yojeh's starting to worry."

After sharing the situation at the palace and inquiring about the training, Seimiya had asked when they would begin breeding more Royal Beasts at the sanctuary. True to Seimiya's character, her words were gentle, but the fact that she mentioned breeding at all—something she'd always avoided—could have meant people were beginning to question Elin's methods.

Knowing how Elin felt about making a Royal Beast corps, Seimiya was probably concerned that none of the Beasts but Leelan showed any sign of breeding. Perhaps she also wanted to confirm Elin's true intentions so she could refute point-blank the doubts of her subjects.

Esalu looked at the Royal Beasts napping in the sun. "Lesseh and the others have certainly grown, haven't they?" she said. The youngest were perched partway up a cliff, their wings spread toward the sun as they warmed their bellies. These were new additions brought to the sanctuary from the wild three years earlier. Of the four, Lesseh and Osseh were males, while Kaseh and Fuseh were females; they were all nearly four years old.

"Do you think they'll take their mating flight this spring?" Esalu asked. Royal Beasts in the wild matured and began breeding at the age of four, but Nola, Ukalu, and Tohba still hadn't mated, even though they'd been brought to Kazalumu Sanctuary many years ago and were closer to Leelan in rank. When Leelan came into heat, they became restless, but they didn't fly and mate. Leelan and Eku were the only mating pair in the sanctuary, and only their offspring increased.

"I wonder what's stopping them from maturing," Esalu said. They had raised all the Beasts just as they had raised Leelan. What could be the difference?

Sunk in thought, Esalu and Elin gazed at the Royal Beasts standing on the snowy plain. Far in the distance, the school bell announced the evening hour. The two stirred and looked at each other.

"I'll tell Lady Seimiya everything we've done so far," Elin murmured.

Esalu frowned, but after a brief pause, nodded. "Yes, I guess you should."

Elin adjusted her grip on the harp and strummed notes that urged the Royal Beasts back to the stables. At the sound, they spread their wings and leaped into the sky.

They're pretty late. Jesse stamped his feet in the snow and gazed at the sky. He'd been waiting a long time. He'd tried shaping the white puffs of his breath on the air and sculpting Royal Beasts from the snow that had collected on the branches, but it was just too cold. Yet he didn't want to go home either.

It was partly because all his friends had gone back to their families for winter break, and he was bored and lonely. But it was also because this was his only chance to spend time with the Royal Beasts, and he'd been looking forward to it. There was no spare time during the school term, but since the holidays had started, he'd slipped through the woods every day to the training grounds, careful not to let his mother or the headmistress see him. There, he'd watched his mother studying and training the Beasts. By now he could guess the meaning of every sound Elin's harp produced.

He cupped his hands around his hot water bottle to warm them, occasionally touching it to his nose as well. At last, he heard the faint sound of a harp far in the distance.

"Ah! Finally!" Through a lace of dark branches, he stared at the snow-laden sky. Soon he heard the soft whir of wings, then saw the shapes of the Royal Beasts against the gray clouds. At this, he shoved two fingers in his mouth and let out a short, sharp whistle. One of the Beasts turned its head and looked down as it crossed the heavens. Jesse's face lit up.

"Alu," he called, keeping his voice low. Alu saw him and, leaving the pack, dropped down, deftly evading the tree branches. The wind from the Beast's enormous wings hit Jesse in the face as he skipped over the snow. Alu landed in a little hollow, and he ran over and buried his face in her chest.

The warm scent of Beast was mixed with a whiff of snow and wind. Of all the Royal Beasts, Jesse loved Alu best. They'd been together since he was little. He thought of Leelan as his mother's, and Alu as his own.

Listening to the rumbling sound of Alu's breathing, he clung to her while she looked down at him affectionately, as if he were a playful little brother. When he'd hugged her long enough, Jesse stepped back and pulled a large paper bag from his cloak. It contained eight baked sweets covered in red sugar. Catching the scent, Alu made a cooing sound as though she couldn't wait. *Shashasha.* She loved sweets.

Jesse popped them in her mouth, and she gobbled them up before licking her nose contentedly.

Jesse brushed the crumbs from her chest. "See you, Alu," he said. He wished he could stay longer, but if she arrived much later than the others, it might make people worry and cause a big fuss.

Perhaps she'd had enough sweets, because Alu flew off without protest when he gave her a shove, following her family to the stable.

The inside of the stable was dark and warmed by the heat of the Royal Beasts. The dinner bell rang. Elin raised her head from the book on her writing desk.

Is it already this late?

Time literally seemed to fly by these days. She'd better hurry home or

Jesse would grumble that he was starving. She folded the sheaf of papers on which she'd been jotting down what she wanted to tell Seimiya and stuffed it into the front of her robe, then stood up and put out the fire. As she always did before leaving the stable, she took the lantern and went to each stall to check on Leelan, Eku, and their children.

Leelan and Eku were sound asleep. She passed their stalls and came to a halt in front of Alu. She stared at the face of the sleeping Beast, who should already have been a mature female, and spoke to her silently.

Alu, you're old enough to be an adult. Why haven't you grown up?

Memories passed through her mind one by one. Alu when she had dropped from her mother's womb, a wet ball of fur. Alu nuzzling Elin insistently and cooing plaintively. In the wild, she would have mated, given birth, and raised cubs long ago, yet she was still like a cub herself. When she wasn't training, she showed no interest in soaring through the air and instead spent her time napping in the pasture. Somehow she reminded Elin of the Beasts in the sanctuary that had dull gray wings and were raised on, and controlled by, tokujisui.

I'm missing some crucial key in their development.

The Royal Ancestor Jeh would have known what kept Beasts raised in the sanctuary from mating even though they weren't given tokujisui. And what was needed for them to mature and mate. After all, she'd bred two thousand of them.

Elin pursed her lips and stared at the Royal Beasts. What had these creatures been to Jeh? She could understand Jeh's longing to avert another catastrophe, and why she had chosen this difficult path to lead her people to prosperity. But her eyes had been fixed solely on her people, not on what was best for the Royal Beasts.

The way Jeh and her descendants had dealt with both the Royal Beasts and the Toda had been cruel. To cement royal power, and later to gain crushing military strength, they'd used these creatures as convenient tools, warping their bodies for their own ends without a thought for their health or well-being. They'd perverted the lives of these creatures to preserve the lives of their people.

Elin took a deep breath. And now here she was, training Royal Beasts to fly into battle.

But her goal wasn't the same as Jeh's. "I cannot set you free," she whispered to Alu. "I may be leading you to your death. Yet, even so . . ." Swallowing the rest of her sentence, she closed her eyes.

Perhaps disturbed by the murmur of Elin's voice, Alu stirred and ran her tongue over the tip of her nose. A sweet scent wafted on the air. Elin's eyes flicked open, and her brow furrowed. Alu hadn't been fed anything that would give off such a sweet scent. Bringing her face up against the cage bars, she raised the lantern. Something glittered on Alu's chest. Squinting, Elin made out grains of red sugar clinging to her fur.

A chill spread through her. Jesse . . .

When he was little, Jesse had always split his sweets with Alu. Elin had made him put the sweets in the feed box, warning him sharply that he must never feed her by hand; it was too dangerous. Maybe he'd fed her by hand when she wasn't looking. She grimaced and left the stables.

2

BEAST FANGS

When Elin approached the house, the younger guard's head was poking out the window, watching for her. He opened the door and let her inside. "It's a cold day, isn't it?" he said. Exposed to the frigid air, the skin on his face was white except for his nose. The middle-aged guard was in the back making dinner, but he looked up and bowed as Elin came through.

"Yes, indeed! It's very cold. I'm so sorry to have kept you waiting," Elin said. "Please go ahead and eat your dinner."

The young guard grinned. "I'm all right," he said, "but young Jesse has been banging his plate with his spoon for some time now."

Elin nodded and strode through the passageway to the door of her house. The living room with the hearth in its center lay beyond the dirt-floored kitchen, which was equipped with a clay oven and sink. Jesse was sitting by the hearth, clanging his spoon against a plate. Catching sight of Elin, he scowled and started banging the plate harder.

"You're so late!" he exclaimed. Noticing the expression on her face, he paused, spoon in midair. He had grown so much he was beginning to look like a youth, but at the moment, his uneasy expression showed he was still a boy.

"Come on. We're going to the stable," Elin said as she turned and left the room.

The guards, who had just sat down and were balancing a bowl of stew on their knees, looked up with curious eyes.

"Where are you going?" one of them asked.

"I'm so sorry, but I must take Jesse to the stable. I'll ring the little bell outside the building when we leave to let you know we're coming back. Please carry on with your meal."

Resting his bowl of stew on the edge of the hearth, the young guard stood up and took down a lantern from the wall. He lit it and handed it to Elin while the older guard rose and opened the door. A cold gust of air swirled into the room with a flurry of snowflakes. The guard glanced at the sky, so black not a star could be seen. "It's snowing pretty bad now," he murmured.

Elin nodded and stepped into the night. She felt Jesse staring at her nervously, but she didn't spare him even a glance. Outside, the brutal cold gripped her body. Although the stable was close, her cheeks and nose burned with the cold of the howling wind. Even when she reached the building, her hands were so icy she had trouble unlocking the door. Stepping inside, she felt her body relax into the air warmed by the Beasts.

Leelan and the others stirred at the sound of the door, but closed their eyes when they saw it was Elin and Jesse who had entered. Elin hung the lantern on the wall and looked down at her son.

"You know why I brought you here, don't you?"

Jesse looked up at her. "Yeah. I know." He bowed his head as if resigned to his fate. "I'm sorry," he said.

Elin watched him without responding. He began to fidget, rubbing his hands against his thighs and stubbing his toe against the ground. "Jesse," Elin finally said, her voice quiet. "Sometimes it's meaningless to say you're sorry. What I want from you is not an apology."

Jesse's face tensed. She could see the confusion in his eyes. What was he supposed to do if she wouldn't forgive him when he apologized?

"When you believe a promise you've made is important, Jesse, you never break it. The fact that you broke your promise shows you don't understand why it's necessary. Am I right?"

Jesse frowned.

"You can't understand why you shouldn't be allowed to go near the Royal Beasts. Isn't that it?"

"Well, yeah," Jesse mumbled. Then he lifted his jaw defiantly. "It's just so unfair. Why am I the only one who's not allowed to go near them? You get to be with them all the time. I want to be with them, too!"

His shrill voice pierced the air. The Beasts stirred, opening their eyes, and Jesse clapped his hands over his mouth. But Elin watched him silently without glancing at the Beasts.

Keeping her eyes fixed on his, she said, "You know that's not true. You're not the only one. In fact, no one but Professor Esalu and I can go to the training grounds. None of the other students can go either. Not even Professor Tomura's allowed in. And, Jesse, I never go near the Beasts without the Silent Whistle. And I would never, ever feed them sweets. In fact, if there's anyone who thinks he deserves special treatment, it's you."

Jesse frowned. "What do you mean?"

Elin's voice was hard. "Are you telling me you really don't know? I can read your mind, Jesse. You're thinking that Alu would never hurt *you*. Right?"

Jesse's eyes wavered. A muscle bulged in his jaw as though he was steeling himself against being told something he didn't want to hear, something he didn't want to know. Elin watched him steadily. His eyes said, 'I know what you're going to say. The same thing you always say. I'm sick and tired of hearing it.' He was just thirteen. When she was his age, she had felt the same way. No matter how hard people had tried to convince her, she hadn't understood. Not when she turned fourteen or eighteen either.

But she had to make him see. Because if she waited until he was ripped to pieces, it would be too late.

Turning on her heel, she walked to the back of the stables, grabbed a long-handled broom that was leaning against the wall, and came back to his side. She looked down at him. "I've lived with Leelan since long before you were born, Jesse," she said. "I love her a lot, just as you love Alu. And I think Leelan loves me, too. You can feel that, can't you?"

Jesse nodded warily, uncertain where this was leading.

"But, Jesse, listen. If I were to smack Leelan with this broom while she's sleeping, she'd bare her fangs and snap at me. If she bit me, she'd cut my fingers off just like that." She held her left hand in front of his face, revealing the stumps of three missing fingers. "When Leelan chomped these off, she was mad with rage. She bit off the nose, lips, and hand of the man in front of her and ate them. If I hadn't blown the Silent Whistle, she would have torn off my head without a second thought."

Shaking, Elin took a deep breath. "That's the kind of creatures Royal Beasts are. No matter how well they know you, no matter how fond of you they are, they could still gobble you up in a reflex action."

Jesse stared up at her, his face white and rigid. Elin gripped the broom tightly. "Grownups warned me so many times, Jesse. But I never believed them. In the bottom of my heart, I was sure Leelan would never harm me. I believed that she would turn her fangs aside so as not to hurt me. I never dreamed she would bite off my fingers and eat them—until she did."

Quietly, Elin turned and walked to Leelan's cage. With the broom still gripped in one hand, she opened the upper half of the door.

Realizing from his mother's face and actions what she was about to do, Jesse opened his mouth to scream, but nothing came out. Before his terrified gaze, she raised the broom and jabbed Leelan in the stomach. Leelan's eyes flew open, and her enormous jaws snapped up the broom, handle and all.

Jesse saw his mother let go of the broom as though she'd been burned and topple over backward. Leelan chewed the broom to pieces, spewing fragments across the floor. Raising her wings, she broke into a menacing growl, waking the other Beasts, who flapped their wings in agitation.

Sprawled on the floor and gripping her right hand tightly with her left, Elin said over and over, "I'm so sorry, Leelan. I'm so sorry." Maybe it was the tone of her voice or maybe it was because she had only hit her with a broom, but Leelan didn't threaten her for long. She grumbled sulkily for a while, then fell quiet. Even so, the fur on her chest bristled, and she shifted restlessly.

Elin rose, gritting her teeth. Cautiously she approached the cage and closed it gently before returning to Jesse's side. Blood seeped from the fingers of her right hand where she gripped it with her left.

Jesse paled and began trembling. "M-mom . . . ," he gasped.

She smiled reassuringly. "I'm all right. She just grazed my finger, that's all. Get me the first aid kit, will you?"

After dashing over to the shelf, Jesse lifted down the kit with both hands and brought it to his mother. She was sitting by the stove stirring the embers in the fire. The flames flared up, and their light fell on her blood-soaked right hand. Sniffing back his sobs, Jesse plunked himself down beside his mother and stared at the crimson stain spreading along her skin.

"Open the lid and get out the bottle of atsune infusion," Elin said. "Yes, that's the one. See that cotton? Soak it with the infusion and give it to me, please."

Jesse did as he was told and poured the liquid over the cloth. His hands were shaking so badly that he spilled quite a lot on the floor. The pungent odor stung his nostrils. He passed the cotton to his mother, and she dabbed the wound with it. No matter how much she wiped, however, blood kept welling up.

"Give me some more of that cotton, Jesse. Just the dry cotton is fine." She pressed it tightly against the wound for some time, then carefully removed it, revealing the cut. There was a deep gash in the flesh between her index finger and thumb. Jesse drew in a sharp breath. Shaking violently, he screwed up his face and resisted the urge to turn away, keeping his eyes fixed on the wound.

Elin reached into the first aid kit with her left hand and removed a needle that had already been threaded. "Take some cotton soaked in atsune and wipe the needle with it, will you?"

Biting his lower lip, Jesse sterilized the needle.

The wind picked up, and the roof rattled. The flames wavered in puffs of air that had forced their way through a crack in the wall. Mother and son huddled around the dim light cast by the fire, tending the wound and saying only what was necessary. The silent Beasts stood like statues shrouded in darkness.

3

VOICE IN A DREAM

The distance from the stable to their home was short, but as they walked, Elin could feel chills coming on. She guessed it wasn't so much from being bitten as from pushing herself for too long. Fatigue assailed her, and occasionally, her body was racked with shudders. Her joints ached. Not wanting to make Jesse feel any worse, Elin hid her discomfort. They ate dinner and went to bed as usual. But lying beside him, the chills that shook her grew steadily worse.

She wrapped the quilt around her tightly and shook uncontrollably until her body flushed with heat and she burst into a sweat. Perhaps her fever had reached its peak. In her fevered dreams, Elin heard Leelan's voice. As a child, she'd dreamed before of Leelan speaking like a human.

"Children must be kicked from the nest," Leelan said. She spread her wings and raised her head to the sky, letting out a roar. Even that sounded like a voice. "When they're kicked from the nest, they become parents."

This scene ran through Elin's brain repeatedly.

She woke. The strange slumber clung to her like the bottom of a muddy bog, and she had to fight to peel herself away. It was still dark, and the house was wrapped snuggly in the stillness of snow. She pulled her right arm from the sweat-drenched covers, and the dull ache in her hand became a vivid throbbing.

Her throat was parched. Reaching for the cup she'd placed by her pillow, Elin took a long pull on the spout. As she gulped the icy water, she felt her body relax. The wind had died down, and the only sound in the darkness was the steady breathing of her son beside her.

Why had she had that dream? Because she was worried about Alu? Because she felt guilty about hitting Leelan with the broom and scolding Jesse so harshly? Placing a hand on her sweat-beaded forehead, she felt her fever. "Children must be kicked from the nest." She ran these words over in her mind. She'd heard them before. But from whom?

Unable to sleep, she searched through distant memories until an old familiar face rose behind her closed eyelids.

I'd hate to be kicked out of home! Good thing I was born human.

She recalled Yuyan's soft voice, the grimace on her face as she'd whispered in Elin's ear. Following that voice, the memory came back to her.

Ah, that's right. It was in class.

A day long ago floated into her mind like a faded picture. Her desk bathed in honey-colored light from the afternoon sun; Yuyan sitting in front of her; Professor Losa, a teacher Elin disliked, lecturing on how foxes raised their young and sent them out into the world . . .

But why would I remember something that happened so long ago? The fever must have affected her brain. After all, there was no way Leelan could have talked to her about children and nests.

Something clicked inside. Opening her eyes, Elin stared blankly at the darkness, watching an idea take shape in her mind.

"Honestly! You never learn, do you?" Esalu said with a sigh.

Jesse had dragged the headmistress to their house, and Elin was now struggling to sit up under her stern gaze. "You haven't changed a bit," Esalu continued. "You get so caught up in things that you never stop to consider your health. If you go on like this, you're going to get really sick. You're not as young as you think, you know."

After scolding Elin roundly, Esalu knelt down and rested a hand on her forehead. "Your fever's not so high."

"It went down after I broke into a sweat," Elin said weakly. "I'm so sorry you had to come out here this early in the morning."

Esalu snorted. "I'm used to it. Children are always getting into mischief at odd hours of the day. Although no one gets into as much trouble as you." She unwrapped the bandage on Elin's hand and deftly examined the wound. "Considering that you were grazed by Leelan's teeth, it's a pretty clean cut. Not much swelling either."

Esalu glanced at Jesse, who was peering at his mother's hand. "Now, boy, when someone gets bitten by a beast and comes down with a fever, what do you need to watch out for?"

Jesse wrinkled his nose. "I haven't learned that yet."

"In that case, remember what I tell you. There are several things you need to keep an eye out for."

Jesse's face blanched as she described the symptoms of rabies and tetanus. "Does she have those?" he asked fearfully.

Esalu shrugged. "Who knows? But I think we can assume she doesn't have rabies by now. You should watch out for signs of tetanus, though. Make sure you take good care of her."

Jesse nodded, looking quite anxious, and Esalu smiled. "Time to start your nursing duties. Go make her some breakfast. She's got a fever, so make something that's nutritious but easy to digest to build up her strength."

"Okay."

"Hop to it!" Esalu snapped. Jesse jumped to attention, then disappeared into the kitchen to escape any further scolding.

Esalu and Elin smiled as they watched him go. "It's good to give him a fright sometimes," Esalu said. "After all, his mother never gave up no matter how many times I scared her."

With a wry smile, Elin nodded. Then she turned serious. "May I ask you a favor?" she said. "Could you please send for Olamu? I want to see him."

Esalu frowned. "Olamu? You mean the Beast Hunter?"

"Yes."

"But what for? He must be quite old now. I heard that his son took over his job."

Elin nodded. "Yes, that's what his son told me when he brought Lesseh here. Olamu may be old, but if his mind's still sharp, there's something I want to ask him."

The gleam of curiosity in Esalu's eyes deepened. "You went and visited him once before, didn't you? With Jesse on your back."

"Yes. Olamu helped me when I was trying to learn about Royal Beasts in the wild. I doubt there's anyone alive who knows them as well as he does."

Esalu's brows rose. "He's pretty stubborn, though."

Elin grinned. "Yes, he is. But all the Beast Hunters are."

"True." Having disinfected the wound, Esalu began winding a bandage around it. "What do you want to ask him?" she said.

When Elin told her, Esalu paused and raised her face. She stared at Elin for a moment, then nodded slowly. "I see. That's a possibility all right," she murmured. Excitement kindled in her eyes. "Are you going to tell the Yojeh?"

Elin shook her head. "No, not yet. I'll describe the current situation, but in a way that lets her know I haven't given up hope that Alu and the others will mature."

Esalu nodded. "Yes, that would be best. I'll tell the messenger to wait a little longer. You won't be able to write properly with that hand, so dictate what you want to say. I'll write it for you."

"Thank you. I'm sorry to trouble you."

Esalu's lips twitched. "I'm sure the Yojeh will be happy I'm writing it. Your handwriting's so hard to read." Although her words were sharp, her expression was bright and cheerful. Elin loved this teacher who never lost her curiosity, no matter how old she got.

4

THE BEAST HUNTER

Olamu came to visit just before the snow melted. He had grown somewhat stooped with age, but with a leather satchel slung across his back and a hatchet hanging from his waist, he still resembled the tough and vigorous hunter who used to dart through the deep forests to capture Royal Beast cubs.

Sitting down at the hearth in Esalu's office, he gruffly accepted the hot tea the headmistress served him. The refreshing citrusy aroma coupled with the hiss of steam from the earthenware teapot reminded Elin of when Joeun had brought her here so many years ago. "Thank you so much for coming all this way to see me," she said.

Olamu pulled in his jaw a little at this. "Ain't much fer me to do right now. It'll be a while before the rulers of our valley start movin'."

The hunters called the Royal Beasts "rulers" and named each one after the territory it controlled. When Elin had trekked through the mountains with Jesse on her back to visit Olamu, he had told her to leave the wild Beasts to the hunters and slammed the door in her face. She was a teacher from the sanctuary, he'd insisted, so she should have stuck to caring for the Royal Beasts they captured. That was her job.

Hunting grounds were passed down from father to son. As these boundaries were considered sacred, it was no wonder that Olamu had taken offense when Elin had trespassed on his territory. But she'd felt crushed, having hoped he would teach her what he knew about these creatures' habits.

Still, she hadn't given up. She forged into the mountains with Jesse, setting up camp in the woods each night after spending the day searching for Royal Beasts. Three days after Olamu turned her away, she was overjoyed to stumble upon a Royal Beast perched partway down a steep cliff. She set up her tent well outside the Beast's personal territory and began watching.

She had been there for about four days when Olamu appeared in front of her tent. Although he looked just as fierce as when he had shut her out of his house, this time he didn't shout at her. Clearing his throat, he said, "My son thinks you're the one who rescued the lord of Akadake. Is that true?"

By the lord of Akadake, he meant Eku, the mature male that had been wounded trying to protect his cub and brought to Kazalumu for treatment. It was Olamu who had accidentally caused the injury, a miscalculation he thought would shame him for life. He had wept when he learned that Eku had not only been healed at the sanctuary, but had mated with Leelan and miraculously conceived a cub.

All this he told Elin. From then on, he had guided her through the mountains, sharing experiences from his long career. Although she had only been able to stay a month, Elin had gleaned much from Olamu about how Royal Beasts lived in the wild.

In Esalu's office, Olamu placed his cup on the table and raised his face. "That talkative chap who brought me here, is that the babe you were carryin' on your back?"

Elin's mouth crooked. "Yes, and my apologies. I hope he didn't talk your ear off."

Olamu's eyes twinkled. "Well, he certainly was full of questions, that one. 'What's that hatchet for? What's in your bag? How d'ya find them Royal Beasts?' Couldn't get a word in edgewise." He sighed. "If your babe's grown that big now, no wonder I feel old." He reached into a small pouch on his belt and took out a roll of tobacco. Lighting it in the hearth, he took a long, leisurely drag. Esalu, who hated tobacco smoke, frowned but said nothing.

"This here's the only good thing about retirin'. Can't smoke when you're a hunter. It's taboo."

Before entering the mountains, Beast Hunters rubbed their bodies with different things to change their scent and erase any human odor. Royal Beasts were extremely smart. Once they knew a hunter's scent, they would be on their guard whenever they detected it again.

The tobacco flared and hissed as Olamu took another pull. His face relaxed. Jutting out his chin a little, he asked, "So? What do you want?"

Elin put down her cup. "There's something I want to ask. Do Royal Beasts do anything to help their young come of age?"

Olamu's forehead wrinkled. "Come of age? You mean somethin' to make 'em leave home?"

"That's right."

Olamu grinned. "You called me all the way here just to ask me that?"

"Yes. I thought if they did, only the Beast Hunters would have seen it. It's a question I never thought to ask before."

Olamu's expression grew serious. "Hmm. So the ones in the sanctuary don't, huh?"

Elin leaned forward eagerly. "You mean Royal Beasts in the wild do, then? They have a way of forcing their cubs to leave?"

Olamu nodded. "Yup. Sure do. Seen it many times. They won't let their cub back in the nest. Pretty rough business. They spread their wings wide, like this, see? And screech. When the cub tries to get at the nest, they beat it off. Bit of a shock I guess. Cubs probably wonder what's goin' on. They keep tryin' to get in, but're driven off every time. Sometimes it gets real bad. The parents even kick and bite their cubs."

A stillness spread through Elin's chest. Just as I thought. Here lay a clue to why Royal Beasts born in the sanctuary failed to mature and reproduce.

Olamu flicked the ash from his tobacco. "Bit heartbreakin' to watch. But that don't happen in the sanctuary, huh? Well, I suppose it wouldn't. Not when you feed 'em all the time like a cub. No need for 'em to grow up and hunt."

Elin nodded. "That's right. The Royal Beasts here don't hunt. I think that everything else may actually be related to that fact." Pouring more tea into Olamu's cup, she asked, "What happens to a cub when its parents chase it away?"

Olamu smiled. "There now. That's the real question. 'Cause wherever it ends up, that's where new cubs'll be born. For us, that's what matters."

"Do they set up their own territory as soon as they leave the nest?"

"Nope. Ain't that easy. They have to fly pretty far. Far enough to find a place to nest where they won't meet up with their parents when they hunt.

But those places're usually already taken. Still, Royal Beasts rule the valley. No need for them to have lots of kids like weaker beasts. Guess in a way, their worst enemy is themselves. They're pretty long-lived, but most only bear about two cubs in their lifetime, probably 'cause it's too hard to find new territory." Esalu nodded slightly at his words and glanced at Elin.

"Leelan was raised at the Kazalumu Sanctuary," Elin said to Olamu. "She and Eku have already had three cubs, but none of them have matured. Not only that, but even beasts brought here from the wild don't mate. I think the environment in the sanctuary must have something to do with it."

"Hmm." Olamu stroked his chin. "Might be it's too small."

"I agree. I also think that having so many Royal Beasts living here together is a big part of the issue. The sanctuary's much smaller than the territory Royal Beasts are used to in the wild, and it's a flat meadow surrounded by a fence. Instead of staking out territory in a river valley with no other Beasts in sight, they're all forced to live in this space where they can see one another all the time. Maybe they form a large artificial family unit so they can live together without fighting and killing one another."

"With Leelan and Eku as the parents and the rest as their children," Esalu murmured. "I see."

Olamu breathed out a long stream of smoke. "Could be. After all, they hate livin' close together. If they see other Royal Beasts in the distance, they make a sound to warn 'em not to come closer. And any that do come close suddenly swerve and fly away, as if to avoid hittin' an invisible wall or somethin'."

He turned and looked out the window. "On a flat plain like this, with all the Beasts in sight, you'd have one terrible battle on your hands if they all began matin'. Wouldn't put it past 'em to figure that out and avoid matin' at all."

His eyes narrowed, as if lost in thought, then he looked at Elin. "Did I ever mention how our territories are made?"

"You mean the hunters' territories?" Elin asked.

"Yeah."

"No, I don't think you did."

Olamu nodded. Fingering his tobacco, he began. "What I'm about to tell you is a secret just for the hunters, so first promise you won't tell anyone." He waited until he saw Elin and Esalu nod before continuing. "The territory of each hunter family's just a single valley that's passed on from one generation to the next. Each valley's ruled by one grand pair of Royal Beasts, and hunters only capture the grand pair's cubs."

Elin's eyes widened. "Grand pair?"

"Yup. Like I said, cubs booted from home fly a long ways away, but they never leave their valley. If they flew into a different one, they'd be in trouble. The offspring of the grand pair that ruled that valley would chase 'em out."

Elin leaned forward. "You mean Royal Beasts born from the same parents stake out territory in the same valley?"

Olamu drew on his tobacco, then slowly exhaled the smoke. "That's right. The grand pair produce a lot of young, but their offspring don't. When the female of the grand pair grows too old to mate, a female in her grandkid's generation usually starts bearing more young. We look at her and her mate and think to ourselves, Ah, there's the next grand pair that'll rule the valley."

Elin and Esalu listened enthralled.

When the female of the grand pair grows too old to mate, a female in her grandchildren's generation starts bearing more young. Excitement stirred in Elin's breast. Even in the sanctuary, Leelan got pregnant as soon as one of the other Beasts died, almost as if she was trying to control the number of cubs she bore to keep from over populating the space.

After another drag of his tobacco, Olamu continued. "Royal Beasts avoid livin' too close, but a mated pair and their offspring get along pretty well. Siblings'll stake out territories next to one another, pretty big territories, so they're scattered throughout a single valley. Kinda like a loose pack.

"Females stay in the same valley all their lives, but when it's matin' season, young males'll fly to other valleys to find mates. If they tried to enter a different valley at any other time of year, all the siblings in that valley would gang up on 'em to protect their territory."

"They cooperate to fight off intruders?" Elin asked.

"Yeah. Well, not really fight. More like chase 'em out. If they see one in the distance, they'll warn 'em not to come close. But they do fight, and fiercely, too, if an outsider trespasses to get food or tries to take over their territory."

Elin stared at him. So I was right, she thought. Royal Beasts live in packs. Probably not very large ones. They looked like solitary creatures because they each had their own large territory and lived scattered through a single valley. But she guessed that if she could view them from above, she'd see the shape of the pack with the grand pair at the top ruling over their children and their mates.

She rubbed her hands, which had grown clammy and cold as a quiet excitement had spread through her. Her hypothesis had been right. Leelan and Eku are the grand pair that rules Kazalumu.

Olamu looked out the window again and exhaled a puff of smoke. It was still early spring, and a gentle light caressed the meadow. His eyes narrowed. "Wind smells like sasha," he murmured. "Means it'll be matin' season soon." He turned his gaze to Elin. "So what're you gonna do?"

For a moment, Elin could only stare at him. Glancing at Esalu, she finally said, "I'll write to Her Majesty, the Yojeh, and ask her to expand the pasture area. There're some good places in the valley where I've been training them. I'll move the younger beasts to those places before mating season begins and . . ."

She swallowed what she was about to say, but Olamu could guess. He smiled wryly. "No need to look so apologetic like. Sure, if you succeed in increasin' the Royal Beasts, you won't be needin' us no more. Some of the hunters'll probably hate you for it." He tapped his tobacco with a finger to knock off the ashes. "But there's no changin' the flow of the times, is there? Maybe I'll be cursed for sayin' this, but everythin' changed the day Her

Majesty wed the Aluhan. I hear the next Yojeh'll have dark eyes. If so, shouldn't be any problem if the rulers of the valley've changed, too."

He ground his tobacco into the edge of the hearth and stood up. "Well, if that's all, I'll be off, then." Without waiting for Elin to stand, he slung his satchel across his shoulder and left the room.

Elin ran after him. He strode so quickly down the corridor that she only caught up with him at the entrance. Outside, he stood gazing at the pasture bathed in the soft light. Here and there, Royal Beasts napped in the sunshine.

"They ain't rulers," he said as if to himself. He flicked his eyes to Elin. "You told me once you wanted to return 'em to the wild. I'm guessin' that ain't gonna work. They got no fangs. Fangs for chewin' up their prey. Ain't no way Beasts used to livin' like this could defend their territory 'gainst Royal Beasts in the wild."

Elin looked at Leelan and the others. "You're probably right. For them, this is the wild."

Olamu opened his mouth as if to speak, but instead raised a hand and turned his back on her.

"Thank you," Elin called after him. He raised his hand again without looking back. Elin bowed deeply as the elderly hunter strode away.

5

LEAF EMBLEM

Kazalumu School, which had many students, attracted a stream of peddlers that came each day to sell their wares. Some sold fish caught fresh that morning in the nearby river; others sold fabric to make clothes and bedding. The early afternoon, when the students sat quietly at their desks studying, was a busy but enjoyable time of day for the dorm mother, Kalisa, and her assistants as they examined the wares and decided what to buy.

Since she had begun living in Kazalumu, Elin also bought everything she needed from the peddlers. Often, however, she was too busy to shop and cook for herself, and she would pay Kalisa a little extra to bring her the same meals she cooked for the students.

On a day when clear spring sunlight flooded the pasture, Elin picked up her shopping basket for the first time in a long while and headed behind the school. From the spring of the previous year, she had spent most of her time settling Alu and Ukalu in a spot far from Leelan and the others, and the lighthearted voices of Kalisa and the other women haggling with the merchants made her heart sing.

Kalisa's plump face broke into a broad smile at the sight of her. "Mistress Elin!" she called out. Although she had aged a great deal since Elin first arrived at the school as a student, she still tackled her duties as dorm mother with the same enthusiasm. Elin recalled how kind she had been to her and Yuyan. When they had come back drenched from playing in the river, she had stripped them down and doused them in hot water from head to toe. Elin felt awkward to be called mistress by her former dorm mother, but Kalisa ignored her pleas to stop.

Elin walked over and gently touched her elbow. "Thank you so much for bringing me meals for the past ten days."

Kalisa laughed and waved her hand. "You've nothing to thank me for. Such an easy task! Have things calmed down a bit, then?"

"Yes, finally! Alu and Ukalu have gotten used to their new home."

The women were gathered around a vendor selling red-haired crabs taken from Kazalumu River.

"Those look delicious," Elin exclaimed. "So it's red-haired crab season, is it?"

Kalisa pushed her way through the group of women, and, grasping a gleaming crab fat with eggs, handed it to Elin. "Red-haired crabs come into season just as the other crabs disappear. Eat well, Elin, and put some meat back on your bones."

"Thank you." Elin took the crab in her hands. Looking at its big red claws, she broke into a smile. "I always think of Yuyan whenever I see these," she said.

"Me too," Kalisa said with a chuckle.

When Elin was a student, one of her classmates who had never seen a crab before wanted to take one home to show his family. After the meal, he had taken an empty crab shell, limbs and all, washed it carefully, and reassembled it so neatly that it looked real. He glued it together with nyukilu, a kind of glue that didn't melt when heated. Yuyan had discovered it and, delighted to find a leftover crab, boiled it up again. When the other students, including Elin, noticed, they spied on her to see what she would do. Eyes shining with anticipation, Yuyan had taken a pair of scissors and cut off one of the legs. Seeing that it was empty, she had exclaimed, "Darn! This crab has shed its skin!" The incident was a standing joke among her friends for years afterward.

"Yes, she was quite a character, wasn't she?" Kalisa said. "She made me laugh so much. Thanks to her, you weren't lonely either."

"That's for sure."

Kalisa's face suddenly grew serious. "That reminds me! I was just waiting until the next time I saw you to tell you something. Did you realize that Jesse doesn't have the leaf emblem embroidered on his belt?"

"Emblem?" Crab still in hand, Elin wrinkled her brow. "Oh no!" she exclaimed.

The women and the merchants all looked up to see what the fuss was about. Elin flushed and waved her hand, crab and all, trying to let them know that everything was fine. "I completely forgot," she said to Kalisa. "He's in the middle level now, isn't he?"

When students successfully completed their first year at Kazalumu, their parents embroidered an unfurling leaf on their school belts during the summer holidays. The emblem expressed their parents' hopes that their budding talents would continue to unfold in the coming year. Most parents splurged on gold thread, so the emblem was also called the golden leaf. The number of golden leaves on a student's belt showed what level he or she was in.

Elin clapped a hand to her forehead. Poor Jesse. How could she have done this to him? She may have been preoccupied with the Royal Beasts, but to have forgotten the emblem for a whole six months. She couldn't believe it.

Kalisa patted her on the shoulder. "Don't worry. Jesse may be a rascal sometimes, but he's very considerate, you know. When his friends teased him about it, he told them that taking care of the Royal Beasts is a lot of work and he certainly wasn't going to bother you by asking you to embroider his belt. That shut them up."

But her words only made Elin feel worse. Crestfallen, she asked, "Do you have any gold thread?"

Kalisa shook her head. "Sorry. I just ran out. The thread merchant won't be back for quite a while, but there's no need to hurry at this point, is there?"

Elin rested her chin against the crab in her hand, then gave a crooked grin. "I'm taking a half day off tomorrow. I'll ask the headmistress if I can take Jesse to town with me."

Kalisa's face crinkled in a smile. "That's a good idea. Jesse will be thrilled. And it'll be good to spend some time together. For both of you. Go and enjoy yourself."

Jesse grumbled that he'd promised to play ozaggu, a ballgame, with his friends that afternoon and that it was embarrassing to go to town with his mother, but his steps were light as he walked beside her.

"Well, I guess this means you've finally realized your duty as a mother, doesn't it? I suppose that at least is a good thing," he said, nodding to himself.

Elin flicked him a glance. "Jesse, do you talk to your friends like that? Don't they hate you for being so cheeky?"

Jesse laughed through his nose. "Are you kidding? Cheeky kids who don't back down get a lot of respect. Sometimes the older kids give me a whack, but I don't care. Never mind that. If you're going to embroider a leaf for me, make it a worm-eaten one, will you?"

Elin's mouth twitched in a wry smile.

"What's funny about that?" said Jesse.

"Is that still a fad?" Elin asked.

Jesse looked puzzled. "Still? It was our level that started it. The older ones never did that. Chikki told us before he went home for the summer that he was going to get his with holes in it, so we all decided to get ours done that way, too."

Elin's eyebrows rose. "Really? Amazing. That means that children come up with the same idea in every generation. When I was a student, it was Kashugan. You know, Auntie Yuyan's husband."

"Oh, yeah."

"When he came back with a worm-eaten leaf, all the other boys copied him."

Jesse looked surprised. "Really? So somewhere there'll always be a kid like Chikki, then."

His face sobered. "That feels kind of funny, doesn't it? I wonder if people will just continue on like this forever. One of them will get the idea and then everyone else will copy them, thinking they're the first to have a worm-eaten leaf."

Elin smiled. "Maybe. It's certainly possible."

The small thread shop sold more than thread. It was crammed with bags embroidered with various designs and bolts of cloth. Spools of neatly wound embroidery thread gleamed in the sun that slanted through the window.

"Excuse me," Elin called out, and a woman who had been sipping tea in the back looked up. Her eyes widened.

"Elin! I haven't seen you for ages! Come in!" Wiping her hands on her hips, she slipped her feet into a pair of sandals and came closer, staring intently at Elin and Jesse.

"And are you Jesse? My, how you've grown!"

"It has been a long time, hasn't it, Yuji? You haven't changed a bit," Elin said.

Yuji waved her plump hands. "Oh, but I have. I've gained weight, and my back hurts."

The smell of thread and the sound of Yuji's chatter brought back another life. Elin had come here often when she lived in town. In those days, there had been time for her to sew clothes for Ialu and Jesse and to embroider little designs on things like the curtains.

After sharing her aches and pains, Yuji suddenly asked, "But what can I do for you today? What do you need?"

"I'd like to buy some gold thread. Do you have any from Chikala?"

"Chikala! You're really splurging, aren't you! Yes, I've got some. Just wait a moment."

Gold thread was expensive, so she probably kept it under lock and key, Elin thought.

Watching the woman disappear into the back of the shop, Jesse whispered, "Chikala?"

"That's a town in Aluhan territory. It's famous for making gold foil. Thread made with gold foil from Chikala is really high quality."

"Oh! Now I remember! I heard that name a long time ago, when father was talking to some huge guy."

Elin looked at him in surprise. "A big man? You mean Jinji? Do you really remember that? You were only about six or seven!"

Ialu had received an order for an expensive cabinet. He had asked Jinji, a lacquer craftsman, to do the decorative inlay. Jinji was a good man, and he and Ialu had hit it off. He had often come to their house to work on the cabinet and had shared stories of his trade, including gold foil, over meals together. But that was a long time ago. Jesse had been small enough to fit snuggly between Ialu's knees when he sat cross-legged.

Jesse stuck his nose in the air and said, "Pretty good memory, huh? I just might be a genius, you know."

Elin sighed. "Honestly, Jesse!"

At that moment, Yuji returned bearing a white box. "Here it is. Gold thread from Chikala. It's really wonderful stuff, and long-lasting, too. But it's expensive." She held it to the sun, and the light slid along the glossy surface. "See? Lovely, isn't it?"

"Yes. Can I have two?"

Yuji's eyebrows shot up. "Two!"

Elin smiled, looking a little embarrassed. "It's extravagant, I know, but I hardly ever make it into town."

"You need it for embroidery?"

"Yes. For Jesse's belt. I'll need to embroider a new leaf on it every year." She placed a hand on her son's shoulder and said with a laugh, "If I keep some around, I won't forget to do it next year, or the year after."

Jesse nodded. "Good idea," he said sagely. "Why don't you leave some hanging from the drawer, too? And while you're at it, paste a sign on the drawer saying 'For Jesse' in big letters. Then you'll remember for sure."

Elin gave him a playful slap on the head.

When they stepped outside, a breeze caressed their cheeks. Although spring was still young, it was a fine day. The rustling leaves on the trees lining both sides of the main street made the sunlight dance, and the sky above was a hazy blue.

Looking up, Jesse said, "It's strange, isn't it? The color of the sky looks different in spring than it does in summer or fall, even though it's the same sky."

"You're right," Elin said, looking at his face as he squinted into the brightness. His resemblance to Ialu was startling. As they strolled through the soft sunshine, she wondered when he had begun to look so grown up.

6

SEIMIYA'S VISIT

On a clear spring day when sasha petals drifted on the breeze, the Yojeh came to Kazalumu. Unlike when her grandmother Halumiya had come, everything about Seimiya's visit was kept secret. She had sent a letter announcing that she wished to be trained in the Handler's Art now that her youngest daughter was five, and Elin had been frantically preparing ever since.

Five years had passed since the Yojeh had agreed to train with Elin.

During that time, a building had been erected behind the school where she could stay for extended periods when she was ready to start. Now that the time had finally come, Elin and Esalu had to meet with many different people to make sure her stay was as comfortable as possible and that she came to no harm. By the time they finished, they were completely exhausted and felt not awe but instead immense relief when the Yojeh's carriage and cavalry troop came into view.

There was no welcoming ceremony. As the Yojeh didn't want her presence to make the students nervous, she had asked the school to suspend classes. Summer vacation had been moved ahead of schedule, and all the students had been sent home the day before.

Wide-eyed, Jesse leaned forward, craning his neck to see the horses prance through the gate, their heads adorned with beautiful plumes. Their cloth headdresses were stitched with gold thread that glinted and shimmered with each step. Led by these beautiful steeds, a brilliant white carriage rolled into the grounds and came to a stop before the school. Servants leaped forward to spread a carpet under the step. Several soldiers dismounted and moved with quick precision to stand guard around the carriage.

Jesse grabbed his mother's hand. "Are those Se Zan?" he whispered. His mother nodded. "Did Dad look like that when you first met him?"

"Yes."

"Did you think he was good-looking?"

His mother smiled as though embarrassed. Looking at the Se Zan, whose eyes scanned and assessed the people gathered there, she whispered, "He reminded me of a forest in midwinter."

"What's that supposed to mean?" Jesse said. But his mother just smiled without answering.

Even before Jesse had asked her that question, the sight of the Se Zan had taken Elin back to a day long ago. Although Ialu had been just one of several Se Zan, he had made a deep impression on her from the very first day. People's hearts are strange, she thought. They hadn't even spoken to each other, so why had his image remained so firmly imprinted on her mind?

The sound of the carriage door pulled her back to the present. A servant reached up to steady Seimiya as she slowly alighted from the carriage. The sunlight caught in her hair and glinted off the gold thread in her robe.

Leaving Jesse's side, Elin walked forward with Esalu and dropped to one knee before her.

"Please raise your heads," Seimiya said. Her tone was gentle, but Elin sensed a ring of excitement in it. Her cheeks were flushed, and she looked far healthier than when they had last met.

"I finally made it! What a beautiful place Kazalumu is." Gazing around at the wide green pasture carpeted with tiny flowers, she took a deep breath. "As we drew near, I saw little birds diving from the sky, almost as if they were somersaulting. I suppose their nests must be in the grass."

Elin smiled. "I believe what you saw were topi, a type of skylark. They do make their nests in the grass, but those nests are not located in the spot where they dive to the ground."

"No? Why is that?"

"They land a little distance away so that their nest won't be discovered by predators. They walk back to it once they land."

Seimiya's face clouded for a moment. "So they flew like that to protect their nest? And I thought they were flying just for the joy of it." She shifted her eyes to Elin. "You've spent your life studying the ways of living creatures like the topi. For the next month, please teach me well."

Elin bowed and said quietly, "It will be my pleasure, Your Majesty."

Morning mist drifted across the field where Elin stood with the Yojeh. For some time now, Jesse had been crouched behind a tree watching them. He had been doing so every day, observing everything his mother did since she had begun teaching the Yojeh.

The Se Zan were scattered through the forest, beyond the reach of his ears and invisible to his eyes. In the beginning, they would appear out of nowhere and glower at him, as if to say, "We know you're here." Now, however, they let him be. He wasn't interfering in any way so they had probably assumed he just wanted to be near his mother.

But that wasn't why he had come. Or at least, it wasn't the only reason. He was driven here by his longing to learn the Handler's Art. The Se Zan probably thought he couldn't hear what his mother and the Yojeh were saying from this distance, but in fact, he could hear quite a bit. He'd been watching his mother for so many years that he knew how voices carried. Obstacles could block sound just like they blocked objects, and voices wouldn't reach him when people spoke with their backs turned either. But when he stayed downwind like this, the wind carried sounds and voices to him with surprising clarity.

Besides, people said a lot with their eyes and body movements, not just with their voices. The Royal Beasts were the same. Having watched his mother interact with them since he was a child, he knew instinctively how she and the Beasts communicated. So even when he couldn't hear their voices, he could guess pretty accurately what his mother was saying. He could also tell from her explanations to the Yojeh whether he'd guessed right. This whole detective process was so exciting that he couldn't stop himself from coming to watch.

His mother had started with the habits and character of Royal Beasts, teaching the Yojeh step by step. Only recently had she begun showing her how Leelan and the others responded to the harp. The Yojeh plucked notes on it eagerly, but although Leelan and Eku listened intently, they didn't respond the way they did when Elin played the same notes. The Yojeh seemed discouraged. "Perhaps I have no talent," she said with a sigh.

"There is no hurry, Your Majesty," Elin said. "They're still trying to decide what kind of person you are. Once you have established a bond with them, they will respond. I promise you."

As he listened to his mother encourage her, Jesse nodded to himself. The Royal Beasts observed people carefully. They would never obey someone they didn't trust. Although they could be controlled by the Silent Whistle, they would never open their hearts to the person who used it.

Someone strong might force them to do their bidding, but they would never truly submit. In contrast, once they opened their hearts to someone, they would respond with great attention. That was one of the things Jesse loved about them.

The Royal Beasts obeyed his mother without hesitation. He knew they would obey her even if she didn't use the harp. Alu was the same. She understood what Jesse said. He had never used the harp like his mother, but when he called Alu to come to him, she would, showing him that she understood. Leelan, however, almost never did what he asked. Though she would let him cuddle up to her and watched over him like a mother over her child, she never responded the way Alu did when he asked her to do something. Instead, she would give him the same tolerant look she gave her own children.

Leelan, Eku, and the other adults obeyed his mother first, and then Miss Esalu. Although it had taken them a long time to accept the headmistress, now when she played the harp, they would do what she asked. But they didn't respond to her words, even when she spoke to them. They had sharp ears and could pick out his mother's voice from far away. To them, she was more important than anyone else. Jesse couldn't help feeling that they were all one big family. His mother was the parent, and the Royal Beasts were her children. And he was probably considered the youngest of the lot.

Jesse remembered how his mother's face had fallen the day he'd told her he wanted to become a Beast Handler. Now he could understand why. To talk about "handling" the Royal Beasts as if they were tools was disgusting. He had often heard the soldiers and the custodians at Kazalumu speaking of his mother with awe as they called her a Beast Handler, so it had never occurred to him that it was bad. Now, however, he felt a flash of irritation every time he heard someone call his mother that.

The Royal Beasts were noble beings. In fact, maybe all creatures were. Maybe there weren't any that people had the right to use as tools. He had never forgotten what his mother had told him about the Toda when she was helping him with his studies. They could talk to one another, she'd said, with voices that sounded like finger whistles. And when one of their fellow Toda died, all the others would mourn with a high-pitched keening.

After that, even the Toda, which he had seen as ferocious beasts, seemed different, and he kept pestering his mother with questions about them. Whenever she spoke of them, however, she looked troubled. She probably didn't want to use even the Toda as weapons of war, although it was the Toda troops that protected the country from invasion.

Humans turned all beasts into tools. Horses and oxen were made to work, other animals were raised to be eaten, and the Toda were trained as weapons. And now his mother was training the Royal Beasts to fight. He knew it couldn't be helped, yet that knowledge warred with the feeling that it wasn't right. A jumble of thoughts and feelings simmered inside him. Not knowing what to do with them, he let them circle around his mind while he watched his mother.

What was the Yojeh thinking, he wondered. She was beautiful yet somehow fragile. There always seemed to be a deep sorrow in her face. Although he knew she was the one who was forcing his mother to train the Royal Beasts, he couldn't help liking her. She looked so sincere as she gazed at the Beasts.

I bet she loves their nobility just like me. I wonder when they'll answer her harp.

He felt sorry for the Yojeh. She tried so hard to talk to them, but they never responded. For the last few days, he had found himself hoping they would show even a little warmth toward her.

When he watched his mother and the Yojeh train, time always flew by, but today, something was different. Although they usually came to the field when the sun was already high in the sky, this morning, they'd come while the mist still clung to the meadow. His mother had been up all night; she'd come home late and then left before dawn. Thinking it must have something to do with Alu, Jesse had waited until she'd gone to get the Yojeh before he climbed up to Alu's new pasture ahead of them. Dawn had only just broken, but Alu was already outside the stable. Perhaps she had spent the whole night outdoors.

Beyond the mauve mountain ridges, the sky was beginning to glow faintly. Suddenly, the sun burst above the rim, its light falling on Alu, who until then had just been a vague shadow in the field. Jesse caught his breath. Her chest was flushed deep pink.

Raising her wings slightly, she stretched out her neck and sniffed the air. Facing her was the young male Ukalu. He was also sniffing the air with his wings slightly raised.

Alu . . .

Although he didn't know what was happening, Jesse could feel the tension between the two Beasts like a tightly drawn string. Standing far apart, they stretched toward each other and inhaled the scent that rode the wind. Jesse had known Alu and Ukalu since he was a baby, yet they seemed like totally new creatures.

His mother and the Yojeh were approaching. They stopped near the tree behind which Jesse was hiding and stared at the two Beasts. When the gently rolling mist had vanished, and the flowers in the meadow shone gaily in the morning light, Jesse's mother pointed to Alu.

Jesse turned to look. The color of Alu's chest began to deepen, turning a bright red as though fresh blood had been spurted across it.

At that moment, Ukalu raised his head toward the heavens and let out a long trilling sound. *Lululululu.*

Alu raised her head and sang a high-pitched note in response. *Lilililili.*

The two beasts spread their giant wings and soared upward at almost the same moment. High in the heavens they came together, blocking out the newly risen sun, and twined their necks as though they never wanted to let go. They collided and flew apart, then collided again, their bodies shuddering as Ukalu mounted Alu's back.

Dazed, Jesse stared at the sky.

7

ALU MATES

"They're mating," Seimiya whispered. She couldn't keep the tremor from her voice. "Alu's finally flown! Oh, how wonderful!"

Turning to look at Elin, she was startled to see tears welling in her eyes as she gazed up at the Royal Beasts. "So this brings you joy, too, does it?" Seimiya asked.

Elin nodded. At last, Alu had done it. She'd taken her mating flight, her first step toward adulthood and making her own family. Even if it brought them one step closer to an army of Royal Beasts, for now Elin was simply glad that Alu had come of age.

When they were done, Alu and Ukalu drifted slowly to the ground. Ukalu sidled up to Alu where she stood languidly on the grass, and licked the fur on her chest while making soothing noises.

"She finally broke free from her parents," Elin murmured. Seeing the perplexed expression on Seimiya's face, she explained, "Alu will turn seventeen this year. Royal Beasts in the wild take their mating flight and bear children by the time they are four. It has taken Alu many times that to reach maturity, most likely because she remained a cub in relation to Leelan and Eku. I think that she's finally come of age because we took her away from them."

"Ah, I see," Seimiya whispered. "So that's why you wanted to expand the pasture area for the Royal Beasts. You wanted enough room to remove Leelan and Eku's children from under their wing and give them a place where they could become independent."

Elin bowed her head. "Yes. I couldn't explain my request in detail in a letter. Forgive me for not being clearer."

"There's no need to apologize. That was a natural precaution. But to think that keeping parents in the same pasture as their children is what stops them from reproducing. Who would've guessed?"

Elin nodded. "It's still just a hypothesis, but I think there are two reasons proximity prevents them from maturing."

"Two?"

"Yes. One is to avoid interbreeding. If Alu had come into heat when her father was ready to mate, Eku might have mated with his own daughter. To prevent that, I think cubs may have some mechanism that keeps them from maturing while they live with their parents."

Seimiya blinked, then blushed and looked a bit flustered. Catching sight of her expression, Elin said hastily, "Pardon me for speaking so bluntly."

Seimiya gave a crooked smile. "Please think nothing of it. And the second reason?"

Elin looked at Alu. "To avoid conflict."

"Conflict?"

"Yes. When cubs come of age, mate, and bear young, they need a fairly large territory to support their family. The pasture at Kazalumu is simply too small. When so many of them are forced to live in the same pasture, I think they choose to create one large family instead of killing one another. One pair becomes the parents of all the others."

Surprise rose in Seimiya's eyes. "You're saying they actually plan that out for themselves?"

"Well, not plan, really. I think it just kind of happened that way. It's not uncommon for living creatures to make such choices. Honeybees, which I got to know very well when I was young, are a good example. To survive in their cramped hive, they also form one big family with the queen bee at the top. Their lives are so completely organized and controlled that it's chilling at times. The queen is almighty. If something happens to her, if she dies or disappears, all the bees in the hive start to shake as if they've lost the center that held them together. I've seen a swarm of bees get so upset that it wandered every which way, not knowing what to do. The bees behaved like little children suddenly separated from their parents. Bees in a hive are all females that can never become independent or bear children. They remain forever their mother's daughters. There were times when I found that quite frightening."

Seimiya's eyes narrowed as she listened. Her face paled, and her jaw tightened. Her eyes on Alu, Elin missed the change in her expression and continued speaking matter-of-factly. "If the only reason the Royal Beasts didn't mate was to avoid inbreeding between father and daughter or mother and son, then there would be no reason for Ukalu and the others, who were introduced later from the wild, not to mature and mate. A system where the parents wield absolute authority over a host of obedient children ensures stability when many individual creatures are forced to live together."

When she finished speaking, the only sounds were the breeze caressing the grass and the cooing noises of the Royal Beasts.

"You're saying that in a system where parents wield absolute authority, their children can live together in peace and stability?" Seimiya whispered.

Elin sighed. "In a restricted environment like that of bees in a hive, yes, I think so. But for Royal Beasts, such a system is abnormal. When Olamu, the Beast Hunter, saw Leelan and the others, he told me they could never live in the wild."

Sadness spread through Elin as she watched Alu and Ukalu groom each other affectionately. "I think he was right," she went on. "By keeping the Royal Beasts in the sanctuary pasture, we've forced them to remain children. Even if they mate and bear young, they can never truly become independent adults. Because they're still dependent on us for food.

"The Beasts raised here have never learned the skills they need to hunt for their own food or to survive a fight with other Beasts. Outside the sanctuary, with no one to protect them, I doubt they could compete with wild Beasts who challenge their territory."

The sun had risen in the sky, and its rays glowed softly on the Royal Beasts' fur. Seimiya stared at them silently for some time as if following a train of thought. Finally, she murmured, "I suppose for them, living here is happiness."

Elin turned to look at her. "Forgive me, Your Majesty," she began, then faltered.

A faint smile played at the corners of Seimiya's mouth. "If you disagree, please say so. There is no need for you to hesitate."

With a nod, Elin said, "I think 'happiness' is too broad a term."

Seimiya said nothing. "It encompasses so much," Elin continued. "But for the same reason, it can conceal a lot. Lumping everything together under that word seems reassuring, but really only the Royal Beasts can judge what happiness is for them. I'm afraid I might use it to convince myself that my actions are right."

Seimiya sighed, and her mouth twitched. "You're very hard on yourself, aren't you?" she said. A strong light gleamed in her eyes. "Because of my position, however, I must decide what is the best system for everyone else and what will make them happy. I must keep an image of what the happiness of my country and my people looks like in my mind at all times. Because I am a parent who must lead many children."

Elin's eyes wavered, and she looked at the Royal Beasts.

"What is it this time?" Seimiya asked. "Tell me your thoughts. There's no reason to stop now."

A sad smile touched Elin's lips. "I was thinking that your ancestor, the first Yojeh, must have shared your point of view."

As the sun warmed the grasses, butterflies and beetles began to whir through the air.

"When she crossed the Afon Noah and assumed rulership to bring an end to chaos and unite the land, the people here must have seemed like children who didn't know what would bring them happiness."

Seimiya squinted into the sun, following the flight of a butterfly.

In a low voice, Elin said, "Every time I look at the Royal Beasts and the Toda, I wonder why the first Yojeh decided not to explain so many things to her people; why she taught them that all they needed to do was to follow the rules. Why did she choose this way? Did the people who live here seem incapable of judging for themselves? Or had she learned from her own experience that people can't understand something unless they've witnessed it with their own eyes?"

Seimiya gave her a long look. "So even now, you're worried about flying the Royal Beasts to battle," she said. When Elin didn't answer,

Seimiya added, "I think you must be. Because you intend to fly them all by yourself without letting anyone else ride them."

"Your Majesty."

"There's no need for you to tell me. Do you think I didn't know how you feel? After spending these last few days learning the intricacies of the Handler's Art, I understand all too well. These skills cannot be acquired overnight. And even if they could, it would take a very long time for the Royal Beasts to learn to trust someone else."

A bitter smile rose to Seimiya's lips. "You know that, and that's why you're giving me only the knowledge of the art. The day is not far off when the Royal Beasts must be flown. But when that time comes, I won't be able to fly them. Miss Esalu could probably do it, but I'm sure you intend to excuse her from battle due to her advanced age."

Her smile faded as she stared at Elin. "You plan to shoulder all responsibility for what may happen on the battlefield alone, don't you?"

The gentle breeze played with a strand of Elin's hair. She shifted her eyes away and gazed at the wide field. "I told you that only the Royal Beasts themselves can judge what happiness is for them," Elin whispered. "But if, as the Ahlyo warned me, a catastrophe occurs that destroys both beasts and men, it will most surely be a calamity for the Royal Beasts. If so, then, without a doubt, I am leading them to grief, not happiness."

Seimiya shook her head. "But by doing so, you are saving the people of this country."

Her eyes still on the field, Elin said, "Perhaps. But that has no meaning whatsoever to the Royal Beasts."

They remained silent for a while, staring at the two Beasts in the field. Finally Seimiya heaved a deep sigh. "Do you really think such a disaster will happen? To me, it sounds like a cautionary tale told by the Ahlyo to keep people from fighting."

Elin stared blankly at the Royal Beasts. "Tokujisui," she murmured. "It's the tokujisui that bothers me. The Royal Ancestor Jeh and all the Yojeh after her, as well as the ancestors of the lord of Amasulu who were invited to come and breed Toda, every single one of them used tokujisui to prevent both Royal Beasts and Toda from being bred by men. Why?"

Seimiya's brow furrowed. "So as not to increase their number. You told me that yourself."

"Yes. But even if we don't breed them, it's still possible to multiply Toda by taking their eggs, and Royal Beasts by taking their young. It's slower of course, but even so, we could increase their number. Our ancestors must have known that. If so, then why?"

Disgust twisted Elin's features. "Tokujisui perverts nature. It warps creatures' growth so that Royal Beasts remain eternal children, never mating, wasting their lives in idleness. And the Kiba die with their unborn eggs inside them. Why would our ancestors have gone to such lengths to control their reproduction?"

She clenched her teeth, trying to keep her emotions in check, but the fury that swelled inside her was not easily quelled.

"My mother chose martyrdom," she said, forcing the words through her teeth. "She chose death by execution rather than break her vow to protect their secret. I, however, have chosen not to use tokujisui. I simply cannot bring myself to use something that I know corrupts living things. As such, it's only right that I should bear responsibility for the outcome of my decision."

Elin paused and took a shaky breath. "But I have my doubts, too. Because I'm not the only one who will be affected by the outcome. If the disaster feared by Jeh should occur, the soldiers in the battlefield, along with the Toda and the Royal Beasts, will all perish."

A bitter smile crossed Seimiya's face. "You need not trouble yourself about that. It is I, not you, who will be held responsible."

Elin shook her head. "Who is responsible is not the point. For those killed, that makes no difference at all."

At these words, a fierce light kindled in Seimiya's eyes. "Regardless, it is my role as the ruler of this land to order my men to lay down their lives for the safety of our people. The best I can do is to avoid making them die needlessly."

Clouds drifted across the sky, casting a fleeting shadow across her face until the light touched her pale cheeks again. For a moment, Elin thought she caught a glimpse of the Yojeh's ancestor in that face, an image of the woman who had determined, at her discretion alone, the lives of men and beasts and the fate of this country; the woman who had sought only to bring peace and security to her people. Although Seimiya was standing right beside her, to Elin she suddenly seemed very far away.

"Just as you have chosen a different path from your mother's," Seimiya said, her voice almost a whisper, "I, too, have sought to break the seals fixed by my ancestors. Because I believed that was the best way to protect the lives of our soldiers. But . . ." She grimaced. "If the catastrophe that you fear should come to pass, I will be remembered for generations to come as the Yojeh who led her kingdom down the wrong path."

There was a tremor in her voice. The image of Jeh that Elin had seen in Seimiya's eyes vanished, and a look of anguish suffused her white face.

8

ELIN'S DIARY

Jesse had no memory of how he made it home. The guard who opened the door for him spoke, and he heard himself answering as though from the other side of a thick fog. Passing through the guardhouse and into his own quarters, Jesse closed the door behind him. As he stood by the hearth in the empty room, words kept echoing inside his head: "You plan to shoulder all responsibility for what may happen on the battlefield alone, don't you?"

The Yojeh's words. His mother's expression as she answered. Everything he had heard and seen from behind the tree spun around inside his head, crushing him.

There was a lot they had said that he hadn't understood, but as he listened, fear had boiled up like a black cloud in his chest and finally taken shape. He turned his vacant eyes to the spot where his mother always sat.

She plans to die . . .

For a long time now, something had been bothering him. He was sure that his mother hated having to train Leelan and the others for war. Royal Beasts were so powerful, he doubted anyone could ever beat them. But the thought of the Beasts dropping from the sky and ripping people to shreds made him wonder how his mother could ever have agreed to do it. "They'll be killing our enemies. What's wrong with that?" his friends had told him. But they'd never seen a Royal Beast bare its fangs. They had no idea how ferocious, how absolutely terrifying they could be.

Even now, he shook violently at the memory of Leelan's snarling face, of her jaws pulverizing the broom. And the thought of what would have happened if it had been a person instead made his stomach churn. Besides, no matter how powerful the Royal Beasts might be, he couldn't rule out the possibility that they could be destroyed if enemy soldiers and Toda managed to surround them. By training the Beasts, his mother might be leading them to their deaths.

At times she looked at the Royal Beasts with such anguish in her face that Jesse was sure she hated what she was doing. Yet she kept on going. And she never showed her pain to others. This is what had been bothering him. With the Yojeh's words, his vague fear had taken shape and pierced his breast.

So that's it. She plans to die to make up for the fate she's forcing on Leelan and the others. But why? Is that really the only way?

Questions tumbled and whirled inside him. Sinking to the floor, he wrapped his arms around his knees. Loneliness stabbed him. If war broke out, his mother and father would leave him here all alone. Tears welled in his eyes, and he buried his face in his knees. Inhaling the scent of his skin, he wept. For so long now, he had kept a lid on the loneliness that lurked inside. The days when his family had lived together in town seemed like a dream. His father leaning over a chest of drawers he was working on, the scent of wood shavings, the smells of food cooking in the neighbors' houses, the shouts and laughter of his friends, his mother chopping vegetables in a corner of the kitchen—he missed it all so much that he could barely stand it.

He had thought that his father would come home when he was finished fighting the Lahza, and they could have their old life back again. But maybe they never would.

His knees were wet with tears. His father and mother were going to go far away and leave him behind. In his mind, he saw their backs receding into the distance.

He clenched his teeth. He was mad at them both. They always did this—left him without telling him what he needed to know, without any thought for how he felt!

He gulped for air and brushed his tears away. He wanted to break something. Plates, cups, anything. He wanted to hurl them at the wall and hear them shatter. But if he did, the guards would come running to see what had happened. He couldn't stand the thought of trying to explain or of listening to them lecture.

With gloomy eyes, he surveyed the empty room. To his surprise, the door to his mother's room was slightly ajar. She always kept it tightly closed, but today, there was a space as wide as his fist. She must have left it open when she went out at dawn so as not to wake him.

He stared absently through the crack. When they lived in town, she had often stayed up writing by the hearth. He would climb onto her back and peer over her shoulder. She would laugh and say, "You're too heavy. Off you get."

"What're you doing?" he would ask. "Writing about what happened today," she would say. She had taught him how to read and write the strange letters she used. But since they had moved here, she no longer wrote by the hearth. Instead, she stayed in her room, studying and writing. When he asked what she was doing, she only smiled and answered vaguely.

Jesse stood up. Walking around the hearth, he put his hand on his mother's door. His pulse beat faster. A voice inside told him that he shouldn't, but he pressed his lips together and opened the door wide. The afternoon sunshine fell upon the small desk and bookshelf. Books jammed the shelves, and more were piled on the floor. Several books bound only with thread lay on the desk. Jesse walked stealthily to the desk, although he knew it would be some time before his mother returned. Suppressing his guilt, he began flipping through the pages.

The top five books recorded the lives and ecology of Toda and Royal Beasts. When he opened the one beneath these, letters written backward from the way he had been taught at school leaped into his eyes.

Mirror script. The one his mother had taught him when he was small. He paused, startled. As a child, he had thought it was a game, but now a completely different thought occurred to him.

I see. Mother uses this so that no one else can read what she writes.

After this realization, he couldn't stop himself. He ran back to the living room and grabbed a hand mirror from the top of the dresser. Angling the mirror so the words were reflected on the glass, he began to read.

The ringing of the bell brought him back to the present with a jerk. Dusk already filled the room. He had been so engrossed in reading, devouring one diary after another, that he seemed to have missed both the lunch and afternoon breaks.

Hurriedly, he gathered the books he'd left scattered about and returned them to their place on the table. Leaving the door open a crack, same as he had found it, he went back to the living room. It was sunk in darkness. As he knelt by the hearth and stirred the embers with a poker, he thought over what he had just read, feeling as though he was returning from a long journey.

The loneliness and anger of the morning had sunk deep inside him. In its place, a leaden feeling weighed down his chest. His mother had written about her life, sharing things he had never known about her past: about her mother and her mother's people; about how she, and now her family, were connected to the Yojeh; about the Royal Beasts and the Toda. His mind was reeling with the knowledge of how she had lost her mother when she was only ten and how she had learned to communicate with Leelan.

Someone had once told him that his mother had Ahlyo blood. He had never thought about what that meant, but now the reality of it thudded in his chest, making him shudder. Just like the Yojeh, the blood of those who crossed the Afon Noah long ago ran in his veins, too. His green-eyed ancestors had been the first to turn Toda into weapons of war, while the Yojeh's ancestors were not gods but a people who had raised Royal Beasts in the Afon Noah. Both had crossed those mountains to reach Lyoza. Even now, remnants of the Toga mi Lyo, who called themselves the Kalenta Loh, lived in a valley somewhere in the Afon Noah.

His mother had written that she wanted to seek them out. What happened long ago? How did the golden-eyed Jeh and the green-eyed Toga mi Lyo, who should have been enemies, become friends and end up helping each other? Why was it wrong to pit Royal Beasts against the Toda? His mother had hoped that the Kalenta Loh could help her find the answers to such questions. When Jesse read why she had been forced to abandon her search for that valley, the magnitude of what surrounded his whole family hit him full force.

To the very last page, which had ended with yesterday's entry, Jesse had felt as if he were walking with his mother. Distant memories had come alive. How long ago was it? They had still been living in town. He remembered the buzzing of cicadas, so it must have been summer. His father and mother had taken him on a long journey, deep into the mountains. Sweating with the effort, they had climbed a steep mountain trail until suddenly they came upon a meadow that spread as far as he could see. It was filled with a profusion of flowers that seemed to brighten everything. Their fragrance was so intoxicating, he had run laughing and shouting through the field and then thrown himself on top of the blooms. His mother had lain down beside him. Holding hands, they had gazed up at the blue summer sky.

Tears fell from his mother's eyes, but she had just let them slip quietly down her cheeks as she looked at a cloud drifting lazily. When he had started to ask what was wrong, his father had swept him up in his arms and started tickling him. He giggled and squirmed, and his mother had sat up and begun tickling him as well. He had laughed so hard tears had run down his face.

Having read his mother's diary, he could now guess why she had cried. She had written about a man named Joeun who had nursed her back to life and raised her as his own child. Every summer, he had taken her to a small hut in that field of flowers. She grieved that he had died before she could repay his kindness. She had wanted to show him that she'd grown up and built a happy life. Maybe she'd been talking to Joeun as she lay in the grass gazing at the sky. Maybe she had brought her family there to show him.

Now that Jesse knew the life his mother had lived, memory fragments from his childhood took on new meaning. Maybe she's writing it for me, he thought suddenly. So that if she vanished from his life, he would understand. If so, then what he had guessed must be true. She was planning to die.

He felt as if his mother's hand had gently touched his hair. The embers in the fire blurred, and Jesse closed his eyes tight.

9

FLIGHT OF THE OCHIWA

It began drizzling at dawn on the day the Yojeh was to leave Kazalumu. The rain signaled the end of spring. Once it had passed, the sky would turn to the color of summer. The Yojeh was scheduled to leave before noon, and the carriage was already standing by, but she seemed reluctant to go. She went to the stable, bidding each of the Royal Beasts goodbye. She left Leelan for last. Looking up at the Beast dozing in the dusky shadows, she breathed a soft sigh.

"In the end, you didn't respond to my voice, did you?" Leelan must have heard, because her ears twitched, but her eyes remained shut.

Seimiya turned to Elin, who was waiting behind her. "Will the day ever come when Leelan responds to me?"

Elin smiled and nodded. "Yes, most certainly."

Seimiya's lips twitched. "You speak with such confidence. Do you have some reason to think so?"

"Yes, I do. Perhaps you didn't notice, but Leelan's behavior has changed greatly since you first arrived, Your Majesty."

Seimiya blinked and looked at the Royal Beasts. They were all napping, perhaps made drowsy by the pattering of the rain. As she watched them, a slow smile spread across her face. "You're right," she said. "They have changed. When I first came, they glared at me and growled."

Every time she had approached the Royal Beasts alone, they had raised their wings and rumbled, staring down at her with a cold gleam in their eyes. Seimiya wondered when they had stopped. The change must have been gradual because she couldn't remember when they had ceased threatening her. Clearly, however, they no longer considered her a danger because here they were, sleeping peacefully in front of her. A warm feeling spread through her chest.

After standing for some time gazing up at the Beasts, Seimiya turned to Elin. "They're amazing creatures, aren't they? Even when they're sleeping like this, I can feel their power."

"Yes."

A light shone in Seimiya's eyes. "It must be a wonderful feeling to control the Royal Beasts so freely."

Robbed of speech by this unexpected remark, Elin could only stare at her for a moment. "To be honest," she finally said, turning her eyes to Leelan, "it is. Frighteningly so. Especially when I'm speeding through the sky on Leelan's back and the Royal Beasts suddenly change course in response to my harp. It always gives me goosebumps."

She turned her eyes back to Seimiya and said quietly, "These magnificent creatures move as I will them, and that's incredibly exhilarating." She took a deep breath and carried on. "But the next moment I am always overcome with fear. Many times the terror twisting inside me has caused me to shake so badly that I can't play my harp until it passes."

Seimiya's brows rose. "But why?"

"Yes, I wonder. Why?" Elin murmured. "Perhaps because I feel I'm doing something that's beyond my capacity. Lady Seimiya, have you ever skied?"

Seimiya shook her head.

"What about riding?"

"Yes, I love riding."

"Then I think you can understand what I mean. Have you ever found that when you set your horse at a gallop, it feels wonderful for a time, then suddenly you're afraid? You feel the horse picking up speed to the point where you can no longer control it, and you're frightened of what will happen if it doesn't stop. Have you ever felt that kind of fear?"

Seimiya nodded emphatically. "Yes, I have." A smile touched her eyes. "When I was a child, there was a very gentle horse that did whatever I asked. That made me so confident, I decided to surprise the guards who were riding with me and urged it to a gallop. It tried so hard to please me, that it took off at tremendous speed. I was petrified. It took everything I had just to cling on."

She stopped abruptly and looked up at Leelan. "Yes, I see what you mean." She paused for a long moment. The sound of the rain on the roof and the gentle breathing of the sleeping Beasts filled the stable.

"I have been so afraid," Seimiya finally whispered, her eyes still fixed on Leelan. "Ever since you came to me that night long ago and told me about my ancestor. Ever since I learned that I wasn't a god but just an ordinary human being." Her voice was almost inaudible, as if she were talking to herself. "It's been so hard, trying to be something I'm not, trying to do something I can't."

Slowly she turned her face to Elin. "But when I met you again and you told me more about Jeh, it suddenly hit me. She also knew she was just an ordinary human being, yet she managed to achieve so much."

Elin said nothing.

"While I was listening to you," Seimiya continued, "I was thinking that she must have been far stronger than me. But then remember? You told me a cornered mouse is neither strong nor weak."

"Did I?" Elin murmured.

Seimiya gave a crooked smile. "Indeed, you did. I remember it clearly." Her gaze was calm as she looked at Leelan. "I may be weak, but I will no longer use my lack of capacity as an excuse to run away. When the time comes, I will send you and the Royal Beasts to subdue our enemies. Still . . ."

Her face twisted, and she turned to look at Elin. "I can't help but be torn by regret. If only the knowledge of the past had been passed down to me, if only I knew what happened when the Royal Beasts were sent to battle! Then I wouldn't suffer such fear and anxiety about what I'm doing!"

Her shoulders trembled. Elin took a step toward her and placed a hand gently on hers. Seimiya's eyes widened, unused to such a familiar gesture, but her fingers pressed against Elin's in response.

"Many times," Elin whispered hoarsely, "I've dreamed that I was an ochiwa flying through the sky to the Valley of the Kalenta Loh, the ones who remain. Each time, I find the green-eyed ones and the golden-eyed ones living together and beg them to tell me what will really happen if I fly the Royal Beasts to war."

Seimiya blinked. "An ochiwa? Why an ochiwa?"

Elin brushed tears from her eyes with her fingers. "Do you remember me telling you that I read an ancient diary when I was staying in the manor of Yoha— I mean the lord of Amasulu?"

"Yes."

"An ochiwa is mentioned at the beginning of that diary." The words were seared into Elin's memory, and she recited them softly. *"While spring is young and snow remains, then comes the ochiwa."* The diary said this exchange of messages was begun 'to cheer the spirits of the young maiden who had once again donned that heavy mantle, her heart troubled by the fate of a people in the lowlands far away.' Our Royal Ancestor Jeh and the Kalenta Loh sent messages to each other by ochiwa."

As Elin spoke, Seimiya frowned suddenly. "What is it?" Elin asked.

Seimiya shook her head. "I had no idea. So that's how the Flight of the Ochiwa started."

"What?"

Seimiya gazed at Elin. "We still do that. We still send the ochiwa. At the hour of dawn as the sun breaks over the horizon on the first day of the year, the Yojeh releases an ochiwa and sends it off toward the Afon Noah. We've continued this ritual every year without fail."

Elin stared at her openmouthed.

"We place a message of felicitation in a band on its leg and release it. And it always comes back. I was taught that by sending a greeting to our home in the Afon Noah, we receive the blessings of the gods in return and bring happiness to the world. But I never knew that was how it started."

Her voice strained, Elin asked, "Do you receive a message in return?"

Seimiya shook her head. "No, nothing. The bird comes back with our message still strapped to its leg. But . . ."

Her face clouded, and Elin urged her on with her eyes. With a bashful smile, Seimiya said, "When we open the letter, it smells like flowers. I always thought that it was the fragrance of the gods."

The perfume of flowers! Tiny lights burst and scattered across Elin's mind.

"What?" Seimiya asked.

"It just might be," Elin said breathlessly, "that the ochiwa still flies to the Valley of the Kalenta Loh."

Seimiya's eyebrows shot up. "Really?"

"My mother wrote in her diary that the valley where the Kalenta Loh live is filled with the fragrance of flowers."

The two stared at each other. Then Seimiya laughed. "But—could that really be possible?"

Elin gave a lopsided smile. "I wonder. Perhaps it's just a coincidence. But still . . ."

Seimiya's face sobered. "You're right. It's worth trying, even if it is a chance in a million."

———

The Yojeh returned to the palace, promising to come again when she could. Upon her return, she attached the letter she had written with Elin to an ochiwa and sent it off toward the Afon Noah. But it returned with the same message perfumed with the faint scent of flowers. It must have flown down to rest in a meadow on its way home, Seimiya decided. That, she thought, was the nature of an answer from the gods.

EIGHT

PARTINGS

I

OLI'S DECISION

It was a cold summer. The rain, which signaled the end of spring, should have lifted in a short time, but it never completely stopped. Staring gloomily at the sky, people in Yojeh territory cursed the clouds. The rain fell for too long on the wheat, which had almost been ready to harvest. When the farmers realized that the yield would not only be scarce but that they might not even have enough grain to save as seed for the following year, they begged the lords of their domains to reduce taxes.

The long rains brought a cold summer even to Aluhan territory. Rice was the staple of its people, but fears were spreading that the crop was going to fail. If it had been just one year, the situation wouldn't have been so serious. But the kingdom had been afflicted with cool summers, pests, and disease for over ten years, and every domain in the kingdom was scraping the bottom of its food reserves.

Domain rulers in both Yojeh and Aluhan territory pondered the question of taxes. If they levied the same amount as every year, some people would starve. But if they reduced the amount, they wouldn't be able to buy grain from the caravan cities. The Yojeh and the Aluhan had no time to rest, spending each day meeting with local rulers who came to the palace to beg for help.

Seimiya was lost in thought, a deep furrow between her brows. Shunan placed a hand lightly on her shoulder, and she looked up at him with a start. "You shouldn't push yourself so much," Shunan said. "Why don't you take a little rest? If the Yojeh collapsed, it would throw the people into a panic."

Seimiya smiled wanly and ran her hand over the document she had been reading. "But how can I possibly sleep? Even when I close my eyes, I can't stop seeing these figures."

Officials had stayed up all night preparing the materials she had been studying. They included a list of remaining emergency funds and assets that the palace set aside for bad years like this, as well as the total amount of goods received as tax from each domain, and an estimate of how much it would cost to buy grain from foreign merchants.

The countries to the east and south had yielded bountiful harvests, and grain merchants from the caravan cities were flocking to Lyoza, having heard rumors of a poor crop. The Yojeh could save her people from starvation if she bought the merchants' grain and sold it in the local markets for a lower price. But if she used the palace's reserve funds to buy grain now, and they suffered another poor harvest next year, there would be nothing left.

Seimiya sighed. "I will ask the nobles of the domains in my territory to present part of their income from tariffs as an offering to the palace just for this year," she said.

The rulers of every domain imposed tariffs on trade goods. Their profits from imported grain would likely increase this year. If the Yojeh ordered them to contribute the surplus, she could prevent the commoners from suffering. But Shunan shook his head.

"That's not a good solution," he said. "They'll just increase taxes on the commoners as they always do to make sure they have something in reserve for the future. People who can afford to buy grain at the market will make it through, but if farmers badly hit by the poor harvest are taxed too heavily, they won't be able to buy enough grain to eat. And besides . . ."

Seeing him hesitate, Seimiya gave a crooked smile and finished his sentence for him. "If the Yojeh becomes indebted to the nobles like that, she'll lose her prestige."

To the commoners, long rains and cold summers were the voice of the gods. They seemed to say, "Your kingdom doesn't deserve to prosper. The Yojeh is no longer pure and divine. Defiled by the Aluhan, she has become a mere mortal."

Seimiya slowly shook her head, her lips still curved in a smile on her porcelain-like face. "You and I together, we have to fix the instability caused by the changes we've made. Otherwise, our children will be forced to deal with even more uncertainty."

Their daughter Yuimiya had inherited her father's eyes, not the gold-tinted eyes of the Yojeh. Seimiya and Shunan would have to build a firm foundation for her to gaze with confidence at her people when she became the Yojeh.

Seimiya whispered, "If the light that the gods shone upon me has dimmed, then I must learn to shine by myself. Isn't that so?"

With his hand still resting on her shoulder, Shunan murmured, "Yes, you're right, but remember that you aren't alone." Seimiya seemed so thin she might collapse. He fixed his eyes upon her as he spoke. "Even should the light of the gods be dimmed, we, your people, are here to support you. Our love for you will make you shine." He paused uncertainly for a moment, but then took a deep breath. "If you can't sleep," he said, "may I speak with you a little longer about the affairs of this country?"

Seimiya blinked. "Of course," she said.

Shunan picked up a handbell and gave it a sharp ring. The door opened and a servant entered. "Tell Oli to come here immediately," he said.

When Oli arrived, she was dressed formally despite the late hour. She seemed subdued and preoccupied, quite unlike her normal bubbly self.

Catching sight of her expression, Seimiya glanced up at her husband. "You mean . . ." Her voice trailed off.

Shunan nodded and then turned to Oli. "Is your mind still made up?" he asked.

Oli nodded. "Yes. Please proceed as soon as possible with arrangements for my betrothal to Prince Tauloka."

Looking at his younger sister, her face taut as a bowstring, Shunan felt a sharp pain pierce his heart. He was well aware whom she truly loved. He had watched the two of them since they were children playing in the mud. There was no way he could have missed it. Rolan. Even though he was a musician, as the adopted son of the lord of Amasulu, he was not unsuitable in terms of rank. But rather than asking to marry him, Oli had asked her brother to arrange her union with the prince of Tolah.

Oli had already visited Tolah several times, deepening her bond with the prince. Confidentially, he had sounded out the possibility of their marriage. If they became engaged, he would offer a substantial bride price. Oli had told her brother that the prince was an intelligent man, fully aware of the significance of rescuing his bride's country from this crisis. Yet he was also considerate enough not to flaunt his actions, but instead to present it as a gift for her hand in marriage.

Although this was surely the best solution, Shunan found it hard to accept. Not only did he grieve for his sister, who must wed the prince of another kingdom to save her own, but he also found it painful to admit that he was cowardly enough to use his own sister in this way. It was Seimiya's words that had helped him to make up his mind. If they were to make this country stable, they needed to build good relationships with their neighbors. As such, Oli's offer was an important step to a better future.

"Thank you, Oli," Shunan said. "Although this is not what I would have wished for you."

Seimiya's chair scraped against the floor as she stood up. "Wait!" she said. She walked over to Oli and clasped her hands in her own. Oli's eyes widened at this unexpected gesture.

"Oli," Seimiya said. "Your offer is most appreciated. But if you mean to sacrifice yourself for our sakes, please don't. There are other options we can choose."

"Your Majesty," Oli protested.

Seimiya caught her eyes with her own. "Rolan is the man you really love, isn't he?"

Oli's gaze wavered, and her eyes filled with tears. She glanced down hastily and remained silent for a moment before raising her head. Seeing a smile on her tear-drenched face, Seimiya looked at her in surprise.

"Thank you," Oli said in a faint voice. "I see that I can hide nothing from Your Majesty. It is true that I love Rolan. I always have, from the time we were children. Although many say he dallies with girls in every town, I believe that he returns my feelings."

As she spoke, her voice grew stronger. "To be honest, for a long time, I agonized over what I should do. But I've come to the conclusion that if Rolan and I were wed, we would strangle each other's potential."

Her eyes were still wet with tears, but her natural brightness had returned. "He's like the wind. To tie him down would kill him. He has a magical ability to bind the hearts of people together wherever he travels and sings. That's his strength. And I, I am the younger sister of the Aluhan, the grand duke of the divine kingdom of Lyoza. If I marry Prince Tauloka, I will one day be queen of Tolah. As such, I can serve as a bridge between our two countries. That is my strength."

She squeezed Seimiya's hands. "Please, I beg of you, permit me to marry the prince of our neighbor Tolah. Prince Tauloka is fascinating and broad-minded. If I were forsaking a man I loved for someone I detested, that would be hard. But if it's Prince Tauloka, I feel I will grow to love him more. I will do my best to ensure that one day our people will rejoice at the union between Your Majesty and my brother and will see how it paved the way for a better future. So please, let me realize my potential."

Seimiya's lips trembled. She nodded silently. Gently releasing Oli's hands, she wrapped her arms around her. "Thank you, Oli," she whispered. "Then let us also support the kingdom of Tolah so that when you become queen, the people of Tolah will rejoice at this union with Lyoza."

Slowly Seimiya released Oli and turned to her husband. "That's the kind of kingdom we should build, don't you think?"

Shunan nodded. "When this crisis has passed, let's begin from scratch and consider what we want Lyoza to be. We'll make products that people from other countries will vie for, deepen our ties with the caravan cities, and build such a solid foundation that poor harvests cannot shake it."

Prince Tauloka was overjoyed when he received word of Oli's acceptance, but the engagement ceremony was conducted privately between the two royal houses, and the announcement delayed until the next spring. If Oli were to marry him now, he said, when everyone was talking about failed crops in Lyoza, the people of both countries would think that Oli had married for the dowry. He didn't want his future queen to be branded with such a vulgar image. Instead, as a sign of friendship between the two countries, he sent a procession bearing a great quantity of grain as a gift. Although it was not enough to completely free Lyoza from poverty, it helped replenish the palace's storehouses. The grand procession, with banners flying and an endless train of horse-drawn wagons piled high with grain, coupled with the Aluhan's Toda troops, which had met the procession at the border and guarded both flanks, made a strong impression on the people of Lyoza and the rulers of its domains.

Thus was the kingdom delivered from the specter of starvation. But when the chill winds brought the first hint of autumn, another dark cloud appeared on the eastern plains.

2

INTERNAL STRIFE

When Ialu stepped inside the entrance to the Stone Chambers, he heard muffled shouts from deep inside. Frowning, he turned toward the noise. Not again, he thought.

Others seemed to have heard the commotion, too. The sound of footsteps rushing toward the voices echoed from the different Chambers where the Toda were kept.

Ialu strode down the dimly lit corridor that was hemmed with thick stone walls. By the time he reached the source of the noise, there was already a group of men gathered there. In the center, a young Rider and a middle-aged Steward were shouting at each other, but their words were incomprehensible. Waves disturbed the surface of the dark pool beyond them. Toda swam around the Pond, their undulating bodies bumping against one another.

A young Steward looked up as Ialu entered, and his face brightened. "Ialu!" Pushing his way through the older men, he came running up.

"Chimulu," Ialu said, but before he could ask what had caused the fight, a clamor rose from the crowd. The Toda Rider had drawn his dagger. Shoving onlookers aside, Ialu sprinted toward the combatants. He grabbed the Rider's wrist in his right hand, swept it upward, dagger and all, and struck the Rider's elbow with his left hand. As the young man's arm gave way, Ialu twisted his wrist outward, using his elbow as a fulcrum, forcing the man to his knees and then onto the rock floor. The knife clattered as it fell from the young man's hand, but still Ialu pressed his wrist to the ground.

At that moment, Ialu sensed a change in air pressure behind him. He whipped his head aside and twisted his body. Something grazed his shoulder, followed by a searing heat. Letting go of the young man's arm, he spun to face his attacker. The middle-aged Steward who had been fighting with the Rider loomed in front of him, holding one of the hatchets the Stewards used to chop the fish they fed to the Toda. Glaring at Ialu with bloodshot eyes, he raised the hatchet high.

A roar erupted from the crowd. The men stamped their feet and pumped their fists, their expressions fierce. Not one of them tried to intervene. The water in the Pond swirled violently, and the Toda raised their snouts from the water. Mouths slightly open, they swam round and round one another. Ialu felt a ringing inside his head, like the drone of hornets, and his gums itched. Blood surged through his body, along with a brutal urge to strike.

The Steward brought the hatchet down as though chopping a block of wood, but Ialu slipped beneath his guard and slammed his fist into the man's spleen. As the man retched and fell forward, Ialu struck him across the jaw with his right fist. He could feel the man's teeth shatter with the blow. The sensation jerked Ialu back to his senses like a bucket of cold water.

The Steward dropped his hatchet and fell to all fours, spitting blood and broken teeth before he collapsed on the stone floor. Curled up like a caterpillar, he lay moaning with his chin cupped in his hands. Ialu stared at him blankly.

The door to the medical room opened. Ialu raised his face to see Yohalu standing in the doorway.

"How's that cut?" asked Yohalu.

Ialu rose from where he was sitting on the bed and bowed. "Thank you for your concern. It's just a graze."

Gesturing for him to sit, Yohalu pulled up a chair and sat down facing him. "I heard you were attacked with a feed hatchet. Chilumu said if you hadn't ducked, your head would've been split open."

Ialu nodded. "Yes. Probably. But I hit him harder than I should have. He'd already lost the will to fight when I punched him in the gut. There was no need to hit him in the jaw."

Dropping his gaze to Ialu's bruised and swollen fist, Yohalu's eyes narrowed. "When they told me what had happened, I thought the same thing. It seems so unlike you." He sat for a moment, head bowed, stroking his chin, then looked up at Ialu.

"The odd thing is that it was also quite unlike the other two to get into a fight in the first place. It started with an argument over something really petty. Neither of them could explain why it escalated to the point where they were trying to kill each other. I just talked with the Steward you punched. He looked at me as though he was haunted, and just kept shaking his head and saying how sorry he was for what he did."

When Yohalu finished speaking, the room grew still. Through the walls came the muffled sounds of voices, and chairs scraping the floor.

The village of Tokala had grown and changed completely since Elin had come to investigate the deaths of the Kiba. Yohalu had chosen it as the site for experimenting with breeding and multiplying captive Toda. There were many new facilities, and, in addition to the local Stewards, it now housed a permanent force of twenty Toda Riders, including members of the Black Armor. Lookout towers had been erected around the village, and the outskirts were patrolled by carefully picked soldiers.

Yohalu had formed a special band of Stewards, most of whom were young with keen intelligence and flexibility, and put them in charge of learning how to breed Toda. The greatest challenge they had faced was determining how much hakujisui to give them. Although it was a much weaker version of tokujisui, the potion that had been used to raise Kiba, too high a dose would prevent the Toda from reaching reproductive maturity. But if they were given too little, they wouldn't grow strong enough for battle.

It was Chimulu who had found a solution. Instead of controlling just the amount administered, he had hit upon the idea of experimenting with timing as well. He tried giving them as little as possible while they were still growing, and then increasing the amount after their first reproductive phase had passed. Through trial and error, they had succeeded in breeding Toda that could withstand the rigors of war.

The Toda produced in this way were clearly different from those raised the traditional way. Their scales were lighter in color, they had bigger bones and fangs, and they were a little larger in overall size. The greatest difference, however, was their disposition, a fact that became evident during training. The Toda were quick to understand their Riders' commands, almost as if they understood words, and followed those commands exactly.

The Toda's unerring obedience made Ialu shiver uneasily whenever he rode them. If such a dramatic change could occur in just one generation, what kind of Toda would be born in two or three generations? He was acutely conscious that the rules governing their care had been designed to prevent such Toda from being bred at all.

When they began training the new Toda, Yohalu had appointed Ialu second in command of the troop. From the time Ialu had asked to become a Rider, Yohalu had openly supported him and helped him to carve a place for himself in the Aluhan's army. Thanks in part to this, Ialu had secured a footing among the Riders and risen in rank to become a member of the Blue Armor, which was second only to the Black Armor.

Ialu guessed that Yohalu supported him for a variety of reasons, but he believed it was mainly because he was Elin's husband. He was one of the few people Yohalu could talk with openly about such things as the Toga mi Lyo, the Yojeh's ancestry, the secrets of the Royal Beasts, and Yohalu's relation to the Sai Gamulu.

One night as they talked after supper, Yohalu compared Lyoza to a butterfly. The Yojeh and the Aluhan were its two wings, he explained, while Yohalu, Ialu, and Elin formed the base of those wings. It was their job to consider what was needed for the two wings to remain strong and for the country to move forward.

As he listened, Ialu couldn't help thinking how dangerous it was to entrust the kingdom's rule to a select few who kept the secrets of the Yojeh and the Aluhan, the Royal Beasts and the Toda, to themselves. Such a system was far too skewed and precarious.

Long ago, when Ialu had worked in the narrow confines of the Yojeh's palace, he had been forced to see everything through a single lens: his duty to guard the life of the Yojeh. He knew from personal experience how perilous such a one-sided perspective could be. Yet he still held the warrior Yohalu in the highest esteem. It was not only that he felt comfortable with the man because he was a warrior. He was deeply impressed by Yohalu's magnanimity in accepting and trying to understand a former Se Zan who had once killed many Sai Gamulu. He was also touched by Yohalu's admiration for Elin.

"That wound will take a few days to heal," Yohalu said, his eyes on the bandage around Ialu's shoulder. "This is a good opportunity. I'll give you ten days off."

Ialu raised his eyebrows. "It's not that serious."

Yohalu regarded him steadily. "Take a holiday. Go back to Kazalumu and see your family."

Speechless, Ialu stared at him. He heard the footsteps of booted Riders in the corridor, and their voices, talking and laughing. The sounds had receded before he finally spoke. "Are the others being sent home, too?"

"I'm giving everyone who will be sent to the front lines a holiday. But finding reasons to send them home can be difficult."

I see, Ialu thought. So the time is coming. Yohalu must have gotten some news. Clearly, he was expecting something different from the small skirmishes they had experienced so far. The Toda Riders were being sent home to see their families before they died a cruel death. But if Yohalu sent them off all at once, they would guess why, and rumors of imminent war would quickly spread.

Which means, Ialu thought, that the situation is still fluid. Yohalu isn't sure if it will come to war yet or not. If rumors that they were preparing for war reached the Lahza, it could tip the balance. That's why Yohalu was looking for excuses to send the men home.

"Autumn comes early to the plateau of Kazalumu," said Yohalu, watching Ialu's eyes as though curious to see his reaction. "The Royal Beasts will look striking against the golden fall leaves."

3

FATHER AND SON

The carriage rolled slowly to a stop, and a guard moved swiftly to open the door. Ialu thanked him as he stepped down. A cool wind that smelled of autumn sunshine stroked his skin. Not all the leaves had changed color yet. There was still some green left on the trees in the forest hedging the pasture. On such a fine day, the inside of the carriage had been hot and stuffy.

Once outside, however, the sun felt pleasant, and the sweat on Ialu's skin dried quickly.

Ialu thanked the driver and asked him to come back in three days. Turning, he saluted the guard who stood stiffly at attention.

"We had word that you were injured, sir! All is well here, so please rest easy!" Although he spoke crisply and respectfully, the young man could not conceal his curiosity. He must be new to the job, Ialu thought. He was staring at Ialu's face as if thinking, 'So that's him.' Perhaps he was intrigued by the fact that Ialu had switched from being a Se Zan to being a Toda Rider of the Blue Armor. Or perhaps by the fact that he was Elin's husband. Smiling inwardly, Ialu thanked him for his work and walked toward the school's entrance.

Muffled sounds typical of classes in session spilled from the building. Ialu scanned a group of students clustered near a goat enclosure in a corner of the pasture to see if Jesse was among them, but they looked a bit older. Their teacher gestured for them to crouch down and look under a goat's belly as he explained something. A few of the children were distracted by a cloud of dragonflies, but the rest listened intently, their eyes fixed on the teacher's hands. One day, those children would return home as beast doctors.

As he watched them, Ialu suddenly realized how different his own childhood had been. These children, even the ones watching the dragonflies, were living the present as a means of getting to the future. They could imagine their lives stretching out before them into the distance like one long road.

When he was their age, he had deliberately avoided thinking of the future. He had kept himself from painting a picture of the life ahead so that death, when it inevitably took him, wouldn't hurt as much; so that he would feel no pain when he terminated someone else's future. He had tried to focus only on the moment, nothing more. In those days, his life had been hard and solitary, like a succession of dots. The lives of these children, however, were a connected line. With a final glance at the clear autumn light playing softly in their hair, he passed on toward the school and stepped into the shadowed entranceway.

Inside, the long corridor echoed with the indistinct voices of teachers that seeped through the thin walls of the classrooms on either side. Ialu proceeded to Esalu's office and knocked on the door. Esalu called out from within. As he entered, she looked up from a book on her desk, and her eyes widened. "Well, well," she said. Laying her reading glasses on the desk, she pushed back her chair and stood up.

"It's been a long time," Ialu said with a bow. "I'm on leave because I was wounded. I just got back now."

Esalu eyed the bandage wrapped around his shoulder. "Yes, the news reached us this morning. But we didn't expect you until tomorrow. You traveled fast." She gestured for him to sit by the fire. "How's your injury?"

"It's just a graze. Nothing serious. It was really just an excuse to give me a holiday."

Esalu lifted the earthenware pot that puffed with steam. "Elin's at the training ground, so have some tea here first."

Ialu sat by the fire while Esalu poured him some tea. "Actually, I'm glad you came just now," she said. "There's something I want to consult you about, although I'm sorry to pounce on you like this when you've just arrived. I was actually going to send for Elin, but I think it's better to tell you."

She paused, then said, "It's about Jesse, you see."

As he took the cup from her, Ialu frowned slightly. "Did Jesse do something wrong?"

Esalu took a sip of her tea and sighed. "He got into a bad fight. I've shut him up in the storage room without his lunch to make him reflect on his behavior." She blew on her tea between sips to cool it down. "I believe it's really the other boy who's to blame. He's in the same level as Jesse and tends to be overly sensitive about people being treated better than him. He often complains if he thinks something's unfair, which gets him into trouble with the other students. The other teachers also think Jesse isn't totally at fault either, but . . ."

She grimaced and looked at Ialu. "It's what Jesse did that bothers me," she said.

"What did he do?"

"He grabbed a vase that was by the window and whacked the other boy in the face with it. Luckily it didn't break, so he was only bruised. But if Jesse had hit him in the wrong place, he could've been badly hurt. And if the vase had broken, his face could've been cut."

Ialu stared at Esalu, barely breathing. If it had been an ordinary fist fight, he would have apologized profusely and told Esalu that he'd make Jesse understand. After all, it wasn't unusual for boys of fourteen to get into fights. But what Jesse had done was different. Even children, Ialu thought, have a strong aversion to punching someone. Although they might flail at each other with their fists, most children would feel fear and self-loathing, not pleasure, if their fist actually connected with someone's face. To grab a hard object like a vase and strike someone's face with it was to cross that deeply ingrained line.

"What did the boy say to Jesse?" he asked.

Pain flashed through Esalu's eyes. "He told Jesse he was the luckiest guy in the world, that he's always protected by guards because his mother can control the Royal Beasts. He said Jesse would get special treatment his whole life."

A bitter taste spread through Ialu's mouth. He stared at Esalu with gloomy eyes.

The custodian unlocked the storage room and told Jesse he could come out. Squinting against the light, Jesse stepped from the room, only to freeze at the sight of his father.

Jesse was not the only one who was surprised. Ialu blinked at the changes in his son. While Ialu had been away, Jesse had turned from a boy into a young man. Before, his head had only come up to Ialu's chest, but he had shot up in height and now stood at nose level. His neck and shoulders were still boyishly slender, making his slimness more pronounced, as though he had been stretched vertically.

The biggest shock, however, was Jesse's expression. The eyes staring up from under his bangs held a bleakness that Ialu had never seen in him.

The surprise on Jesse's pale, rigid face gradually gave way to a sullen scowl.

"I hear you were in a bad fight," Ialu said. Jesse shrugged.

"Why did you hit him with a vase?" Ialu persisted quietly, but again got no response. Keeping his mouth firmly closed, Jesse fixed his eyes at Ialu's shoulder level, never looking up into his face. Ialu stared down at him for a while, then turned abruptly on his heel. "Follow me," he said.

He walked quickly, sensing Jesse following behind at a distance. Leaving the building, he crossed the pasture. The long yellow grasses, bathed in the autumn sunlight, swayed in the breeze. Ialu nodded at the guard who stood at the edge of the forest before he strode in among the trees. The light was dim, and the earth smelled damp where the trees kept their foliage, but where the branches were already bare, the light dappled their faces and the air smelled of freshly fallen leaves.

Ialu turned onto a trail that was invisible except to those who knew it was there and walked deeper into the forest. When he heard the sound of running water, he veered off and made his way down a leaf-strewn slope toward a rushing stream. Jesse followed, slipping on the leaves. Ialu glanced up to check on him and then stopped at the river's edge. He sat on a sun-warmed stone, feeling the heat beneath him. There was a little waterfall just up the river, and the sound of the rushing stream mingled with the sound of the water plunging into the basin below.

Jesse had reached the riverbank, but he simply stood and scowled, making no move to sit down.

"Turn your head and look up the slope you just came down," Ialu said. Jesse turned and gazed up the slope. He grimaced at the sight of a soldier standing among the trees at the top, but Ialu waved a hand at the man, who bowed in return.

Ialu shifted his gaze to Jesse. "Here we can be seen but not heard," he said. "The river drowns out our voices."

Still standing, Jesse blinked.

Ialu looked up at him. "How've you been?" he asked.

Jesse slid his eyes away and shrugged. Ialu sighed. "You've grown a lot since I saw you last. But I guess you've only grown physically. Inside, seems like you've become a coward."

Jesse's jaw clenched and his nose grew pinched. With his eyes fixed on his face, Ialu continued. "You won't look me in the eye. You shrug your shoulders. You refuse to speak. That's what cowards do. They build a wall to keep people from mentioning something they don't want to hear. If anyone dares to mention it, they hit back in a low-handed way. In the past—"

"I'm not a little kid anymore!" Jesse interrupted, his eyes flashing. "Don't talk like you know who I am when you only come home once a year!"

Ialu raised his eyebrows. "The other students only get to see their parents twice a year. Is there that much difference between you and them?"

Jesse fell silent as though taken by surprise.

"In fact, you can see your mother every day if you want," Ialu continued. "If someone says you're lucky, they're right, don't you think?"

Jesse's face flushed. "Me? Lucky?" he snapped, gritting his teeth. He was trembling so hard that even his tightly clenched fists shook.

"Does it make you that angry to be told you're lucky?" Ialu asked quietly.

"You bet it does!" Jesse snarled. "What's so lucky about me?"

Ialu looked him in the eye. "What's so lucky? You have three meals a day. You have a roof over your head when you sleep at night. You can study as much as you want. And if you become a beast doctor, you'll never have to worry about having enough to eat. It's true I'm away a lot, but that's the same for the other students. And you have your mother nearby."

Jesse shook his head violently. "You just don't get it, do you? You don't understand anything! Other parents think about their kids all the time. Even when they're far away, their kids come first. To them, their kids matter more than anything else in the world."

"You think we don't care about you?"

Tears welled in Jesse's eyes. "You expect me to believe that you and Mom care about me? Really? I don't know what matters most to you. Mom? Or maybe the country. But I do know this: I'm not the one Mom cares about most!"

"That's not true."

"Yes, it is!"

"No, it isn't."

With tears streaming down his cheeks, Jesse yelled, "It is too! If she cared about me, then why would she plan to go off somewhere and die? I get that she feels responsible for Leelan and the others. But if she really cared about me, she'd choose to live, wouldn't she? Even if it meant giving up everything else."

For a moment, Ialu was at a loss for words.

Jesse . . .

When and how had Jesse realized what Elin had steeled herself to do? With grief in his eyes, Ialu gazed at his son, who was brushing away his tears with both hands as he hiccupped and shook with sobs.

Ialu knew too well the bone-crunching pain of learning he was not first and foremost in his mother's eyes. Even at the age of eight, he had understood that his mother had no other choice. Her husband had just died and left her with a suckling babe. But he could still remember what he had felt when she reached out to take the bag of gold in exchange for him. Nausea and loathing, the sensation that his guts were melting inside him. Though it would have meant starvation, he had longed for her to say she wouldn't give up her son, to tell those men that this child meant the world to her. He would rather not have known that there was something more precious to her than him.

Ialu stood up and, reaching out his arm, pulled Jesse close. Rather than resisting, Jesse clung to him. Wrapping his arms around him, Ialu said, "For your mother and for me, there is nothing in this world more precious than you."

Jesse tried to shake his head, but Ialu held him still. "Listen!" Holding

Jesse's head firmly against his chest, he took a deep breath. "Your mother and I," he said, "we knew that this would happen, yet we still had you. We knew that we would cause you pain, yet we still chose to bring you into this world. From the moment you were born, the most important thing to us has always been you. All we've thought about is how to ensure your happiness and your future."

Tears slid down Ialu's cheeks, but he didn't wipe them away. "It's true that the things we've done have trapped and bound us," he said hoarsely. "What I'm doing, what your mother's doing, is like fighting in a fog. We have no idea what the outcome will be. But even so, we're doing it so we can live in peace as a family someday."

Jesse shook his head. "But Mom—"

"I know, Jesse. I know." Ialu loosened his hold and looked down at him. "But even that decision is for you, Jesse. We don't know what will happen if she flies the Royal Beasts to battle. But unless we find out, we can never escape from the situation we're in. We'll spend the rest of our lives guarded by allies and hunted by enemies. That's why your mother decided to follow this path to its end. She chose to obey the wishes of the Yojeh and the Aluhan so that we could see where that path will lead.

"Flying the Royal Beasts into battle may precipitate a disaster. For that very reason, she's decided not to let anyone else ride the Royal Beasts. Just as you fear, she alone wants to bear responsibility for whatever happens. Ironically, if no disaster occurs and the Royal Beasts achieve some astonishing feat, we'll spend the rest of our lives under guard for the sake of the country. But if there is any sliver of hope—if there is any chance that our family and the Royal Beasts can be freed from this situation—it lies only at the end of the path your mother has chosen."

Ialu spoke slowly and deliberately. "Jesse, please. Try to understand. Your mother didn't choose this path because the Royal Beasts are more important to her than you. She's trying to find a way for us all to be happy."

Jesse's face twisted. Screwing his eyes shut, he bit his lip.

"Your mother's doing her best to find a way for you to grow up and have your own family who won't have to live like this, constantly being watched, always in danger of assassination."

Jesse wrinkled his nose. "Who says having my own family's going to make me happy anyway? If that's what she's worried about, I don't care if I ever marry."

Ialu's lips crooked. "All right, don't, then. But do you really want to spend the rest of your life like this?"

Jesse opened his eyes and gazed up at his father. "If it means that Mom won't have to die, then yes, I'm fine with it." His lips were trembling. "More than anything else, I'd rather she lived."

For a long time, Ialu stared at him without speaking. Finally, he said, "Me too, Jesse. Me too."

Jesse added quickly, "The same goes for you, you know."

"What does?"

"I would rather you lived. Why'd you have to go and join the Toda Riders?"

Ialu released his son with a faint smile. "Because there wasn't anything else I could do."

Jesse looked at him questioningly, and Ialu's smile faded. "If the Toda troops can become powerful enough to defeat the enemy on their own," Ialu said, "then the Royal Beasts will never have to fly to battle, will they?"

Jesse's eyes widened. "Oh, I see!" The bleakness that had filled his eyes when he had come out of the storage room had vanished.

There was another reason Ialu had applied to become a Toda Rider, but he didn't feel like sharing it. He prayed fervently that Jesse would never have to experience the brutal possibility that haunted his mind.

4

WHITE LIGHT OF MORNING

As Ialu approached the house near the Royal Beast stable, the door opened, and a guard stepped out. Snapping to attention, he saluted and stood aside to let Ialu in. A narrow ray of westering sun shone through the window, striking a spot beside the soot-blackened oven. The guards must have just finished their meal because there were a few scraps stuck to the inside of a pot that rested on the floor.

Although they took turns, living in this narrow hut and guarding the house must be suffocating, Ialu thought. And if anything happened to Elin or Jesse, the guards would be severely punished. They had to live with that fear constantly in the back of their minds and weren't even allowed an occasional drink to help them relax.

Ialu bowed. "Thank you for watching over my wife and son," he said. "I'm indebted to you."

The young guard flushed. "Thank you for your kind words. Be assured that we will protect them with our lives."

The middle-aged guard in the back room also saluted. "At this time of year, your son sleeps in the dormitory, so your wife often spends the night in the stable. She just informed us that she'll be staying there tonight because the Royal Beasts are unwell."

Ialu nodded. Esalu had told him at dinner that some of the Beasts were suffering from indigestion, and Elin's meal had been taken to the stable. Esalu had told him wryly it happened quite often. Jesse couldn't be given special treatment just because his father had come home, so he was staying in the dorm. Having injured his friend, he had been deprived not just of lunch but of dinner as well, and he hadn't been in the dining hall. Ialu had sat with the teachers as a guest of honor. With the students casting frequent glances his way and the teachers peppering him with questions, he couldn't remember what he had eaten.

He slipped the leather satchel from his shoulder and pulled out a large package of ogalu, dried cakes of sweetened sticky rice. "This is for you," he said. "I'm sorry I've only brought sweets."

The men's faces brightened, and they thanked him profusely. Although ogalu was common in Aluhan territory, it was hard to come by in Kazalumu, and the two men beamed as they accepted his gift.

Ialu walked through the narrow passageway and opened the door to the house. The living room on the other side of the dirt-floor kitchen was shrouded in dusk and the hearth was cold, yet it still smelled faintly of Elin and Jesse. When he put his satchel down, he felt he had come home. He took another package of ogalu from his bag and left the house.

The door to the stable was bolted from the inside. Ialu rapped on it.

"Yes?" Elin called out.

"It's me," Ialu said. He heard the sound of muffled footsteps and the jiggling of the bolt. Then the door opened and Elin's surprised face appeared.

"Ialu!" she exclaimed. "I thought you weren't coming till tomorrow!"

Ialu smiled. "I had a good driver. He got me here a little past noon. Can I come in?"

Elin nodded and stepped aside. A faint warning growl came from the stalls. The younger Royal Beasts stared at him, their eyes glinting. "Quiet," Elin said, and the sound ceased abruptly.

"Amazing," Ialu murmured, and Elin cast him an amused glance as she barred the door. "I heard they've got indigestion," he said. "Are they all right?"

"Yes. It was just Lesseh. He swallowed a bird whole while flying. He does that quite often, but he's got weak intestines. It gives him a terrible stomachache until the laxative starts to work."

"So the Beasts have stomach trouble, too, do they?"

Elin smiled and looked at Lesseh. "Of course they do. Just like us, some have weak intestines while others can eat anything with no problem. If Lesseh was in the wild, he would probably have died quite young."

Ialu looked down at her as he listened. She was so thin. Perhaps sensing his gaze, Elin glanced up. Her eyes caught his for a moment, then slid to his shoulder. "I heard you were cut with a hatchet," she said.

"It's nothing serious. The wound has already closed."

"Let me take a look."

Without responding, Ialu ran his eyes around the stable. There was a small, wood-floored room on one side with a pile of folded bedding, a hearth, and a brazier with glowing coals. Beside it was a tray of untouched food.

"You didn't eat supper?" he asked.

Elin shook her head. "No, I didn't feel much like eating after dealing with the aftermath of Lesseh's indigestion. I often don't eat supper, you know. Then in the middle of the night I'm so ravenous that I toast some fahko over the fire and eat it."

"I've got something better than fahko." He pulled the package from his shirt, and Elin's face brightened.

"Ogalu! It's been a long time since I've had any."

They took off their boots and, stepping up into the wood-floored room, began to toast the rice cakes on a metal grill over the brazier. Biting into one of the sweet, fragrant cakes, Elin closed her eyes with a sigh. "Mmm. Tastes just the same. I used to beg my mother to get some whenever the merchants came to sell their wares in the village."

Ialu reached for the teapot on the table. Elin looked up and said, "Oh, sorry. The tea's already cold. Here, I'll boil up some water."

"No, don't bother. Cold tea is fine." Ialu poured it into the cups, and for a while, the two of them sat silently munching ogalu and sipping tea.

When they finished, Elin rose to her knees and reached out to touch Ialu's shoulder. "Show me," she said.

"It's nothing, really," Ialu protested, but he removed his top as she asked. Elin undid the bandage and peeled away an ointment-smeared cloth.

"It's a clean cut," she murmured, probing gently around the edges. "There's no swelling. You should be able to remove the stitches soon."

"Will you take them out for me tomorrow?"

"Yes, it should be all right by then."

He felt her breath on his shoulder. Looking at her intent expression as she examined the wound, he felt a sharp pang of tenderness. He reached out and cupped the back of her neck in his hand. Elin looked up in surprise, then stretched out her arms toward him.

Listening to the soft patter of the rain on the roof, Ialu stared blankly at the ceiling. Beside him, Elin stirred.

"Rain?" she asked.

"It'll stop soon. The birds are warbling."

Elin stretched luxuriously. "It's been a long time since I slept so soundly."

"Me too. I didn't even dream." The thought that this could be their last time together brushed Ialu's mind, and a deep sorrow filled his chest. He wanted to let everything about this moment permeate his body.

"Have you seen Jesse yet?" Elin asked.

"Yeah. I was surprised to see how much he's grown."

"He's been acting strangely lately," Elin said in a low voice. "When we pass each other, he pretends he doesn't see me."

Ialu smiled. "Yesterday, he went without two meals for hitting his friend."

"What?" Elin sat up with a jerk.

"It's all right. We had a long talk."

"About what?"

"It's a secret. Between men. I promised him I wouldn't tell you, so I won't."

"Ialu . . ."

Hearing the anxiety in her voice, he said, "Don't worry. It'll be fine. He's going to be all right."

"But I want to know. What did he talk about?" Ialu cocked an eyebrow and said nothing. Elin sighed, pouting. "Honestly. You always clam up like that when it's something important."

Ialu gave a wry grin. "Have to keep my word as a man."

With a snort, Elin rose and began putting on the clothes she had left folded by her bed. Ialu rose, too. "How long can you stay?" Elin asked as she tied her sash,

"They gave me ten days, including traveling."

343

Elin's hands paused. "Ten days? For such a minor wound? That's an awfully long time, isn't it?"

Ialu slowly tied his belt. "It's just an excuse. The Black Armor and Blue Armor units are being sent home for ten-day periods over the next half month. I got to leave a little early thanks to this injury."

Elin's face went blank. "So. The war is about to start," she whispered.

Ialu nodded. "From the little that Lord Yohalu told me, it sounds like the Lahza offered us some deal concerning the caravan cities in the eastern plains. But it's probably an offer we can't accept."

Elin frowned and bowed her head. The blood drained from her cheeks, and her lips grew tight. Taking a deep breath, she raised her face and fixed her gaze on Ialu. Her eyes gleamed, and she opened her mouth to speak, but no words came. She knew there was no point in voicing her plea. If she begged him to quit the Riders, if she pleaded with him not to go to war, he would say that if she found a way out herself, so would he. With trembling fingers, she pushed back a strand of hair from her forehead, then buried her face in her hands.

A breath of wind stole through a crack in the wall to stroke Ialu's cheek. The paper that had wrapped the rice cakes fluttered as it passed, and he stared at it vacantly. Even without physically touching, the pain he and Elin shared joined them together. The only way to erase the agony that seared his insides and tortured Elin was for both of them to survive and return. For both of them to come back to Jesse and grow old together. He knew what an impossible dream it was. But he couldn't help but hope.

Even if it's not possible for me to survive, if at least Elin can, he thought as he watched the paper flutter. Jesse was only fourteen. Ialu had to at least make sure that Jesse's mother came back.

He closed his eyes at the thought of his son staying behind alone. Although Esalu would make sure he didn't want for anything, Ialu couldn't bear to let him suffer the grief of losing his mother. He couldn't let that happen. That was why he had chosen to become a Toda Rider and spend these last six years away from home.

But a battlefield was a maelstrom of madness. No matter how much he might prepare or how hard he might wish for it, there was no knowing if he and Elin would make it back alive.

He opened his eyes. Elin had raised her face and was gazing at the Royal Beasts. The rain had stopped, and the white light of morning was shining through the skylight. How would he feel when he saw the morning's light on the battlefield? The thought rose slowly in his brain as if it belonged to someone else, then disappeared.

5

IN THE FIELD

The grass was wet with the rain that had fallen early that morning. Ialu's boots were soaked as he strode through the field toward the cliff.

"Do you want to see the Royal Beasts train?" Elin had asked. There was no longer any hesitation in her eyes. Until now, afraid of getting him involved, she'd never let him near the training grounds. But today, Ialu reflected, she'd probably decided that it would help him on the battlefield to know how the Royal Beast corps moved.

There was no sign of anyone on the cliff top; just a cluster of brilliant dots flashing between the clouds far in the distance. As they drew closer, the specks of light expanded, revealing the forms of Royal Beasts. They flew in a perfect V formation as though drawn by the one in front, its wings propelling it forward with powerful strokes. Ialu's stomach and legs began to quake as they loomed nearer, and he backed away to the edge of the forest.

Perched on Leelan at the front of the pack, Elin raised her arm and then lowered it sharply. Instantly, the enormous beasts raised their wings with a crack that split the air like thunder. Curling their claws, they swooped down to land.

Leelan glided gently onto the top of the cliff. The wind from her wings bent the grass and whipped up a powder of crushed leaves. Behind her, the others alighted one by one without breaking formation. Some of them perched on ledges below the cliff top so that only their heads were visible. Elin climbed down from Leelan's back.

A sense of awe gripped Ialu, squeezing his chest. There were only ten Royal Beasts, but seeing them shoot like arrows toward him had been breathtaking. That sight would have captivated the heart of any leader or statesman. He was struck by the magnitude of the situation in which they were trapped. And the reason Elin couldn't escape. Some things have to be seen to be truly understood, he thought. This was one of them.

Elin swung her arm in a circle while calling out to the Beasts. The tension drained from their bodies. Some rose and flew off to a distant cliff, while others glided down to the river below. Leelan lowered herself onto the grass in the sun and began grooming her fur.

Ialu stared at Elin wordlessly. Having been exposed to the cold wind, her cheeks were ghostly white, but her eyes gleamed. "Aren't they beautiful?" she said breathlessly.

Ialu nodded. "Yes. And fast, too."

Elin's face broke into a smile unlike any Ialu had ever seen. "Aren't they, though!" she exclaimed. "It depends on the wind of course, but they can fly as far as Lazalu in about one hour."

Ialu's eyebrows shot up. Even with a fast horse, it would take him a day to get to the Lazalu Sanctuary in the capital. "Really?" he asked.

"Yes. Only Esalu knows, but I've already flown them to Lazalu three times. I've been training them to make night flights. That's one of the reasons I've been staying overnight in the stable. So that people won't notice I'm gone and become suspicious."

Ialu stared at her. If she's been training them that rigorously, he thought, it's no wonder she's so thin.

"If I let them fly at the speed they wanted," Elin continued, "we could get there even faster. But I couldn't endure it. The wind's incredible."

In a rush of words, she told him how she navigated by the moon and the stars, how high the Beasts flew, and how she communicated her commands while in flight. As he watched her, Ialu's face clouded. She was like a stranger. When she spoke about the Royal Beasts, her face became sharp, and her eyes glittered strangely, as though she were possessed.

Catching sight of his expression, she broke off and stared at him. Sucking in air, she let out an unsteady breath and shook her head. "I'm sorry," she said.

Still frowning, Ialu looked at her. Her eyes seemed hollow and vacant, and she absently wiped away the sweat that beaded her brow. "Elin," he asked gently. "What's wrong?"

She blinked. "It's always like that. When I ride the Royal Beasts in formation, I feel strangely exhilarated." She began to tremble, her arms flopping uselessly, then slumped to the ground.

Ialu knelt beside her and slipped his arm around her shoulders. Her skin was icy cold yet clammy with sweat. "Are you all right?" he asked.

Elin nodded weakly, as if speaking were too much effort. For some time, she leaned against him with her eyes closed. Finally, she opened her eyes and let out a slow breath.

"Sorry," she said. "I'm okay now."

The flush of excitement had drained away, and her cheeks were pallid. Ialu suddenly recalled the faces of his fellow Toda Riders after training exercises with the new breed of Toda. Once they dismounted, they often trembled violently. Even veterans of the Blue Armor unit, who'd seen mortal combat many times, told him they'd never experienced anything like it when riding other Toda.

Stroking Elin's back, Ialu shared this anecdote with her. Her face tightened. "You mean the degree of excitement is different?" she asked.

"Well, I guess that, too, but I think it's more the quality that's different." He searched for words. "Men get really wound up in combat. It agitates and excites them. It's not uncommon to get battle fever. But when I'm riding the new breed of Toda and training in formation, I feel strangely on edge, as if my blood is raging inside me. I'm filled with an urge to kill. It's at its worst when we're training to storm a building. Then the sensation becomes like a buzzing in my ears. It makes my teeth ache and my skin crawl."

Elin frowned as she listened.

"A few veteran Riders say they've experienced something like it before," Ialu continued, "but most never have." He paused suddenly. "You know," he said, "I just realized that I sometimes feel that same irritation when I'm in the Stone Chambers with the new breed. Maybe that's why there're so many fights among the Stewards and Riders these days."

"You mean like the one you tried to break up?"

"Yeah." The fight reminded him of something Chimulu had said. "Elin, I forgot to tell you. Chimulu wanted me to ask you a question."

"Chimulu?"

"Yes. He wants to know if the Silent Whistle emits something invisible to the human eye." Ialu's mouth crooked. "He said he knows it's a weird question and you may just laugh at him, but it's really been bothering him. He thinks if we can identify what the whistle does, we could find a way to calm the Toda without using it to paralyze them. He's a lot like you, you know. He says the craziest things."

But Elin didn't laugh. She sat motionless, gazing off into space.

"Elin?"

"What does the Silent Whistle emit?" she whispered. She shook her head slightly, then said, as if to herself, "Chimulu's amazing." She stared at the ground, remaining silent for a long time. Finally, she raised her head and said in a low voice, "Sound is intricately related to the secrets of the Royal Beasts and the Toda. I think Toda would respond much more sensitively if we controlled them with sounds rather than with their horns."

Ialu stared at her pale, strained face. She found the manipulation of Royal Beasts and even Toda repellent, yet his job was to breed and improve the Toda. A chill spread through his heart at the thought of what she must have felt as they discussed these things.

Elin's face relaxed. "Don't look like that," she said gently. "Even if I kept this to myself, Chimulu is bound to realize it sooner or later. I'm sure he'll keep discovering what the restrictions imposed by the Law prevented us from seeing."

She glanced over at Leelan who was still lazily grooming. "Leelan and the others control the Toda with sound," she said. "Not just to kill and eat them either. They use it in more subtle ways.

"I've been flying them one at a time to areas with wild Toda and training them to stop attacking at my command. But during this process, I noticed something interesting. When there's only one Toda, Leelan won't make the sound that renders them helpless for the kill."

Ialu listened, absorbed by her words.

"Olamu, the Beast Hunter, once told me the same thing. Royal Beasts in the wild only paralyze and devour Toda that are trying to attack their nest, or when they run into a whole swarm of them."

Ialu's jaw dropped. "So when Leelan attacked the Toda during the ambush of Her Majesty Halumiya and at the battle on Tahai Azeh it was because there were so many of them?"

Elin nodded.

"Are you sure they won't attack if there's only one Toda? Unless it's attacking their nest?" he demanded.

"Yes. If they aren't hungry and there's only one Toda, they won't attack. But it depends on the situation. For Leelan, the pasture is her territory and the stable is her nest. Even so, if a Toda on its own is behaving aggressively because it's mating or egg-laying season, she'll threaten it, warning it not to attack."

"Threaten? How?"

"With her voice. The cries of a Royal Beast, which sound like notes on a finger flute, are incredibly varied. Even within the range of what I can hear, she distinguishes between many different sounds. Interestingly, Toda also use a varied range of sounds to communicate. I've been studying wild Toda these last six years, and the males have a special intonation to attract females, while their young have a cry to call for their parents. Toda are fascinating creatures, you know. Lizards and snakes don't raise their young, but Toda actually spend quite a long time raising and protecting them. As a pack. They have a strong instinct to protect hatchlings within the pack, even if they aren't their own."

She breathed a short sigh. "The Toga mi Lyo must have studied all of the Toda's cries in great detail and used that knowledge to develop the Handler's Art."

Ialu saw grief rise in her eyes.

"I'm sure that art is still passed down among the Ahlyo," she said hoarsely. "But I don't even know the real meaning of the song my mother played to save my life. Toda and Royal Beasts are mysterious creatures. They're different from other animals. The more I learn about them, the more I'm sure of that. If Toda bred by men are different from those in the wild, there must be a reason. But I would need far more time to find out. I'd have to spend years studying and comparing them."

She looked down and rubbed her chilled fingertips to warm them. The autumn wind shook the grasses and stroked her hair. Far away, she heard a bird call twice, then silence. She raised her head and gazed sightlessly at the swaying ears of grass. "What I've managed to find out so far has just scraped the surface. But thanks to that, I've learned a lot. Toda are such powerful creatures that, except for other Toda, Royal Beasts are their only predators. Without the Beasts, they would soon overproduce and end up eating each other, or starving to death. They don't produce as many young as lizards or snakes, but compared to Royal Beasts, which only bear an average of two cubs in a lifetime, they're far more prolific. That's probably why Royal Beasts wield such power over them. For Royal Beasts, Toda are the only creature capable of killing their cubs. And if their cubs are eaten, they could be wiped out."

Turning her face up to the autumn sunshine, she narrowed her eyes. "The relationship between Toda and Royal Beasts is deep and complex. I'm certain the catastrophe we were warned about is connected to that relationship in some way."

She turned to Ialu. Frustration burned in her eyes. "Even though I've managed to find out that much, I'm still missing crucial pieces. For some time now I've been pondering the same question Chimulu asked. Because the Silent Whistle is unique to the Toda and the Royal Beasts. It doesn't affect any other animal. Dogs and humans aren't paralyzed by it, so why do both Royal Beasts and Toda freeze when someone blows it?

"And why," she whispered as if chasing her own thoughts, "can Royal Beasts tell how far apart they are in heavy mist or avoid rock formations in the middle of the night? How do they pick up on such things without using their eyes? If the Whistle doesn't make a sound, then what knocks them rigid when we blow it?"

She stared off into space, thinking, then looked at Ialu. Her eyes gleamed with an uncanny light. "You said that the strange irritation becomes stronger when you're inside a building or the Chambers, didn't you?"

"Yes."

"Then maybe the Toda are emitting something that bounces off the walls or objects." Her voice rose with excitement. "I've been wondering if that might be the case for a long time. If they measure the distance between themselves by emitting something invisible and inaudible to us, then the training I've been doing may not have been wasted!"

Ialu frowned. "Is there anything that we can't see or hear?"

"Yes. Lots of things in this world exist even though we can't see them with our eyes. Just think about tokujisui. To us it simply looks like a liquid, but the solution contains elements that react with something inside Toda and Royal Beasts to change them. From the outside, we can't see the effects of tokujisui or the changes it causes. If only they *were* visible!"

Ialu's eyes narrowed. "That reminds me. Speaking of changes, the body fluids of the new breed are more toxic."

Elin's eyes widened. "Really?"

"Chimulu told me. According to him, one of the Stewards accidentally cut his hand on a scale. He went rigid and collapsed, and the cut bled profusely even though it was quite shallow. Maybe the bleeding helped wash out the poison, because the rigidity soon wore off and he recovered. But I've never heard of that happening before when people came in contact with Toda fluids. Have you?"

Elin shook her head, her eyes gleaming. "It sounds like the toxins are not only stronger but also produce different symptoms," she said. "I wonder what could've caused such a change in the nature of the poison. I'll have to look into it."

The excitement in her face faded. To investigate the cause would mean staying in Tokala village for an extended period. She couldn't do that and still continue training and studying the Royal Beasts. If Ialu told Yohalu how important this research was, he would appoint someone to do it. But she would prefer to see the nature of the change with her own eyes.

She shoved her hair back from her forehead and looked at the sky. "I need more time!" she exclaimed. "Time to find out all the things I want to know! Human lives are just too short."

Clouds swept like thin brush strokes across the autumn sky. Gazing at them, she let the tension seep from her shoulders. "At times like this, I always remember what Yuyan used to say: 'You haven't got eight brains and eight hands y'know, Elin. You've just got one head and one body. It's only natural that you can't do everything.'"

Ialu smiled. Elin's face always softened when she spoke of her old friend. They used to exchange letters frequently. Yuyan would tell her all about her eight kids, her husband, Kashugan, and all the little village intrigues. Her cheerful disposition came through in her writing, and they would all burst out laughing when they read her letters. Jesse loved it whenever they got one. As for Ialu, each time he came in contact with Yuyan's unhurried, pragmatic approach to life, it made him keenly aware of the speed at which he and Elin were living their own lives.

Elin had stopped sending letters once she began training the Royal Beasts for fear of repercussions on Yuyan and her family. But even now, her friend remained in her heart, reminding her to slow down when she was going too fast.

"Ialu," Elin murmured, still gazing at the sky. "Is there any meaning to what I've been doing? Did I accomplish anything?"

Ialu stared at her. He didn't bother searching for words to respond. Even as she asked this question, Elin knew there was no answer. They sat together in the autumn field for a long while, staring up at the light blue sky and feeling precious time slipping away.

6

THE TODA OF LAHZA

Stars glittered like grains of sand in the broad heavens. Omilu glanced up at the night sky above the buildings as he trudged along the dark road.

That last pub was one too many, he thought. The pungent odor of spices lingered in his mouth, making him feel queasy. The whole town reeked of it. Everything about this place, the buildings, the women's skin, smelled different from his hometown. When he was first posted to the caravan city of Ulamu, it had all been new and exciting. His eyes were drawn to the women with their long slender necks and firm, high breasts, and the tenderly stewed meat marinated in spices had melted in his mouth.

But the novelty had since worn off, and he had grown tired of this place. Things that at first had seemed exotic now seemed cloying. Whenever he saw children running in the streets, where multi-hued fabric flapped in the breeze, he would think of his daughter, who must have been playing back home, and each night he spent time with a woman whose skin was slick with fragrant oil, he recalled his wife's hair, which smelled of the hearth.

Five more years. That was how long he had to go before he could leave this foreign place. The thought made him sigh. Maybe they'd let me go home if I got sick, he thought. But it would take him a month and a half by carriage to get there. Even on a fast steed, he would need at least twenty days. The reality of the distance pierced his heart.

He turned onto the main road. His face clouded. It seemed abnormally quiet. It should have been bustling with groups of soldiers off duty on their way back to their quarters, but there wasn't a soul in sight.

Am I the last one?

Just as he had thought, he should never have gone to that last tavern. He should have gone back with his comrades instead of being greedy and insisting on going to another spot. If he was late getting back and arrived on his own, the senior officer might notice and berate him.

The night wind blew down the wide thoroughfare. Somewhere in the distance a dog barked. The road led to the thick outer wall of the city and the imposing main gate. It was known as the Thunder Gate because of the noise the chains made when the heavy drawbridge was lowered across the moat that protected the city against invasion. As he approached it, Omilu frowned. It was still open. It should have been closed at sunset, and there were no guards or Toda to protect it. Even more surprising, the drawbridge was down.

His scalp crawled, and he sobered up instantly. Placing a hand on his hilt, he moved into the shadow of the great stone wall circling the city and broke into a dash, heading for the guardhouse. The sweet odor of Toda wafted toward him, but there were still none in sight. Nor did he see any of his comrades. He peeked inside the guardhouse. The light of the candles illuminated the space to the back of the room, but all he saw was a deck of cards scattered across the table.

Rather than walking through the towering main gate, he opened a wooden door on one side of the guardhouse as he always did, and stepped onto the drawbridge. The wind struck him forcefully, bearing the scent of Toda and something that reminded him of copper. Blood. His pulse hammered like a gong.

No one was there. Sinking into the darkness, all that was visible were the moat filled with dark water, the Toda stables—ten stone structures along the edge of the moat, and the fort that also served as the soldiers' living quarters. As he started across the drawbridge, the smell of blood grew stronger. Peering over the railing, he let out a little scream.

A corpse floated in the moat. Or half a corpse. Its torso was gone from the midriff up. For a moment he thought that the gatekeeper's Toda must have gone mad and eaten him, but then he noticed a huge log-like shape floating beyond the body. Dead. A dead Toda floating in the moat!

His head felt numb. Everything seemed to warp and pull away from him, as though he were in some kind of nightmare. He broke into a stumbling run, drawn toward the fort where his comrades ought to be. His mind kept telling him to go back, to run for it, to hide in a cheap inn or tavern in the town, but he couldn't stop his feet from moving.

He ran across the bridge and onto the grass beyond. As he passed the first Toda stable, he thought he heard something moving. Cautiously, he approached the half-open door and peered inside. His eyes widened. Bobbing in the large Pond were the corpses of Toda and men. At the edge of the pool stood a large Toda, and on its back . . .

A sharp blow struck his temple, and he knew nothing more.

When Omilu came to, the first thing he noticed was the smell of cold stone. Opening his eyes, he saw wet paving stones and beyond that, the Toda Pond. The raw odor of blood and the musk-like scent of Toda wafted toward him from its surface. Nausea gripped him, and he cleared his throat. His head was pounding. He tried to touch it but couldn't move his hands. Each time he struggled, ropes bit into his wrists.

When he understood that he had been tied up and rolled to the edge of the Pond, memory came flooding back. Breathing shallowly, he tried to make out what was going on. For several minutes, his mind had registered sounds, but now that he was fully conscious, he realized the sounds were voices.

"The lucky soldier appears to be awake." The man's voice was startlingly close. Although he was speaking Omilu's language, the accent was so thick he sounded as if he was twisting his tongue as he spoke.

"Sit him up." With that command, he heard footsteps coming toward him. Someone grabbed his arms roughly and forced him to a sitting position. Omilu's head jerked and pain shot through his skull. Bile rose in his throat, but he forced it down. Gradually the world stopped spinning around him, and three men came into focus. Two wore leather vests and had a sword slung at their hips. One of them, a fierce-looking warrior with skin tanned a deep copper, gripped Omilu's arms, while the other, a stocky, middle-aged warrior, stood gazing down at him. They were both Lahza.

Omilu's flesh tightened from his stomach to his chest. Shaking, he stared up at the older man in front of him. Beside him stood what looked like a musician. From the lakkalu slung across his back and his loose robes, it was clear at least that he wasn't a warrior.

The stocky man turned to the musician. "This one's yours. Take him back with you as a living witness, a remnant of the Lyoza army."

The musician, his face haggard, looked down at Omilu. He was a young man, bronze-skinned like the Asheh. When he began to speak, however, he sounded like a native of Lyoza. "What about the others?" he asked. "Will you not let even a few more prisoners free?"

The warrior shook his head. "They're hostages. Whether we set them free depends on the Yojeh's answer." He stroked his beard and continued in a soft voice. "Minstrel with the eyes of an Asheh and the heart of a Lyoza, tell your father just how easily we took this town tonight. Tell him with that silvery tongue of yours that the plains belong to us and the fearsome Toda are no longer his kingdom's alone."

Cold sweat trickled down Omilu's face as he listened to the conversation above his head. Slowly it dawned on him that he wasn't going to be killed after all, and a warmth spread up from the pit of his stomach. At that moment, however, he was yanked to his feet and, for the first time, his eyes took in the whole Pond. He began to shake again. Before, he had merely registered that there were corpses in the water. Now, however, he could see their faces and their uniforms. These were the bodies of his comrades that he had bid farewell to at noon. Or what remained of them, for they had been ripped and chewed by Toda jaws.

Two Toda sat on the other side of the pond, their long tongues flicking in and out of their mouths. They looked a bit different than usual, but the light was too dim for Omilu to see clearly. One thing he knew for sure, however, was that the men mounted on them were Lahza warriors. Mesmerized, he stared at this nightmare, barely breathing.

Turning in his saddle, Omilu saw a red glow spreading along the horizon, and the green grass of the plain emerging from the dark. Dawn was breaking.

He kept his horse at a gallop, ignoring his aching head. The musician who rode in front looked over his shoulder. "Are you okay?" he asked.

But Omilu couldn't answer. Although the pounding in his head grew worse, he kept spurring on his horse. He was petrified that no matter how fast or how far they ran, the Lahza would soon come galloping up behind. Desperate to put as much distance between them as possible, he dared not ease his pace.

The musician brought his horse closer. "Slow down," he said gently. "That was a hard knock you got to the head. You don't want to shake it too much."

"But they—" Omilu said in panic.

"The Lahza won't come after us," the musician said flatly, cutting through Omilu's fear. "I guarantee it. They want us to go back to Lyoza and tell everyone what happened."

When his words finally sank into Omilu's mind, something deep inside him loosened. He pulled back on the reins, slowing his pace. Panting, he wiped the sweat from his brow. The musician took a flask hanging from his saddle and passed it to him. The cool water slid down Omilu's throat, and his mind cleared. "Thank you," he gasped as he handed back the flask.

The musician took it with a nod, and Omilu snuck a peek at his profile. His eyes looked fierce, and his gaze was fixed on some far-off point across the grassy plain. "Pardon me," Omilu asked hesitantly, "but who are you?"

The man glanced at him. "Rolan," he said quietly. "Rolan Amasulu."

Omilu gaped. Several pieces of the puzzle that had been bothering him fell into place. "I see," he murmured. Every Toda Rider knew that Yohalu Amasulu of the Black Armor had adopted an Asheh as his son, and Rolan's fame as a musician was so great he was known in every caravan city. Omilu couldn't help but stare at him.

"You were lucky," Rolan said, his eyes still on the plain. "If you'd returned on time, you'd have been thrown into the dungeon like the other off-duty soldiers. Or killed by Toda if you happened to be on duty."

Shuddering, Omilu gripped the reins tightly. "What on earth . . ." He swallowed audibly, and tried again. "How could they have overcome fifty Toda so easily?"

Rolan's expression hardened. "Poison."

"Poison?" Omilu's voice squeaked.

"Yes, they poisoned the sheep carcasses that were fed to the Toda. By the time the Lahza arrived, the Toda had gone into convulsions and were unable to fight."

Omilu gave him a hard stare. "How do you know that?"

Rolan looked at him. "Ozkula, the older warrior with the beard, told me. He's a senior officer under the grand chief Nozgula of Western Oolish. He held me captive for a long time. I was wondering why he kept me alive, but now I know. He wants me to tell my father in person just how easily the Oolish Oh subdued the caravan city of Ulamu."

Rage suffused his face. "It's all because of Ola," he said, cursing the governor of Ulamu. "He was such a careless imbecile! I warned him time after time, begging him not to become complacent. He governed Hoza for so long, he thought he knew what he was doing, but Ulamu and Hoza are totally different. I told him he should dine with leading figures in the city to gain their trust. But he wouldn't listen!"

Rolan's face was tight and his eyes burned as he spilled forth everything he had dammed up inside. "Unlike Imeelu and Hoza, Ulamu was built by the kingdom of Hajan and most of its leaders are Hajan descendants who see us as invaders. They appear friendly on the surface, but their hatred for us runs deep.

"The only reason the city held fast this long, despite repeated attacks from the Lahza, was because Ola's predecessor, Kassomu, worked hard to develop close connections with the city's leaders and gain the cooperation of Ulamu's citizens. That fool Ola made no effort to nurture those connections. Instead, he treated the people with contempt. No wonder they betrayed us!"

Omilu listened openmouthed to this scathing criticism of the governor. He wondered why Rolan was telling him all this, but guessed he probably didn't care who was listening. He just needed to vent his pent-up frustration.

Oblivious of Omilu's thoughts, Rolan continued his rant. "It's the people of Ulamu who deliver food for the Toda. Ola stopped having dogs test the food for poison. I suppose he figured that everyone was so grateful for our protection, they'd never do something like poison the meat. But the citizens of Ulamu chose to abandon us in favor of the Lahza."

He turned and glared at Omilu. There was such a wild light in his eyes, that Omilu tensed. Even though Rolan was staring straight at him, he seemed to be talking to someone else. "The caravan cities are strung on a delicate thread," he said. "If the news that Ulamu sided with the Lahza reaches the other cities, they might make the same choice."

Omilu licked his lips. "You mean the other cities are at risk, too?"

Rolan sighed. The rage drained from his face, replaced by deep fatigue. "I suppose not yet. The governors of the other cities aren't as stupid as Ola. And they're still testing the Toda's food for poison."

Omilu breathed a sigh of relief. "We'll be all right, then. As long as they can't poison our Toda, no one can withstand us."

Rolan frowned and stared at Omilu as though he were some strange creature. "But you saw them with your own eyes, didn't you? Didn't you notice anything?"

Notice what, Omilu was about to ask, when he realized what Rolan must be talking about. "You mean the Toda?" he asked. "The ones the Lahza were riding so proudly? They took our Toda and . . ." His voice trailed off, realizing that what he had just said was impossible: If any of their own Toda had survived, his comrades would never have been so easily defeated. Which could only mean that the ones he had seen belonged to the Lahza.

"But that can't be," he breathed.

Without responding, Rolan turned his face forward. A ray of sunlight struck his back. Staring at the edge of the plain ahead, which still lay in darkness, he dug his heels into his horse's flanks.

7

THE YOJEH'S WORDS

"It's time for tea," Seimiya announced.

The nobles of Yojeh territory turned to stare at her aghast. They were in the middle of a meeting. Consumed with anxiety, they had been arguing heatedly, each insisting on his own point of view. Her words quenched this feverish exchange like a bucket of cold water. Although they could not hide their displeasure, they scraped back their chairs and, with a deep bow to the Yojeh, filed from the room. The warlords of Aluhan territory followed after. When the door snapped shut, a hush fell over the room like the silence after a storm.

Seimiya sighed and looked up at Shunan, who sat beside her. A wry smile touched his fatigue-worn face. "If only there was a Silent Whistle that worked on humans," he said.

Seimiya gave a weak laugh and gazed around the room. The heat of the gathering still lingered in the air. "Instead, the Yojeh uses tea time," she said. "When my grandmother taught me how to conduct these kinds of meetings, I didn't understand what she meant, but now I do."

Her grandmother's soft voice sounded in her ears: "When you think that all possible opinions have been shared and the discussion has come to a dead end, announce that it's time for tea. It's very important to get the timing right. If you miss the moment when everything that can be said has been said, people will go on repeating themselves until everyone is weary. Be sure to end the meeting nicely before that happens."

Traditionally, the Yojeh listened to the opinions of the warlords and the nobles, and when she judged that she had heard them all, she declared that it was time for tea. This tradition had begun with the Royal Ancestor Jeh who had always had a cup of tea before making a major decision, and each successive Yojeh had followed in her footsteps. As Seimiya sipped the fragrant tea, she thought once again that the past Yojeh must have known human nature very well.

To ensure complete control over the final decision without making anyone feel slighted—that is what this custom was for. Not only that, but when Seimiya sipped her hot tea and reflected quietly on the content of the meeting, it helped her see the main points and get a clearer picture of what needed to be done.

The nobles of Yojeh territory were mean-spirited, motivated by self-interest, yet even so, because their rule benefited their domains, it also benefited the country as a whole. The warlords of Aluhan territory would have protested just as vehemently if they felt their own profits were threatened. But Seimiya knew that the reactions of both were really inspired by fear.

Although Lyoza had managed to scrape through the crisis precipitated by the year's poor harvest, there was no guarantee that next year or the year after would be any better. Everyone in the country was probably afraid that they would slide into poverty and famine.

Seimiya clenched her jaw. I changed this kingdom by marrying Shunan. I can't let this reformation lead to decline. I mustn't let my people think it was a mistake. If we're to live in peace, we can't afford to lose the prosperous caravan cities.

There was really only one choice that would please them all. She placed her cup on the side table with a click and turned to her husband.

"Have you come to a conclusion?" he asked.

Seimiya sighed. "It seems that war is the only way."

Two months ago, a secret messenger sent by grand chief Nozgula of Oolish Oh had delivered a letter to Aluhan Ula, Shunan's castle. In it, Nozgula had proposed that they enter into an agreement. If the kingdom of Lyoza would renounce all territorial rights to the three caravan cities of Ulamu, Ikishili, and Togulamu, which were located closest to Lahza, Lahza would recognize the territorial rights of Lyoza to the caravan cities of Imeelu, Hoza, and

Kasholu, which were closest to Lyoza; in addition, Lahza would order the clans loyal to Lahza not to attack Lyoza.

Nozgula had also stated that he would first demonstrate the wisdom of accepting this agreement. True to those words, Lahza warriors mounted on Toda had attacked and conquered Ulamu, the caravan city farthest from Lyoza.

Half a month earlier, Rolan had arrived in Ikishili, the caravan city nearest to Ulamu, and told those in charge what had happened. Soldiers from the Toda troop stationed in Ikishili were sent to Ulamu to find out if his report was true. They discovered the city gate guarded by warriors wearing Lahza armor and mounted on Toda decorated with unfamiliar headdresses. They also saw Toda swimming in the moat. Although smaller than those raised in Lyoza, they were swift and agile. Having confirmed that Ulamu had fallen, the soldiers decided their first priority was to defend Ikishili. Abandoning any attempt to infiltrate Ulamu, they hurried back to their base.

Messengers and carrier pigeons sent from Ikishili had reached the Aluhan just five days earlier. Around the same time, a detailed letter addressed to the Aluhan and Yohalu had arrived from Rolan, who had reached Imeelu, the closest caravan city to Lyoza. News that the Lahza had developed a Toda army capable of defeating Lyoza's seasoned troops was a major blow. Summoning the warlords of Aluhan territory, Shunan had spent the last five days consulting on strategies without rest.

For the last twenty years, the Lahza had harried the farthest protectorates: Ulamu, Ikishili, and Togulamu. Many soldiers from Aluhan territory had lost their lives defending them. These cities were flourishing trade centers to which goods flowed from many eastern countries for processing and distribution. The taxes levied for their defense brought the kingdom such prosperity that the advantage of protecting them was far greater than the cost of maintaining forts and stationing Toda troops nearby.

Faces flushed, the warlords and the nobles had insisted almost unanimously that accepting the terms of Nozgula's proposal was inconceivable. In all the skirmishes fought to date, Lyoza had never suffered a clear defeat. Ulamu may have been taken temporarily in this surprise attack, they said, but that was no reason to start compromising now.

Their indignation was fueled by shock and fear. They were terrified by the thought that the Lahza were capable of defeating their elite Toda troops, but they were ashamed to admit their terror in front of the Yojeh and the Aluhan. To cover up their consternation, some nobles began calculating the impact on the country's finances of lost tax income from the three cities.

Only two men disagreed with the rest: Lord Saluma from Jiki, a domain on the southern edge of Aluhan territory neighboring Tolah, and Lord Yohalu from Amasulu on the edge of the eastern plains. While basically opposed to accepting Nozgula's proposal, they argued that it would be wiser to show a willingness to negotiate.

Although the three caravan cities named by Nozgula provided substantial tax income, discontent among the soldiers protecting these far-off lands was leading to corruption within the Toda ranks. In addition, these three cities were populated largely by Hajan, who harbored a deep resentment toward Lyoza for bringing about their kingdom's downfall long ago. Lyoza soldiers stationed in these cities lived in constant fear of revolt by the local people. Yohalu and Saluma recommended exploring the possibility of compromise to gain time before engaging in a decisive battle, while in the meantime communicating secretly with influential people in the caravan cities to win them over to their side. They proposed finding a new approach to governing those cities that would satisfy their leaders and encourage their citizens to work with Lyoza to defend themselves against the Lahza.

Few people, however, agreed with this idea. Even if Lyoza were to seek a new approach, they insisted it should only be done once the Lahza had been routed. To try and placate the Lahza in the hope of buying time was foolhardy.

Saluma continued to argue against open rejection, but when it became clear that the majority was opposed, Yohalu said that if they insisted on routing the Lahza first, he would accept their decision on one condition: If they failed to achieve a resounding victory over the Lahza, he asked that they accept his and Saluma's proposal to explore possible concessions while developing a new approach to running the protectorates.

It was just as people were beginning to protest that the Yojeh had announced it was time for tea.

"Yohalu presented his argument in that way to push his proposal for compromise and a new way of governing," Shunan said in a low voice. "He told me about this idea some time ago." Shunan lowered his voice even further. "But he also told me that if we're going to go to war, it's probably better to do it sooner rather than later."

Seimiya nodded. "Before the Lahza Toda troops grow even more powerful."

"Yes. The reason he started off by insisting that we should avoid confrontation was to make the nobles of your territory and the warlords of mine push even harder for war."

"And by doing so, he made it clear where responsibility lies if there's no resounding victory," Seimiya said with a smile. "He really cares about you, doesn't he?" Thanks to Yohalu, she thought, the nobles of Yojeh territory wouldn't be able to blame the Aluhan after the fact for starting the war.

With a wry smile, Shunan cocked an eyebrow at her. "Yes, indeed. But his words didn't just save me, did they?"

Still smiling, Seimiya said nothing. He was right, she thought. Yohalu's words had saved her, too. She'd been forced into a position where she'd have to declare war. This wouldn't be a skirmish like the many battles fought before, nor a defensive action required to protect her country from invasion. To rebuff the hand extended by the enemy and declare war for the sake of national interest would be to change the very nature of the divine Yojeh, who had always rejected bloodshed as defilement. Yet this is what she had to do. Thanks to Yohalu and Saluma, she could at least excuse herself by claiming she'd made that decision in response to the entreaties of her people. By offering her this escape route, Yohalu had demonstrated his sincere desire to support the Aluhan and, for his sake, to avoid defiling the position of the Yojeh.

I know I should be grateful, she thought. But Yohalu was a warrior.

To him, war was a necessary means for resolving conflict. That was fundamentally different from the view held by the Yojeh of every generation. She could her hear grandmother's voice in her mind: "No matter what the reason, never try to justify bloodshed. Drill that into your bones."

This way of thinking, which had been passed down from their royal ancestor Jeh, is what made the Yojeh who she was.

Grandmother, Seimiya thought, addressing that kind, gentle woman who was now long gone. I will command my people to fight, but I will never seek to justify war.

For generations, the Yojeh had trained her people to revere her as a god, attempting through that reverence to instill in their hearts an aversion to war. Yet, at the same time, every Yojeh had profited from war, while pressing the sin of killing onto the Aluhan and his people. This hypocrisy made it impossible to successfully guide the country's affairs.

We will never find an alternative to war until every one of us—nobles, commoners, and even warriors—is convinced that bloodshed must be avoided at all costs.

To convince her people: that was her real task as the Yojeh who, resolved to bear responsibility for war, had married the Aluhan.

For some time, she fixed her melancholy gaze on a ray of sunlight that fell on the long table in the middle of the room. Finally, she sighed and looked at Shunan. "Let me follow the example of Lord Yohalu and Lord Saluma and take a step to deepen the bond between us."

Shunan raised his eyebrows in surprise, but Seimiya said coolly, "For the Yojeh to declare war is lunacy. The least I can do is to make a change for the better, no matter how small it may be. You once showed me the tragic sacrifices your soldiers make. The people of Aluhan territory are expected to give so much for me. And for the people of my territory, who reap the benefits without sacrificing anything themselves and without any gratitude. The warlords and commoners of your territory resent this injustice, so let me at least help relieve some of that ill feeling."

Shunan's face clouded. "Are you sure? That's bound to upset the nobles in Yojeh territory."

The smile that lit up Seimiya's face seemed incongruously bright. "They're already upset because I married you. Don't worry. I won't handle this so clumsily as to make life difficult for our children."

A strong light gleamed in her eyes. "Those who wish to profit must bear the responsibility involved. I will simply make sure the nobles pay what is due."

After tea, the Yojeh summoned all the warlords and nobles back to the meeting room. There she asked them if they truly wished her to reject the agreement offered by Nozgula of Oolish Oh and whether they were resolved to accept the outcome if rejection should lead to war. The nobles placed their hands over their hearts and declared that this was their will. To them, she said, "In the past, when the Hajan attacked this country, my ancestor chose not to fight and expressed her willingness to offer them her head. I have the utmost admiration for my ancestor's wish."

Her voice was thin but piercing. A shadow of unease crossed the faces of the men at these unexpected words.

"To the Yojeh," said Seimiya quietly, "the shedding of human blood is a sin. I detest war with my whole being. If, in order to avert conflict, I should take the hand that Nozgula has extended to me and give him the three caravan cities he demands, would you respect my decision?"

The men blanched, and their expressions froze. Then with bewildered looks, they searched the other faces in the room. Observing their consternation, Seimiya continued, "Or would you dissuade me, as Yaman Hasalu, the ancestor of my husband the Aluhan, once dissuaded the Yojeh of his time by offering to accept the defilement of bloodshed in her stead and expressing his willingness to lay down his life?"

A murmur arose and spread through the room. Color returned to the men's faces and they nodded, glancing at one another. Seimiya turned her face to the nobles of the oldest family lines. "Toiyala? Somaya? Akizalaku? Which path will you choose?"

Asked point-blank, they blushed, but Toiyala said, "Your Majesty, I humbly beg your forgiveness, but I wish to dissuade you."

Somaya and Akizalaku immediately chimed in. "For the sake of this country, we also wish to dissuade you. This impure decree has not come from Your Majesty. Rather it is our wish."

They had regained their composure, and relief showed in their faces. Having read behind Seimiya's words her desire to keep the position of the Yojeh unsullied, they had concluded that all they needed to do was respond to her wish.

With her eyes fixed on theirs, Seimiya drove her point home. "So," she said, "you wish to emulate Yaman Hasalu, the Aluhan's ancestor. Is that correct?"

Only Somaya showed a trace of apprehension at these words. The other two nodded magnanimously. "That is correct, Your Majesty," Toiyala said. "As sincere and loyal subjects, we are concerned for Your Majesty and for the country."

Seimiya nodded and shifted her gaze to Akizalaku and Somaya, then to each of the other nobles. A few looked troubled, but when she gazed into their eyes, they all nodded without exception. She rose from her throne. "Not only the loyal vassals of Aluhan territory but my own nobles are urging me to declare war. I ask you, my people, should I choose to fight?"

They pressed their hands to their hearts and declared in unison, "Yes."

"My people, I do not wish to drag you into the chaos of war. I ask you once again. Do you truly wish for war in which your own blood may flow?"

With their hands still on their hearts, they declared that they did.

Seimiya nodded and let her eyes sweep the room. "I understand. If you truly wish to shed blood for the sake of profit, then I, the Yojeh, will respect your wish. Oh, nobles of my realm, I have heard this plea from your heart. Let me reject the hand that Nozgula has offered. If war should result, then so be it. And, my faithful nobles, I hereby give you permission to ride into the battlefield as Yaman Hasalu did of old."

The nobles, who were listening to her words with flushed faces and shining eyes, froze. Giving them no chance to speak, Seimiya said, "Until now, the Yojeh has made the Aluhan and his people shed blood for her sake, but see how blessed I am to have such loyal subjects as you. Your high-minded ideal that those who seek profit should bear equal responsibility and pay the same price for their actions is truly noble. It is my intention to join my husband in the battlefield and stand by you in this decision. So that there may be no one who profits without sacrifice."

As her words rang through the room, the nobles of Yojeh territory were not the only ones who paled. The warlords of Aluhan territory looked as though they had been struck by a lightning bolt.

At that moment, everyone knew: The Yojeh stood with the Aluhan. That was her wish.

8

THE COURIER COMES

Elin was feeding Leelan when she heard someone pounding on the stable door.

Ever since bidding Ialu farewell, she had felt hollow. No matter what she did, she couldn't dispel the emptiness. She looked up at Leelan and sighed. Although there was still meat in her food box, Leelan had turned away and begun preening herself. She had less appetite than usual, and her coat of fur and the hairs around her muzzle had lost the luster of youth.

Whenever she noticed signs that Leelan was aging, Elin felt a pang of loneliness. The average lifespan of Royal Beasts in the wild was unclear, but those in the sanctuary lived about twenty years. And while thirty years was possible, it was considered a remarkably long life. Leelan was already past twenty. Looking up into her gentle eyes, Elin thought how quickly time had passed.

It was at that moment that she heard the knock on the steel door. Someone called her name. After wiping her hands on her apron, she raised the bolt and opened the door. One of the guards stood in the morning sunlight, his face strained.

"A courier has just arrived with an urgent message from Her Majesty, the Yojeh. You are asked to read it and respond immediately."

Elin broke the seal and spread open the pages inside. As her eyes followed the words, a chill numbness spread across her forehead. Written in a code that only Seimiya, Shunan, Elin, and Esalu could understand, the message described the defeat of Ulamu in a surprise attack by a Lahza Toda troop, the Yojeh's rejection of a proposal from Nozgula, grand chief of the Western Oolish, and the fact that she and the Aluhan were preparing for war. Elin read as far as the Yojeh's request that she fly the Royal Beasts to the capital, but got no farther. Her eyes kept skidding off the page.

She raised her face. "Please tell the courier that I received the message and will begin composing a reply immediately," she said to the guard. "But it will be faster for me to take the Royal Beasts and deliver my reply in person, so please tell him that I'll take it myself."

The guard saluted sharply, then turned on his heel and dashed away.

Elin did not fly the Royal Beasts that day. Instead, she spent hours at her desk in her room. The Yojeh and the Aluhan had asked her to gather the Royal Beasts immediately at the Lazalu Sanctuary in the capital. Assuming that the main battle would take place near one of the caravan cities, they were now building enclosures at each city to station the Royal Beasts. Once it became clear where the battle would be fought, they would ask her to fly them from Lazalu to the battlefront.

To the Royal Beasts, Toda were just Toda. They couldn't distinguish between friend and foe. A clear plan of action was needed to prevent them from attacking their own side. The Aluhan and his men had studied each potential battlefield and had developed a number of plans, which were conveyed in the letter.

Elin examined each one and wrote detailed comments about which might be difficult and about adjustments that should be made in consideration of the Royal Beasts' nature. By the time she finished, it was already late afternoon, and the light slanting through the window onto the edge of her desk had turned a rosy hue. There was a dull ache deep in her eyes. She pressed her fingers against her temples as she carefully reread the words she'd written. With a sigh, she rolled and sealed the letter tightly.

She had been requested to leave Kazalumu within the next two days at the latest. Today she would have to tell Esalu everything and prepare her luggage. Had they given her so little time to pack because it was so urgent, or because they didn't want to give her time to think?

Elin gazed out the window. The setting sun gilded the treetops. In her mind, she imagined the Royal Beasts shooting up like fireworks at a single command and scattering across the vault of the evening sky.

I have done what I could.

That thought dropped into her breast and spread through her being. She had studied the nature of Royal Beasts for a long time. Based on that, she had pondered what kind of disaster might have happened beyond the Afon Noah. She had added to this all that she had learned from Ialu about the habits of the Toda to make her own deductions and train the Royal Beasts so that she could respond to whatever happened on the battlefield. There were still some things she would have liked to try if there had been a little more time, but she had no regrets about what she had done so far.

A ray of red light bathed her bookshelf. On it were all the documents that she had written and bound roughly with thread. Records of the characteristics and nature of Toda and Royal Beasts, as well as a record of her own life and the path that had led her here. She had written these accounts, hoping to give them to Jesse when he was old enough to read them. Their paper spines were fuzzy because she had flipped through them many times, adding passages. She stared at them for some time. Then, slipping the scroll she had written inside the front of her robe, she stood and opened the door to her room.

The living room with the hearth had already sunk into blue shadow. The sight of the cold hearth reminded her suddenly of Jesse, who usually sat there waiting for her, and a sharp pain ran from the pit of her stomach up to her chest. They would have to part so soon. When she left tomorrow, she might never sit around that hearth with Jesse again.

Her skin grew cold, and she felt as though her body was shriveling up and sinking deep into her chest. She fumbled for the wooden post with her hand, and when she found it, pressed her forehead against it. A huge wave of grief rose inside her. She couldn't breathe. Clinging to the pillar, she pressed her forehead against the smooth wood surface and gasped for air. Even now, some corner of her mind told her not to cry out loud because the guards were in the next room. For a long time, she clung to the post, breathing raggedly through her mouth.

When his teacher told him to spend the night at home, Jesse felt the world around him recede into the distance. Everyone had been talking about the special courier from the palace who had arrived that morning, and Jesse's friends told him they had seen his mother go into the headmistress's room. He had worried all day that the courier's message had something to do with his mother. So when he heard that an exception was being made to the school rules and he was being allowed to spend the night at home, he knew that what he had feared had now come to pass.

As he opened the door to his home, the aroma of fresh-baked fahko tickled his nostrils. Elin was kneeling in front of the oven removing a thin baking sheet.

"Oh, there you are," she said. "Welcome home. Perfect timing, too. Would you get me that big plate?"

Jesse hurried over to the sink and quickly washed his hands, then got out a large plate and held it out for his mother to slip the fahko on it. It was a large thin disk like those sold in the stores, rather than the kind she usually baked. Noticing thin slices of boar meat on a cutting board in the kitchen, he guessed what she must be making. "We're going to have charcoal-grilled boar?" he asked.

Elin nodded. "Yes, we are. Although I'm a little late getting started."

A pot hung over the hearth, filled with piping hot vegetable soup. Wrapping a towel around the handle, his mother removed the pot and put it off to one side, then placed a four-legged metal grill over the coals. She greased the pan with a chunk of fat and arranged the slices of meat on it. They made a sizzling sound.

As he watched, Jesse spread mazu, a sweet-and-spicy miso, on the steaming fahko and topped this with leafy greens. He loved this dish. Well-grilled boar, a little burnt around the edges, wrapped in fahko spread with mazu. When they'd lived in town, his mother always used to make this for him on his birthday and for special occasions.

"It's done," Elin said. "Here." When she placed the sizzling meat on top of the greens and fahko, Jesse's eyes blurred, and he could no longer see. Keeping his head down and gritting his teeth, he forced himself not to cry.

He heard his father's voice in his ears: "When the time comes, don't make your mother sad. Send her off without tears." He sucked in his breath repeatedly, determined not to let her see him cry, but a sob caught in his throat, and he couldn't hold back his tears any longer.

The plate was lifted from his hands and placed beside him, and he was wrapped in his mother's arms. Clinging to her, he wept. He pressed his head into her chest, just as he had done as a child, and sobbed. The thought that he might never see her again burned his chest, and the tears wouldn't stop. He cried until his head swam. Feeling the strength of his mother's arms as she held him to her, Jesse stayed wrapped within her warmth. Finally, like the receding tide, something drained from his heart, leaving only a hollow loneliness. Once again, the words his father had said before he left Kazalumu rang inside him:

"When the Yojeh gives the command, your mother must leave. No matter how much you might cry, there's nothing that can be done to change that. So Jesse, don't cry. When the time comes, don't make your mother sad. Send her off without tears."

Jesse took a deep breath and gently withdrew his arms. Looking up at his mother through tear-drenched lashes, he saw that her face was also streaked with tears.

9

MOTHER AND CHILD

"Is the war going to start?" Jesse whispered.

"Probably. But nobody knows yet what's going to happen. Or if I'll need to fly Leelan and the others. I was told to wait at Lazalu for further orders."

"When are you leaving?"

"Tomorrow night."

"That soon!" Elin nodded, and Jesse's face twisted. "Are you taking them all? Even Alu?"

"I'm leaving Alu and Ukalu here. Because Alu's pregnant."

When Jesse heard this, he clenched his teeth and looked down for a moment. Raising his face, he said, "You'll come back again, won't you?"

She was about to nod but hesitated, something Jesse didn't miss. A hard light gleamed in his eyes. "You can't die, Mom! Promise me you won't!" he cried. "You're taking Leelan and the others to war because that's what the Yojeh and the Aluhan want. It's not your fault! There's nothing you can do about it, so don't go thinking that you have to take responsibility for it!"

Elin looked at him in surprise. "What are you talking about, Jesse?"

"I know what you're thinking, Mom! You feel guilty for training Leelan and the others as weapons of war, don't you? You feel you've betrayed them. If they're killed on the battlefield, you plan to die with them to pay for what you've done, right? Don't think I don't know! I heard what you told the Yojeh. I've been thinking about it ever since.

"Father said you're trying to find a way for our family and the Royal Beasts to live in peace, but if you die, we'll never be happy. Don't you get that?" His voice had risen shrilly.

"Hush, Jesse. Lower your voice," Elin whispered, glancing at the door, and he fell silent. "So you heard us talking, did you?" Elin asked.

Jesse nodded defiantly, biting his lip. I see, Elin thought as she stared at her son. That's why he's been acting so odd lately. The tension inside her ebbed away, replaced by a strange peacefulness.

"Jesse," she said quietly. "I'm not going to die to pay for what I've done."

Jesse pulled in his chin as though caught off guard. "Really?" he said.

She nodded. "Really. How could I even think of such a thing when you're here? I won't choose death to pay for what I've done. If I want to make amends, I'll do it by living, even if I have to crawl to do it. What I meant by taking responsibility is that I won't shove that burden onto anyone else just to escape from it." She paused, then added, "Jesse, ever since I was your age, I've dreamed of returning Leelan and the others to the wild. I've always believed we should let creatures born in the wild live as they would have. But when I tried to do that, I ended up twisting the bonds that bind the Royal Beasts even tighter."

She turned her eyes to the hearth and stared at the red coals. "Even now, I still don't know what was the right thing to do. If I hadn't interfered, if I'd given the Beasts tokujisui, they would never have had to go to war. But left like that, they would never have flown, or mated, or borne cubs either. They would have spent their lives waiting to die."

She turned her gaze back to Jesse, a bitter smile on her lips. "In the end, I couldn't return them to the wild, and I couldn't stop us from going to war either. But there is one thing that I can do. And it's something only I can do."

"What?"

"Expose the truth."

Jesse frowned. "Expose the truth?"

Elin fixed her eyes on his and said quietly, "I can reveal the truth that the Royal Ancestor Jeh and my own ancestors sought to hide."

Jesse blinked. "You mean the disaster that killed all the beasts and humans?"

"Yes. If that tale is true, I may actually cause such a disaster." She looked straight at him. "But I've been searching this whole time for a way to prevent it. You've watched me train Leelan and the others to fly together, haven't you?"

Jesse nodded.

"If what I've done is right, and I'm able to stay connected with Leelan and the others on the battlefield, I might be able to avert disaster." Her voice trailed off huskily. If only she could make that dream come true, how much easier she would feel. If only she could close with her own hands the door she had opened when she was a girl and get through this crisis without hurting anyone, man or beast . . .

She closed her eyes for a moment as longing filled her chest. Slowly, she opened them again. "Yet no matter how hard I might try to foresee what will happen when a pack of Royal Beasts falls upon a thousand Toda, I just don't know. What happens may exceed anything I could ever have imagined. So if a catastrophe does occur . . ."

She looked at her son, her face pale. "I will stand witness to what happens when Royal Beasts are used as weapons."

Jesse's eyes widened. Gazing into them, Elin said, "If we choose to use the Royal Beasts like this, despite knowing that a catastrophe may occur, then we must accept the consequences. Those who decided to wage this war, and I, who couldn't stop it, we must bear responsibility for it."

She paused, then drew a deep breath and whispered, "I want everyone to know this, Jesse. All of it."

Jesse listened silently, frowning.

"The Royal Ancestor Jeh and the Ahlyo hid the true nature of Royal Beasts and Toda so that men, driven by greed, wouldn't do something foolish. Like putting blinkers on a cart horse. My mother died to protect that secret." Her voice trembled slightly. "But you know, Jesse, I think hiding the truth was a mistake. I think that people need to be aware of their actions and of the consequences. Regardless of what it is, I don't think it's right to hide knowledge. Even if humans are stupid. Even if they're so foolish that they'll use the knowledge they gain for the wrong purpose."

She heard a door close outside. The guard was leaving to do his regular rounds. Listening to that familiar sound, Elin reached out her arm and gently clasped Jesse's hand in her own. "I once told your father that if humans can't maintain a balance except by killing one another, then let

375

them. Even if it means they all perish. For a long time, I kept this cold, cruel thought in my mind. But I don't think so anymore."

She smiled faintly. "People will never stop killing one another. There will probably always be war. We're separate. Although we have words to communicate, we can never adequately convey what we think and feel to one another. Yet humans will keep looking for a way through. That's the kind of creature we are."

Jesse listened silently as Elin continued.

"When people know, they think. Many different people, each with their own perspective and motive, will keep on thinking. When one dies, another will look for a new path to avoid extinction. That's how the human herd has survived this long.

"But we can't explore such questions if we're ignorant. We need knowledge to think. It's only when we have thought everything through to the end, when we've studied how we came to cause such a catastrophe, what stupidity drove us to it, why we behaved the way we did, that we can ever find a meaningful way to prevent it.

"And that's why," she said quietly, "I'll never give up, Jesse. I will never choose death for myself. If what I'm doing causes a catastrophe, I'm going to fly into the midst of it to see if there's a way through to the future. And I'll do my best to tell everyone what I find out."

She reached over and stroked his cheek. "Just watch me, Jesse."

A bird chirped a high-pitched note. Shadows flitted across the evening sky as birds flew home to roost. The remnants of the sunset still lingered in the west, while the east was already sunk in blue darkness. "He's late. What on earth can that boy be doing?" Esalu muttered, turning to look back toward the school with a frown.

Behind her, the guards stood quietly at the edge of the forest watching Elin and the Royal Beasts preparing to leave. Perched on the cliff top, the Beasts appeared unperturbed. They loomed beautiful and majestic like snowy peaks, their fur shining golden in the last rays of the sun that was disappearing below the rim of the mountains.

Gazing at their figures, Elin reflected that it was their beauty that had first captivated her and drawn her to this point in time. Even now, she vividly recalled the brilliant silver forms of the wild mother and cub she had seen with Joeun so long ago. She had longed to return Leelan and the others to the wild where they could mate and bear children, where they could rule the mountain valleys and be masters of their own lives, not tools of men. But in the end, she had failed.

In her mind, she spoke to the Beast that towered like a statue above her. What are you thinking right now, Leelan? she asked. They had taught each other their language and could now understand from the slightest gesture what the other was going to do. Yet she still didn't know what went on in Leelan's mind.

These creatures would now fly at her command and devour the enemy. If she ordered them to dive into the jaws of death, they would obey without protest. Yet even then, she would never know what they thought. How often she had wished that they weren't so obedient. If only they were like cats, if only they would ignore her commands and live as they pleased, she would never have had to lead them to their deaths.

"Alu will be entering the more stable phase of her pregnancy soon, won't she?" Esalu asked.

Elin turned to look at her and nodded. "Maybe it's a good thing the order to fly came now," she said.

"You mean we can at least save those two," Esalu said with a shrug.

Elin gave a wry smile. "Yes. And besides, I doubt they could fly with this pack anymore."

Esalu's eyes widened slightly. "Really?"

"Yes. I tried bringing Alu and Ukalu close to Leelan and the others, but they all raised their hackles and began to growl."

Watching Leelan groom her fur, Elin said, "If they formed their own separate pack and flew some distance apart, it would be possible, but to do that . . ."

"Someone other than you would have to lead them," Esalu said, finishing her sentence. Elin nodded. "I see," Esalu murmured, her eyes on Elin.

"So you've come to another line. If you don't cross it, you can keep others from being dragged into the conflict. What you're really saying is that being summoned now means you can bear this burden alone." There was a hard ring to her voice.

Elin gazed at her aging teacher. Her hair was much grayer now, and although her back was still straight, she seemed somehow smaller. Seeing Esalu's thin lips tremble, Elin felt a deep emotion well up and spread through her chest. Stepping closer, Elin hugged her shyly. "Thank you," she said.

Elin had never known her father's face and had lost her mother when she was very young. Despite this, though, she'd been happy, because of the affection with which Joeun had raised her and the stern yet profound love with which Esalu had nurtured her.

Esalu squeezed Elin tightly, then pulled herself away. "Don't say things like that," she snapped in her typical fashion. "It's bad luck!" Her face was wet with tears. "If you really want to thank me, come back. Come back and let me see you again."

Elin nodded, brushing her tears away with the palms of her hands. At that moment, she heard a commotion behind her. Turning, she saw Jesse push through the guards and come running toward her, bearing a bundle in his arms.

"Mom!" Gasping for breath, he placed the bundle on the ground and began undoing the cloth that bound it. Various things started tumbling out. Jesse grabbed a large parcel wrapped in wax paper and handed it to her. "I asked the dorm mother to bake these for you. They just came out of the oven. Cookies rolled in red sugar. They're still hot, but it's cold up there, isn't it? Eat them on your way. There're some for Leelan and the others, too. Give them one each when you get to Lazalu. They taste good even when they're cold. And this is a scarf. I've already warmed it with a hot water bottle, so put it around your neck before you fly."

He shoved the scarf into his mother's hands and then gazed up at her. "You don't have to worry about Alu," he said. "I'll take good care of her. You said you weren't able to return these ones to the wild, but you don't know that yet. It might still be possible. When you get back, I'll help you. Let's find a way to free Alu and the others." A fierce light burned in his eyes, and his mouth was firmly set.

Esalu cleared her throat and rapped Jesse lightly on the top of his head. He looked up at her in surprise. "I'll give you credit for your good intentions," she said with a scowl, "but only students in the upper level are permitted to take care of the Royal Beasts. Remember that, young man. You aren't anywhere near old enough for me to leave Alu in your care."

Jesse looked put out, but Esalu fixed him with a beady glare. She brought her hand up to Elin's eye level. "If you want to help your mother, work hard until you at least measure up this high. There are no shortcuts in studying. You'll never understand all your mother has learned these many years unless you knuckle down and study. Once you've mastered all your subjects, then you'll start to grasp what she has written. That's the nature of science and learning, so do your best, Jesse."

Although Jesse looked at her with a puzzled frown, in the end he nodded reluctantly. Seeing his expression, Elin burst out laughing. A leaden pain had weighed on her heart, but now she felt warmth radiate to every corner of her body.

She pulled him close. "Thank you, Jesse," she murmured. "Please watch out for Alu." Holding him tightly, she tried to imprint on her being the warmth and even the scent of him. In her heart, she whispered, I'll give you a new future. I promise.

She gritted her teeth. She didn't want to show him any tears right now. She released him slowly, as though peeling away her longing to stay, and bowed deeply to Esalu. "Please take care of Jesse," she said.

Then she turned to the guards standing at the edge of the forest and bowed her head low. They looked at her as if surprised and saluted.

Tying the bundle that Jesse had given her onto the riding harness, Elin settled herself on Leelan's back. The wind caressed her hair. With the two fingers remaining on her left hand, she grasped the worn and battered harp

379

that was attached with a long rope to the saddle. With her right hand, she plucked a string. It reverberated sharply. Instantly, the Royal Beasts raised their heads and, spreading their wings, leaped into the air.

Jesse and Esalu stood staring after them until they vanished into the sky, where distant stars were beginning to twinkle.

NINE

MADNESS

I

TO AMASULU

When Elin reached the Lazalu Sanctuary, she had asked a servant to deliver her message to Seimiya while she tended to the Royal Beasts. Seimiya read it while waiting for Elin to arrive. The window of her room was slightly open, and the chill night air drifted through. The scent of the outdoors mingled with the aroma of freshly brewed tea.

When a maidservant finally ushered Elin into the room, Seimiya stood up from her chair. "I'm glad to see you arrived safely."

Elin dropped to one knee and bowed formally. Seimiya acknowledged her greeting and gestured toward a desk in the center of the room. A large map was spread across it. Seimiya's eyes were on the map as she walked toward Elin, when suddenly she raised her face. "You smell lovely," she said.

"I do?"

"Yes, sweet and somehow delicious."

"Oh." Elin blushed. "My son gave me some baked sweets for the journey, and I just ate them."

At this, Seimiya's face relaxed into a smile. Turning once again to the map, however, her expression grew serious. She had already communicated with Elin in writing and so plunged straight into the subject of concern. "The palace is here," she said placing a finger on the map. "This is Amasulu, and here are the caravan cities." She moved her finger to each city as she said its name.

Imeelu was closest to Amasulu on the grassland highway that led straight from the eastern plains through Imeelu to Amasulu. Hoza was situated above the plains on the northern highway that skirted the edge of a mountain range, while Kasholu was situated south of the plains on the desert highway that passed through the drylands and branched off toward the kingdom of Tolah. Ulamu, which had been taken by the Lahza, as well as Ikishili and Togulamu, were located much farther east near the city of Hajan, which was once the capital of the Hajan kingdom.

"Ikishili is on a road leading to the northern highway, while Togulamu is on one leading to the desert highway," said Seimiya, "and Ulamu is on the grassland highway that passes through the plains."

The terrain through which the grassland highway passed was quite hilly in places, and although there were several small post towns scattered along the route, the only large settlements were Ulamu, followed by Imeelu and then Amasulu.

"Our soldiers stationed in Ikishili and Togulamu haven't reported seeing any Lahza troops. Nor have those in Hoza or Kasholu. We did hear, however, from soldiers in Tsualu over here." Seimiya pointed to a small post town between Ulamu and Imeelu. "They said there're about two thousand Lahza cavalry on the move."

Two thousand. The number seemed so huge Elin couldn't imagine the scale.

"The Lahza have been attacking both Ikishili on the northern highway and Togulamu on the desert highway quite frequently. They excel at surprise attacks, and the topography of those areas lends itself to such tactics."

Seimiya stopped and bit her lip. "Shunan once showed me some soldiers who had been wounded in battle." Elin noticed that she used her husband's name rather than calling him by his title, the Aluhan. "One young man had lost an eye and another an arm at Hosalu Pass, near Ikishili."

Seimiya's words brought back a night long ago when Ialu had staggered into the Royal Beast stable, badly wounded, and Elin had hidden him. He'd told her that Shunan had brought some injured soldiers to show the Yojeh.

Seimiya stared blankly at the map as if she, too, were lost in memories of the past. Finally, she took a breath and said bluntly, "As you know, I've rejected Nozgula's proposal to cede Ulamu, Ikishili, and Togulamu. Shunan and his advisors thought that Nozgula, having conquered Ulamu without losing any men, would try to take Ikishili and Togulamu next and establish a strong foothold in these three cities, rather than moving to attack us directly. I thought so, too. But it appears we were wrong."

Seimiya traced her finger along the map from Ulamu to Tsualu and then to Imeelu. "As soon as he conquered Ulamu, he moved straight toward Imeelu. He'll probably try to gain control over the highway that runs through the plains."

She tapped her finger on the place where the word "Imeelu" was written on the map. "Imeelu is just four days by carriage and only two days by horse from Amasulu, our eastern border. If Imeelu falls, it will be a disaster."

She raised her face and gazed at Elin. "We must protect Imeelu at all costs. Our largest Toda force is already stationed there, but we've ordered the new Toda troop to join them as well." She paused for a moment. "Ialu must have reached there by now," she concluded.

Elin nodded. Having worked so hard to build up the new Toda force, Ialu had been appointed second in command. Elin stared at the red spot on the plains that represented Imeelu and imagined Ialu astride a Toda riding into that foreign town, home of the intelligent and beautiful Kuriu, the woman she had met in Yohalu's hall.

"Shunan has set up base in Amasulu territory," Seimiya said calmly. "Tomorrow, I will leave the palace to go and join him."

Elin stared at her in shock. "Your Majesty?"

Seimiya smiled. "If I ride out to join them, the nobles of my territory won't be able to complain that they've been sent off to war."

In her smile, Elin thought she caught a glimpse of Seimiya's grand-mother Halumiya, the previous Yojeh.

Seimiya pointed to Amasulu. "You've just arrived and haven't had time to rest, yet I must ask you to lead the Royal Beasts to Amasulu tomorrow night. We've already prepared beacons along the road to guide your way."

Elin nodded. "I understand," she said. In her mind's eye, she saw the great river that Yohalu had once shown her from the top of a hill. The Amasulu River, across which Shunan's ancestor, Yaman Hasalu, had ridden the Toda given him by the Yojeh's ancestor to stop the Hajan invasion; the place near which Yohalu's ancestor, who came from a valley in the Afon Noah, had built the first Toda village.

Now she and Yohalu, descendants of the green-eyed ones, and the Yojeh, descendent of the golden-eyed ones, would converge on Amasulu, where their ancestors had first used Toda to fight for the kingdom. And to that same spot, Elin would take the Royal Beasts.

2

THE CARAVAN CITY IMEELU

Imeelu spread along the edge of the River Sahfa. It was surrounded by a high wall with only two entrances: the bridge gate, with a port where riverboats could dock, and the east gate, for merchants arriving via the highway through the eastern plains. Both gates were manned by Lyoza soldiers. When the bells rang the evening hour, the thick gates closed, and no one was allowed to leave or enter until the next morning.

Ialu had visited Imeelu twice before, and each time he was struck by the beauty of the white city, which seemed to float like a mirage on the slow, wide river. He guessed that the white walls of the buildings contained crushed quartz, because they sparkled in the sunlight.

The thirty Toda stables scattered along the outer wall and the semicir-cular turrets that jutted out at regular intervals marred the city's beauty like alien growths. The walkway on top of the thick wall surrounding the town was patrolled by Lyoza soldiers, whose numbers had recently been doubled.

Ialu entered the dimly lit Toda stable with the rest of the Blue Armor unit and let his Toda slip into the Pond. "Ialu, come," his commander, Oluku, said from behind. Ialu followed him to the door. There they quickly removed their tsuppa, thick leather leg guards, and handed them to a servant before exiting the stable.

Grooms waited for the two men at the Bridge Gate, leading their horses, and held the stirrups for them to mount. The horses balked and rolled their eyes when they came close, perhaps frightened by the scent of Toda that clung to their bodies. Ialu swung himself into the saddle and gentled his horse immediately. Still struggling with his own mount, Oluku cast him a wry grin. "You must be a Se Zan after all. You look much more at home on a horse than on a Toda." Ialu smiled.

Once the commander had gotten his mount under control, they passed through the gate and into town. The main boulevard that ran through Imeelu from east to west was surprisingly broad and lined on both sides with stores that opened onto the street. But the normally bustling thoroughfare was quiet. Rumor of war had spread quicker than wildfire, and there were far fewer caravans than usual. The people passing along the streets showed great diversity in the shapes of their faces and the clothes they wore.

When they reached a large building beside a temple that towered in the center of the town, the commander and Ialu dismounted and, handing the reins to grooms that came running up, climbed the broad stone stairs. Inside, their boots rang on the polished stone floor. With the sound echoing behind them, they strode toward a door guarded by soldiers.

"I am Oluku, commander of the new Toda troop, and this is my second, Ialu," Oluku announced. The guards saluted and opened the doors. Ialu followed Oluku into a large, high-ceilinged room.

The windows were open, and sunshine poured in. Potted plants stood in each corner of the room, and red berries on their branches glistened in the light. In the center stood a large desk surrounded by a group of people. They all turned when the two men entered. Ialu's eyes were drawn first to a tall musician.

So that's Rolan, he thought. He had heard a lot about him, but it was their first meeting. When Ialu introduced himself, he saw a look of surprise and recognition on Rolan's face. Fatigue was also etched there, indicating the hardship he had been through, but his eyes held a clear light.

Beside him stood an elderly woman, tall and slender, and beside her was a middle-aged man. The tattoos on their upper lips showed that they were pathfinders responsible for guiding the affairs of the city. That striking woman must be Kuriu, the one Elin told me about, Ialu thought. She was staring at him, and he bowed in acknowledgment. Her face lit up in a smile, and she inclined her head gracefully.

The others on Kuriu's side of the table were all people who wielded influence, while on the side nearest to Ialu were the governor-general, his deputy, and the general in charge of the entire Toda army in Imeelu. The latter now asked, "Did the regiment of new Toda all make it here without incident?"

Oluku saluted sharply and said, "Yes, sir. They all arrived safely."

The general nodded and gestured for him and Ialu to approach. Standing beside him, Ialu saw that small wooden markers had been placed on the map.

"The Lahza are now about here." A red marker, which Ialu assumed represented the Lahza cavalry, had been placed on a spot about two days' journey from Imeelu. "They're moving very slowly, but we hear they've been plundering villages as they go, so I think we can assume they'll continue at the same speed. Which means they won't reach here until the day after tomorrow at the earliest."

Oluku nodded. "Are the Toda troops traveling along with them?" he asked.

At this question, everyone in the room looked uncomfortable. The general cleared his throat. "That's exactly the problem. So far, the Toda army is nowhere to be seen."

Oluku's head jerked up. "Do you mean you've stopped receiving reports from our outposts?"

"No. We've been getting messages by courier pigeon daily from our soldiers stationed along the highway. The Lahza cavalry are avoiding our Toda garrisons as they approach. Seems like they don't want to lose any of their force before attacking Imeelu. As there's been no combat yet, my guess is that these reports are accurate. Plus our scouts have been bringing news as well. But there's been nothing to indicate the presence of a Toda army anywhere near the highway."

The general's thick eyebrows came together in a frown, and he cast Rolan a quick glance. Rolan had remained silent throughout, but now his lips curved in a wry smile. "You all think I was deceived, don't you? You think that Nozgula's clever right-hand man, Ozkula, showed me what he wanted me to see, completely fooling me into believing I'd seen Lahza Toda Riders."

The governor-general spoke placatingly. "No one would blame you if that was true. Under those conditions, there was no way for you to check whether they had just left a few of our Toda alive and put Lahza soldiers on them for you to see."

Rolan shook his head slowly. "I may have chosen to become a musician, but I am still the adopted son of Yohalu Amasulu of the Black Armor. As such, I have seen many Toda at close quarters ever since I was a child. I am convinced that what I told you is true. Those were not our Toda. The color of their scales and their build were different, even if that difference was slight."

The general cleared his throat. "But the inside of the Toda stable was quite dark, wasn't it?"

Rolan turned to look at him. "Yes, it was. But there was the light of several torches to see by."

The governor-general raised his hand, silencing them. "Whatever the case, as I said earlier, our first priority is to decide how to defend ourselves against the two thousand Lahza cavalrymen headed toward us. At the same time, we must keep our minds open to the possibility that there is a Lahza Toda army. That will have to do for now."

After that, the governor-general and the general took the lead in discussing how to protect Imeelu. When they had reached a conclusion, Kuriu spoke up. Her tone was mild but firm. "My dear comrades from Lyoza, I and the people of Imeelu are sincerely grateful to you for protecting our city. For that very reason, I believe we should share with you the truth of our situation. May I have your permission to do so?"

The governor-general nodded. "Of course, Lady Kuriu. Frank communication between us is crucial, particularly at such a time as this. Please tell us what you have to say."

"Thank you. I must regretfully inform you that it has become extremely difficult to gather goats."

Those assembled looked puzzled at first, but then understanding dawned on their faces. "You're talking about feeding the Toda, aren't you?" the governor-general said.

"Yes. We sent notices to nomadic herders in this area requesting them to supply us with goats. But they consider their livestock precious property. Rumors that the Lahza are going to invade have spread quickly, and many nomads are heading deep into the mountains with their herds. Some of the craftier herders have come to us, guessing that their livestock will sell for a higher price. But they're asking twice the normal rate. On top of that"— Kuriu flicked her eyes toward Ialu—"a fresh Toda regiment has arrived so we now have three times the number of Toda to feed."

The governor-general groaned. In times of war, the caravan cities were responsible for providing food for the Toda. Under these circumstances, however, this would clearly be an oppressive burden on the local people. Considering what had happened at Ulamu, they needed to avoid turning the local people against them.

"I understand," the governor-general said. "We'll consult about this immediately."

"Thank you," Kuriu said with a gracious smile.

3

SUBTERRANEAN RIVER

By the time the council of war ended, the sun was already tilting in the sky. Ialu was following Oluku to the door, when someone called out to them from behind. Turning, he saw Rolan approaching with his lakkalu slung over his back.

"May I come with you?" he asked Oluku. "I'd like to see the new Toda breed."

Oluku, who was from Amasulu and served Rolan's father, knew Rolan well. "Of course," he answered casually, and Rolan fell into step beside them.

"Allow me to introduce myself," he said to Ialu. "I'm Rolan Amasulu."

"I'm Ialu. My wife has told me that she's in your debt." At this, Rolan's eyes twinkled. "What?" Ialu asked.

Rolan blushed. "My apologies. It's just that I've heard so much about the swift-footed Ialu. I was expecting someone a little more imposing, not as quiet as you."

Ialu's lips twitched in a wry smile, and Rolan smiled in return, looking a little embarrassed, perhaps realizing he'd been rather blunt. "They often say," he added, "that man and wife resemble each other. There's something about you that reminds me of Elin."

Ialu's eyebrows rose. "Really?"

"Yes, though I can't quite put my finger on it."

They went down the steps to the plaza in front of the shrine. Rolan stopped and squinted up at the soaring temple. Great white pillars rose at the top of the broad staircase supporting the large roof. But it was the shape of the roof that drew the eye. Tiled with white slates embedded with blue and green polished stones, it was shaped like the prow of a ship. As he gazed at it, Ialu thought of the Shalamu people, who had built Imeelu. They had accumulated tremendous wealth doing trade on the great river.

He remembered hearing that they had designed the city as a large ship and built the temple as a prayer for a safe voyage.

The plaza was almost empty. On the wind, he heard a warbling so sweet and clear, he searched to see where it came from. Rolan pointed to the temple pillars. "There's a bird cage attached to each one. What you just heard is the song of the rihan, a beautiful sky-blue bird. The god of this temple loves music, and many musicians come to donate instruments. My grandfather was a traveling musician who always came here on the festival day. And this is where he died."

The westering sun shone on the roof with a dazzling light. Shading his eyes with his hand, Rolan said, "I found him under that round pillar there. He was cut down. A tribe of Lahza warriors broke through the gate, and he got caught in the conflict. There were fires scattered all over the city that night. I was only nine and had run into the temple to escape. My father was protecting the city with the Black Armor unit when he rescued me."

He sighed and turned away from the temple. "That was more than twenty years ago."

They mounted their horses and proceeded along the main road, which was filled with foreign scents. Ialu's thoughts drifted to the musician riding beside him, to the prosperous city over which foreign powers continued to fight for control, and to the many people who flocked to it. In some distant future, when the present became the past, would travelers passing through talk of the battle that took place here?

Entering the Toda stable where the new breed was kept, Rolan winced. "What's wrong?" Ialu asked.

"Can't you hear it?" Rolan said, still grimacing.

Ialu looked at him in surprise. "You mean you can hear something?"

"Well, not 'hear' exactly. It's more like a sensation in the middle of my forehead." He rested his gaze on the Toda swimming in the pond. They swam round and round, perhaps unnerved by their new environment.

"We've also experienced that sensation," Ialu said, "although we don't hear it as a sound. The Toda seem to emit something inaudible to our ears. Particularly when they're agitated. It goes away when they calm down."

While he was speaking, the Toda's pace began to slow. "Ah, you're right," Rolan whispered. He lowered his hands, which he had been pressing against his temples.

The Toda swam to the edge of the pond and crawled up one after the other onto a shallowly submerged ledge. There they stretched out, with their stomachs and jaws still underwater, and closed their eyes. Looking at their exposed backs, Rolan's expression sharpened. "Is that the color of the new breed?" he asked.

"Yes."

Rolan turned his gaze to Ialu and then Oluku. A fierce light gleamed in his eyes. "Their color, and their build as well, are very like the Toda the Lahza rode in Ulamu, although theirs were a little smaller."

Oluku's brows shot up. "Are you sure?"

"Yes. And now that I think of it, I heard the same sound in that Pond. Or not so much a sound as a vibration that set my teeth on edge."

Ialu and Oluku looked at each other. "But that can't be," Oluku protested. "We only managed to develop these Toda recently through repeated trial and error. They couldn't have developed such Toda with the skills shared by the Steward they abducted from Oohan village."

Rohan shook his head. "You're right that if a Steward of Oohan had raised them, they would've been small and black, but the Toda I saw weren't like that."

"In Lahza," Ialu said quietly, "there were never any rules for raising Toda. If they took what they learned from the Steward and experimented with it freely, adding their own ideas, it wouldn't be strange for them to end up with a similar type."

Oluku stared at Ialu in disbelief. If the Lahza had raised them in the way Ialu suggested, they could have bred a thousand by now. Oluku shifted his gaze to Rolan. "I can only pray that you were mistaken in what you saw," he said.

At that moment, a soldier named Tohlu entered the stable. Although he had been born and raised in Amasulu, his merchant mother was an Asheh like Rolan. Tohlu could speak Asheh and Shalamu fluently, which made him the troop's prized interpreter. When he saw Ialu, a look of relief suffused his face. He bowed and said, "May I speak with you for a moment?"

Ialu cocked an eyebrow at him. "Me? Of course, but why?"

"It may not be that important, but still, I thought I should tell you."

Guessing that it would be hard for him to talk freely in front of the commander, Ialu led Tohlu to a corner of the stable.

"As I said, it really may be nothing at all, but something's been bothering me."

"Go ahead. Tell me," Ialu urged him.

"I was just talking with the men who bring food supplies for our troops when an Asheh shepherd happened to walk by. He complained that our soldiers were letting the Toda loose in the river and demanded that we stop."

Ialu frowned. "In the river? But we don't do that, right?"

"That's right. I was going to brush him off, thinking he was just an idiot, but we've been told to maintain good relations with the locals. So instead, I asked him questions and listened to his story. He wasn't talking about the Sahfa, but a different river, in the hills far to the north. He said his goats are afraid to go near that river because it reeks of Toda. He was quite upset that the goats wouldn't drink the water."

An icy chill spread through Ialu's chest. A river in the northern hills! He stared at the young man for a moment, then turned on his heel. "Come with me," he said. Striding over to the commander and Rolan, he called out to them. "Pardon me for interrupting, but please follow me."

Oluku cast Ialu a puzzled look. "What's going on?"

"One of the nomadic herders said that the water in a river up in the northern hills smells of Toda."

"What!"

"I'm going to check where that river is on the map. Please come."

Oluku nodded, and Rolan fell in behind. They left the stable and entered the fort. Some scouts were poring over a map. "Could you help me a moment?" Ialu asked.

The scouts looked surprised to be addressed so suddenly by their superiors, but they quickly stepped aside so that Ialu and the others could see the map.

"Tohlu," Ialu said. "Show me the river the herder was talking about."

Tohlu frowned as his eyes swept the map. "Um, I think he called it Tsukalu."

"Tsukalu?" Rolan said. "That means 'trout' in the local language. In the Shalamu language it would be 'tohkool.'" He pointed to a hill a little northwest, rather than due north. "Here it is," he said. "That's Tohkool River."

Ialu ran his eyes swiftly along the river to see where it led, then he raised his face and looked at his commander. "I think we may have fallen straight into the Lahza's trap," he said.

Oluku paled. The river flowed through the hills to join a tributary of the Amasulu.

"The cavalry advancing along the road through the plains may just be a feint," said Ialu.

Oluku groaned. "You think they've drawn the main Lyoza force to Imeelu while they swing around behind us to attack Amasulu directly?"

The other soldiers in the room stared dumbly at the officers.

"But that's a lousy strategy," Oluku protested. "Even if they have their own Toda troops, they've never been tested in battle. To attack Amasulu where the Aluhan's army lies in wait? And without any cavalry or archers for backup? They'll just lose their precious Toda army."

"They may be thinking in longer terms than that," Rolan murmured.

Oluku frowned. "What do you mean?"

"Amasulu is a symbol. It's the field where the Hajan fought the battle that resulted in their defeat and destruction. For us, it's a field of glory, but for the Hajan, it's a field of shame. Maybe the Lahza want to demonstrate to caravan cities like Togulamu and Ikishili that they already have a Toda army capable of directly attacking Amasulu."

His face pinched, Rolan continued, "Like Ulamu, Ikishili and Togulamu were built by the Hajan. They've never really accepted us. If the Lahza can attack Amasulu, the place associated with the Hajan's shame, they're bound to move the hearts of the Hajan."

"But if they lose, there's no point," Oluku said.

"Yes, there is," Rolan said impatiently. "They may attack even though they know they're likely to lose. Maybe it's hard for you to understand because you've never lived with the people of those cities, but deep down, they hate the Lyoza. On the surface, they obey us because they're cowed by the overwhelming force of our Toda army. But that just makes their resentment stronger and more twisted."

"Like the Sai Gamulu," whispered Ialu.

Oluku and the scouts jerked their heads to stare at him. He turned to them and said quietly, "I think you in particular would understand. It's the same feeling the people of Aluhan territory have felt toward the Yojeh's nobles for generations. A firmly rooted, complex resentment toward those who benefit like parasites from your sacrifices."

The room fell silent. "If that's how the Hajan feel about us," Ialu said flatly, "when the Lahza, mounted on their own Toda, charge our army at Amasulu, they'll rejoice."

Ialu looked at Rolan. "That's what you meant when you said they might be prepared to lose this battle, isn't it? Even if they lose, they'll have tested their Toda army against ours. And in doing so, they'll have captured the hearts of the Hajan in Togulamu and Ikishili. In the long run, they have much to gain."

Rolan nodded. "Exactly! That's what I was trying to say. I'm sure you've heard the Hajan expression 'uri kimu.' 'Uri' means 'the heart,' and 'kimu' means 'to show.' Literally, it means to show your sincerity. But it's much harsher than it sounds. If you claim to be speaking and acting sincerely but in fact are not, the Hajan will never trust you again, ever. If, however, you do what you promise, even at great personal sacrifice, they'll put absolute and almost fanatical trust in you. The Lahza understand this characteristic of the Hajan very well.

"By attacking Amasulu, the symbol of Hajan's shame, even though it may mean self-destruction, the Lahza will have demonstrated to the Hajan how seriously they take their past humiliation at our hands and the kind of relationship they intend to build with them."

From the others' expressions, it was clear that his explanation still wasn't getting through. Rolan leaned forward. "Don't you see? The Hajan living in Togulamu and Ikishili hate the Lyoza, but that doesn't mean they like the Lahza. While they may hate us as their conquerors, they've been under our protection for a long time and are used to the way we do things. They'll have significant doubts about welcoming new rulers."

Understanding began to glimmer in Oluku's face, and Rolan continued more confidently. "For the Lahza, the support of the Hajan, who run those three caravan cities, is crucial, because it's a long way from the Lahza's home base to Lyoza. A very, very long way. Without support and supplies from the Hajan, the idea of them launching a serious invasion of our kingdom is no more than a dream of a dream. They won't get anywhere if they continue fighting small skirmishes near our protectorates the way they've been doing so far."

Rolan looked Oluku in the eye. "Now that we know the Lahza have their own Toda army, they can't take Togulamu or Ikishili by surprise the way they did Ulamu. But if they can win all the inhabitants of those cities over to their side, we'll lose the advantage we've enjoyed so far. Do you see?"

Oluku's eyes narrowed, and he looked down at the map. The caravan cities were very far from home. It was the people of those cities who kept Lyoza's troops supplied with food, water, and lodgings. And it was thanks to that firm foothold that they had never before lost to the Lahza. If the people of those cities were to become their enemies, that foothold would crumble.

One by one, Rolan pointed to the caravan cities. "If the Lahza can gain control over Togulamu and Ikishili, just as they've done in Ulamu, they can raise up an expeditionary force to attack Hoza, Kasholu, and Imeelu. And once they take Imeelu, they can attack our kingdom.

"To gain the advantage over Lyoza, they need to demonstrate their sincerity to the Hajan of Ikishili and Togulamu and win them over. An attack on Amasulu, even if it means the loss of two thousand Toda and their Riders, would be a significant strike in their favor."

For some time, Oluku stared intently at the map without speaking. Finally, he raised his eyes and looked at Ialu. "It could be that this is true. But right now, it's still just a possibility. It would be too risky to move our troops on the basis of a single herder's report. Ialu, take several men up to this river and see if you can find any traces of Toda."

Clicking his heels together, Ialu saluted, then beckoned the others to come with him. Time was of the essence.

Ialu spurred his horse toward the hills, racing the sun as it slid down the sky and dyed the grasslands red. Just as the world around him began to melt into dusk, a cluster of hills came into view. Mostly bare rock with only sparse clumps of grass, the hills were fading into mauve. Ialu found it hard to believe there could be a river among such rocky outcrops, but as he approached their shadow, the smell of water reached him on the wind.

Rolan led the way over the bumpy terrain, his horse pushing through the scraggly shrubs. Following after, Ialu heard the gurgling of water. They passed through a field of waving reeds and stepped out onto a riverbank. A sweet scent wafted toward them. Toda.

Ialu called out softly to Rolan, then gestured for everyone to dismount. Tying their horses' reins to nearby shrubs, the scouts spread out in four directions and came back stealthily. "No signs of anyone here," they reported.

Ialu nodded. There may not be any men here, he thought, but the smell of Toda lingered. "Light the lanterns," he ordered. "Cover the tops so that the light doesn't escape. Search for traces of Toda, particularly on the stones in the river."

Even in the dark, such traces were easily found. Many of the rocks had been scraped by sharp claws. The shallows also showed the marks of multiple claws where they'd scratched the bottom, and the tracks of running

Toda were discernable along the banks. There must have been so many that they couldn't all fit in the river.

At least several hundred, Ialu thought.

The sun had vanished, and the icy wind seeped through Ialu's skin. Shivering, he turned his face heavenward. Even if they rode the Toda through the night, it would take his regiment two days to reach Amasulu.

Let us be in time!

With this plea in his heart, Ialu leaped onto his horse, gesturing for the men to follow.

4

IN THE CAMP

Hemp curtains had been stretched on poles to create enclosures on a hill overlooking the Amasulu River. Standing outside the entrance to the largest enclosure, Yohalu called out, "Elin, I have brought His Excellency, the Aluhan. We're coming in." The instant he grasped the curtain, however, loud growls rose from inside, and he froze with the cloth still clutched in his fist.

Footsteps sounded from inside, and he heard Elin speak. "Hush now." Although her voice was not loud, the growling ceased instantly. Yohalu, however, remained rooted to the spot, goosebumps prickling his scalp.

Elin raised the entrance flap. "My apologies," she said. "Please come in."

Yohalu cleared his throat. "His Excellency is with me. Is it all right for both of us to enter?"

Elin smiled. "Of course. However, I must ask that you stay just inside the entrance without coming in any farther. This curtain is really the outer limit of their territory, and you both smell of Toda."

"Ah, I see." Yohalu wiped the sweat from his brow and ducked cautiously under the curtain with Shunan following behind. Once inside, they were rendered speechless.

A Royal Beast towered in front of them, and more stood behind it, each separated from the others by an even interval. Hackles raised, teeth bared, eyes flashing, they glared down at the two men.

"Shhh-shhh." Elin made soothing noises as if calming a child until the Beasts gradually settled. At last, they averted their eyes and began licking the fur on their chests.

His face tense, Shunan whispered to Elin, "Is it all right to talk here?"

Elin smiled apologetically. "Yes, but please refrain from making any sudden moves."

Shunan let out a slow breath. When angered, a Royal Beast could devour a person from the waist up in a single bite. Standing before them, Shunan felt that possibility so acutely, he could hardly breathe. "Terrifying. Absolutely terrifying. I thought Toda were frightening, but I've never experienced anything like this. Not even when I rode on Leelan's back all those years ago."

Shunan's lips crooked. "I just wanted to see them, and never gave it a second thought. But now I'm petrified."

Yohalu nodded, his eyes glued to the Royal Beasts. "Me too. I still have goosebumps." He shook his head. "They truly are the king of beasts."

Elin placed the feed pail she had been holding in one hand on the grass, and the two men looked at her as though waking from a dream. "Oh," Yohalu said. "I forgot. Part of the reason we came here was to tell you that Her Majesty, the Yojeh, has arrived and asks if she can visit the Royal Beasts now."

Elin nodded. "Yes, certainly."

Yohalu lifted the flap and went outside. Not long after, voices approached. Hearing Yohalu warning the Yojeh to be sure to keep her voice low, Shunan and Elin caught each other's eyes and smiled.

"Elin, may I come in?" Seimiya asked.

Elin reached out and raised the cloth. "Yes, please do."

Seimiya ducked inside. The Royal Beasts raised their heads to look at her, but instead of growling, they regarded her silently.

"Well, that's a surprise," Shunan murmured. "They don't growl at you."

Seimiya put a hand to her heart as though relieved. "You still remember me, do you?" she said to the Beasts. "I'm so glad."

Holding the Silent Whistle ready, Elin took the Yojeh's hand and led her to Leelan. Shunan and Yohalu tensed as they watched them walk so close to Leelan they could have touched her. Seimiya raised her head to look up into the Beast's face. Picking her harp up from the grass, Elin passed it to Seimiya, who looked at her with a surprised expression.

"Please. Speak to them," Elin urged her.

Seimiya nodded. Hesitantly, she began plucking the strings. Leelan cocked her head and listened, then slowly she began to wave her head and sing notes very similar to those Seimiya played on the harp. Seimiya's eyes widened. The sound of the harp mingled with Leelan's song, becoming one voice.

Tears welled in Seimiya's eyes and trickled down her cheeks. Gently she placed a hand on the strings to still them. "Thank you, Leelan," she said.

When the Yojeh and the Aluhan left, Yohalu remained behind. He told Elin to carry on with her chores, saying that he just wanted to look at the Royal Beasts a little longer. Elin began her regular routine, but as she passed Kalu, he lowered his head and butted her in the shoulder with his nose. She staggered. "Kalu, stop that," she said, pushing his nose away.

He wanted her to pet him. The eldest son of Leelan and Eku, he had always wanted attention as a cub. Although he was now grown, he hadn't changed. Rubbing the side of his nose, she thought that if they could return home, she'd like to give him his own territory. She was sure he'd make a good, affectionate father, like Eku.

She began raking together the manure with a hoe. "Surely there's no need to do that here in the field," Yohalu said in a surprised tone.

Elin stretched her back and looked at him. "In such a small space, to leave it messy will make them irritable. The odor of manure and urine is what they use to mark their territory. Besides, the manure tells me a lot about their physical condition."

She gathered the manure into one spot and examined it, then dumped it into a pit dug in a corner of the enclosure. Yohalu watched her silently for a while. "You seem very calm," he remarked.

Elin turned. "Is that how I appear to you?"

"You mean you're not?" he asked.

Elin gave a wry smile. "I didn't sleep a wink last night."

Yohalu grinned. "I see. But there's no need for you to worry. I doubt you'll need to fly the Royal Beasts. Although we asked you to come here, the defenses at Imeelu are impenetrable. Even if the Lahza have a Toda army, such untried troops couldn't possibly defeat our battle-hardened forces."

Elin listened silently, resting her hoe on the ground.

"Although I'm sure you object to us breeding Toda at all," Yohalu continued, "the new breed has incredible mobility and striking capacity. With them on our side, you'll never need to fly the Royal Beasts to war."

Elin shifted her gaze from Yohalu and looked up at Kalu beside her. "From the day I lost my mother," she said quietly, "I decided not to believe in lasting happiness, but instead, to prepare for the misfortune that was bound to come. That's how I have lived my life." A faint smile touched her lips. "I don't like to be caught off guard by fate. I'm really a coward at heart."

"That's an important mentality," Yohalu said gently. "But tonight, you can rest easy. I'll have them bring you a nightcap to help you sleep."

Elin smiled. "Thank you," she said.

After Yohalu left, the breeze creaking in the branches of distant trees and the flapping of the camp enclosures sounded loud in Elin's ears. She walked over to Leelan and pressed her face against her belly, just as she had done when she was a child. The soft warmth of Leelan's fur and the rumble of her breathing calmed Elin's mind like waves lapping the shore. To live was such a simple thing. This thought rose in her mind, then receded.

Elin's eyes flew open at the sound of footsteps running by the enclosure where she slept. It was still dark but the shadows of people outside, backlit by torches, flitted across the curtains. She reached for her clothes, which lay folded beside her pillow. She had just finished dressing when she heard a man's voice. "Lady Elin, are you awake?"

"Yes," she responded.

"You are requested to come immediately. I will wait here to accompany you, so please come out once you are ready."

Slipping her feet into her shoes, Elin stepped outside. "I'm ready," she said. "Please lead me there."

Whatever had happened, it had thrown the whole camp into an uproar. Lanterns burned brightly in the large enclosure that housed the Yojeh and the Aluhan, and grim-faced soldiers surrounded it. When Elin's arrival was announced, the flap was raised immediately. It was so bright inside that her eyes were momentarily dazzled.

"Elin, over here," Yohalu said. He took her arm and drew her to the large table in the center. The Yojeh and the Aluhan stood across from her flanked by the warlords of Aluhan territory. The nobles from Yojeh territory stumbled into the space after Elin, many of them rubbing swollen eyes, as if they had been rudely awakened from a deep sleep. From their disheveled hair and hastily tied belts, it was clear that many of them had never had to get ready on such short notice. To be summoned in the middle of the night like this would have seemed very rushed indeed.

After confirming that everyone was present, the Aluhan said, "A short while ago we received an urgent message via Lord Yohalu's hall. A report arrived there by courier pigeon from a lookout tower on the banks of the Makan River. A host of Lahza was seen coming down the river mounted on Toda."

The nobles erupted in loud exclamations, but the Aluhan's solemn voice cut through the clamor. "The two thousand Lahza horsemen advancing through the plains appear to have been a ruse. The enemy's main force is heading straight here to Amasulu."

The nobles froze, robbed of speech. With his eyes fixed on their faces, the Aluhan said, "I've already explained the situation to our commanders and ordered the Toda troops that remained here to prepare to move out to the Amasulu River. The main force will be led by Muhan of the Black Armor, son-in-law of the lord of Amasulu."

When the Aluhan finished speaking, the Yojeh looked at each of the nobles. "It's time to go to war," she said.

The nobles stared at her with stunned expressions. Until this moment, they and their families had condemned war as unclean, while believing it was their inherent right to profit from bloodshed. Each family had been ordered to send one representative. Many had chosen to send their second or third sons, but some, afraid to lose any of their heirs, had come in person, leaving their eldest in charge.

The Yojeh urged them to look at the map. "You've all brought a company of archers with you. Lead them upstream from where our Toda troops will defend the river." She pointed to a spot on the map. "The forest cover is quite thick here, making it hard to land. To leave the river, the Lahza will ride beyond this point to the shallows downstream. Tell the archers to shoot the Lahza as they ride their Toda past them."

Looking at their pale, silent faces, Seimiya continued, her voice firm. "Once you've positioned the archers among the trees, lead your cavalry to close off the rear of the Toda troops. The city of Amasulu must be defended at all costs."

She waited until they had nodded their assent, then turned toward Elin. "Elin," she said. "Stand by on the hilltop with the Royal Beasts ready to fly at a moment's notice." She paused for a moment, her fair porcelain-like features taut and strained, making her look like a stranger. "I'm sure the seasoned troops of our kingdom will never be defeated by the inexperienced Lahza," she said. "But even so, we should be prepared."

Elin returned her gaze steadily. "I understand," she said.

"Your Majesty," Yohalu said in a low voice. "Please allow me to speak as a former member of the Black Armor. At this time of year, the temperature drops dramatically before dawn. Our Toda won't move until the air warms up, even if we pull on their horns and order them to. I'm sure those ridden by the Lahza are the same. The Lahza will likely have made camp and be letting their Toda rest on the riverbanks."

The Aluhan nodded. "Yes, before dawn will be the perfect chance for the archers to catch them off guard."

The Yojeh waved a hand at the nobles. "You heard him. Gather your men and move out!"

The nobles bowed, then hurried from the room. After watching them leave, the Aluhan turned to the warlords. "You know what you need to do. They won't be able to manage on their own. Take your archers there, too."

The men saluted and left. Elin was following after them when the Aluhan called her name. She stopped and looked at him. "Rest until dawn," he said. "It's quite far from the Makan River to Amasulu. The enemy won't reach here until after sunrise."

"Thank you," she said. "I will do so." She bowed deeply to the Aluhan and the Yojeh, nodded to Yohalu, and left.

The night air was cold and clear, and her breath turned white. Far off across the dark plains she could see the low shadows of the mountains. And far beyond them was Ialu.

Stay safe, she thought. The words rose in her mind like a murmured prayer. If they could end this battle quickly, Ialu wouldn't need to fight. Just for now, she was glad that both Ialu and Jesse were far away. Turning to the soldier who had guided her here, she said, "Before going to bed, I wish to visit the Royal Beasts." The soldier nodded and set off at a quick pace.

When she reached the Royal Beast enclosure, Elin went inside and looked at the sleeping Beasts one by one: Leelan, Eku, and their son Kalu, and those captured from the wild, Nola and Tohba, and the youngest, Lesseh, Kaseh, Osseh, and Fuseh. Alu, who was pregnant, and her mate, Ukalu, as well as Mina, who had recently injured her leg, and Leelan's youngest cub, had been left behind in Kazalumu. But even the small number of Beasts here could butcher hundreds of Toda in moments if they weren't restrained.

Elin looked up at Leelan, who slept with her jaw nestled in the fur on her chest. Will all that training work? She had drilled them to respond instantly to her commands. If her theory was correct, her ability to save them depended upon their complete obedience under any conditions. For most of her life, she had wanted to free the Royal Beasts from the prison of the Silent Whistle and the Canon, yet for the last six years she had done just the opposite.

The moist night air caressed her cheeks. A faint blush of color touched the lower edge of the sky. Soon it would be dawn. Once day broke, the war would begin. She might have very little time left.

Chills spread up from her knees, and she began to shake. She strove to remain calm, but the fear that lurked behind her rational mind and twisted in her gut spilled over, shaking her in its grasp. Unable to stay on her feet, Elin crumpled to her knees on the grass. Curling up, she buried her head in her arms with a moan.

I don't want to die.

She couldn't die and leave Jesse behind. Not when she knew how that would grieve him. There was so much she still hadn't taught him, so much more she wanted to say. She longed to hold him in her arms just a little longer, to walk beside him as he lived his life. She wanted to be with him and Ialu, wanted all three of them to live and grow old together.

Ialu . . .

She clung to his image in her mind. She screamed to him in her heart.

Help me . . .

No one could change this situation. She was here by her own choice. She knew that, yet she couldn't quell her agony, her longing to reach out for someone. Hugging herself as if clinging to Ialu, who was now so far away, she wept.

There was a snort behind her, and something nudged her in the back. Looking up, she saw Leelan's face looming above her. Leelan stuck out her huge tongue and licked Elin's face. Elin pushed her muzzle away with both hands, but still Leelan didn't stop. Slowly and deliberately, she licked Elin's arms, her hands, her face, just as if she were a newborn cub.

What's she thinking, Elin wondered. Overcome by a strange sensation, she closed her eyes and gave herself up to Leelan. As she did so, an old memory surfaced. Leelan had done this before. Long ago, when she had plucked Elin up in her mouth and flown her to safety. She had lowered Elin onto the grass at the top of a hill and licked her all over, refusing to let anyone near for a long time.

A warm feeling oozed from a point in Elin's chest and spread through her body.

Two different creatures can still connect like this. Despite the insurmountable gulf between us, we can still reach out and touch each other.

This bond. It would probably never have been formed in the wild. As a member of the human herd, she should never have longed for such a connection. It was this relationship that had caused everything to warp and twist. But still . . .

Elin opened her arms wide and hugged Leelan's muzzle, praying that some of what she felt would reach her. Leelan had given her so much, so very much.

Leelan rumbled comfortingly for a while, then gradually the sound receded. Slowly, Elin removed her arms and sat down on the grass, gazing at the sky.

A strong wind seemed to be blowing across the heavens. Clouds flowed by, blocking the stars. Elin thought of all the countless lives under that sky. Mites burrowing in the earth, winged insects dancing like dust motes in the air, honeybees, fire ants, and humans. All those lives breathing in this darkness like myriad pulsating points of light. In its struggle to pass life on to the next generation, the human herd had extended its territory to the ends of the plains, spreading across the earth like stars scattered across the heavens. She was just one human among many; her life, just one brief moment. What would she achieve with that life before she vanished?

Herds of different creatures intertwined in an infinite number of ways, so that she couldn't even tell what or where her tiny hand was touching. Would the actions she was about to take change anything?

Beginning with all her mother had given her long ago, she had received so much from the many lives she'd encountered along the way. Cradling each gift, she had carried on, thinking, always thinking, to reach this place.

All this is what I'm made of.

She opened her arms toward the heavens and took a deep breath. The smell of night expanded inside her. A thought rose and quietly filled her mind.

May all things be set free. All those things entangled in the long stream of history.

May the Royal Beasts be released to soar in this illimitable space.

May Jesse, Ialu, and I be freed from the fetters forged by the inexorable flow of time.

Because that is why I came this far.

She lowered her arms away from the dark, endless void through which she and the Royal Beasts had often flown. Nestling herself between Leelan's legs, she buried her face in the Beast's belly. Wrapped in the scent of this creature with whom she had shared so much of her life, Elin closed her eyes.

5

THE KALENTA LOH

In the afternoon of the day that Elin reached Amasulu, two men and a woman dressed in deep-hooded gray robes arrived at the Kazalumu Sanctuary. When the guard demanded to know who the three travelers were, they responded that they were Elin's distant relations. Of the three, two had green eyes, which convinced the guard that they spoke the truth, and he allowed them into the school, although he accompanied them to the headmistress's office.

As he led them down the corridor, which echoed with the sounds of teachers' voices, the guard glanced repeatedly at the third traveler, a woman whose face was once again hidden by her hood. When she had removed it a moment earlier, the guard had been startled by her eyes. Impossible, he thought to himself. It must've been the light.

They reached the headmistress's room, and he opened the door to let the travelers pass through. When the woman removed her hood, he took one last look at her eyes. He had not been mistaken. One of her eyes was green, but the other was golden.

When he was told to report immediately to the headmistress's office, the first thing that occurred to Jesse was that something had happened to his mother. Breaking the school rules, he dashed down the hall and burst into the room. Three strangers sat by the hearth. They turned to stare at him.

Esalu beckoned him to her side. Placing a hand on his shoulder, she said, "This is Elin's son, Jesse."

The three strangers rose, regarding him solemnly. Jesse looked at them, wide-eyed. Green eyes, and golden, too, he noted.

All three were tall and slender with finely chiseled features. The man on the right was elderly while the one on the left was young. Both somehow resembled his mother. But the one who drew his attention was the middle-aged woman between them. The light from the window clearly showed that her right eye was green while the left was golden.

The green-eyed Ahlyo and the golden-eyed Yojeh. Suddenly, Jesse remembered a strange tale he had read in his mother's diary. "Are you Kalenta Loh?" he blurted out.

Their eyes widened, and Esalu jerked her head to stare at Jesse. The elderly man gave him a stern look. "Did you hear that name from your mother?" he asked.

Jesse nodded hesitantly. The man's eyes were hard, as if he thought Elin had told her son something she shouldn't have. "Well, only sort of," Jesse added hastily. "I overheard her talking to Her Majesty, the Yojeh, about it."

At this, the visitors and Esalu looked satisfied.

"I'm Nason," the elderly man said to Jesse. "I'm an Ao-Loh, one of the People of the Law. But these two, as you guessed, are Kalenta Loh. They have traveled for several months from a valley deep in the Afon Noah to meet your mother and the Yojeh Seimiya."

With a determined set to her jaw, Esalu interrupted. "As I said earlier, is it not sufficient that I alone hear what you have to say?"

Nason shook his head. "I knew before we came that Elin had already left. We must see her and the Yojeh as soon as possible. But I have taken time from this precious mission specifically to come and see this young man."

He looked at Jesse, a bitter smile rising to his lips. "You don't know me, but I know you very well. I have watched you all these years as you snuck through the forest to spy on your mother when she was training the Royal Beasts, although the soldiers kept such a strict guard that I couldn't speak to you."

The hairs rose on the nape of Jesse's neck, and his eyes narrowed.

"I was close to your grandmother and have talked to your mother before. I watched them both break the Law and take the path to destruction."

Anger flared inside Jesse, and he scowled at the man. Seeing his expression, Nason turned to Esalu. "You see," he said. "Look at his face. He's still young, yet he's his mother's child. These two must share what they have to say with this boy now. If we wait until after his mother is dead, his mind will be closed, and he'll be unable to judge clearly. This is the critical moment when we may still prevent him from following in her footsteps. That's why I asked them to come here with me."

As Jesse listened, the words in his mother's diary clicked with the words this man had just spoken. Fury welled up from the pit of his stomach as he remembered who Nason was and what he had said to his mother.

"After she's dead? So I won't follow in her footsteps?" Jesse shouted. "How dare you, old man! No matter what you say, I'll follow her! Do you expect me to listen to someone who treated my mother the way you did!"

Nason looked at him unperturbed. "And so, like your mother, you'll take countless lives, including your own?" he said quietly.

Jesse flushed bright red and tried to retort, but no words came.

"If we don't stop her," Nason continued, "your mother will end up killing thousands and meet a horrible end. I brought these two here to prevent such a tragedy." He sighed. "The Ao-Loh have abandoned hope for your mother. With the number of Royal Beasts and Toda you have now, we expect that several thousand people will die if there's a battle. While that's a terrible tragedy, it's still small compared to what happened on the other side of the Afon Noah. If your mother dies here to atone for her sin, she'll take the Handler's Art with her to the grave, and no one else will be able to ride the Royal Beasts. If she dies now, neither Seimiya nor you will be able to fly them as you please. My people see this timing as a blessing, and so they've chosen not to intervene."

His voice faltered, and he stopped to take a breath. "But if possible, I would rather save thousands from dying." Anguish rose in his face. "I realize now that when I told your mother about the catastrophe, I should have told her the whole truth. If I had told her then, she might have chosen a different path. But at the time, I thought I shouldn't because to do so would be to reveal that Toda can be bred by humans."

He shook his head slowly and sighed. "In the end, my precaution was not just in vain, it made things worse. So when I learned that these two had left the Afon Noah and were traveling the Road of Mist to reach this country, I offered to guide them."

The two travelers, who had been listening to him speak, barely stirring, looked at each other. "Nason," the younger one said, "may we share the rest ourselves?" His voice was resonant with an odd inflection that sounded as if it vibrated deep in his throat.

Nason nodded and gestured with his hand for them to go ahead.

The young man turned to face Esalu and Jesse. "My name is Lyoza. My mother here is Sohyon. We have come from Paleh, the valley."

"Lyoza? Sohyon?" Esalu whispered. "I thought Sohyon was Elin's mother's name."

Nason shrugged. "It's a name heard often among the Ao-Loh, although no one I know is named Lyoza."

Esalu nodded and turned to the young man. "Lyoza. The same name as this kingdom?"

He nodded. "Yes, so I've heard. For us, Lyoza is a very common name. Do you know where it comes from?"

Esalu shook her head with a puzzled look. "No. I didn't even know there was a source for it."

"I see. In that case, I should start there. Although, to be honest, for us this tale is no more than a legend. We don't know how much of it is true."

The woman beside him spoke up, her voice soft. "But first, you should know that while we share the same roots as the Ao-Loh, we're not one people. We've stayed in limited contact with people like Nason, here, but we never leave the mountains the way he and his people do. The Ao-Loh call us the Kalenta Loh because our ancestors who survived the catastrophe chose not to wander as they do, but rather to settle in one place and live in peace. To them our name means 'the ones who remain in the valley.' But for us, the name Kalenta Loh means 'the ones who survived.'"

She paused and then continued quietly. "Our homes are scattered in the mountain range you call the Afon Noah, the mountains of the gods. We'd never been to this side of the mountains, so until now, we had no idea what kind of lives you lived, what oral histories you had, or what kind of worldview."

Esalu suddenly seemed to notice that they were still standing, and she gestured for them to sit. When they had taken a seat, the woman continued. "Concerning the origin of the name Lyoza that my son mentioned earlier, this legend is the one that has been passed down in my home village. It's deeply connected with the young woman named Jeh.

"After Jeh left the valley, she used to send a message strapped to the leg of an ochiwa every year to share news of her life. This custom of exchanging letters by ochiwa continued even after she died. If there's anything that has connected my people and yours, it's just these letters.

"But even though an ochiwa still bears a message to us every year, at some point in the past, the words written in that message changed to a language we couldn't read and the content became very short. To be honest, these messages have become more of a ritual than actual communication for our people. According to legend, our ancestors believed that the same thing must have happened on the other side of the mountains due to the passage of time."

She glanced at Nason. "Talking with Nason, that riddle was solved. It seems that the script you used suddenly became reversed."

Esalu frowned, but Jesse let out a little yelp. He blushed as every-one's eyes turned to him. "Sorry, it's just that I realized something. My mother used to write while looking into a mirror. I always thought she was writing in a secret language, but now I know she was writing in your language."

Nason sighed. "That's right. It was Jeh, the founder of this country, who created the mirror script. But then, for some reason, she taught it to the people here as their regular script. I don't know why she would have done so." Nason looked at Jesse, then at Esalu. "Our people, of course, still write the same way we used to. Elin probably learned that way of writing from her mother, Sohyon. But the descendants of Jeh forgot how to read and write it."

"Ah." Esalu murmured. "That knowledge was lost in the fire set by the Sai Gamulu."

The woman smiled politely. "Yes, it seems so. But we knew nothing of it. Because of that, we viewed the message borne by the ochiwa simply as a New Year's custom, and returned it with the scent of flowers while offer-ing our prayers for the happiness of Jeh's descendants in that far-off land. However . . ."

She stopped and looked at her son. He nodded and took up the story. "This year the ochiwa came not only in the new year but also again in early summer. Moreover, it came bearing urgent questions written in our own language. Surprised, we consulted about what to do."

Lyoza smiled at Jesse. "You see, to answer the questions asked by your mother and your ruler Seimiya, we needed to write such a long explanation that it wouldn't have fit in the tube borne by the ochiwa."

"Also," Lyoza's mother chimed in, "as I told you before, we've been out of touch with your people for so long that we weren't sure how to explain."

Her son nodded. "Their questions seemed to be about something that happened so long ago it was more a myth or a folktale. We couldn't under-stand why they would be asking us such questions now. And they sounded so desperate, like they were sending a plea to the gods. We were quite bewildered."

Esalu nodded. "I see. If you hadn't had any contact for centuries, their message must have seemed to come out of the blue."

The woman's face softened. "Exactly. We realized that the best way to answer would be to send someone over the mountains to meet whoever wrote that message. To be frank, not everyone agreed it was necessary. But I felt strongly that if someone had sent that ochiwa believing in the promise of our ancestors to help them in need, we should go to them."

Jesse gripped his knees with his hands. The words of this kind woman touched his heart, and he felt his chest grow hot. "Thank you," he said, bowing his head.

The woman looked at him as though startled. She smiled gently, but her expression quickly turned to one of regret. "I'm sorry," she said huskily. "If we had come sooner, we could've met your mother before she left and stopped her. Until we met Nason, we had no idea what was going on in this country."

Jesse opened his mouth to speak, but Esalu cut him off. Placing a hand on his shoulder, she said, "So if the Royal Beasts attack the Toda army, a catastrophe will occur. Is that correct?"

With a pained expression, the woman nodded. "Yes."

Esalu leaned forward. "We tried to imagine every possibility and trained the Royal Beasts to respond to Elin's commands no matter what the situation. Won't that mean she can prevent it?"

The woman shook her head. "Unfortunately, no. I don't think that's possible. Because when the Royal Beasts come in contact with an army of Toda, they go mad."

Esalu threw on her mantle, but her fingers fumbled on the strings at her throat so that she couldn't tie them. She clicked her tongue in disgust. Her hands were shaking too badly. Sohyon's tale kept running through her head, and she couldn't keep herself from trembling.

She clicked her tongue once again. She'd forgotten how far along she was in her packing. She paused and took a deep breath. "Honestly. Pull yourself together," she told herself.

Sohyon and the others had planned to take the mountain roads to keep out of sight, but Esalu had stopped them and told the guard to bring her a fast horse. If she rode through the night, she would reach the palace a little after noon the next day.

Having finally managed to tie the strings of her hood, she slung a cloth bag over her shoulder. She turned to make sure she had put out the fire in the hearth, when she heard a knock on the door.

"Miss Esalu, everything's ready." It was one of the custodians.

"Coming." She opened the door and was confronted with the man's worried face.

"I gave Jesse the saddle as you asked, but do you really intend to fly?"

Esalu frowned. "What did you say?"

"You told Jesse to put the riding harness on for you, didn't you?"

"Absolutely not! I'd never do such a thing!"

The man's face blanched. "But Jesse said you did. He's taken the riding harness to Alu's stable—"

Without waiting to hear the rest, Esalu broke into a run. Her knees hurt, but she gritted her teeth and rushed toward the Royal Beast stable. The sun had set, and the evening star was beginning to twinkle in the sky. Beneath the blue vault of night, she could see the stable door standing wide open.

Backlit by the lantern inside the stable, a huge black shadow ducked under the lintel and into the open.

"Jesse!" Esalu screamed, just as the shadow spread its wings. It sank onto its haunches and then shot up into the sky. For a second, Esalu glimpsed the tiny form of the boy clinging to the Beast's back. Then Alu turned and vanished into the night.

6

THE MORNING OF THE BATTLE

The wind moaned in Jesse's ears. When he raised his head, it slammed him in the chest and threatened to blow him off. It was hard to breathe. He pressed himself against Alu's back and clung on tight. He had to use not just his arms but his whole body to keep from being ripped away. Worse still, it was freezing. Even with his thick gloves, his hands gripping the harness were so stiff with cold he could no longer feel what he was holding.

He had thought it would be easy to ride as long as the harness was on. What a mistake. Yet his mother seemed to ride the Beasts so effortlessly. For years, he had watched her fasten Leelan's harness and fly into the sky on her back. When he realized that they had to warn his mother as soon as possible, he had immediately thought of riding Alu to get there.

Alu had been restless when he was fastening her harness, as though she sensed that something was unusual. Once he was on her back and told her to fly to Lazalu, however, she seemed to recognize this familiar order and flew without protest. His heart had thumped wildly in his chest when she leaped into the sky. The ground fell away abruptly, and when he could see the whole of Kazalumu from the air, he had felt like letting out a loud cheer. But now, he was frozen and sore all over. It was so painful, he wanted to cry. If it weren't for the urgent need to warn his mother, he would've asked Alu to turn around and take him home.

Pressing his face into Alu's soft, warm back, he closed his eyes and turned his thoughts to his mother.

Mom. You mustn't fly!

The story told by the woman with one green eye and one gold was far more terrifying than the one his mother had written. The woman had spoken as though telling a folktale to her grandchildren, but Jesse had been so petrified his head had gone numb.

If the Royal Beasts went mad, then all their training, no matter how thorough, would be useless. Icy cold gripped him at the thought of his mother being torn apart when the Royal Beasts clashed, of his father crushed beneath the Toda.

As for Toda bred by men, when faced with Royal Beasts would they really undergo the transformation that woman had described?

He must stop his mother. But even if she knew that the Royal Beasts would go mad and the Toda would undergo a horrible change, she would probably still fly. She'd still fly to show everyone what would happen.

If so, then I'm the one who must stop it. Like the young man Lyoza in the woman's story. But he must not think about what would happen if he did what Lyoza had done. Otherwise, he'd be too afraid to go through with it. He must not think . . .

Just then, he felt a change in the way Alu flew and heard her gasp for breath. A chill spread through him. She was pregnant. Such a long flight would take its toll on her. "I'm sorry, Alu," he said, stroking her back. Her wings slowed and made loud flapping noises, but she flew on. "I'm so sorry, Alu. Just a little longer. You can do it."

How much farther was it to Lazalu, he wondered. Below him, the earth was dark except for the occasional village where a few lights were shining. He tried to remember the time his father had taken him to the capital many years ago, but the scenery viewed from the air was quite different from that viewed from land, and he had no clue as to where he was. He could only pray that they would reach Lazalu soon. Finally, in the distance, he saw a broad cluster of lights. Alu's wings began to beat more strongly. Drawing on her last reserves of strength, she flew toward the Lazalu Sanctuary, which she knew so well.

When they landed, Alu dropped down on her haunches, as though exhausted. Men came rushing out, alarmed by the noise. They stood staring from a distance as Jesse slid from Alu's back. He landed on his feet, but his knees buckled, and he ended up on his bottom.

A stocky, elderly man approached cautiously and asked, "Who are you? Is this one of the Royal Beasts from Kazalumu?"

Gasping for breath, Jesse answered, "I'm . . . Jesse . . . Elin's son . . . from Kazalumu."

The man's eyebrows shot up. "What?"

"Is my . . . mother here? I have to . . . see her . . . immediately!"

The man's face clouded. "Your mother's no longer here. She left for Amasulu with the Royal Beasts."

For a moment, everything went dark. Jesse pressed his forehead against his knees and tried desperately to breathe. A cold sweat broke out on his face. Raising his head, he said, "Amasulu . . . It's east . . . right?"

The man knelt and patted Jesse on the back. "Yes, but you can't fly right now. If you need to tell your mother something, we can send a courier pigeon."

"Courier pigeon?" Jesse whispered.

"Yes. It'll reach Amasulu by dawn."

Trembling, Jesse said, "That won't work. I have to go myself."

"You can't."

"Yes, I can. If I rest a little first."

The man shook his head. "You may be all right, but that Royal Beast is in no condition to fly. That's Alu, isn't it? Her belly seems a little swollen."

Jesse looked up at Alu. Her tongue was lolling out, and she was panting heavily. Her face showed just how hard the flight had been for a Beast bearing young. Impatience burned Jesse's chest, but he couldn't force the exhausted Alu to fly any farther.

Elin woke with a start to the sound of a shrill whistle.

Dawn had already broken. A chill wind bearing the scent of rain brushed against her cheeks. Thick clouds streamed across the leaden sky, but no rain fell as of yet. Shafts of sunlight streaked from a break in the clouds, and the cloth enclosure shone a dazzling white.

That she had slept so deeply came as a surprise. True, she had been exhausted, but that was not the only reason. The uneasiness that had gripped her for so long seemed to have vanished. All worries, fear, and anguish had sunk to the bottom of her mind, leaving the surface as still as water.

Listening to people bustling about the camp, Elin stepped outside and gazed down upon the broad plain of Amasulu. Cloud shadows raced across it. The wide Amasulu River wove through those shadows, light glinting on its surface. From its upper reaches, dark log-like shapes rode its waters.

Toda . . .

Foreigners straddled them, red feathers flickering in their hair like flames. Their number was overwhelming. Elin wondered if the archers sent by the nobles to intercept them had had any impact at all.

The Yojeh and the Aluhan stood side by side watching them come. One step behind, Yohalu kept his eyes fixed on the river. Seimiya turned as Elin approached. Her face pale and tense, she looked at Elin but said nothing. A stray wisp of hair danced in the wind, touching her cheek. Elin stood silently, watching troop after troop of Toda glide down the river.

Raindrops fell randomly at first, then turned into a thin sheet of water that joined earth and heaven. The gray autumn fields glowed dully, and waves chopped the river's surface. Rain shrouded the boats pulled up along the banks. Seimiya never took her eyes from the invading Toda hosts even when a servant brought her an umbrella.

Yohalu's son-in-law led the Aluhan's Toda troops, and he had drawn them up on the near bank to shield the farm villages and the city of Amasulu behind from the invaders. With the main force still in Imeelu, there were perhaps only a thousand Toda Riders assembled below, yet to Seimiya, they still seemed to outnumber, at least slightly, the enemy forces speeding down the river toward them.

"It's all right," Shunan murmured. "It looks like we're evenly matched in numbers. If that's all they've sent, we should still come out on top."

Seimiya nodded, her shoulders relaxing a little.

Just as the invaders approached a landing spot, Shunan raised his right hand high. Below the hill, a hand-flag rose in answer. Like a flock of butterflies taking to the air, a flurry of flags flapped in succession, heading in a straight line toward the Aluhan's troops. When the last white hand-flag shot up, the blare of hundreds of war horns shook the earth and ascended into the air. The troops advanced to envelop the enemy Riders as they clambered from the river. Dust and water swirled into the air and spread outward as the two Toda forces collided.

Shunan suddenly leaned forward with a puzzled frown. "Wait a minute. What's going on?" From his vantage point, it looked like the Toda formation had begun to warp. Instead of falling upon one another with tooth and claw, they seemed to be circling each other as though reluctant to come in contact. At first, he couldn't see what was happening through the thick haze of dust and mist, but once the entire enemy force had emerged from the water and begun moving ponderously toward the hill where he stood, he could make out their movements more clearly.

"But that's . . . impossible," he whispered. The wind blew wet strands of hair into his eyes, and he shoved them aside. "Toda. Do they not attack their own kind?"

The beasts weren't fighting. Although the Riders grasped their horns and pulled frantically, trying to steer them, the Toda reared or shied away whenever they drew close to one another.

"But why?" Yohalu said hoarsely. The rain had plastered his gray hair to his forehead. "They'll rip one another to shreds if there're more than ten of them in one Pond."

"It might be because this is an open space," Elin said. Everyone turned to stare at her. "In a Pond, they attack one another because their territory is too small to support more than ten. Here, they have lots of room, and it's not their territory. Maybe that's why they won't attack one another." Even as she said this, however, she felt there was more to it.

Frowning, she looked down at the Toda. Although it was hard to tell at first because they were moving quickly now, it seemed as though they were maintaining an equal distance from one another. Whenever they came too close, they bounced away, like two magnets when their poles repel each other. It reminded her of the way Royal Beasts behaved when they flew too close to each other.

A soundless sound . . .

Ialu's words came back to her. Men felt a low buzzing in their ears when they rode the new breed of Toda, he had told her. Their teeth ached and their skin crawled. Her heart began to pound. The Aluhan's men protecting Amasulu were mounted on the new breed. What if the Toda ridden by the Lahza shared this same characteristic?

As the Toda struggled to avoid one another, resisting their Riders' attempts to make them attack, multiple swirling eddies began to form within the mass of beasts gathered on the plain. Figures began to spill from the edges of the eddies. One after the other, Toda bearing enemy Riders with red feathers in their hair were ejected from the vortexes. They stood looking dazed at first, but once they grasped the situation, they turned their mounts and charged straight toward the city of Amasulu.

At that moment, everything changed. Quick-witted Lahza Riders burst from the edges of the swirling of Toda. Caught off guard, the Aluhan's troops tried to follow in pursuit, but their mounts rebelled, turning and twisting to avoid approaching the Lahza's Toda. The eddies broke, and a thousand enemy troops stampeded toward the city with the force of an avalanche.

Cavalrymen stationed beyond the city's outer wall began chasing the Lahza, arrows flying from their bows. But they only succeeded in killing a few Toda Riders. They couldn't slow the thunderous charge.

"Elin!" Seimiya swung around to look at her.

With a quick nod, Elin turned, but then she stopped and looked back at Seimiya and Shunan. "Promise me one thing," she said, her voice strained. Raindrops trickled down her cheeks. "Please. Promise you will witness what takes place today and never again conceal what happens. So that everyone can know the truth and think for themselves. Promise me that the truth will never again be hidden."

Seimiya placed a hand over her heart. "I promise to do what you ask," she said.

Elin held her eyes, then bowed deeply and ran to the enclosure where the Royal Beasts waited.

7

MADNESS

Perched on Leelan's back, Elin plucked her harp, and the Royal Beasts rose as one into the sky. She hadn't plugged their ears. There would be times when they couldn't see her hand gestures. If she wanted to coordinate their movements, sound was the surest way to communicate her commands. It was a gamble. If a Toda Rider blew his Silent Whistle, the Royal Beasts would fall from the sky. But she knew that the Riders would have plugged the ears of their mounts. They would have left their whistles hanging from their chests, rather than holding them in their mouths, so that they could call out to one another. And earplugs couldn't block the song of the Royal Beasts. When the Royal Beasts attacked and the Toda rolled over, the Riders would have almost no chance to let go of the horns and blow their Whistles.

Even so, to be on the safe side, Elin with Esalu's help had repeatedly tested just how far the effects of the Silent Whistle could travel. It was much farther than the "ten adult steps" she had been taught at school, but she now knew instinctively the distance needed to prevent the Royal Beasts from being paralyzed.

Leelan's hackles rose. She had caught sight of the Toda troops ahead and entered fighting mode. The others also bared their fangs. Filled with a savage fury, they were tensed as taut as bowstrings, but they kept to the speed Elin had commanded with her harp, resisting the urge to accelerate. Repeated training with Toda in the wild appeared to be paying off.

The city of Amasulu spread out below, and the Royal Beasts flew swiftly over the clustered buildings. The Lahza force had reached a farm village on the plain outside the city walls. In seconds, the Toda had trampled through the recently harvested fields and plowed into the storehouses. The wooden walls cracked and burst. The farmers had already left with their tools to take refuge within the city, but their livestock remained behind. White feathers flying, hens scattered before the onslaught, only to be crushed underfoot.

A thousand Toda fell upon the wooden houses of the village. Fences and buildings collapsed in a churning cloud of dust that left only wreckage in its wake. The horde of Toda sped toward the city without slackening its pace. Archers on the wall showered them with arrows, but although enemy soldiers fell, this had no effect on the Toda. Once they reached the wall, they would quickly scale it with their sharp claws and pour into the city beyond. The Lahza would conquer Amasulu just as they had planned. Soaring across the city, Elin could see people climbing onto roofs, clinging to one another as they stared at the invading force.

The Toda mustn't clear the walls.

If a battle between Royal Beasts and Toda was going to cause a catastrophe, then she must stop the Toda forces before they reached the city. Otherwise, the people would be slaughtered.

The Royal Beasts reached the outskirts and flew beyond its walls. On the plain below, the Toda raced toward the city. Steeling herself, Elin plucked a different sound on her harp. In response, the Royal Beasts tilted their wings and began their descent.

How will it start? And at what distance?

She now guessed that the calamity must have been caused by some kind of sound emitted by Toda and Royal Beasts when they came too close. Somewhere, an invisible boundary existed. Whatever happened would start when they crossed that line.

Leelan led the way. She dropped toward the advancing horde, emitting a long, trailing whistle. As the high-pitched sound echoed through the air, the Toda in the front lines reared upward and flipped, landing belly-up. Their Riders were crushed beneath them before they could even scream. Alighting on the hapless Toda, Leelan began ripping their flesh, taking her time. The smell of blood assailed Elin, and she heard the crunch of breaking bones. Leelan lowered her head, hunching over the Toda to feed. Over Leelan's shoulder, Elin saw the face of a dead Lahza warrior. His eyes were open wide, as if surprised. He looked so young, not even twenty.

Elin screamed at Leelan. "Up! Up! Get away from the Toda you've killed!"

With a sulky expression, Leelan spread her wings.

Nothing happened. Even though we came into contact with the Toda.

As this thought was flitting through her mind, Eku and the other Royal Beasts, which had spread out over the Toda horde, began dropping from the sky while trilling a high, piercing melody.

The Toda, their bodies mutated by hakujisui and repeated breeding, were now face-to-face with their natural enemy. Overcome by fear, they emitted a voiceless scream. When the Royal Beasts' song collided with that scream, it all began.

The Toda host morphed. Pressing against one another, the Toda picked up speed. Each one leaned into the other as though the angle of their bodies had been perfectly measured to move in a circle. They revolved in a clockwise vortex that generated a thick cloud of dust. The cloud rose and radiated outward, but it contained more than dust.

The Toda, a thousand strong, burst into a high-pitched wail like wind shrieking through a cracked pipe. Rather than one long sound, it came in short, repeated bursts that grated on the ear. Each time Toda bumped one another, a secretion triggered by fear and excitement spurted from the gaps between their scales. This was swept up with the dust and dispersed like mist into the air.

The Toda Riders suddenly arched backward as if they had been struck by lightning. Bodies rigid, lips puckered like the mouths of fish unable to breath the air, they bounced about limply on the backs of the running, shrieking Toda.

Although she didn't know why, Elin was certain that every single Rider on those whirling Toda had died.

Something strange was happening to the Royal Beasts as well. Lesseh and Fuseh recoiled from the Toda they were attacking, springing into the air. They twitched and flapped like shrimp, opening their mouths wide as though in a scream. Shaking their heads, they shrieked soundlessly, yet still they plunged back among the Toda as though pulled by an invisible string.

Elin stared mesmerized by the sight when suddenly she felt her body lift. Leelan was swooping down toward the Toda. "No!" Elin shouted, but Leelan didn't stop. Elin saw Toda with Riders' corpses lolling on their backs, rushing toward her. When Leelan hit the layer of whirling dust, a mist touched Elin's cheeks. Pain shot through her face as though it was being pierced by a thousand needles. She screamed, but something caught in her throat as she inhaled. She couldn't breathe. The searing needles of pain swept beyond her face to jab every inch of skin.

Instinctively, Elin leaned back, pulling with all her might on the riding harness. Leelan shook her head and, with a voiceless cry, twisted her body and soared upward at an angle. The same voiceless cry burst from the other Royal Beasts as they writhed in agony. The soundless sounds overlapped one another, resonating and repeating as they collided with the Toda's screams of terror.

Crazed, the Toda charged round and round in circles, and the Royal Beasts, wings tilted, revolved with them. Earth, grass, and feathered hair ornaments were whipped into the cloud of dust, which roared as it gyrated upward. Rain steamed like smoke and swirled, whistling, up into the air. Caught in this maelstrom, the bodies of the Toda Riders were reduced to mere objects that would never scream again.

Blinded by tears, Elin desperately plucked her harp. Even that sound seemed warped to her ears, but Leelan responded. Groaning, she flapped her wings and twisted her body, fighting to break free of the vortex, then flew up into the heavens.

"To the sky! To the sky! To the sky!"

Elin plucked the strings so hard she worried they would snap as she tried to pull the Royal Beasts back from the maelstrom. By the time the strings finally broke with a twang, Eku had joined them, and Nola, Kaseh, and Tohba were struggling to follow. But for Kalu, Lesseh, Osseh, and Fuseh, it was too late. They had already gone mad. Blood spurted from their eyes, ears, and noses, yet they continued their wild circular flight. At that moment, the Toda that bore the Aluhan's troops finally caught up with the Lahza force, and the four Royal Beasts dove down into them.

The Aluhan's Toda were swept into the frenzy, joining the others in their anguished scream.

Who was from Lahza and who was from Lyoza no longer mattered. Every living creature on the plain, man or beast, pulsated in unison as they were swept up and crushed within a mortar of ever-magnifying fear. The Royal Beasts, the berserk Toda, circling and undulating like a whirlwind, became one tortured mass. Blind and deaf to the world, the mass smashed into the city's outer wall.

"There were no longer any victors or losers."

As he pressed his face into Alu's back to protect it from the rain into which they flew, the woman's words kept ringing in Jesse's brain.

"When tens of thousands of Toda collided with thousands of Royal Beasts, this is what happened. The Royal Beasts went mad. Men and Beasts touched by the mist generated by the Toda were killed instantly. Buildings collapsed, crushing women, children, and babies beneath. In minutes, the deadly mist that rose from the horde had covered the land.

"For the few that survived, there were no enemies and no allies. When Lyoza saved them, our ancestors banded together and, leaving the ruins of that country, fled deep into the mountains. Since that time, the golden-eyed and the green-eyed ones have lived as one family."

Lyoza was the name of the younger brother of Jeh, the woman who had flown the Royal Beasts and caused that great catastrophe. At the cost of his own life, he had finally stopped the Beasts attacking the Toda. A hundred people had been saved. Jeh left the valley and built another country, giving it her brother's name.

Mother . . .

Surely nothing bad will happen, Jesse told himself. His mother probably hadn't flown the Royal Beasts yet, and even if she had, she'd survive.

But he couldn't suppress the horrific images that kept bubbling up like foam in his mind. No matter how many times he tried, he couldn't keep them down. He prayed that he would find his mother in Amasulu. Alu couldn't go any farther, not when she was pregnant.

The rain had lessened and no longer struck his face. Raising his head, he saw clouds hemmed with gold. It seemed like a good omen, and he felt his heart lighten.

8

THE SILENT WHISTLE

Elin couldn't hear. Sounds came to her, but they had no meaning.

Her mouth gaped as she gulped for air. Even trying to open her eyes was agony. Tears streamed from them, and her lids twitched uncontrollably. She managed to force them open a crack but could see only a wobbly band of light. When she wiped away the tears, red blood from her nose stained her palm. That color was the only thing she could see clearly.

The gray clouds covering the sky flowed on the wind, and a ray of golden light fell through a gap onto the earth below. It dappled the gyrating, undulating sea of crazed beasts. Kalu, Lesseh, Osseh, and Fuseh rose and fell, arcing over the Toda as they attacked them over and over. Each time they attacked, the Toda tried to escape, only to collide with one another. Panicked and crazed with pain, the writhing mass of Toda, no longer distinguishable as individual beasts, slammed repeatedly against the outer wall of the city. Those in the rear continued to throw themselves against those that were already pressed limply against the wall. With each impact, stone dust rose like a cloud of white smoke.

The main gate to the city shuddered. The thick slabs of cedar, which fit seamlessly together, groaned, and the iron spikes that fastened them loosened from the frame. As Lesseh swooped down yet again, the Toda below twisted violently and crashed against the gate. Its heavy bolt snapped, and the gate splintered. Bursting open, it was trampled beneath the Toda that poured into the city. Those that stumbled or fell were crushed underfoot, while the rest plowed down the wide street, toppling the trees along the boulevards. Above them swooped the Royal Beasts.

Fuseh dove down and sank her fangs into a Toda's back, then suddenly reared, her body contorting and twitching. She toppled to the ground like a stone and did not move again. Wild with pain, their faces streaked with blood, Kalu, Lesseh, and Osseh threw themselves repeatedly against the Toda, the source of the noise that was driving them mad.

Archers defending the city let loose a hail of arrows from the windows and rooftops of two large buildings facing the main gate. But they merely pierced the corpses of the Lahza warriors still lolling in their saddles. Toda crashed into the buildings where the archers stood, and a thick mist rose. Archers collapsed at the mist's touch. Dropping their bows, they plummeted to the ground.

The strong wind and intermittent rain diluted and dispersed the mist, but even so, those who had sought refuge on the roofs began to cough. If the wind changed direction, the mist would kill them, too.

All this Elin saw from a world where sound had vanished.

She knew that she must stop Kalu and the others. As long as they kept attacking, the Toda in their terror would continue to emit the deadly mist. But the four Royal Beasts were now deaf to her voice and blind to her gestured commands.

Elin raised her eyes to the heavens and wept. She had known this catastrophe would happen. She had told herself that to witness it was the only way through to the future. But for the beasts and men dying in agony below, there was no future.

She clenched her teeth to hold back a scream. She had to stop them. Now. This was no time for weeping.

The mist that rose from the frenzied Toda as they tried to flee the Royal Beasts was deadly. Toda in the wild, and even the army of Toda on Tahai Azeh, hadn't emitted any poison. But the Toda whirling below were clearly generating a toxic mist. Elin bit her lip.

They aren't the same as Toda in the wild or the ones on the plains of Tahai Azeh. They were bred by the hands of men.

She remembered what Ialu had said. When the new breed of Toda were agitated, the men around them not only became quick-tempered and vio-lent, but also went into convulsions if they came in contact with their bodily fluids. Over several generations, breeding must have resulted in more con-centrated toxins, while fear or anger accelerated the Toda's metabolism. When the panicked horde pressed against one another, the poison spurted from their bodies and dispersed as a deadly mist into the air.

The Royal Beasts and the Toda. Unless she could sever the chain reaction of fear and madness, the toxic mist would continue to spread. She had to end the madness before that poison wiped out the entire city.

Eku, who was flying beside Leelan, shuddered. Even at this distance, the screams of the Toda were reaching him, Elin thought. Something in that sound was driving the Royal Beasts insane.

She had to get him and the others to safety. She raised her hand high and waved it repeatedly. "Eku! Go! Get out of here! Nola, Kaseh, Tohba! Fly!"

Eku looked at her hand, shook his head once, and flew away, head-ing straight toward the hill. Nola, Kaseh, and Tohba followed. When they were just tiny specks far away from the whirlpool of Toda below, Elin saw another tiny speck hurtling toward her from the hill. For a moment, she thought that Eku must be flying back, but she realized immediately that it wasn't. She peered at the approaching figures, trying to make them out, then gasped.

Jesse? Impossible! Why?

Elin spurred Leelan toward him. Soon she could make out his face. He was clinging to Alu's back and staring at her. Shifting his gaze to the Toda and Royal Beasts below, he moved his hand and brought something toward his mouth. When she realized what it was, Elin cried out. "Jesse! No!"

Jesse wept. Below him, the gentle, timid Kalu had gone berserk. Fangs bared, drenched in blood, he fell upon the Toda, ripping them apart. Lesseh and Osseh were slamming their bodies against Toda, slashing and writhing as they tried to pull themselves away.

His eyes full of tears, Jesse looked at his mother. As she drew nearer, he raised the Silent Whistle that hung at his neck and placed it to his mouth. It felt cold against his lips. His mother was yelling something, trying to stop him, he guessed.

He could end this. All he had to do was fly into the midst of the Royal Beasts and blow. He knew that, but he couldn't do it. If he did, Alu would fall to her death. And her unborn cub would die with her.

Leelan and Elin raced toward him. He saw his mother raise her palm and heard her yell as she waved her hand. Instantly, Alu swerved aside and flew up into the sky. "No!" Jesse screamed. "Alu, no!" But Alu didn't stop. She passed Leelan who was on her way down. For a moment, Jesse saw his mother's face, ghostly white, then she was gone.

He twisted his body, trying to follow their flight. As Alu banked away, he saw his mother bend forward to whisper something in Leelan's ear.

The instant Elin saw Jesse raise the Silent Whistle to his lips, she knew what she must do.

Thank you, Jesse, she thought.

As they passed each other in midair, she seared his face on her mind. She closed her eyes for a moment, then opened them again. "Let's go, Leelan," she murmured in her ear. "Let's go to your children."

Leelan obeyed without protest. Watching her back as they descended, Elin wept.

If you'd never met me, you could've escaped this fate.

It was Elin, not Leelan, who had rebelled at the idea of this Royal Beast ending her days dozing in the meadows of Kazalumu. Yet even if she could live her life over again, she would probably choose the same path. She would've tried to free the Royal Beasts to live as they would in the wild—to mate, bear young, and die. Remembering the life she had shared with Ialu and Jesse, a warmth spread through her.

The pool of beasts filled her sight, undulating, swirling, colliding. Leaping into the thunder that rose from the crashing bodies and flying between the frenzied Royal Beasts, Elin raised the Whistle to her lips and blew.

Like a thread that has been cut, all sound vanished.

Kalu and the others froze like statues, wings spread wide. Rocking from side to side, they dropped to the ground. The Toda froze, too, then collapsed on the spot. For as far as the Silent Whistle reached, every beast toppled over, severing the chain reaction generated by the screams of the Royal Beasts and the Toda.

When the Royal Beasts hit the ground, they smashed into the Toda with the sound of shattering bones. Elin had blown the Whistle in Leelan's ear. She froze, wings spread wide as her body hurtled to the earth. Elin's hair rose. The wind whistled in her ears. The Toda had fallen outward, leaving a hole in the middle of their ranks. Elin saw the ground rushing toward her and squeezed her eyes shut.

The next moment, Leelan slammed into the earth.

9

ASH-COLORED CITY

By the time he reached Amasulu, Ialu could see small specks flying in the air above the city—Royal Beasts. They dropped from the sky like eagles attacking their prey, then flew up and dropped, again and again.

"Move it! The battle's already begun!" The commander blew his war horn, spurring on the Toda and their Riders, who had raced through the night without stopping to sleep. Ialu rode beside the commander, and together they plunged into the river. Spray shot up into the air, drenching them. Beyond the white curtain of water, they could see horsemen galloping, not toward the city where the battle was taking place, but toward the river. One of them pulled ahead of the rest and waved his arm frantically, shouting at the approaching Toda troops.

"I'll go on ahead," Ialu said. He urged his mount to the riverbank where the horseman waited. When Ialu was within hearing distance, the man yelled, "Stop! Don't go to the city!"

Frowning, Ialu said, "What do you mean? Get a grip on yourself!"

The Rider took a deep breath and tried again, his shoulders heaving. "The Toda and the Royal Beasts! They've gone mad! Anyone, friend or foe, who gets caught up in that whirlwind spits blood. It crushes everything in its path. Turn back, or your Toda will be driven insane!"

There was a wild look in his eyes. "When the Royal Beasts attacked, the Toda went totally berserk. And then so did the Royal Beasts, with blood gushing from their eyes and noses. You've got to turn back!"

Fear stabbed Ialu's heart like an icy blade.

Elin . . .

He took a quick glance at the Royal Beasts, swooping and soaring between earth and sky, then leaped from his Toda and whacked it on the back to turn it toward the river. Running over to the horseman, he shouted, "Lend me your horse! And tell the commander over there everything that happened!"

The man tumbled to the ground. Ialu leaped into the saddle and took the reins. Squeezing his thighs against the horse's flanks, he pressed his body against its neck and spurred it to a gallop.

It was a swift steed, and the autumn fields raced by. Speeding across pastures churned into mud and littered with the splintered fragments of shattered farmhouses, Ialu closed in on the horde of Toda. It looked like an enormous, shapeless lump. As he approached, the scent of Toda mingled with the stench of blood and offal. Particles of fine dust pricked Ialu's throat, and he coughed. His horse balked and reared, rolling its eyes. Ialu pulled back on the reins and retreated a few steps to survey the scene before him.

The city's outer wall trembled, and smoke rose above it. The main gate had burst inward, and Toda were flooding through the opening. Those still outside were being pushed along, and their Riders, both friend and foe, were trapped within the seething mass, their faces raised in agony. Within the walls, Royal Beasts swooped down again and again to attack the Toda, while high above them hovered a single Beast.

Ialu leaped from his rearing horse and broke into a run, the howling, stabbing wind at his back. A strange odor pricked his nostrils as he neared the wall. He held his breath and climbed over the fallen Toda, slipping through the gate into the city.

At that moment, all sound ceased.

Shadows plummeted to the ground. Looking up, Ialu saw the enormous winged beasts fall from the heavens like stone. On the back of one fluttered a familiar robe. Then the Beast collided with the ground.

"Elin!" he screamed. He ran toward the spot where he had seen her fall, her hair flying in the wind.

Wails of mourning rose into the sky, like wind whistling through broken pipes. The surviving Toda raised their heads to the heavens and cried as one.

Alu had alighted on top of a tall building. She stared motionless at the ground, without raising her voice in answer. Jesse stood in the saddle gazing down, his breath coming in shallow gasps.

Mom!

She had to be down there somewhere among the broken bodies of the Toda and the Royal Beasts. But if he flew Alu there, she might drive the remaining Toda crazy again. Making up his mind, he slipped off her back. "Stay here, Alu," he whispered, his voice shaking.

He ran along the roof, searching for a staircase. The only one he found was broken in places. He climbed down it gingerly, clinging to the wall, occasionally sinking to his hands and knees as he searched for a foothold. At the bottom, people milled about fearfully inside the entranceway, but Jesse ignored them and ran outside.

The wind was so strong, he could barely stand. Fine dust stung his face, and when he tried to breathe, it stabbed his throat. Hacking violently, he staggered and flailed his way through the dust toward where the Toda raised their mournful cry. Blood-drenched Toda lay with their bellies pressed against the ground. Those that were still alive didn't even glance at him when he passed. On their backs, bodies drooped like rag dolls, their arms and necks contorted into impossible positions. This scene stretched on and on, all the way to the main gate.

In the ash-colored landscape something moved. Someone was striding toward him, pushed by the strong wind as he climbed over Toda carcasses. Jesse stood wide-eyed, gazing at his father. In his arms was Jesse's mother. Her body hung limply. Jesse stared at her pale skin and at his father's face.

The wail of the Toda ceased abruptly. Silence enveloped the city along with the gray dust.

ELIN'S TREE

"My mother lived for four more days," Jesse said, resting his hands on the desk as he looked at his students. They were all in their final year. The spring sun shone through the window, softly lighting their faces as they listened intently.

"Thanks to the strong wind, the poisonous mist didn't kill me or my father. As for my mother, she lived a little longer because my father ran to her rescue as soon as she fell. Of course, he hoped to save her life, but that was impossible. You've already learned that when someone's limb has been crushed, they may live for several days fully conscious, only to take a sudden turn for the worse and die. That's what happened to my mother. When Leelan fell, she was thrown from her back, and her thigh was pinned beneath Leelan's body. Even so, thanks to my father's quick action, we had those four precious days."

Jesse's expression softened. "When she opened her eyes in the infirmary, my mother stared at us for a very long time, as if trying to decide if she was dreaming. Then she asked what happened to Leelan."

Jesse had been tasked with telling the oldest students this story every year. With each telling, the scene came back to life. His mother, lying silently on the bed in the large, dimly lit room, tears sliding down her face as she learned that Leelan, who had been almost a part of her, was dead.

"My mother closed her eyes," he continued. "Then she opened them and told us to call a scribe. I can still see her bloodless face and hear her voice. She spoke of the Toda, and of the Royal Beasts. She told us why they went mad when faced with a situation that would never have occurred in nature."

The Yojeh had compiled the record taken at that time into a book and made it compulsory reading for every teacher responsible for training those involved in running the country and for every person who aspired to become a beast doctor. It had already gone through many printings.

After the scribe had left, Jesse had clung to his mother. She had wrapped him in her trembling arms and held him tight. "It was thanks to you, Jesse," she had said. "Because of you, I could achieve what I set out to do."

He had longed for time to stop right then. In that dark room, with his head pressed against his mother's chest, he had learned for the first time that some things can't be changed, no matter how desperately he might wish otherwise. Maybe that's why not just the pain, but also the brilliance of those last four days remained engraved on his mind.

His father never left her side, even though his body was wracked by tremors. Although the fallen Toda discharged no more toxins, he'd still been exposed to some when he climbed over them. His life had been saved through repeated application of shilan solution, which neutralized the poison. It was in that state that he had come and stayed with Elin. She didn't let go of his hand, or of Jesse's, until her last breath.

Although the story of how the first handlers of Royal Beasts and Toda came to this country remained unknown and so was never recorded in her book, Elin did get to meet the Kalenta Loh before she died. The woman with one green eye and one golden, along with her son, Lyoza, spoke with the green-eyed Elin, the golden-eyed Seimiya, and Yohalu. Shunan, Esalu, Jesse, and Ialu sat nearby and listened. Jesse could still hear his mother's voice as she asked, "Are there any handlers of Royal Beasts and Toda in your valley now?"

The woman had smiled and shaken her head. "No. There are none left," she had said. "They remain only in our books along with the memories of our distant ancestors."

The smile that had lit his mother's face, and Seimiya's tears, remained etched on Jesse's mind. His mother was tormented by remorse for having opened the door to a disaster that claimed so many lives. By breaking the chain of fear and madness, she had saved the people of Amasulu. But no matter how many times she was told this, her burden never eased. Remorse for sending so many men to such a horrible death weighed even more heavily on the Yojeh, the Aluhan, and Yohalu, because they were the ones who had chosen to wage war and forced Elin to use the Royal Beasts as weapons.

Seimiya prostrated herself before Elin and vowed to set the Royal Beasts free. Never again, she promised, would they be raised as symbols of royal power. She wasn't the only one chastened by the horror caused by a pack of Royal Beasts falling upon Toda hordes. That terror had been carved into the bones of the Lahza as well. Those who survived were sent back to their homeland with the bodies of some of the Toda and their Riders preserved in salt. These bore far more eloquent testimony to the terrible disaster than any words.

To her last breath, Jesse's mother grieved that she had killed Leelan, Kalu, Lesseh, Osseh, and Fuseh, Royal Beasts she had raised with care and affection. But in the end, she had succeeded in freeing the others.

As his mother had said, war never ended, and conflicts still continued. Yet this kingdom was changing little by little. The bond created by the Aluhan's younger sister's marriage had paved the way for prosperous trade with countries to the south, the disparity between the territories of the Aluhan and the Yojeh had been erased, and the possibility of negotiating with the Lahza was being explored.

To Jesse, who had witnessed his mother's struggle at close quarters, it was clear that the heroic actions of a single, clear-sighted person could not prevent war. Humans were herd creatures. Until each member of that herd understood their own actions and thought for themselves, major changes could never take place. Just as his mother had told him in the sun-dappled forest, some things could only be changed by passing on the torch from hand to hand to spread the light.

For years, Jesse pondered what she had taught him. At the age of twenty-seven, he compiled his ideas into a plan and presented them to the Yojeh, asking her to establish schools of higher learning where every commoner could study. Although Seimiya knew full well the potential consequences for a ruler of giving commoners access to knowledge, she supported his proposal wholeheartedly.

The first school was built in the capital where Jesse's father and mother had lived. Graduates spread throughout the country so that now schools were beginning to spring up even in small farming and fishing villages. Jesse didn't know if the small flame that had been passed on to them would one day become a great light. But he knew that through learning, people begin to think. Through repeated trial and error, the herd of creatures known as humans would keep passing life on like a vast river.

Hearing the chime that signaled the end of the day, Jesse tucked his books under his arm and stepped outside the school. The gentle spring breeze caressed his cheek. It smelled good.

Just as he did every time he taught this lesson, Jesse walked to where the Royal Beast stables had once stood. The site of Leelan's stable was now covered in grass, and beside it was the grave of Esalu, who had passed away at eighty-two years of age. The Royal Beasts that Jesse's mother had raised and loved were all buried in this wide pasture: Leelan and Eku and their children, as well as those brought from the wild when they were still cubs: Ukalu, Tohba, Nola, Lesseh, Osseh, Kaseh, and Fuseh.

Two trees rose tall and slender, nestling together at the edge of the pasture where the Royal Beasts lay. Beneath them slept Jesse's father and mother. His father had lived for twenty-two more years after his mother's death. Eight of these he had spent with the Blue Armor. After that, until his death from illness many years later, he had worked as a carpenter. Having finished raising Jesse, who could be quite a handful, he lived a simple, peaceful life, and enjoyed his grandchildren.

Jesse sat under those two trees, their branches laden with white blossoms, and watched the sunlight dance and sparkle each time the petals trembled in the breeze. When the blossoms fell, young leaves would burst forth, and in the fall, the branches would bear small fruit—mountain apples for which his mother, Elin, was named. They were hardy trees that still bore fruit even after the frosts came.

Squinting against the dappled light, Jesse picked up the blossoms' faint fragrance on the breeze. At her bedside, as she lay dying, he had asked his mother how he could return Alu's children to the wild. "Listen to Alu," she had said. "If you try to understand her words, even though they seem incomprehensible, it will open the way." Her face softened in a gentle smile.

After repeated trial and error, he had finally succeeded. How he wished she could have been there to see the young Royal Beasts gliding off into the valley that day. After Alu and the others died, there were no more Royal Beasts at Kazalumu, and the students had never even seen one. The school now trained aspiring beast doctors and would continue to send out many more into the world.

The sound of footsteps jolted Jesse from his reverie. A student came running up, red-cheeked and out of breath. "Professor Jesse, Yuma has gone into labor!"

A smile lit up Jesse's face, and he rose to his feet. "That mare has done well. For a horse, she's pretty old to be having kids. Let's make sure she gives birth to a healthy foal."

Jesse gave the student a light pat on the head, and together, they dashed off toward the barn.

AFTERWORD

When I wrote *The Beast Player*, I considered that tale to be finished. It is the tale of one who strives to communicate her feelings to a beast, the distant "other," and when I reached the ending, I felt there was nothing more that could be said. Even now, this feeling hasn't changed.

But then Tadako Sato, an author I greatly admire, wrote to me. "I want to read more," she said, "even if it detracts from the perfection of this perfect story."

Reading Sato's letter, I realized that Elin was still alive. So alive, in fact, that she inspired this kind of longing. The thought that readers wanted to read more, to know what happened next, not only made me very happy, it made me want to write that story.

Still, it took me a long time to get started: In my mind, *The Beast Player* was like a beautiful, closed circle. I couldn't bear to write something that seemed as if it had been tacked on. The spark I needed came in the summer of 2007 with the unexpected offer of turning *The Beast Player* into an animated series. As I worked with the director to dissect the story, I was hit with a jolt of revelation. It may seem odd to discover something about a story I wrote myself, but that's what happened. I saw the road that led Elin to become the Beast Player, the road that led on from there, and the wide, inexorable flow of the herd of creatures we call humans.

When the "history" of Elin's world rose in my mind, I knew instantly that this was the tale I needed to write. As Elin began to breathe once again inside me, the cheeky little boy Jesse was born, and the story swiftly took shape.

If *The Beast Player* is the tale of one human and a beast, then *The Beast Warrior* is a history of humans and beasts. The tale is now complete, this time for certain. But the sound of that great river flowing still murmurs in my ears.

I am deeply grateful for the assistance of many people in writing this story. Seita Fujiwara of Fujiwara Apiary, which I visited for background research when making the animation, explained the nature of honey bees in such a way that it stimulated a wealth of ideas. Likewise, reading through and rethinking *The Beast Player* with the animation staff, including the director Takayuki Hamana and the scriptwriter Junichi Fujisaku, provided tremendous impetus, helping me complete this final volume. I cannot thank you all enough.

To Joji Nishimaki, who shared his thoughts on Immanuel Kant's educational theory over dinner so long ago. Looking back on it, I realize that what you told me then runs through this tale from start to finish. Thank you so much.

My cousin, Takamichi Matsuki, a medical doctor to whom I often turn for advice, gave me valuable suggestions for the symptoms described in the last battle scene.

Professor Shoichi Ishiura of the University of Tokyo provided much appreciated advice on heredity, while Professor Kentaro Nakamura of the Tokyo Institute of Technology instructed me in basic acoustics and provided careful and thorough descriptions of how sound changes in different situations for each scene. I am indebted to you both. I was also greatly influenced by the enjoyable episodes shared by Nanae Nishi from her own experience of observing creatures in the wild. Thank you.

Of course, this story is a fantasy, and any divergence from reality is solely my responsibility. But just as Elin was nurtured and grew through the many lessons she received from Sohyon, Joeun, and Esalu, this story also grew and developed through the precious lessons I received from so many professionals in a range of fields that encompassed animation, apiculture, philosophy, and acoustic engineering. I am deeply grateful to all of you.

I must also express my appreciation to Etsuko Moriyama, the editor in charge of the Kodansha paperback edition, who gave me invaluable advice on the first draft; to Misa Mizumachi for her meticulous editing work; and to Naoyuki Kanoya for his careful proofreading.

Last but not least, I am profoundly grateful to Kaori Nagaoka, my wonderful editor, who accompanied me on this journey and did everything possible to support this author—who never talks about the content of what she's writing until she's finished—during a horrendous slump. That Elin and I finally reached the end of this arduous journey is thanks to Nagaoka, who stuck by my side throughout and never stopped encouraging me.

Because of all of you, I was able to write this book. Thank you!!!

July 10, 2009 in Abiko
Nahoko Uehashi